Also by Robert Holdstock from Gollancz:

Mythago Wood
The Mythago Cycle Volume One
The Mythago Cycle Volume Two
Avilion

THE MERLIN CODEX

Celtika
The Iron Grail
The Broken Kings

MERLIN'S WOOD

or

The Vision of Magic

ROBERT HOLDSTOCK

Copyright © Robert Holdstock 1994
All rights reserved

The right of Robert Holdstock to be identified as the author of
this work has been asserted by him in accordance with the
Copyright, Designs and Patents Act 1988.

First published in Great Britain in 1994 by HarperCollins

This edition published in Great Britain in 2009 by
Gollancz
An imprint of the Orion Publishing Group
Carmelite House, 50 Victoria Embankment, London EC4Y 0DZ
An Hachette UK Company

5 7 9 10 8 6

A CIP catalogue record for this book is available
from the British Library

ISBN 978 0575 08419 3

Typeset at The Spartan Press Ltd,
Lymington, Hants

Printed and bound by
Clays Ltd, Elcograf S.p.A.

The Orion Publishing Group's policy is to use papers that are
natural, renewable and recyclable products and made from wood
grown in sustainable forests. The logging and manufacturing
processes are expected to conform to the environmental
regulations of the country of origin.

www.orionbooks.co.uk

To Scott and Suzi Baker
Phantasmes de l'Opera

Contents

Then in one moment, she put forth the charm
Of woven paces and of waving hands,
And in the hollow oak he lay as dead,
And lost to life and use and name and fame.

Then crying 'I have made his glory mine',
And shrieking out 'O fool!' the harlot leapt
Adown the forest, and the thicket closed
Behind her, and the forest echo'd 'fool.'

From 'Merlin and Vivien'
part of *Idylls of the King*
by Alfred Lord Tennyson

PART ONE

Broceliande

A storm was coming, but the winds were still,
And in the wild woods of Broceliande,
Before an oak, so hollow, huge and old
It look'd a tower of ivied masonwork,
At Merlin's feet the wily Vivien lay . . .

From *Idylls of the King*

The People on the Path

(A time in childhood)

The boy's voice woke Martin from a spirit haunted sleep. It was pitch dark. A fragment of gravel cracked against the bedroom window, and again the voice: 'Martin! Martin! There are people on the path. *Martin!*'

People on the path.

Martin flung back the blankets and ran to the window. Below, in the faint moonlight, he could see his fair-haired brother Sebastian, pale-faced, and excited. He was pointing to the forest. 'Martin, there are three of them. Quickly.'

Martin pulled on his jeans and a grubby white jumper. He opened the window, dropping effortlessly to the ground. The old dog whined and yapped in its kennel, dreaming of the chase, too far away in other lands to be disturbed by this second escape from the farmhouse. Martin ran through the darkness. He vaulted the gate and chased after Sebastian.

'Wait for me!' he hissed, not wanting to raise his voice and perhaps disturb the people on the path, though he knew this had never happened.

Where was Sebastian? The moonlight waxed and waned as light cloud drifted over the forest, over the farm. Something ethereal flowed and glowed distantly. Faint birds seemed to be flying upwards, spiralling around the dark shape of a slowly spinning figure.

The boy who danced was Sebastian. Martin watched amazed as his brother, arms outstretched, danced among the people on the path, moving through the three milky forms, a man, a woman, a tall child with long hair. The child was looking back, nervously. Martin thought it was a girl, but the spectral features were hard to discern. All three moved in slow motion. Their ghostly shapes shed light like streams of plasma, where Sebastian passed through them, his voice a thrill of laughter.

'It feels cold. I can hear their hearts beating – it's weird. Their breathing too. The man smells of grease and smoke. Come inside, Martin. Quickly. It's the best yet! It feels like I'm flying and running and swimming all at once – I can fly like an eagle, Martin – come and feel what it's like.'

Martin followed his brother up the old path, but he felt apprehensive. There was a shifting, lurking movement in the wood and Martin thought at once of the old *bosker*, the murderous woodsman who lived among the pools and rocks of the deeper forest. Or perhaps it was Rebecca, spying, always spying on her brothers when they went out onto the path by moonlight.

The night air carried the strong sour smell of earth, emanating from the spectral figures that had emerged from the edge of Broceliande. The man, looking over his shoulder as he moved slowly along the path, seemed to be watching Martin. His mouth worked as if he was speaking, his face contorted as if in warning. Then he raised an arm and pointed, the pale finger freezing Martin in his tracks. The woman turned slowly. She too seemed to stare at the boy who followed them, unaware of the blond lad who laughed and danced within her insubstantial form.

At length, Sebastian left the inside of the people on the path. He was shivering, almost ecstatic. 'It felt *strange*! The man's so frightened. They've had a *vision* of something. Like a long, thin bottle, with trees and earth inside. Like the one I drew last time. They're running away from something. How old, d'you reckon?'

Martin knew his brother was referring to the historical age of the figures. The people who walked the path sometimes looked quite modern, sometimes came in the uniforms of the cavalry from the time of Napoleon, or even earlier; Martin had once seen a Greek warrior on the path. The women occasionally wore dresses that swirled and sparkled with glass as they moved, but more usually were wrapped in heavy cloaks, or thick furs. But the people he watched tonight were wearing peasant's clothes and carrying rough sacks over their shoulders. Their hair was long and they had no weapons. They could have come from one of many times.

Martin shrugged and shivered, walking slowly behind the ghosts on the old track as they steadily ascended the hill to the ruins of the church. There, as they crossed the thorny hedge to the right of the lych gate, the figures began to fade.

Swinging on the wooden gate, aware of bright moonlight cutting an edge across the hollow tower and the broken walls of the chapel, Martin and Sebastian watched as the figures began to descend into the earth. The ghosts were outside the defining wall of the cemetery, beyond the hump of the prehistoric mound on which the church had been erected.

When they were waist high the boys waved and called 'goodbye'. Soon only the heads could be seen, bobbing through the thistles, and then they too were gone.

Where the people went from here, none of the children of this or any other time had ever discovered.

The path from Broceliande continued south into another realm.

The Stoneshifter's Tale

(Fifteen years later . . .)

A storm was coming, Martin noticed, as he followed the cart and the coffin along the path around the forest. And yet the winds were still, the air apprehensive, sharp with the first scents of autumn, seeping from the wild woods of Broceliande. As he drifted onwards to the graveyard and his mother's cold earth home, he watched the dark oaks in the green. Hollow, huge and old, their towering trunks veined and snaked with ivy, they might have been old men, their smooth and spreading roots the shapely limbs of women sprawled at their feet in careful, drowsy thought.

In those days, as in all days, Broceliande was a terrible place, a 'glooming' forest growing over boggy dells, forgotten stones, a place of hidden pools, falls of water and strangling thickets. Cut through by the village road from Gael to Guer, still the true heart of Broceliande could not be found, although the stink of that heart's corruption oozed from the edgewoods to lie, a sour miasma, over all the farms and hamlets to the west, the direction of the wild sea coast at Quiburon, of the

7

stone-tattooed land at Carnac, the direction of the source of storms.

Yes, something lay rotting at the heart of the forest, a death that had been known for generations. It was a decaying place, shedding ghosts like autumn leaves. It held the farmsteads in a root-strong grip, the minds of the families too, though sometimes a youth escaped the shadow (to wait too long was to be lost) and Martin was one of these. He had fled that shadow from the forest. He had been sixteen. He had promised that he would return only at his mother's death, a sad event which had now occurred, calling upon his conscience and his courage.

Again, then, he walked the slow path by Broceliande, a grieving son, a frightened man, confused by the flow of feeling from the wood.

Off the western shore the tide was turning, and with the ebbing flow the traveller was finally lowered to her cold earth home. The storm passed to the south as the priest spoke words over the grave, then walked through the two small fires to embrace and commiserate with Martin. The bell in the renovated tower tolled slowly.

'I'm sorry your sister couldn't be here. Eveline loved her very much. After little Sebastian died . . .'

Martin saw how the priest swallowed back the words, but he knew well what the man meant. Sebastian had been a special child to his parents, the deeply loved one; when he was gone, Rebecca had inherited the mantle of affection. Martin, too, would have liked to have seen his sister by the cold earth home, but she was lost, some-where in the outback of Australia, following songlines, always following songlines.

Father Gualzator hesitated, shivering slightly as the chill wind blew, sending smoke swirling from the fires, the applewood sweet, the hazelwood smoke more acrid. Behind him, Martin's uncle Jacques and aunt Suzanne stood in respectful, watching, waiting silence, the old man's beret clasped at his groin, his long grey hair disturbed by the breeze. His watery eyes were filled with an odd longing; he was longing, certainly, for a cigarette, and to remove the too-tight shirt and tie. But there was something more disturbing him and Martin was aware of it. The priest was agitated, his rosy complexion now brighter with the embarrassment he was feeling. Martin asked him, 'What is it?'

'There are people on the path. I think they've followed us from the wood. Before I sing the hymn, I'd like to let them go.'

Martin looked back, to the place where the people used to sink below the hill. He could see nothing, sense nothing. The priest was blind to them too, but aware of them. He was a Basque, estranged from his strange land, and his language had given him a form of vision that was denied to the likes of Martin. *To speak old was to see old*, he had always said, and when Martin had been a boy he and Sebastian, watching the ethereal flow of people on the path, had tested the priest's 'old' eye, and found it unerring.

A few minutes of strained silence later the priest

relaxed. 'They've gone,' he whispered, and turned back to the cold home. He tugged the rope that held the lid of the coffin and exposed the three linen-wrapped packs. He sang softly as he poured spring water along the length, then the breadth of each part of the traveller. Martin watched, remembering, as red berries and white were dropped carefully onto the wet linen. The flask of honey and the sack of meat were lowered, and then the small sun-wheel, resting on the traveller's chest. The lid was replaced, earth was scattered and more familiar words were uttered: 'Dust to dust, flesh to the fire . . .'

It was over. Jacques steered the ageing dray back to Eveline's farm, the cart riding smoothly on newly greased axles, the priest leaning forward on his knees, staring back at the rebuilt church. Martin was comforted by the over-attentive Suzanne, whose black veil continually blew in his face as she held his arm, held the side of the cart, and talked non-stop about the traveller, Eveline, and the years of her trials and tribulations. Martin was not unaware that he was being gently criticised for having stayed away so long and he repeatedly tried to change the subject, talking about Amsterdam, the design business he ran – but Suzanne was quite single-minded.

Jacques had prepared a stew of rabbit and pheasant in red wine; the priest offered a whole *coeur de brie*, a succulent cheese which Martin had not tasted in years;

and Suzanne had baked bread. There were several stone jars of still cider, and brandy wine.

They sat at the pine table, warmed by the smell of cooked wine and fragrant wood burning on the open fire; they raised their glasses to the traveller and spoke her full name aloud, 'Eveline Mathilde la-coeur-forte Laroche'.

Jacques was then allowed his single cigarette, which he smoked silently, curling the cigarette inside his fingers as he pinched the tip, inhaling deeply and staring at his empty plate.

When he announced that he wished to smoke another he was told sharply that he couldn't, but he glanced at Martin, defied Suzanne and rose from the table, lighting-up as he moved and cocking his head meaningfully to the door. Suzanne poured herself more cider. Father Gualzator reached for the brandy, which he blessed (with a mischievous grin at the woman) before tipping the bottle to his glass.

Outside in the cold dusk, Jacques said, 'I don't know if you're intending to stay, but if you are you should come to the Quiburon peninsular with me. Maybe tomorrow, although I think it'll be a stormy day. What do you think? Will you stay?'

Puzzled by the man's words, Martin nodded, accepted a cigarette and lit it. Distantly a fox barked, and the wide scatter of hens moved suddenly towards the shelter of the shed. 'I have to stay. I have to sell the farm, clear up the paperwork, settle the taxes. I'll be here for a few days. Why Quiburon?'

'It's where your grandfather died, just after the war.'

'Oh yes. Of course. Eveline would never take me there . . .'

'Your mother was only twelve. My little sister. I was only a year older but I felt a lot of responsibility for her. How things changed!'

'Why go back now?'

'I want to tell you what happened to me. And to Eveline. I've never spoken about it, and nor did she, not as far as I know. But now I think I must. If only to encourage you to leave Broceliande, and not endanger your own life.'

'That's what Eveline said to me in her last letter.' Martin drew the envelope from his jacket pocket and removed the single sheet of blue writing paper. His mother's handwriting was neat and precise. He read aloud, '*You were always the sensible one. You avoided the path and I think you must have avoided the danger. I do hope so. If you come back to Broceliande, please don't stay. I have always enjoyed the trips to Amsterdam. You have always been a loving presence in my life. I don't need you at the farm when I finally travel on. It would be better to avoid danger and stay in the city where you have made such a good life for yourself. Please think carefully about these words and say the same to Rebecca, if you ever find her.*'

Jacques lit his third cigarette, glancing almost guiltily back at the house, but Suzanne's voice was raised with laughter and the glasses were clinking.

'For a reason I don't fully understand she was very

worried about you coming back. There are so many strange things about this place – the ghosts, the wood, the lost memories. We've all experienced them. They are part of life, *our* life, we take them for granted. But there's something not quite right. Something wrong. Something has changed in the last few years. I can't explain it. The priest has seen it. We probably all felt it when Eveline died, seven days ago. She seems to have been *acutely* aware of it. She was very concerned for you.'

'The evil in the heart of the wood . . .' Martin mused aloud, staring into the night.

'As I say – it's hard to know. But I would like you to come to Quiburon. Hear my own nightmare. It may help, it may not. It might help you understand your brother's death a little more. I don't know. But Eveline didn't want you to stay here. And the only way I have of persuading you to leave is to share my nightmare. It's up to you, then, to decide whether you should handle Eveline's affairs from here, or from your house in Amsterdam.'

The next day Jacques drove Martin to the sea-drenched cliffs of the western coast of Brittany, arriving in sleeting rain, below a grey sky that moved effortlessly over them from sea-horizon to misted hills behind.

As Jacques drove, he hunched forward in the seat of the old Citroën, peering through the running water on the windscreen, occasionally recognising a place name and exclaiming, 'There! It's OK. Now I know where I am!' or 'Hell and damnation. That last signpost must have been wrong. These damned coastal people.'

Through hamlets, closed against the rain, through country lanes, winding between grey fields and gleaming trees, they traced an erratic course southwards, driving near the cliffs, then looping inland, then back to the edge of the great sea. It was a journey in which they regularly passed the signs of habitation, yet saw not one single human being.

At last the road dropped towards a pebble beach. The restless sea curled and whitened as it heaved against the dark rock of the small bay. Stones, like a ring of black fingers, probed from that swell, out below the waves.

'There,' Jacques said, turning off the engine. 'There at last!' He took a moment to light a cigarette, then remembered to offer Martin one. The paper was damp, but the sharp smoke made Martin heady and relaxed. They peered through the rain for a while in silence. After a few minutes Jacques wound down the window and flicked the smouldering butt into the abyss. Martin did the same, then squirmed and twisted into his oilskin. He followed the older man, out onto a path that looked down on the drowned stone circle.

'There!' Jacques said again. 'You see?' He pointed through the rain beyond the circle. 'You see the stones of the second ring? Two rings together, side by side, stretching into the sea, one of them more drowned than the other. *Can* you see?'

Two dark fingers of smooth rock appeared then

disappeared beneath the swell, a long way out across the ocean.

'Yes,' Martin said, adding, 'How old are they?'

'The rings?' Jacques shrugged. 'Six thousand years, some say. Or maybe only a few years.' He chuckled. 'It depends on how you think of them. When we built them, when we put them upright, they marked a land that was hallowed, but has now been swallowed. Maybe people around here are descended from the builders, eh? Who knows. The stones wear the sea like a skin. You can see how it gleams on them! At low tide, during the hot summers, you can walk among them. It's muddy, they're crusted—' he meant with barnacles, 'but you can touch them. I've heard stories that they sing, some that they dance, and some that they feed on the blood of young girls.' He laughed again, glancing at Martin curiously, green eyes narrowed against the wind and rain, but watching for a reaction. 'And of course, under certain circumstances, or maybe in certain minds, they do. They do. Everything is true. I've always believed in spirit,' he said. 'But it's something you just accept, not make into daft ritual. Do you have them in Amsterdam?'

'Girl-eating stones?'

'Ritualisers. The people who sing to the stones. The people who think that aliens made them. Crystal gazers.'

'We call them The New Age. The Age of Aquarius, in the sixties. People then used to long for it to come. I've worked with many of them. Most of their dream was

15

hope, expectation. If their dreams *had* come true, they'd anyway have grown older, moved on . . .'

Jacques laughed throatily, then hawked and spat away from the wind. 'I agree with you,' he said. 'Dreams are for dreaming, not living. But that said, there's one dream I'd like to have come real, which is why I asked you here. I've lived my life with it. I stood here and hoped it. I longed for it. I dreamed of my father for years, for decades. If I could switch back the clock . . .'

Martin wasn't following his drift and said so. Jacques pointed out to sea again. 'There. Right there. Follow my finger . . .'

He was pointing to the outer ring of stones, perhaps to the tallest stone that could be glimpsed at the ebb of the swelling water.

'I was fourteen years old,' Jacques said. 'The storm had come in fast. The far horizon darkened, but Eveline and I kept playing on the beach. My mother seemed alarmed, but we kept playing on the beach. The blackness spread like colour soaking through water. It swept towards us, although where we played was still in the sunlight. My father was on the small boat. Eveline and I had each had turns with him. Now he was alone, and enjoying a few minutes of peace away from us. The sail was full and he was turning to come back to the bay. The darkness was like a veil, like a net being flung towards us. The sea began to rise, and we were called from the beach and taken up this very path. Soon the sea began to heave into the rocks. The stone circles were awash. We watched the swirl of cloud, the blackness. It was flowing very fast. I had never seen a storm like it.'

Jacques was suddenly speaking strangely, almost dreamily. Martin felt that this story, this memory, had been rehearsed for years. He spoke as if reading from a book.

'My father got tangled in the rigging. The boat was very small. It seemed to skip for a moment in the sea-wind, nosing up then down and the man seemed to be sitting very precariously. He was drenched, his thick white hair draped about his face. The boat was awash. He saw his family, safely up on the path, and waved, then made signals with his hand.

'I remember my mother shouting something; I can't remember what. The boat was twisting on the sea, too far out for safety, the sail full one moment then flapping the next, and he hauled and tugged at the ropes as the ocean broke across the bows. Again my mother shouted to him, her words lost in the wind that was now beginning to scream from the west.

'Above us, the black swirled over, and the rain struck us, and our eyes became half blind so that all we could see was the white of the sail, the dark hull, and the black shape of the man who struggled to guide the small vessel into the haven of the bay. When the boat tipped over it happened so fast I missed it, even though I was watching and shouting and crying for my father. One moment the white sail was a proud balloon, the next there was just the sea, and something splashing, a shape splashing.

'That was the moment when the sea became a monster, when the wind hit it, when the storm changed the cold water into a beast.'

Jacques was in a dream, his eyes almost closed, tears squeezing from the corners, his words oddly stilted, his description strange for this charcoal maker and handy-man.

'It became a monster of many backs. The backs rose and heaved, green and scaly, flecked with white, shining as the monster rolled below the surface. You could see the muscles, the writhing limbs. On the beach, the monster's teeth exploded upwards, white enamel, sucked back into the tide just as the monster was trying to suck back the desperate man who was swimming for the shore. Around him, as he swam for his life, the limbs of the creature rose and fell, its huge back following him, trying to throw him, then suck him down as it subsided.

'He reached the stone. Do you see it? That stone there, yes, the dark one, the sharp one, you can see it now as the waves drop, the outermost stone of the second circle. It rises twelve feet from the sea bed. It was his only haven. And he reached it by sheer guts and reached around it, embraced it, and clung there. All the while the monster in the sea raged at him, sucked at him, tried to draw him back.

'I believe, or I have dreamed, that I saw him smile. He certainly waved. Believing himself to be safe, if cold, he clung to that great stone, to that great past, to the spirit of land, defying the sea. He clung like a limpet. Have you ever tried to prise a limpet from the rock it lives on? You need a chisel. When the creature sticks and grips, it cannot be dislodged, it cannot be sucked into the maw of the monster. And like a limpet embracing the old stone, my father resisted the tide that sucked at him, drew at him, tugged at him. It surged around him, it broke across him, it pulled and dragged at his legs, but he held on, he held on.

'So the ocean, seeing that it would not draw him back, now changed its tactics. It was the moment my mother knew we had lost him. It began to smash him against the friend who had found him. It lifted him and smashed him; it twisted him, drew at him, then flung him to the very stone to which he clung. His head became a bloody mess. It concentrated on his head, of course. It crushed his bones against the rock, stunned him, bruised him, broke him bit by bit, until soon his strength had gone and his whole body was lifted and broken on the circle.

'Three times, maybe four, the sea cracked my father against the rock to open him. And then the pulp was drawn away, down and gone from us, gone for ever.

'He never came back, not a single trace of him, not even the boat. Nothing.'

The rain beat down. It had found a way through Martin's oilskin and was freezing against his shoulder. Jacques had finished speaking and they scurried back to the car, squirming and twisting out of their waterproofs, flinging the wet garments onto the back seat before spending a few minutes smoking, listening to the drum of rain, to the odd silence that is invoked by that hollow sound.

'Why do you dream of him?' Martin asked at length. 'I don't understand. If you *could* turn the clock back, how could you help him?'

'I could have flown to him; or I could have moved the

stone closer to the shore. I had the power to do it. For a year or more I'd known I was a stone-shifter, ever since I'd danced on the path. But I was too frightened . . . perhaps too young. I didn't trust myself to do it right.'

'I don't understand.'

'I could have *flown* to him. I stayed on the earth. I could have moved the stone. I didn't even try to grip it. My father died, but in my heart I know he *knew* that I could have saved him. That's why he waved. He trusted me. I had danced among the people on the path – the magic was in me. He knew this, he'd heard me talk. I failed him. That's all. And I think that's all I can say for the moment.'

Jacques opened the window and tossed his cigarette into the storm.

'I don't understand,' Martin said.

'I didn't expect the sea to change its game. I wasn't ready to take on the sea. I thought he could do it on his own.'

'And you thought you could move the standing stone?'

'It was a *gift*! I'd danced and played inside the ghosts. And sometimes you get a *gift* if you do that, and it lasts a while then goes. Like 'Old Provider's' Christmas presents, though, there's always a catch. Like nearly every child, I was too afraid to use the gift, and now it's gone, and your grandfather died when he might have lived.

'Eveline was there too and she too felt helpless, and yet she felt she *could* have helped. And whatever it was happened to *her* during that terrible storm later made her frightened for you and Rebecca, which is why she encouraged you to go away and *stay* away.'

Jacques fumbled for the starter and the Citroen shuddered into life. Martin sat back, cold and confused, and let the rain and the saturated land drift past as his uncle drove him home.

The Songliner's Tale

Four days after the interment, Martin dressed warmly against the chill weather and walked through the drizzle up the path to the cemetery. He'd had a restless night, waking at one point to the sound of movement downstairs. Half dreaming, half alert, he had imagined that someone was prowling about the house, at one point even entering the bedroom where he lay. Indeed, in the morning he found the back door swinging free, and the signs of sandwich-making. Not knowing his mother's routine, nor lifestyle, he was not unduly concerned by this intrusion.

He approached the old church, with its half-shroud of scaffolding, and as he reached for the gate, so he saw a crouching figure by the hump of green-cloth covered soil, the new grave. It was a woman, he thought, from the drop of auburn hair around the figure's shoulders, but he didn't recognise her. She wore a heavy lambskin coat, green cord trousers, and black leather boots that were scratched and muddied. She was hunkered down and singing softly, her arms folded across her chest, her head raised slightly, as if looking above the top of the gleaming marble headstone.

Her voice suddenly made contact!

'Rebecca?' Martin whispered. Her singing voice came clearer, sharper through the fine rain. 'Rebecca?' he called more loudly, and the woman turned to look at him. Martin stopped walking, shocked by the face that stared at him.

Slowly Rebecca rose to her feet, rubbed at the backs of her knees and came over to her brother. Her long hair was damp, framing a strong and handsome face, aged by sun and dust. She was as hard as stone, as carved as wood; when she smiled she revealed the absence of a canine tooth, something that the younger Rebecca would have never allowed to go unfilled. But the smile was a genuine gesture of pleasure, the wry turn of the lips, gladness conveyed in every movement of face and hands as she reached for Martin and hugged him.

'You look lean,' she said, stepping back to inspect him after the embrace. 'You've not been eating.'

'I try to keep fit. Genes for fatness run in the family; have to keep them at bay, like wild dogs. Not eating twenty-course Indonesian meals every day helps as well, excellent though they are.'

'*You'll* get fat,' she said with a smile. 'Just like daddy, it'll happen suddenly. But you look good now. Nice complexion.' She pinched his cheek. 'And no drugs, I think. No shadows. That's good.'

'I don't take drugs,' Martin agreed. 'You look rugged,' he went on. He touched the deeply etched lines about her eyes and mouth, his fingers gentle. She shrugged.

'I'm a rugged lass. The outback is a hard place. The land wants to take your water. Take my hand . . .'

They walked to the iron gate, then suddenly Rebecca ran, childlike, to leap and swing on the rusting hinges, looking out towards the village and the old forest – Broceliande, hazy in the rain, dark on the horizon. Martin stepped onto the gate as well.

Rebecca said, 'It's odd to be back. I can't tell whether I like it or hate it. I hate this bloody weather, of course. But the smells, the colours . . . I've been bleached yellow, burned red and charred umber at various times over the last few years. And I've heard the songs, such wonderful old songs, Martin . . . But I've missed the colours, the greens. The *real* colours.'

'Can you hear songs now? Are there songs in this earth?'

She glanced at him, her expression one of deliberate if unfelt contempt. 'Don't be an idiot. Of course there are. The song is everywhere around us. It doesn't sing *from* us, Martin, it sings *through* us; which is why we forget so easily in this hemisphere.' She stepped from the gate and folded her arms, her characteristic gesture. She watched him through jet-lagged eyes, across the years of absence. 'I don't want to talk about the songpaths. I came here to watch my mother into her cold home and I missed it. I'm really sorry that I wasn't here. I missed dad down, ten years ago, and I promised myself not to repeat the negligence.'

Martin said, 'You must have got my letter . . .'

'I did! It came fast. And I got the first flight available,

but the bloody *engine* failed in Bombay. A day and a half in Bombay, confined to the airport, paying three kids a tip each every time I needed a piss, and all the cash I had was in Australian dollars! I tried to ring, but the lines just wouldn't connect.'

She laughed and clutched her brother's arm. 'That's funny, isn't it? Twelve years of my life I've spent connecting the lines, the lines between different shapes of spirit, but I can't connect with France Telecom from Bombay Airport. I like that. It's sort of ironic.'

'Pompous little bag of bones,' Martin murmured, echoing a childhood taunt, and Rebecca put him in a headlock, laughing as they struggled through the rain until Martin declared a truce.

'I *am* a bag of bones. But I'm five times stronger than *you*, my man.'

'Damn right. I said *pax*!'

'Can I stay with you?' she asked a while later, as they straightened clothing and returned to the rough road back to the village.

'Of course. The house is as much yours—'

'Can I *stay* with you!' she repeated, and Martin felt the thump of his heart. It had been a long time and he flushed as he anticipated the renewed relationship. But there was no-one in his life in Amsterdam at the moment. 'I suppose so.'

'You suppose so. Great. You suppose so.'

'Yes. You can *stay* with me. It's been a long time, Beck. We've moved apart.'

'Of course we have! But the line is still there between

25

us. Lines like that don't break. And I need to be close. That's all. That's it. I need to be close. To you. To them. I should have been here to watch them down.'

'I wasn't here when either of them crossed,' Martin said quietly. 'So they wouldn't have known you weren't here for the interment. They knew you'd be sent for. Eveline actually didn't *want* us here. Anyway, I watched them down. They were guarded. I swear it.'

Rebecca sighed as they walked, now linking arms, almost hanging on to Martin, jet-lag beginning to creep into her muscles. 'She'll be with little Seb. That's nice . . .'

'Not for thirty days yet,' Martin reminded her, and she glanced at her watch.

'Oh yes. I'd forgotten. Well . . . she soon *will* be with our little brat brother. It's so *odd* to be back,' the last statement made in a forceful tone of voice, the subject changed abruptly.

Martin felt the same shudder of realisation. He too was something of a stranger in a familiar land. His life had changed, he was out of place here, and yet he was needed.

'I know,' he said grimly. 'I think I have to stay. The farm needs sorting out. I hardly know where to begin. It would be good to have some help, Beck.'

Martin was aware of her hesitation as they walked, the slight loosening of his sister's grip on his arm, the sudden tightening of her fingers again. Rebecca said, 'I'll stay as long as I can. I'll do what I can. But if the songs get too—' she broke off, then smiled and shrugged. 'I

26

can't explain it, Martin. My line isn't here anymore. The sounds confuse me. If I get called back, I'll have to go.'

'Stay as long as you can. It'll be good to have you here.'

'I'll try. But when I go, I'll be gone before you know it. It's the way with me.'

'How very New Age,' he said with a smile.

'No. Just the way I am.'

He looked at her across years, across age, knew that the moments together would be short, that this sad reunion was an event in a life, hers, as rich and complex as any tapestry; he knew that Rebecca was here because her lines had brought her here, and that in her own world she would soon be so far from him that not even the sound-wires would be able to connect them, and again she would be gone.

His voice dropping, his voice resigned, he said simply, 'I know.'

Martin built and stoked the applewood fire until the small parlour was glowing with light and warmth. He spread a blanket on the hearthside, undressed and lay back. Rebecca finished her bath and ran naked into the room, clutching a bath sheet which she flung over the two of them, shivering beside him. Martin felt the steam and heat from her body, a cooling dampness. When the attack of shivering had passed she sat up, the towel around her shoulders, looking at the man, smiling and shaking her head. 'You *are* lean. You used to be so chubby! I don't think I've ever seen so flat a stomach.'

'Come on. Flynn is the most athletic man you've ever met. *Your* words, five years ago, last letter I ever had from you.'

Rebecca laughed, leaning her head towards the fire so that her coppery hair could start to dry. 'What are you talking about? I wrote every week. Didn't you get my letters? Obviously a bad postal service.'

'Obviously.'

'Besides, Flynn is nothing but bone and sinew. Athletic but not aesthetic, not that I give a damn. I don't want to talk about Flynn. I want to talk about us. So just get me warm. Please?'

'This reminds me of that first night. When I came here? Do you remember? I was a sad, bedraggled soul, and you and Sebastian hated me.'

Martin smiled as a vague memory of Rebecca's arrival in the family entertained him. 'They made such a fuss of you. They kept comparing you to me. I got really angry . . .'

'They were teasing you. I could see it so clearly. It was obvious. I thought it was funny—'

'What was funny?'

'—the way you *couldn't* see it. You were such a sheltered boy. Such a cautious boy . . . But I was hungry, and defensive, and new, and confused. I was missing my own home, my own parents. Dad – *my* Dad – was

28

always teasing. I loved his teasing. It's what I missed most when he died. And then I found that my "new" Dad was just as bad – just as good! It was like coming home again. I missed it all so much when I went to Australia. Flynn is so straight . . . "if it's irony it must be metal". "Say what you mean and mean what you say". It comes from having to dissect the literal from the symbolic in reconstructed languages, I suppose.'

'Do what?'

'It's his job. What he calls digging out the hard foundations below the crumbling ideas of walls and towers. And he's good at it. But he's: So! Serious! He's learned to cherish the clear signal of a clear statement. I'm not criticising him, you understand.'

'Of course you're not. Perish the thought.'

'Bastard! Anyway *you* were always easy to wind up.'

'Who's denying it? I didn't like you. Not at first. I didn't want you in the family. I didn't like the way you and Seb teamed up to dance through the people on the path. I felt excluded.'

'You *were* excluded. Which isn't to say that I didn't fancy you even then. You intrigued me. But you were a pain in the butt.' She looked at the fire. 'Poor little Seb. What the hell did he do, I wonder? What did he do that he had to die like that?'

Martin was surprised by her comment. 'You sound as if you think it had something to do with the path.'

'Do I? I'm not sure. But I am sure he went inside the people once too often. I bet every child around here still does it, of course. But most of us stopped seeing them after a while. As if we'd been . . . as if we'd been contacted. Or maybe completed. I don't know. Something like that. But Seb, he kept *on* seeing them. And he kept on drawing those funny bottles. Do you remember? Long, thin bottles, with little trees and little men inside them.'

'I do remember.'

Martin leaned towards the fire, puzzled. 'Contacted? Completed? What does that mean, Beck? Do you feel completed in some way?'

Rebecca wriggled closer, her hand resting on his warm skin, just above the knee. She seemed to be shivering again. 'I think so. I don't know so. There's something in Broceliande that is seeping out. Merlin's spirit, of course. We've always known that, haven't we?' She smiled, then spoke the local lore, the belief based on forgotten legend. 'Merlin sleeps in the heart of the wood, trapped by the enchantress Vivien in a thorn tree, or an oak tree by some accounts, inside a column of air that hides him from all eyes but hers. His dreams, his nightmares, creep to the edge to provide for us, to divide us, to test us, to seek out the true hearts among us.'

'That's fairy-tale. The people on the path aren't dreams, or nightmares. And they don't interfere with us.'

'Don't they? But that's not the point. The point is, this is a haunted place, and it always has been. We take the ghosts for granted. Not everyone sees them, just a few, and all of us stop seeing them after a year or so and start to doubt our memory. But we never talk about them *outside*. Why is that? Why do we keep quiet? Is something *stopping* us? Have you ever spoken to anyone in Amsterdam about the people?'

'Never. They'd think I was mad.'

'But *why* do you say that? *You* know you're not. You're no more mad than everybody else. We share a common experience and we share a common fear of communicating that experience. It's as if we've become afraid of what happened to us as children, when we saw them, when we danced inside their skins. Except that you never did, of course—'

'In fact, I did. Just once. It was terrifying. It felt as if I was gliding on a cold lake, and there was a woman singing, but it only lasted an instant.'

Rebecca frowned, staring at him for a moment. 'I didn't know that.' She turned away. 'Yes. I think I remember.'

'No you don't. This is the first time I've mentioned it.'

'Well, my point is, most of us saw them for months. Some only got a glimpse. And for all of us there was a moment when we got frightened . . .'

'Christ. That's what Jacques told me . . .'

'Jacques? Is he still alive?'

'Very much so, still building sheds and making charcoal. He was at the cold-earthing, four days ago.'

'The funeral, Martin. We call them funerals in the outside world, these days.'

'I like the old terms. Anyway, he took me to Quiburon, out on the coast where the stones are. Told me about my grandfather . . . about how he'd felt that he could have saved him from drowning, even though he was a child at the time . . . And he said just what you've just said. He had suddenly got frightened, and known that it was time to stop the encounters.'

'With the path . . .'

'Yes.'

Rebecca sighed, stretching out across the rug, dry and warm, her hands behind her head as she stared at the black beams of the ceiling.

'To go away is to see more clearly, Eveline said, but she was trapped. She wrote to me – just once – she said she loved me but for my own sake, stay away. *We get blinded in this place*, she said. *We take too much for granted. We don't see how trapped we are, how used we are. All that protects us is that we are afraid to talk about it. But who's trying to stop us talking about it?*'

'You never talked about Broceliande to Flynn?'

'A little. I didn't find it easy.'

When I first arrived in your home, I didn't believe in the people on the path. I thought you were all crazy, dancing around at midnight, describing thin air as if there were human figures in it. I used to watch you from the garden. I was watching you the night Seb danced into the frightened people, the week before he died. You thought I was in bed asleep, but I never slept in the middle night; I was too frightened. There were too many prowlings and breathings, too many noises, and I was new to the house, and my new father still scared me a bit, even though I had no reason to be frightened.

I'd seen other children playing with the ghosts – do

32

you remember Thierry? What a crazy boy. Always shouting, always calling to them: 'Tell me your story! Tell me your story!' And Suzi. Always nattering away, happy with all the people, always urging them to stay, having a *real* relationship with them. And all I could see were my new friends, and my new brothers, addressing the emptiness. But I'd also heard adults talking about their own childhoods, and the way they'd followed the people on the path, and some of the terrible and wonderful things that had happened to them shortly afterwards. So I was intrigued. I assumed it was just because I didn't know how to *look*. My eyes were wrong, which is why I started to rub them, and screw them up. It was so painful. I became so obsessed with seeing that I became crazy. When I finally cut the eyelids to let in more light – remember that? – I was finally taken in hand. I still have the scars, but they're lost in the skin-lines now, thank God.

I suppose Eveline knew that I was trying to see the things which she herself had once seen, and long become blind to. She locked me in my room at night, although she always came back two or three times to cuddle me. The one night she didn't come and check on me was the night when you followed Seb dancing up the path inside *three* ghosts, although I didn't know this at the time. Eveline was ill, remember? And I managed to get out through the window when I heard Seb disturb you. He was always outside. I don't think he ever slept. It was as if he'd got some magical energy that kept him hunting, hunting the spirits.

I ran along behind you, hiding in the tree-line when

the moon came out, and heard Sebastian shouting something like, 'This is the best ever. I can hear their hearts!'. You were hanging back; you always said you'd never go inside one of these ghosts. You were probably wise. I could only see you walking slowly and nervously, and little Seb twisting and laughing. The moon went in, everything was dark, and that's when I saw *my* person on the path.

He was right at the point where the track leaves Broceliande, where the tangle of rose-briar and hawthorn thins, that marshy area, with the aspens and broken oaks . . . He was standing there, holding a horse by the reins. Then he stepped forward, and I could see that the horse was heavily packed and that the man, who was young and lightly bearded, had some strange bagpipes over his shoulder. There was a stringed instrument on the side of the packhorse, a piece of curved and decorated wood and a small soundbox. I didn't recognise it, and I never heard it played, but that this ghost, this shimmering man, was a musician was all that I could think of.

He drew back into the woods as you and Sebastian came running back to the farmhouse. He watched you carefully, and you didn't see him. That's odd, isn't it? Usually the ghosts are unaware of us.

When you'd gone, he led the horse forward up the path, hurrying slightly, although he was moving slowly, like a slowed film, but the haste was conveyed clearly. He knew I was behind him, following. I had never seen anything like it. I was enchanted. The glimmer, like fairy glamour, flowed from his edges. It filled the night air, and I tried to touch it, but felt nothing.

I caught up with him. I felt so alive, suddenly I forgot about my eyes, which were still hurting from the way I'd slashed the skin. I can recognise now that I was aroused, that my body was aroused by imagination, by the experience of seeing a troubadour, a ghostly one, but a sort of dream recreated on that autumn night. I was thrilled by the encounter, and desperately wanted to hear him sing. So I entered him, and copied Sebastian, turning and swirling inside the dewy ghost.

There was nothing but rage. It was terrifying. I was caught in a whirlpool of fear, of anger. The man was escaping. He was frightened of something, and secretive. The rage in him seemed to crush me. Every squirt of blood in his veins was the rushing of a waterfall; his heart was thundering. I was deafened by this man's retreat from some terrible encounter, or so it felt. I was strangling, gasping for breath, turning desperately to find fresh air as he carried me with him, up to the hill. It was like being buried alive.

Then, just at the last, just as I thought I was going to die, I heard the sound of pipes. He wasn't playing them, he was *remembering* them. He was singing to himself in his own language, remembering the skirling notes of the pipes he carried, and I shared that thought, that moment of internal music. I touched an ancient music. I was treated to such an old song, and a song filled with such despair . . .

I became haunted by that music, just as Sebastian had been haunted by his own encounter. I couldn't sing it. It made no sense. It made sense only in my head; I could jig to it, I could twirl to it, but it was inexpressible, except in dreams.

How old was I? I can't remember, now. Fifteen, maybe. I spent the holiday weeks of the next two years among the stones at Carnac, hating the tourists, the wretched families who came to picnic, to photograph, but not to listen. I was listening for the dreamsongs of that time, for the old tunes, for some clue to the magic that was now in me. But I realised that even that ancient earth wasn't old enough. To articulate the music that flowed inside me not so much like blood, more like . . . like a benign but omnipresent parasitic worm, invading my spaces, pulling back when it hurt me, growing inside me but as I say, *inexpressible*, because it was pure feeling, eroding me, fighting me, but carefully . . . to find out how to exorcise that music, to get rid of the ghost that something in Broceliande had driven into me, I had to go further back.

Which is why I went to Australia, to the place of songlines, and songtrails, and a way of singing that you would never understand, because it isn't singing at all, nor singing up the world of rocks and creatures as happened in the dreamtime, but being sung *through*. I can't describe it.

The other side is easier: I never had a good voice. I was always gravelly, you remember? The groaning background, Daddy used to say. But suddenly when I sang I seemed to have an effect on people. Whatever I sang, wherever I was, whatever the country.

I silenced the chief (and his family!) of the Memoragas

people – the thunder people – out behind the Mann Ranges. They were singing to the sleeping rains and asked me to join in. I was already flowing with them, they seemed to be singing through me, and when I sang it was dizzying, it was like falling, then flying. Suddenly I was the only voice. They were entranced and puzzled, watching me in silence. I seemed to fly among them, and there were so many of them, and the land shifted and changed, the light, the colour, the warmth. I was travelling *through* the song, some silly ditty from childhood, 'Frère Jacques' maybe, I've now lost the words, I just remember how the world dropped away when I sang, and how my song went through those watching people.

In the morning I felt hungover, though I hadn't been drinking. There was so much excitement outside my private space that I got up, quite naked, and peered out.

Flynn was there, crouching with the chief and looking at water flowing from below their painted rock. There had never been a spring there, now there was new water, very cold, rich in calcium and magnesium – Flynn did the analysis – a new spring, which had come during the night.

My song, they said, had called the sleeping water to their hunt trail. They were amazed at the new spring. They made me bathe in it. They all wanted to wash me. I sat in the muddy stream for an hour, while I was anointed and sung to, and questioned, and played to with kazoo and bark drum. They put eucalyptus leaves on my head and insisted on daubing me with the image, in yellow ochre, of a gerbil, a creature that seems to find water everywhere. It was their totem creature.

The only truly embarrassing moment was needing to go to the toilet. Everything that I *didn't* want, they *valued*, collecting it and burying it below a small stone.

After that I got frightened. I was singing to people, singing anything, any rubbish, and it was affecting them profoundly. There was a touch of magic in my voice and I had no conception of it, only the knowledge that it worked. Flynn was both apprehensive and loving. He was never exploitative, although we did earn a few meals in the lean times by my singing in small town bars. I think he knew there was a spirit in me, he simply had no idea what it was and had no idea how to use it. We went into the desert for five years, built separate shacks, and entered our own Otherworlds. We'd meet on occasion to eat a ceremonial meal (of whatever we could find, or obtain), and spend a few hours on the mat, but most importantly we talked about our dreams. We'd end each visit by going to the small stream and bathing, then follow our separate lines again.

That was ten years ago. It was a hard time for me, a time in which I came close to death on several occasions. But with the song in me, this song, this magic, I always came back.

Then Flynn drowned – a terrible accident. I ran twelve miles to the billabong when I was told the news, and dragged his body from the muddy pool. He'd been dead when he was found, so they'd left him there. He was bloated with water, naked and fat, his skin fishbelly-white. He was quite dead. But I crouched on him and sang to him and the water started to ooze from him, came out of his mouth, his ears, his eyes, nose, out of his pores, his arse, even out of his cock. The water drained from him, a steady sweat, a steady flow in the cold dawn, and soon there was room in his body for the air again. He started to breathe and his body danced below me. The air went in, his eyes opened and stared at me, and I stopped the song.

If he was frightened of me before, he was terrified of me then!

It was the moment when my time with Flynn became fatally defined. I mean in terms of its intimacy, its . . . longevity? We were dying together from that moment on. But only because our time together was now defined by the *song*. He hadn't known he was dead. But when people come up to you to congratulate you on being alive again you tend to get the idea that something weird has happened. Flynn was as muscular and lean as the desert where we lived; every part of his mind was trimmed to the bone. He had no time for doubt. He heard the story – that he'd had a stroke and fallen into the drowning pool – he heard the story of the songlady bringing him back to life, he knew that our friends in the wanderlands, the desert, weren't liars; and he accepted.

At that moment he was a dead man alive again; at that moment my song was magic. At that moment he was at a distance from me, because his own curiosity now extended not to the land which we loved, or to the past which we were trying to recreate in our minds, but to me, to a French woman, born near the forest of Paimpont, orphaned when fourteen years old, now a *possessor* of magic, not just an explorer of magic tradition.

The Lake-finder's Tale

The old 'bosker', Conrad, came to the farmhouse shortly after dawn, a dark figure moving effortlessly along the path, the early sun catching on his small, silver spectacles. Martin had been unable to sleep, his mind full of Rebecca's story and the idea that to dance inside the ghostly figures from Broceliande was to become possessed by some shadow of the past. Rebecca slept soundly in the bed behind him. Martin peered down as Conrad rummaged in the long grass by the hedges and found two eggs, which he inspected and pocketed. He was wearing a wide-brimmed leather hat – he had made it himself – and a long, grey overcoat which flapped around him as he moved. He carried two short wooden staffs, slung on his back like rifles.

Seeing Martin at the bedroom window he waved, then let himself in to the warm kitchen below. Martin came downstairs. The old man stood, hat in his hands, white hair combed back into a long pigtail, tied with grass-twine. He was looking around sadly.

'I watched Eveline as she went to her cold home, the other day,' he said. 'I was by the wood. I didn't want to intrude by the fires.'

'I wish you had. You'd have been very welcome.'

'I'm going to miss her. She was just a girl when I came here first, but she helped me build my houses in the forest. She always let me have eggs – and bread, sometimes. I traded foxes, after your father died. She couldn't bear to kill them, but they have to be controlled.'

'I understand,' Martin said quickly, feeling uncomfortable. 'But please stop controlling them from now. I'm more than happy to let you have eggs whenever you want.'

As Martin picked a dozen of the larger eggs from a wicker basket, placing them carefully in Conrad's sack, the old man said carefully, 'You're a fox lover, then?'

'Always have been.'

'So am I at heart. But trade is trade.'

Martin offered the remains of yesterday's heavy loaf and a farm cheese that was now over-ripe. The old bosker seemed delighted.

'Would you like some breakfast?' Martin asked him.

'I ate in the forest at first dew. Thanks all the same.'

Conrad seemed to relax. He pulled on his hat and lifted the pack to his shoulder. He was staring at Martin curiously, grey eyes bright in the weather-etched face. 'Are you still frightened of me, Martin?'

'Good God no.'

'You used to be—'

'Kids are always frightened of hermits. *And* you were once an enemy soldier, left behind by the war. We used to make up terrible stories about what you did in the woods.'

'A living demon, eh?' Conrad laughed. 'Yes, I remember. I used to listen – I could hear you all from a long distance. It's a talent I seem to have developed since coming here,' – he sounded wry – 'Sometimes your fantasies amused me, sometimes – not often – they made me sad. I was a long way from my first home, and harmless to everything inedible, which included children—'

'Ah yes, but we didn't think so.'

'All except Rebecca, your special friend Rebecca.' Conrad winked. '*She* wasn't afraid of me. Anyway, I would watch you children chasing the ghosts from the forest as they walked the path. I couldn't see them, of course, no adult could. But I could hear them. It was an extraordinary experience. It still is. Which is chiefly why I came to see you. There's something I want to show you . . .'

'Shall I wake Rebecca?'

The old man glanced back. 'No. This is for you alone.'

Conrad might always have been a part of Broceliande. He was as eternal, as familiar, indeed as elusive, usually, as the strange ruins that could be found just inside the forest's skirts. But he had not been born here, nor come into existence here. In his own words, 'There comes a moment in every person's life, I now realise, when as they are marching forward they become aware that in fact they are running away. At that moment, home is where you are standing, and this place, this gloomy edgewood, became my second home.'

His army column had been marching past Broceliande. Conrad was sixteen, not particularly frightened, not particularly lonely. He was just a soldier in a column, moving forward towards the coast. There were not enough trucks to transport all the troops, in those early winter months of 1944, and so like Caesar's legions they tramped the rough roads to the west, sometimes aware that a watery sun was leading them on.

'But I had no faith, no real belief. My father had always talked of duty, and of family, but his words, sincere though they were, were of no comfort to me. I wonder sometimes if there can be any greater pain than realising that you are no longer part of a family that once was your whole life.

'As we marched past Broceliande my First Home broke into shattered memories. Everything simply fell apart. I hated where I had come from. I loathed that savage war. I despised the principles that drove it. I was not alone in this, of course, but the forest took me and me alone.

'I deserted quickly. I used a strip of oilskin to wrap my weapons and bury them; the rifle was a bolt-action Lee Enfield, more like twenty pounds in weight than nine, or so it seemed, and I was glad of the freedom from this burden.

'That first day, I walked a wide circle, walking to the limit of what I felt I needed. That circle, I discovered later, was more than two miles across.'

This disc of land had become Conrad's Second Home.

He walked its circumference five times, first entering the dark forest, then emerging and skirting the villages, crossing the fields and the farmlands before entering the woods again. All of this was done at night because he was in fear of his life, now, and his uniform would certainly have been an invitation to murder.

In all the long years since then he had never once stepped outside the circle, as he had defined it during those February days. 'I belong here. I made it right that I belonged here. I became accepted, eventually welcomed. I don't belong across the circle, but I've lived long enough, and circled hard enough, to make this small land *my* land. My home.'

Now Conrad led the way into that small land and into the forest, following a wide, winding path that was tall with wet, webbed grass and purple thistle. He stopped occasionally to listen. The air was moist, almost stifling.

His first house was a shack constructed out of corrugated iron, wooden panels and old doors. It was covered with black oilskins. Around it, on a picket fence, hung thirty or so carcasses of grey squirrels, in various states of decomposition. Two foxes' heads on poles were a grim reminder of Conrad's main usefulness to the farms around the wood.

'Come in, come in,' the bosker said with a chuckle, glancing back at Martin. 'Into the place which terrified you once upon a time.'

Martin pulled aside the oilskin door, ducked through

the small entrance space into Conrad's living quarters. The floor had been hollowed out and lined with sandbags and turves. His bed was at one end, in a stream of light from the only window, a gap below the metal eaves. His fire was at the other end of the small room, built out of bricks, with an iron chimney to the outside world. The walls were hung with skins and furs; hooks and leather ties dangled from the ceiling, ready for hanging game. He had a chair and a table, and a small chest on which stood two tiny, framed and faded photographs, one of a shy, fair-haired girl, holding a cat, the other of two people sitting on a garden chair, a couple who looked out of the frame with solemn expression.

As Conrad stored his new supplies, Martin noticed that above the bed were five crude paintings, all of the girl, all from different angles: one of each profile, her full face laughing, her face looking coy, a discreet nude, they had been executed in crayon on smoothed and chalk-whitened wood.

Light spilled suddenly into the shack. Conrad had pulled back the doorflap, waiting quietly for Martin to finish his inspection.

'Just a ghost,' the old man said, and Martin felt embarrassed, stepping quickly away from the portraits.

'I'm sorry. That was an intrusion. I was too curious.'

'No intrusion at all. She's long gone, now. Long changed. But she keeps me in touch with my younger spirit.'

They continued inwards, the track narrowing and becoming more difficult, the oaks crowding from the sides.

'Be careful,' Conrad called, as he smacked at wet briar to clear the route. 'This is the way the ghosts come. If I say get off the path, do so immediately. They sometimes move very quietly.'

'What does it matter?' Martin called back. 'I can't see them or hear them any more. I'm too old. They can't harm me . . .'

Conrad's voice as he moved ahead was steely. 'They can harm you. Just do as I say. For Eveline's sake, for your mother's sake.'

The path spilled out into a clearing below the spreading branches of three massive beeches. The ground here was soft and golden brown, streaked through with the green of fern. Here, Conrad had his second home, a hemisphere of bent willow branches, covered with hides.

'Hunting lodge,' he said quickly, skirting the clearing. 'We've not far to go, now.'

Not far to go?

For an hour that seemed like ten, Conrad led them deeper into the wildwood, through half-lit dells and marshy, silent glades, down stone escarpments and over massive, mossy rocks which caught the shifting sun with a vibrant, emerald luminosity. Muddy watercourses wound through crushing woods of oak and holly; springs spilled from ragged ledges, misting in the thin light from the glistening canopy.

'We're lost. We must be lost.'

'Not lost at all. Look!'

And suddenly they had come through the wood to the rush-fringed shore of a wide lake, and the bosker's third home – a series of tarpaulins, slung between trees, open to the water.

'Fishing lodge,' Conrad announced, stooping to enter the shelter and beckoning Martin to follow him.

The lodge was full of dried and drying fish, crude rods and nets, a harpoon and a further pile of skins, rabbit and fox; the cured hides of two small deer were stretched on frames and could be pulled across the open front to block the wind.

They sat, squeezed together, and watched the gentle water. Mallards and moorhens wriggled through the rushes, dipping and pecking below the lake. The forest was solid on the other side.

'They come across in small boats, or sometimes on rafts,' Conrad said after a while. 'When I'm here at night, sometimes the water is covered with a low mist, and it swirls where the boat comes, the only visible sign of their passage from the heartwood. I hear the oars dipping, and the rustle of the sedges when it comes to the bank. I hear the murmur of voices, and on occasion the breathing of horses. The ghosts, which are invisible to me, follow the path by your farm, then up to the church and over the hill. The boat returns to the dark wood, after which there will often be nothing for months.

'Over the lake is the heart of Broceliande but it is an older forest than the forest behind us. It doesn't belong here.

'My circle of land ends as far out onto the lake as I need to go to spear pike, perhaps twenty yards. I would never dare go further.'

*

I had lived in the wood for ten years before I found the lake or perhaps I should say before the *lake* found *me*. There was no sign of it when I first came here. I had probably walked across its edge fifty times since I first circumscribed my land. It had hidden from me, or *been* hidden from me, but one bitter winter morning I heard the sound of moorhens and gently splashing water. I was curious, aware that there should have been a grove of trees there. I pushed through the dense holly to find the lake very much as you see it now. It was covered with ice, though, almost to the edge itself, where the rushes were white with frost.

This was the second event that convinced me of a source of magic at work, deeper in the forest. I'd already seen the strange behaviour of you children, at night on the path, your clear belief in ghosts and your parents' reluctance to contradict you. More than that, when hunting deep in the wood I had occasionally heard the sound of a man crying out. The wailing came from a great distance, and quite soon I realised that the distance was further than I'd thought, since I discovered I could also hear the whispered words of children from a mile away. That crying voice haunted me, though. It drifted through the glades, seemed to flow down the paths through the wood, and was usually followed by a woman's voice, laughing.

So when this lake miraculously appeared, one morning, I could no longer deny that I'd stumbled into a place which, to put it mildly, was quite out of the ordinary. The strange way of speaking among the farmers and villagers now became more important. The traditions, the rituals that I had watched from the edgewood, all had seemed eccentric, perhaps just local habit; now they seemed to echo an older thought: the fires you put at the head of each grave, the procession of the twelve trees, the drowning of grass images, with the hair-filled puppet of a child inside . . . They'd never been sinister, but now they became more meaningful, although I've never really understood that meaning.

I wasn't aware, when all this was happening, of the association of Merlin with this forest. I hadn't read Tennyson or Chrétien de Troyes, knew nothing of Thomas Mallory, or the *Vitae Merlinis*, or the other sources. The priest talked to me about all of them. He lent me books. But before that education I only knew that there was a vision of magic, somewhere across the lake, and that it was seeping from the forest, shrouded in the ghostly forms of the people on the path, and in that terrible moaning.

You know how the seasons bring different scents, different feelings in the air? So it was with the wailing voice, as if there was a season for the agony, a certain day for the distress, an hour, just after dusk, when the moment of true desperation could be remembered and the air of the forest filled with the cry.

On one such evening, when the pain of that voice had gone, I crept from my hunting lodge again and heard the wildwood speak, an odd echo, like a girl's voice, but curiously slow. It seemed to breathe a word. I wasn't sure, but I thought the word was 'Fool', and moments later the word was repeated. 'Fool!'

I waited, fascinated, and soon a girl from the village came running and twirling along the path. I knew her by sight, though she had never entered the wood before. She was a slight thing, fourteen years old or so, her hair almost orange in the half light, her clothing a simple dress and a loose grey cardigan.

As she ran she seemed to dance, exactly as I have seen the children dance among the ghosts. She was murmuring as she moved. 'I have it. I have it now.'

She approached the clearing where I waited, unaware of me. Then she stopped and crouched, snarling and shaking her head so that her hair was wild. Laughing, she suddenly launched herself at a tree and scratched and bit at the hard bark, tearing with her fingers, stripping away whole lengths of wood. Embracing the torn trunk she flung back her head and howled and bayed, then laughed and again exclaimed, 'I have it!'.

I felt terrified of this feral child and inadvertently drew back, drawing attention to myself. She raced across to me, coming very close, then folded her arms about her body – her fingers were bloody – cocking her head as she peered at me. Then she leered forward, lips hideously drawn back from pearl-white teeth to expose the death in her head. 'I have it!' she hissed, and proceeded to dance a little jig, arms still folded. 'I have it,' she murmured, almost singing, delighted with herself.

At that moment a boy laughed from the darkness of the wood. The girl turned quickly, crouching slightly, then took off like a hare towards the source of the sound. The boy stepped into the half light and taunted her. 'No you don't! No you don't!'

'I *have* it,' screamed the girl.

'You have *nothing*. You took *nothing*!'

And at once his crowing ceased and his youthful face took on a look of great age, and great amusement, the amusement of an old man, listening to the pretensions of someone younger and still naive.

'Fool . . .' he added quietly.

It was the wrong thing to do, perhaps. The girl leapt at him and in a second had torn her nails across his grinning face. They struggled. He held her hair, but she was taller, stronger, and she hunched above him, bending him and crushing him, finally sinking her teeth into the back of his neck. She shook him, worried at him, like the wolf whose shape now seemed to envelop her. Girl-like, hair tossing, legs thrashing inside her simple skirt, the hunched form of a wolf was shadowed around her, an evil glamour.

The screaming boy was dragged away by this monstrous creature. I ran towards her, but she turned and looked at me, the struggling boy still held in those perfect teeth. I felt as if I'd been struck by falling sickness. I couldn't move. I was on my knees. My arms fell heavily and I stayed there, watching the savage death, the boy dragged back towards the ponds, close to the village, close to the farm where the poor child lived.

Yes, Martin. I'm sorry. The child I saw murdered by the girl was your own brother. Sebastian.

I didn't regain the use of my limbs until after dawn of the following day. By the time I reached the edge of the forest I could hear the dogs, and the voices of searchers, and then the terrible cry of pain, your mother's voice, followed by the splashing of men in the shallow pond, dragging the body from its grave.

Later I came close to your farm and listened to the grieving voices. It was clear that a wolf was being blamed – as if a wolf would have treated its prey in such a way! Even if there had been any wolves *left* in Broceliande!

The children were more courageous in their suspicions, and I heard one of you say, 'The old woodsman. He's got one of us at last.' And someone answered, 'Let's get him. We'll burn him on the hill.'

But these were just the fears of you, your friends, still reconciling yourselves in your childlike ways to the loss of your littlest friend, Sebastian.

I approached the farm, very apprehensive, my mind a mist of uncertainty as to how to describe the events that I had seen. Eveline was on the garden seat, you on one side of her, comforting her even as you planned revenge on me, your sister Rebecca on the other, her face wet with tears as she held Eveline's arm.

Your father approached me quickly. He had two questions: had I seen or heard anything, and how should we organise a wolf hunt?

I was about to tell him what I'd seen the night before when Rebecca turned towards me. In an instant a *charm* fell away from my eyes, or perhaps away from her, it's impossible to tell. All I know is that she was revealed instantly as the girl in the woods, even wearing the same skirt and cardigan. I had simply not recognised her in the forest the night before.

I was speechless for a few seconds, then became terrified again as your tall sister ran towards me and hugged me, looking up through sorrowful eyes as she said, 'Don't listen to what the boys say. I'll always come and visit you. I promise. I promise. I'll not leave you alone for an instant!'

My head and heart had turned cold with fear. To this day I have no idea whether I was addressed by the true girl or by the wily sylvan monster. But I know she came and visited me often, before eventually she went away, to pursue new studies in Australia.

And I know that all thought of revealing my vision faded. How could I tell Eveline, mourning the death of her younger son, that it was her adored adopted daughter who had dragged him to the reed pond, and held him down?

The Shape-shifter's Dream

Martin was being shaken gently. He surfaced out of a dream in which he floated at night through drifting mist, the water of the lake lapping gently below his small boat. He woke with a shiver to find that he was still in Conrad's fishing lodge, the lake burnished with orange as the sun began to set. A swirling flight of dark birds crowded the sky above the heart of the wood.

'We should go back,' the old man said urgently. He looked very anxious. 'You've been asleep all day.'

'All day?'

'I couldn't wake you. We must get away from here.'

Martin was shocked by what he heard, and was still disturbed by Conrad's tale, and the revelation of the cause of Sebastian's death. He stood stiffly, groaning as he unlocked his knees. Conrad laughed sympathetically and held his arm, then offered one of his staves for support.

They returned to the iron-roofed shack and the bosker shed his overcoat and sheepskin jacket, stoked up the fire before uncorking a flagon of cider brandy. Martin sipped the potent drink with circumspection, not knowing who might have brewed it. Conrad was less careful, shuddering as the spirit burned its way to his cold bones.

'Will I make us supper?' he asked, but Martin shook his head.

'I should get back to Rebecca.' He hesitated, realising that suddenly the thought frightened him. 'Are you quite sure of what you've told me? About Rebecca?'

'Quite sure. Perhaps the possession was just a brief encounter. She grieved for Sebastian like all the rest of you. I felt no evil in her when she visited. I'm sure she had come from the lake, that deadly night, but she was completely unaware of it. Perhaps, as I say, the possession was brief. I do know that later she danced through another ghost and heard song, ancient song, and became obsessed with it . . .'

'Yes. That's why she went away.'

'And she must go away again. And you must too.' Conrad drank heavily from the flask again, then replaced the cork. 'Your mother sensed danger for you, just before she died.'

'That's what my Uncle Jacques said. But what danger?'

Conrad shrugged. 'She began to see the people on the path. She lay in bed, looking down, and saw their outlines again, just as she'd been able to see them as a child. Something she saw made her determined that even if you came for the funeral, you shouldn't stay.'

Martin rose from the floor by the crackling fire and turned to go. Then he asked, 'Why did you take me to the lake? Wasn't that a dangerous thing to do?'

'Yes. But if you take no heed of Eveline's wishes, then you may need to know it's there.'

Lights were on in the farmhouse, and the warm smell of garlic, herbs and red wine was on the air, suggesting a casserole under preparation.

Rebecca was at the wood stove, shaking an iron pan which sizzled loudly. The table was set, a candle in the middle, a bottle of claret opened, one glass half full. She glanced round and smiled as Martin entered staring at her in some shock. 'Won't be long,' she said.

There was a note from her, discarded on the sideboard. It read, '*Hi early riser! 9am. Gone to Vannes for clothes food hair a few special little things. No idea how long I'll be. Hope you're having fun.*'

'I'm sorry. I should have left a note for you before I went out . . .'

'Why?' she said, wiping her hands on her apron. 'If you'd wanted me to share in what you were doing you'd have woken me. I hope you're hungry. I bought far too much beef.'

'I'm starving. I appreciate it. I haven't eaten all day. Beck, you look . . . wonderful.'

She removed her apron and stood across the table, grinning, her arms outstretched. 'A transformation, eh?'

'Very sexy. Not that you need clothes to be sexy, of course. I didn't mean . . .'

She laughed as he contorted through the words,

saying, 'Burble, squirm, burble. I know what you mean. Shut up and feast your eyes. It won't last.'

She'd dyed her hair jet black, cut the fringe in a straight line and made three thin ringlets on each temple, each strand decorated with golden amber beads. Her black silk blouse left her arms bare. It was cut low over her breasts. Her skirt flowed fully from below her tight waist, a green fabric patterned with lines of tiny red and purple squares. She'd rouged her lips and applied make-up to her face. The etching of her skin was hardly visible, now, and in this illusion she had shed ten years of age.

Amused by his scrutiny she laughed, 'One small nod to vanity, one huge dent in the purse. Don't worry, it's just for fun.'

'You look very . . . er . . . Romany?'

'Earlier than that. A lot earlier than those travellers. You'll see decorations like this on Bronze Age vases. But it's how my mother looked, it's how I remember her. A traditional look in the group of families. I wish you'd met her. I wanted to share a touch of her memory with you. May I please have a welcoming hug, now?'

She came round the table, oak-brown eyes flashing with pleasure, a hint of passion. Martin reacted apprehensively, his whole body stiffening slightly. She saw this and frowned, then put her arms round him and kissed him, holding the kiss for a few seconds then pulling away, turning away.

'Some wine? I opened it an hour ago. It should have caught its breath by now.'

'Mm.'

She passed him a glass, then raised her own. 'To health.'

'Health,' he echoed and sipped the wine appreciatively. He raised the glass again. 'To the traveller.'

'Bright path, Eveline.' She drained her glass and set it down, then leaned back on the table and folded her arms, looking at him curiously. 'The question, then, is this: do you tell me now, or after we've eaten?'

'Tell you what?'

Rebecca laughed, but there was little humour there. She shook her head, saying, 'Anxiety is a song that sings from eyes.'

'French proverb?'

'Thunder people *spiritlook*. It's part of a long chant teaching how to read the inner songs when the words are unclear. In other words, body language and heigtened sensory perception. What's made you apprehensive all of a sudden? You seem almost frightened of me. You're not regretting last night, are you?'

'Of course not.'

She came over to him quickly and put her arms round him, fixing him with her level gaze, dark eyes searching. 'Where did you go today?'

'Into the forest. With the old bosker. Conrad.'

Rebecca smiled, 'I'm glad he's still around. I want to see him. How is he?'

'An old man, living rough. People round here look after him, clothes, barter, disgusting cider brandy. It's hard to remember the ogre in him. In fifteen years I don't think he's changed a bit.'

After a moment Rebecca said, 'Let's eat. I've bought haslet. Your favourite, if I remember.'

Sitting across the table they ate the thick slices of brawn in silence. Rebecca was about to fetch the casserole when Martin said, 'Where were you the night Seb died? Can you remember?'

She sat down, quizzical, then ran a finger and thumb down an amber-beaded ringlet. 'I was with you and your friend Peter, chasing the woman and child on the path, the ones who were running . . .'

Martin felt his face go cold. Rebecca hadn't been with him that night. He'd been with Peter, but the people on the path had been two men with staffs and unstrung longbows, one of them a heavy set man with bushy beard, the other aristocratic looking, dressed in half armour. Martin had watched Peter dancing inside them, but as usual simply ran in circles round the figures, studying them in great detail.

He told as much to Rebecca, who said angrily, 'Nonsense. I was there. We went back home together, climbed through the window together, and the next morning woke up to the shouting. What the hell is this, Martin? What's going on? You're white as a sheet. What's frightened you? What's going on?'

His heart thumping, unexpectedly anxious, he said, 'The bosker said he'd seen you by the lake in the forest the night Seb drowned.'

Rebecca frowned for a moment. 'What lake? Do you mean the pond?'

'No, the lake at the heart, the big lake.'

'There's no big lake in Broceliande. Not that I know of.'

'He says he saw you there. The night Seb died. You were dancing in the forest, behaving like a wolf.'

'Like a wolf?'

'That's what he said.'

'Why didn't he speak to me, then? Why didn't he contact me? I wasn't afraid of him, I was the only one of you who wasn't.'

'I don't know,' Martin said. 'I don't know why he didn't speak to you about it.' He regretted the lie as he spoke it and so transmitted the lie instantly.

Rebecca looked disgusted. She picked up a napkin and wiped the make-up from her face, an angry, pointed act. The years, the sunburn, the hard side of her came back. She was upset, clearly confused, aware that Martin was keeping something back from her but frightened by something deeper.

'Have you seen this lake?' she asked.

'I saw it today for the first time.'

'He took you there?'

'For the first time. Yes. It's a long way in, and it's a difficult route, but I'm damned sure it wasn't there when we were kids.'

Rebecca stared across the table, thinking carefully. 'Everyone knows there are ghosts on the path. So why not a lake that magically appears? Maybe it's an adult vision. Maybe as we age we can start to see things inside the wood. It's just that we never look.'

'That's more or less what Conrad said. He thinks he's a lake-finder.'

'Nice talent. But I still don't understand why thinking I might have been in the forest when Seb died should make you upset.'

She grasped the point suddenly, leaning forward on the table, beads rattling in her hair. Her eyes gleamed with a terrible, controlled fury. She spoke in a whisper. 'Or maybe I do. You say Conrad saw a girl. He must have thought it was me – and he thinks I might have seen him . . . that's right. Not a wolf at all, then . . . Not a wolf that killed Seb. The old bosker's been guilty all these years, and he's made you suspicious of me. He's trying to implicate me.'

Her voice rose in pitch. 'And you believe him. You believe him. You unbelievable shit!'

Martin said quietly, 'Beck – I'm telling you plainly: you were not with Peter and me that night.'

'Liar! You know I was.'

'We were alone, Beck. The encounter you're talking about was a week or more before. You weren't with us that night. And your fingers were all torn at the ends, as if you'd been scratching at rough bark, which is what Conrad claims he saw.'

She was silent for a long time, looking at Martin, yet somehow through him, fiddling with her hair, then shaking her head. 'I scraped them sliding down a trunk after watching the two of you on the path.' She too was speaking quietly, almost sadly. And suddenly her eyes closed and her face grimaced with pain.

'My God. Oh my God.' She looked at him again. 'You do think I killed Seb. You think it was me. Don't you? Why don't you speak? Don't just stare at me. Oh Christ,

I feel sick. I'm going to be sick. How could you? How could you think such a thing? I loved Seb. I loved him. I wouldn't have hurt him.'

She stood slowly and left the kitchen, closing the door slowly behind her.

Later, Martin heard her moving around upstairs. He thought she might be packing her things to leave, but eventually he heard the bed-springs, and then silence.

'I've lost her,' Martin said to the silence after she'd gone, experiencing an aching despair as this fear became a reality. But later he woke suddenly, cramped up on the small sofa, a blanket over his clothed body. Moonlight streamed into the sitting room, illuminating Rebecca, who sat on the sofa's edge, her eyes sparkling as she watched the waking man.

'Beck?'

'After Seb died,' she said softly, 'I had a recurring dream. It was very strange, quite frightening, and I never told it to anybody. After what you said this evening, I can't get it out of my mind; I think it came back again, I probably woke in the middle of it.'

Martin sat up and made more room for her, reaching out to touch her arm. She sat motionless, unresponsive. He said, 'Beck – forgive me. I'm confused. It's this place, the old fears. And the old man confused me . . .'

'Be quiet – please – be quiet. Let me tell you the dream.'

She turned away from him, arms across her chest.

'I'm in a clearing, a glade in an old forest. I'm running

63

round the glade with a torch, and everything is burning, the flames sweeping high, the smoke billowing, and cloth and skins and parchment are being consumed by the fire, burning brightly, shedding charred fragments into the air. There's the tall, thick shaft of an old thorn lying on the ground. I've hacked its branches down to stubs, then decorated it with bracelets in bronze, and torques and brooches, and there are bones around it, and clay pots filled with stinking liquid and coloured powders. All of them are melting in the heat. And I'm dancing around a swirling column of earth that rises above me. A man is screaming. The more I dance the faster the rising tower of earth spins, the louder the cries, and the more I laugh!

'Then I'm dancing with a man, spinning round among the flames, only it isn't a man it's a stone statue, a horrible effigy, the ears cut off, the eyes gouged out, the nose slit, the mouth gaping tongueless, no fingers on the hands, no toes on the feet, the sex has been broken from the groin. I twirl this gruesome statue across the glade, and around the rising earth, singing all the time, even kissing the cold stone lips. There is a feeling of terror. A cairn of stones holds the centre of the glade and I fling the dancing stone across it.

'I run from the burning grove, swim hard through dragging, sucking waters, shaking myself dry on the shore, then running through the forest, swerving and ducking, but dancing all the time. Only I'm not a woman, now . . . I'm on all fours, my tongue lolling. I howl and scream at the sky as I run, I bay at the moon,

I bark at shadows, I scratch at bark. It is a run of great triumph, and great delight.

'But suddenly a man is there, naked and blind, blocking my path. He is the man of the statue, stripped of senses, sex and touch; but his presence ahead of me – laughing! – fills me with fear and I plunge off the path and into the bushes. The land gives way into a pit and I fall, screaming, spinning in the air, endlessly falling, reaching for the branches and the stone outcrops that will save me, reaching for safety but always missing, falling and falling until I wake up terrified!'

She turned back to Martin.

'I felt a moment of that wild dance and the wild wolf run tonight. It woke me up. It brought the dream back to me.'

She was trembling. Martin sat next to her and enfolded her, feeling her tears as a cool moist touch on his neck.

'Perhaps it *was* me,' she whispered. 'Perhaps I *was* possessed.'

Suddenly she sat up, strong again. 'I'm frightened, lover. I think we should get the hell out of here. First thing in the morning. What do you say?'

'The paperwork will take two days. Don't go near the path. Avoid the bosker. We'll be safe for two days. Come on, I'll take you back to bed. We'll talk more about it in the morning.'

PART TWO

The Unquiet Grave

My breast, my love, is cold as clay,
My breath smells earthly strong;
But if you kiss my cold clay lips,
Our days they will be long.

From *The Unquiet Grave*
(folksong, variant ca. 1750)

The Unquiet Grave

I

A child was laughing, outside in the night, running along the path towards the church. Martin got out of bed and watched the small boy, visible by moonlight. It was Adrien LeConte. He whirled and slipped in the darkness, his eyes alive with the vision of enchantment, his head filled with the sounds of ghostly hearts and voices.

'It goes on,' he whispered, and turned to look at Rebecca, realising at once that she had gone. Her clothes were no longer over the chair.

With an apprehensive glance back through the window, over the field to Broceliande, Martin murmured, 'Don't go to the forest, Beck. For Christ's sake, don't go to the forest . . .'

He couldn't eat breakfast. He fed the chickens and the ailing retriever, walking the dog for a few hundred yards, but the creature was long past her prime and preferred the warmth by the wood stove. Jacques called by, his Citroën belching exhaust fumes, his breath even stronger with tobacco smoke. He had brought a pile of boxes for packing, and a suitcase for the clothes that he would be taking for his and Suzanne's own use. He stayed for coffee, then went back to his house. Martin took the opportunity to enter the forest's edge and look for the bosker, but Conrad was off hunting, or fishing, perhaps exploring.

Bess's barking brought him running back to the farm. The bitch was up on her hind legs, forepaws on the gate, barking towards the path. She was not normally disturbed by the phantoms from Broceliande, so perhaps she was aware of something in the woods themselves. Martin scratched the animal's head and patted her, calming her, and the barking changed to a nervous wheezing. 'What did you see, old girl, eh? What did you see?'

There was someone in the house, the door was open. 'Rebecca?'

She called back, and Martin found her inside drinking coffee and reading a magazine.

'Where did you go?'

'Up to Seb's cold home.'

'Don't you mean his grave?' Martin was trying to be light, but Rebecca stared at him, unsmiling.

'It feels cold up there, Martin. It's a cold home. I wanted to make my peace, in case I *did* have something to do with the death.'

She was very matter of fact, and Martin nodded, irritated with himself for not having thought of something so obvious.

'*Is* he at peace?'

She sipped at her cup and nodded, eyes skimming the

text of the magazine. 'I think so. I know *I* am. But it still feels cold where he lies.'

'I thought you might have wanted to talk to Conrad.'

She closed the journal and looked up thoughtfully. 'I do. I think I'll wait for a while, though. But I do want to talk to him. Last night I was afraid, very afraid. That dream, your story, your hostility . . .'

'It wasn't hostility, Beck. I was frightened too.'

'Yeah. Well . . . it was all suddenly overwhelming. But the fact is, *I* didn't kill Sebastian, even if my fingers did. There's the ghost of that moment inside me, and that's why I felt so frightened, but I don't see why we should run from here because of the past. It feels good to be here, I feel I belong again. I thought the songpaths would be too weak to keep me, but now I'm not so sure.'

What was she saying, that she wasn't going to return to the outback?

'And Flynn?'

'Flynn is dead,' she said, looking at Martin sharply. 'I don't mean physically. I mean, he and I are dead. The songpaths are a closed part of my life. Eveline's death was the final marker of that experience, the defining moment. I had to come back when she died, and now I have to stay. I feel quite calm about this, Martin. If you want to leave, you go ahead. But I'm staying.'

There was a certainty about Rebecca that was so intense it was almost stunning. A few moments before, Martin had been clear that he would sort out the affairs of the small estate and then leave for Amsterdam, or perhaps for a long vacation by the southern shore. Now he was confused. Eveline's urgent demand, through her letters and the mouths of friends, that neither he nor Rebecca should risk their lives in Broceliande was still a powerful consideration, yet he felt himself weakening, his resolve to depart going.

This was his home. This was the only place, in all the world, where he truly belonged. Rebecca belonged here less than he did, and yet she, too, was finding that old spirit again, the attachment to a place of ghosts, farms, rural existence and peace.

'Why don't we stay for a week,' he said, 'then review the situation. Eveline was quite adamant that we're not safe here. There must have been a reason for it.'

'Have some coffee,' Rebecca said, filling a wide cup for him. She was smiling as she spoke. 'Eveline was afraid for us, Martin. But she's gone, now. It's up to us to be aware, to be cautious. Whatever she was afraid of, maybe it had only to do with little Seb's death, all those years ago. Maybe she knew that I had something to do with it – but what she couldn't know was that whatever the possession at that time, whatever was in me, it's gone. My new possession is song, ancient song, the songs of the earth, call it what you like, you know what I mean: song was always used in magic, and a little of that song-magic came into me from the people on the path. You couldn't know it because you never went inside one of them. Well, only for an instant. And perhaps that was wise. I can't in my heart feel any danger here.'

'But we should be cautious,' Martin said, and Rebecca smiled at him.

'Of course. What else?'

Martin worked on the details of the estate with Uncle Jacques, and a solicitor from Rennes, a jocular man, with bushy side-whiskers and a florid complexion, ill-at-ease with the pin-stripe of his suit.

Eveline had left an estate valued at two million, two hundred thousand francs, of which a quarter was in investments, insurances and savings. The farm stock accounted for very little of the remaining value, which was substantially contained within the building and outhouses, and in the land, twenty five acres, including woodland, that was divided between grazing and broccoli. There was a good water source, a spring that had been enclosed and channelled in the Middle Ages, and only two tumuli cut into the useable cultivation space.

The farm was, of course, heavily untended. In her later years, Eveline had concentrated on pigs and chickens, with Uncle Jacques and another farmer, raising broccoli and maize in rotation on five acres. For the first time, reviewing the estate, Martin became aware that his father had had a not unreasonable business sense, since the investments he had made out of the very meagre profits from the farming business had performed excellently on the Paris stock exchange. His mother had lived comfortably in her last years, and there were sufficient disposable assets almost to cover the taxes due upon the transfer of her estate.

Martin and Rebecca were the main beneficiaries under her will, and the stipulation that they receive

their due inheritance only when they had left Broceliande was discreetly, at Rebecca's persuasive insistence, deleted from the document, witnessed and
approved, albeit against his better judgement, by Uncle
Jacques.

Martin quickly organised the selling of land to cover
the balance of the death duties, negotiated rental deals
for the remainder of the farm space, and within two
weeks the paperwork was more or less completed.

The old retriever, Bess, was ailing and had taken to
uncontrollable, pointless barking, and though it broke
their hearts to do so they put her down, Rebecca taking
care of the difficult arrangements.

It was mid-October by now, and the weather was
generally bad, a series of rainstorms, grey days, the
occasional crisp, frosty morning. When the sun shone,
one Saturday, and the air was sharp and scented, the
woodlands alive, the fields flowing with bright shadow,
Rebecca went quickly around the houses in the
neighbourhood inviting everyone to the farm. Martin
dug a fire-pit, Jacques rigged up a spit to take a whole
piglet, a vat of cider was wheeled from the LeContes,
bread was made, salads fabricated, or bought ready-made
from the nearest hypermarket, and Martin and Rebecca
hosted their first garden party as a couple.

In the late afternoon Father Gualzator blessed the
succulent and roasted creature and reminded everyone
of the old custom by which the priest received the first
cut from the best meat, the neck fillet, a tradition that
was rapidly challenged, and which proved to be inven-
tion. Amidst the hilarity, as the priest staked his claim

with wilder and wilder stories across the fire-pit, each outmatched by Johann deClude, a storyteller of wild exaggeration, the snout and tail of the pig were prepared on a bed of lettuce and presented, with ill-restrained giggles, to Father Gualzator.

'I *will* eat this!' he declared solemnly, holding the plate before him, 'but only if I can have the squeak as well.'

'Long gone,' someone said.

'Not at all! I believe I saw it earlier. There it is – hiding in the *fillet*!'

The roasting, the feasting and the hours of horseplay helped to create a special warmth on this cold, hard day. Then the fire was stoked and fed to make a warm place where there could be dancing until darkfall. Martin was very drunk. Rebecca danced alone, wide skirts swirling, hair flowing as the accordion wheezed out its jig, and feet stamped on the stone flags at the edge of the field, where the pit had been dug.

'We haven't had a party like this since 1946,' said Father Gualzator, as he bobbed to the accordion and nibbled at a finger of cheese. 'By the way, Conrad is over there, in the gloaming. Do you see? By the well. He's watching us. But he won't come into the fire-glow. I've asked him, but he's staying out.'

Martin couldn't see the shadow that the priest had seen. 'Have you taken him something to eat?'

'No. I didn't like to.'

Martin cut four thick slices of meat from the pig, and two of bread from the heavy cob. The salads had all been consumed. He found a small china flagon and filled it with the raw cider from LeConte's vat. As he began to walk across the field to the copse, Rebecca stopped him.

'It's for the bosker. He's up in the trees.'

'I'll take it. You're very drunk,' she laughed.

'And you aren't?'

'Out of my skull. But I want to say hello. Where is he exactly?'

'The copse, by the stone well.'

With the words, 'Don't expect me back too quickly,' she took the plate and flagon and strode off across the night field, to become a shadow among shadows.

It was after midnight before Rebecca crept into bed. She was naked and bitterly cold. She pressed her feet against the complaining man, warming her hands on his stomach, laughing as Martin struggled. They soon relaxed below the covers and eventually turned to face each other, kissing gently, savouring the fumes of garlic and cider.

'You were a long time. I would have been worried, but I passed out. Must have had a lot to talk about to Conrad.'

'He didn't stay long. I think he was still a little frightened of me. He ate what I took him, and we shared the cider and remembered old times. He didn't want to talk about Sebastian and the wolf-thing that had killed him. I told him you'd told me and all he said was, "Then everything, now, is in its cold home. It's done with, and with Eveline gone, and the lake so quiet, perhaps the storm has passed." Then he went back to

76

the forest, asking me to thank you. I stayed by the well. It's a nice place, there. You can smell the water rising through the hill. Everything by that well is vibrant, very pure, very clear. I spent a long time thinking.'

'Thinking about what?'

Her touch was suddenly intimate. He felt aroused and reached around her to draw her body very close.

'Thinking about what?' he repeated.

As they kissed, Rebecca whispered, 'About staying in Broceliande, learning how to run a small farm. About you, how much I love you, now that I allow the feeling to surface. About us, how natural it feels to *be* us. About a child . . .'

Martin was stunned. His lips found Rebecca's, his hands found hers, fingers entwining as she wrestled him underneath her, to lie on him, her hands, then, holding his face, her mouth a moist presence on his eyes and cheeks as she took him into her, holding him close, holding him tightly until first light, first dew, and the first call, an urgent one, for the bathroom.

The first green had been on the woods for a week, now, and the last of winter had been seen off.

Martin waited by the gate as the eight horsemen cantered towards him, doffing his beret as they swept past leading a riderless mare. One blew a short, brass horn, the others waved flowered staves and screamed at the tops of their voices as they passed. Laughing, they wheeled around and trotted back, resplendent in their short white jackets and black trousers. Bells on the spurs of their black boots made a constant jangling as they waited for the groom.

Martin climbed into the saddle of the ninth horse, feeling the strength of the animal below him, holding her head back as she tried to stretch. Further away down the path, towards the village, the bride's canter was approaching noisily, the five horns sounding their high-pitched, sweeter notes. Rebecca, in the centre of the gallop, was a tall shape, robed in green and white. The women in her entourage were trousered in black, with white jackets and wide-brimmed, rose-decked hats. The arc of flowers-and-ivy, held between them, wobbled as they approached, and the groom's party kicked-off for the church, mud spraying, laughter punctuating the high-pitched challenge of the party.

Father Gualzator opened the main gate to the church grounds as the groom's riders cantered through and reined-in. The horses were led aside, and Martin and Jacques (who was battered, bruised and stiff from the ride) walked into the church, which had been cleared of the pews and chairs, a wide hall, the thorn and the cross in the centre.

When Rebecca rode through the open doors, cantering noisily around the edge of the stone-flagged floor, she streamed confetti behind her as was the custom, but watched Martin all the time with eyes that were radiant and longing. The child inside her was almost unnotice-able below the green dress, although she held her belly carefully as she swung from the saddle by the door, and was escorted to the thorn and the cross.

In the light from the high windows they were

78

married. The child kicked as they kissed and took the two blessings. They went outside into bright, cool sunshine and paid respects at the cold-earth homes of Eveline and Albert, and then of Sebastian. The horses were straining at the tethers. Martin led Rebecca to the carriage. The riders mounted and led the way through the gate and along the path to the first village, and for two hours, with the sounds of car-horns, hunting-horns, klaxons, timbrels and the ululating voices of the younger women, they paraded the countryside and villages near Broceliande, collecting the presents and offerings of flowers, money and charms that were flung to them.

Daniel Tristan Laroche was First Named at the moment of his birth; ultrasound scans had confirmed the child's sex some months before, but Rebecca was superstitious and no items relating to the child, not clothes nor crib, nor bath were allowed in the house until the safe delivery.

Daniel was an enormous infant, over nine pounds in weight at birth, eyes bright in the red, wrinkled skin. He was completely silent, no cry, no breath of complaint as he was confronted with the world. He took to the breast with fervour, and remained calm and compliant during his Welcoming as cold water was splashed on him at the stone well, among the hazels. The name given to him was *fort de vie*. Since he was fit, and grew normally for the first few weeks, feeding avidly and lying contentedly below the spinning objects on the playframe, it was easy for a while to feel no real concern at his silence, or his seeming unawareness of what was happening around him. Indeed, it was a boon, since Martin had anticipated disturbed nights and short tempers.

But quickly the mood changed. Rebecca became frustrated by the silence, and Martin's concern grew as well. Daniel slept solidly for hours at a time. He woke on being touched, and fed normally. He lay quiescent on being placed down and stared into space. Sudden sounds didn't alarm him. Sudden movement had no effect.

Four weeks after his birth the health visitor was able to say with certainty that something was wrong.

Daniel was taken to a paediatrician in Vannes and Rebecca's worst fears were rapidly and thoroughly confirmed. Daniel was without sight, without hearing . . . and therefore it was necessary to entertain realistically the possibility that he would be without speech. Genetic tests taken by amniocentesis had shown no irregularities, and in every other respect Daniel was a perfectly healthy child.

Rebecca was devastated, Martin depressed and frightened. They returned to Broceliande and closed the door of their house against the world, keeping the shutters up throughout the summer, shadows living among the shadows of their home, cradling and nursing the beautiful, silent creature who was their son.

Rebecca was singing in her sleep. It was an odd sound, drawn out, a single note that faded as each breath was exhausted. It was enough to wake Martin, however, and he sat up, running his fingers through the heavy sheen of sweat on the woman's pale features. She stirred restlessly at the touch and turned away, curling into a foetal position, beginning to breathe more heavily.

Now that he was awake, Martin heard two more sounds: the tap-tap of metal on glass, and the same note that Rebecca was singing, except that it was higher in pitch, a single, sustained tone.

'Daniel?' he whispered, puzzled. 'It can't be . . .'

He wriggled his feet into slippers and went to the window. Two children were on the path, the Breques girl, Cathy, and her elder brother, a gawkish lad of ten. It was the girl who was relating to the invisible travellers, her raincoat swirling as she danced and spun around, exposing thin, naked limbs below. She was in a trance, her brother loping after her, his eyes wide with the wonder of what only they could see.

Again, the tap-tap of metal on glass, and Martin crept stealthily to Daniel's room.

The two-year-old had somehow crawled out of his high-walled cot. In pyjamas, hair awry, he was spread-eagled against the window, his arms stretched above him, his fingers, one with a metal thimble on it, rapping on the pane. His face was pressed to the glass, his mouth gaping and emitting with every exhalation the single, musical note. His eyes were wide, sightless, reflected in the window.

He jumped suddenly when Martin touched him, then turned and let his father cradle him. Small fingers traced the features of the man who lifted him into his arms. Daniel's chin was wet with saliva. He was smiling and silent, now. He was heavy for his age, dead weight as he curled into a ball, carried back to his cot.

Rebecca was suddenly in the doorway, dishevelled and sleepy. 'What's going on?'

'He was singing,' Martin said, his heart racing, his mind still unable to grasp fully that Daniel had made this sound! *He was singing!*

'I suppose you could call it singing . . .' he added.

She came over and brushed fingers lightly over the silent boy's brow.

'I was dreaming of him,' she said. 'We were sitting together below bright stars, on a wide, cool desert. It was a dream of Australia. Together we were singing up a path, rocking side to side, but aware of each other. He was an older boy in the dream, Daniel as a grown lad, with good sight and a vibrant life. We sang together . . .'

With a shiver of recognition, Martin said, 'You were singing together just now. You in your sleep, Daniel by the window. A single note, not very musical.'

Rebecca smiled sadly. 'There you are then. Mother and son on the same wavelength, the same line. What was he doing at the window?'

'Kids on the path. The Breques children. He was tapping the window as they passed with one of Eveline's thimbles, but he couldn't have been aware of them. Could he?'

'I'm sure he could,' Rebecca murmured. 'Christ, he's got to be aware of something . . .'

Exhausted, they took Daniel into their room, and as always the boy fell into peaceful sleep between them, even though his eyes were open.

The two years since his birth had been terrible, more for the failure to make a decision on Daniel's future than for the fact of his disabilities. Should he be sent to a home, nursed by professionals, where his blindness and deafness could be addressed at every hour of every day? Or should he stay with parents who loved him, but who could do nothing practical to improve his physical condition? Daniel was not difficult. He loved being outside. He walked with Martin, hand in hand, and seemed, oddly, aware of that which was surely beyond his senses: the forest, the rolling sky, the passing storms, the animals in the fields.

The boy never complained. His worst moments were at night, when sometimes he would howl ferally, or scream in an hysterical way, always becoming silent after a few moments in either of his parent's arms.

Father Gualzator had blessed him and prayed for him. Yvette Valence, the local herbalist who lived above the local post office, had prepared all manner of rubs and potions, from camomile to dogwort, from belladonna in honey to the crushed skull of an owl, whose night sight was the most perfect in the animal world. No amount of sympathy had allowed this sympathetic healing to have effect.

Yvette, like the priest, was from Basque country. After feeling 'called away' from the high passes and airy forests of her native land, she had followed the path that wound north, through the painted caves of the Perigord and the dense oakwoods of the Dordogne, to where Broceliande straddled the way to the coast, cutting across the ancient route. The place had felt right to her, and she had settled. She had been a close friend of Eveline's, and was a doting friend and helper for Rebecca and Martin now, but she became frustrated with Daniel, perhaps confused and distressed by the failure of even the simplest of her healing cures. It was as if, she said, Daniel was aware of the charm she used and was blocking it.

Even the wart on his left thumb – which ought to have vanished within two days – remained obstinately in place, until one day he dipped his hand into the well water, by the hazels, and the crusty excrescence disappeared within an hour.

Yvette's time with Daniel ceased abruptly when Martin forbade her to come back to the house. She had arrived in a lather of fury and fear, holding fresh herbs in black, cloth packets, and a cross made from the branches of a yew.

'The boy is dead,' she said in hushed tones. She would not cross the threshold into the house. 'I realised it suddenly. The boy is dead. A traveller is inside him. I can't help you any more.'

To Martin and Rebecca's fury, she didn't keep this information to herself, but spread it through the villages.

Daniel, however, was far from dead. Senseless, literally, he showed otherwise every sign of vibrant life. And he had started to sing, single notes but different notes, singing them until he was breathless and exhausted, singing them with gusto. Where the conception for such sound came from was not readily answerable, but Rebecca, who was giving classes in song at the local school, sang to Daniel at every opportunity. Perhaps he was aware of the melodies through some other sense, a synaesthetic appreciation of the creation songs of the Australian aborigines, and the corrupt creation songs – the folk songs – of old France and England, with which Rebecca was now very familiar. So the house was a musical place, although at times the double act of tuneful and single-note singing, an eerie sound that lasted for hours, was too much for Martin, and he was glad of his job, at a small design studio in a town an hour's drive away.

A second letter arrived for Rebecca from Flynn. The first had been a short note, transparently sad, yet filled with best wishes, received shortly after Daniel's birth. As ever, with Flynn, it was not so much a question of knowing more-or-less where he was as of waiting for him to come to the small town and check the post office for any mail. He wrote sparingly, using an old fountain pen that spilled more ink randomly than it dispensed in the tight lines and folds of the words he expressed. Rebecca savoured the two letters, as if they were fragments of a lost shroud. Martin saw this but did not interfere. He was never in any doubt as to her love for him, nor her loyalty, and try as he did, on one occasion, he simply could not arouse in himself any sense of jealousy for the outback-traveller, reaching through space and time for his once-love, the Live Alone Lady as he called Rebecca.

Rebecca had written to Flynn, describing the odd way in which Daniel sang despite profound deafness and the way in which he seemed aware despite his blindness. Perhaps she had been seeking some intuition or insight that she remembered from her outback-travelling days.

She was rewarded with a letter, certainly helpful, but far from what she expected.

Jesus, Beck, your letter frightens the fucking life out of me. God knows how long since you wrote it. Time never meant a great deal here, but I guess you're in the summer when this is happening, as you describe it, and that's a solid strand of time or so ago, so I guess you've walked the line a good way since then.

But don't you remember anything that happened around you on the songlines here?

Jesus! If this boy, your Daniel, is singing, then he's taking! So the first thing to do, Beck, is stop singing. Christ, I wish our times were crossing, but we're adrift by months, and that makes me concerned.

Beck, stop singing. Remember the Three Lady

Macbeths, as you nicknamed them? Well, there's a lot to remember in what those three ladies were all about. I can't get to you, Beck, or else I would, and you know I would. I'm hurt inside, and I miss you, but you wouldn't be my old Live Alone Lady if you weren't sure that what you were doing was the right thing, and I guess you've found a new line or two to travel, maybe those old teeth-from-the-earth stones you always told me about, and the dreamtime songs of the Celts, or whoever the hell it was that lived there at the time.

Beck, when a Man Walking reaches a songline, he sits down for a rub or two, and chews some sweet wood, and listens to the wind, then listens to the song, and maybe sings up a little of the old line. But the song is big in the air, and it's too big to take away, so he maybe sings a bit of it, and chews off a bit before he crosses, but there's plenty left to get inside the next Man Walking.

But a Lady Macbeth is out to take the song that was born. She'll walk around a puddle, walk through a hut, walk around a sit-down place, and when she sings the song, someone loses the song. Because that's what she's all about, a gatherer, a collector. What she does with the song only the Dream knows, but I've seen children stripped of music, and a young man lose the song that he'd been born with, and an old lady, in rags and with sticks, walking out across the dry places, full, fed and bloated on what she'd taken and making patterns on the land that only the tribe could see. So you beware, Beck. I don't like the sound of this Deaf Son Singing of

*yours and this Other guy or no, song is soul, and where
the soul is lacking, the taking game is strong.*

*I send my love to you, Beck. God knows I miss you,
and for more than just the jumping up and down,
although, Jesus! those were good nights in the old hut,
you truly are magnificent, and never to be forgotten,
especially for your spirit. But I know you'll come back if
the lines turn right for us again. In the meantime, God
Bless and keep you, and that lucky bastard who sleeps
next to you. And keep writing. I need to know you're
OK.*

Martin folded the letter and slipped it back into the
envelope. Rebecca had Daniel in her lap, and was rocking slightly as she watched the news on the TV. The
boy waved his hands in the air, sightless eyes on the
ceiling, a glistening of liquid on his chin. He seemed to
be reaching for something, but it was simply a reflex
action. Rebecca glanced across the kitchen to where
Martin was tapping the letter against the table.

'I don't mind talking about it, if that's what you
want.'

'The letter?'

'Are you upset by it?'

'*Upset* by it! Not at all. You know me better than
that. It's these "Lady Macbeths". I don't understand the
references to "Lady Macbeths" . . .'

Rebecca used the remote control to switch off the
television. She hefted Daniel in her arms and stood
up, then sat the murmuring boy on his home-made

'stimulus truck', a wheeled cart with dangling objects, some soft, some hard, some noisy. At once Daniel started to use his feet to move around the wide kitchen, batting at the shapes and making incoherent howling sounds. He never laughed.

'Lady Macbeths are both the destroyers and builders of the songlines, at least in the remote tribes that Flynn is studying, and which I visited for a while. There's a lot below the surface in any culture, and sometimes you just get hints about how the rituals are governed. It's not that they're secret – they sometimes are – just that they're obscure. You can think of a songline as a barrier, or as a marker for a moment in the dreamtime, or as a place perceptible only to a particular form of consciousness. If you take the example of a wall, you need to maintain the fabric of the wall, or it rots and falls away. If the wall is made by song, and the songs define both the land and the totemic spirits of that land, then that wall still needs to be sustained and maintained by new song.

'Where does that song come from? It's born, of course, born in certain children of the tribes. The Lady Macbeths scour the tribes for those songs, and they literally *sing* them out of the child, then take them to the line, and sing them out, sing them back, make the songline strong again.'

Martin considered this as he drank his way through a full pitcher of cider.

'Is Flynn suggesting that Daniel is stealing your songs?'

'He's afraid of that. I can't think why. The songlines work differently here . . .'

'Sing to me,' Martin said, and after a moment, perhaps recognising the concern in his face, Rebecca leaned forward on the pine table and sang.

Her words filled the warm space. The tune made Martin shiver with recognition until he, too, was joining in, two voices gently singing in the kitchen of the farmhouse, while Daniel was silent, his arms relaxed, his gaze fixed on nowhere, as if he, too, was listening to the melody.

3

But Flynn's intuition, from half the world away, had been right.

Martin had been up to Paris for the day to meet a small orchestra company interested in employing him to redesign their logo. He had taken the opportunity to buy artist's materials, then went to the Place D'lena, to the Oriental collection of the Musée Guimet, seeking inspiration if not for the new commission, at least for future work.

It was after ten at night before he arrived back at Broceliande. He was surprised to find Jacques sitting, half-dozing by the wood stove, the television tuned to a riotously unfunny gameshow.

Daniel was awake but silent, curled up on the sofa,

thumb firmly in mouth, apparently oblivious even to the sudden draught from the door.

Martin woke the old man, and Jacques stood up, walking stiffly to the lad and stroking fingers on the pale face. He smelled of brandy.

'I must have dozed off. He seems fine, though. Good as gold. He's even been humming a tune. You're making progress, obviously.'

'Where's Rebecca?'

'I'm not sure. She was upset about something. Asked me to come and look after Daniel. I'll be off, now, if you don't mind. It's been longer than I expected. That's not a complaint,' he added hastily. 'Any time. You know that. It's just that my joints, these days, do seem to like bed by about nine o'clock. Goodnight, Martin.'

'Goodnight. And thanks.'

Jacques walked awkwardly to the door, closing it behind him. Daniel stirred and made sounds, reaching into the void. Martin lifted him and hugged him and the boy relaxed again.

After a moment or two, as Martin rocked him, holding the long-legged child to his chest, Daniel started to hum. It was not tuneful, but it was familiar. Martin felt a dual reaction: of delight, and of apprehension. It was the song Rebecca had hummed and voiced those few nights before, after Flynn's second letter.

'Enough, now. Enough,' he said suddenly, putting a finger on the boy's lips. Daniel squirmed, frowning, watery eyes unfocused. But he did not object when he was laid down on the sofa and covered with a blanket.

Rebecca came home at midnight. She was dishevelled

and distressed, the hem of her skirt filthy, her boots caked with mud. There was moisture on her greying hair, and apple blossom, which Martin picked away.

'What's happened?'

'How was Paris?'

'Paris was fine. I have some work, not much, but something. What's happened?'

She went round to Daniel and kissed him. The boy shifted restlessly. She was whispering something to him and Martin stepped closer. 'What the hell's going on?'

Her look was one of fear and anger, a challenge to him to stay back.

'I'm telling him that I don't begrudge him anything, that he can take what he needs. What else can I do? He'll take it anyway.'

'Song?'

'He's taken it, Martin. It isn't there any more. Flynn was right . . .'

'One letter from the outback and you succumb to the suggestive power of it? How can he possibly steal a song? Maybe he's learned it—'

'He's stone *deaf*!'

'We assume that. But we don't know that he doesn't have some other way of receiving information! You can't have lost the song!'

'Well I have.'

'This is nonsense.'

'It's not nonsense to *me*, damn you.'

She began to cry, sitting by her son, her head in her hands. When she looked up, through moist eyes, she was grim. 'I'm frightened. For three years I've been willing life into this boy. It never occurred to me that he might take part of *me*. I offered it, but now that it's happening, I'm afraid of it.'

'He's not taking your life, Beck. Every child copies, learns by imitation.' He looked at the peaceful boy. He thought, *every normal child, that is*. How could Daniel absorb the experience of his parents, when he was so blocked off from normal sensory experience?

'Sing the song, Beck. Sing "The Unquiet Grave".'

'I would, Martin. If I could I would. But it isn't there any more.'

Martin sang it. At once, as if aware of the sound, Daniel started to hum the tune, tunelessly, a ragged accompaniment. 'Join in, Beck.'

And she tried. She opened her mouth, she watched Martin's mouth, she struggled to find the song, but the song was gone.

Later she sang 'Frère Jacques', demonstrated that it was not something affecting her language, she had not had a stroke . . .

But almost at once, little Daniel began to hum the same old French tune, the music behind the roundelay. Rebecca kept singing, and Martin joined in, but after a few minutes – and it was now very late – Rebecca fell silent.

When she picked up the boy, she was crying. She started to carry him to his room, he was dozing now, but turned at the door from the kitchen. Grimly, yet with some humour, she said, 'I never did like that song. So it's no loss. But it's gone, Martin. It's gone like "The Unquiet Grave" . . .'

There was *life* in the boy. In his dark world, with all tests suggesting that he had no sight at all, and no language ability, he began to flourish. He began to sing, and in a matter of weeks his thin voice was in tune, the sounds crisp and haunting, even though no words accompanied the melodies he vocalised.

Rebecca declined. After a period of fear she became unnervingly complacent about the theft she believed was occurring. 'He's my son. What's mine is his. What's a song to me if it helps him break down his own walls?'

Next to go were the songs she had sung as a child, the Christmas carols, the simple hymns, the nonsense rhymes, the folk songs that Eveline and Albert had taught them.

The words remained Rebecca's. It was strange for Martin to see the doting mother and the langourous, lean child draped across her lap, the child intoning 'Once in Royal David's City', while Rebecca spoke the words in rhythm with the infant's humming.

Where once Rebecca's head had been filled with music, now it was a wasteland. She could imagine Mozart, but not articulate it. She could give voice to a note, to a meaningless sequence of notes, even to a scale, but when it came to singing, she was lost. Her appreciation of music remained the same, in fact became a source of solace. In a state of melancholy she would lock herself away in the bedroom and play CDs, increasingly loudly, of Fauré, Mozart and Mahler, composers whose work could create in her heart a feeling of great strength. But she could no longer sing with the recorded sound, she could only hear it, gaining and maintaining a spiritual strength that allowed her to caress and adore her growing son. What truly concerned her was that she seemed to be suffering a sort of tinnitus – her ears rang, her voice echoed in her head when she spoke and her hearing was slightly dulled.

Daniel was more active than ever. At night, he would bang on the window, most particularly when there were people on the path. Martin took him out, one black, cold morning, leading the lad, well-wrapped against the chill, in a quick pursuit of the local children who were dancing through some spectre of their own envisioning. Daniel gave no sign of seeing that ghost, but he reached out to the source of activity, and babbled meaninglessly in his childish tongue.

The specialist in Rennes could well understand Martin's anxiety, when Daniel was presented for examination. 'Whatever is at fault with his sight, I'm afraid you'll have to live with it, short of a miracle. But the acquisition of language is a complex process, and it comes as a surprise, but not a shock to me, to discover that your son is approaching language through song. I'm quite certain that he'll begin to talk within a very short time.'

'The boy is deaf! He can't hear. How can he start to speak?'

'I know! This is what is so beguiling. As far as our

tests are concerned he has no response to auditory stimulation at all. Nevertheless: he *hears*. And everything suggests he'll soon start to talk coherently.'

Indeed, the day before the boy's fourth birthday, Martin entered his room in the early hours to find again that his son was pressed against the window.

'Come on, Daniel. Back to bed, now.'

He lifted the boy down, then felt the tug of a fist on his shirt collar. Dead eyes stared vaguely nowhere in the half-light, but from the boy's mouth hissed the words, 'Put me back!'

'Daniel . . .' Martin breathed, shocked by the sound, instantly suspecting that he had simply dreamed the words.

'Put me *back*,' Daniel said determinedly.

'Can you understand what I'm saying? Can you hear me speaking?'

'*Back*!' hissed the boy.

'Back on the window? What are you doing there?'

'Put me *back*.'

Martin lifted the lad back to the sill. Daniel flung himself against the glass, his breath misting, his nose flattening, his fingers spread out like the suckered pads of a frog. He stood there, trembling, breathing gently, and every so often his head jerked, as if he was listening.

As far as Jacques and Suzanne were concerned, this was a miracle and to be celebrated as such. Father Gualzator came round and listened to the boy's sharp, staccato speech. Daniel sat back in the chair, his legs drawn up against his chest, his eyes unfocused; he shouted words, random phrases, each uttered in a tone of delight: 'Eat! The woods! Bright water! Bubbling. The well. Keep him in. Here they are! Food, please. Falling, always falling. Hah hah!'

'This is quite remarkable,' the priest whispered. 'I've watched a hundred children start to talk – signals first, then grammar, slowly becoming coherent. Daniel seems to be using scattershot. His pronunciation is excellent. The words clearly have meaning for him, but no meaning to the rest of us.'

'Kill bird! Stone sinking. Into the sea! Storm coming. Keep him down. Shadows!'

'It's as if he's creating his vocabulary from scratch. There can be no meaning to these shouted words; it has a curious feeling of Tourette Syndrome, but he communicates a sense of understanding, which I find powerful and alarming . . .'

'The dell! The shaft! Drowning! Bread on the table. Cold home down. Getting free! Sing song, sing song. Hah hah . . .' a curiously knowing laugh and a body posture that suggested listening. 'Oh yes! The shadows! Dancing on the path! Almost out. Cheese!'

Daniel stumbled from his seated position and reached the table, scrabbling among the plates for the ripe brie, gouging it with his fingers until Martin eased his small hand away, led him to a chair and guided his touch to a slice of the food, with a soft piece of bread. Daniel ate and laughed, bobbing on the chair, dark hair flopping about his pale face, as if sharing some secret joke.

He had also discovered the TV, now that he had

acquired a rudimentary degree of hearing, and he laughed furiously at some of the programmes, even when the subject matter was serious or completely inane.

These were the weeks leading to Christmas, and it seemed that each day something new that was also odd occurred. The children who occasionally ran the path, dancing with the spirits, now took to screaming with terror, disturbing the early hours of morning with their fear as they scattered and ran. None of them would talk to their parents about the cause of the panic, but it was clear that the apparitions, once so benign, now seemed nightmarish.

This change for the worse didn't last very long. Soon there was just the drifting, dreamy dancing, again, and the sound of laughter and excitement.

Conrad became very ill. He would come to the house, wheezing badly, and beg food and medicines, but any attempt to take him in, to nourish and nurture him through these bouts of illness, was met by his instant departure. A pale man, his eyes hollowing out, his lips drawing back to expose the cold, blank skull behind his kindly, canny face, he would accept expectorants, aspirins, and vitamin pills, but not hospitality.

Elsewhere, near Broceliande, he treated himself with infusions of various herbs, bringing the petals and leaves to Yvette, who created the potions for him.

The man was dying, and Rebecca in particular felt a strong sense of loss as Conrad moved, edgy and remote, through the scrub wood, and along the lesser paths about the area.

For a year or more, Rebecca had earned a small amount of money, and gained a great deal of pleasure, by teaching two local children folk songs, and music in general, using the small piano at the farmhouse. These lessons stopped when she discovered she could no longer sing; indeed, as she struggled for the final time with one of the girls, she realised that she could no longer focus clearly on the music.

'I need glasses,' she moaned. 'Thirty years old, perfect vision all my life, and suddenly I'm getting short-sighted.'

4

With four days to Christmas, the church bell intoned the dawn hour to signal Winter's Deep. From all over the region, people came by car and cart to the church on the hill, arriving for midday, wrapped well against the frost. The sky was brilliant azure, the sun low to the south and west. The forest of Broceliande glistened whitely. Breath hung in the air, streamers of mist behind each walking human shape. When noon came, the congregation, spread around the base of the hill, joined hands. Daniel, between his parents, laughed as the whole circle stepped carefully, with many a collapse, many a trip, much humour, once around the hill, while the priest lit the fire at the porch entrance and the flame streamed high into the crisp day.

At the end of the clumsy dance, the children raced up the hill, scrambling over walls and through the hedge to be the first to carry the fire to the villages. They set off, thirty mufflered shapes, torches held high streaming black smoke. The adults crowded into the warm church and gathered round the copper cauldron of warm, spiced red wine.

As usual, the talk was of presents, and the extortionate price of computer games, radio-controlled cars and the other sophisticated toys that the little horrors of the villages were demanding, from Saint Nicholas in most cases, or from Old Provider in just a few.

Old Provider had been Rebecca's choice of gift bringer, with his one good eye, riding his black dog at dawn and with his wailing daughter stumbling after. He was an ogrish figure ready to take the child's head if the offering of fowl and fish at the doorstep was insufficient. Rebecca had always enjoyed the sense of terror associated with the gifts from Old Provider, and as a child had dismissed Saint Nick, in his white fur robes with his moon-chariot pulled by eight white harts, as just a fairy-tale.

Daniel had indicated that Old Provider was his choice. The gift he would risk his head for was a collection of Disney songs on disc – he was an avid fan of TV and radio, now, sitting with his left ear pressed to the sound box – with bendy models of some of his favourite Disney characters Baloo the Bear, Dumbo,

One Eye and Three Eyes, and the Seven Little Miners (he didn't want Snow White!).

The proper way to summon Old Provider was to write the gift-request on paper, wrap the paper round a black stone and throw it into Broceliande (or whichever was the child's local wood). One child in every hundred was supposed to be able to hear the Black Dog growl as it snatched the stone, before bounding through the tangle-wood to where its master, the one-eyed man, lay sleeping below a pile of stones.

Daniel enjoyed this ritual, although his first attempt to throw the rock almost knocked Martin unconscious, the shot, from the blind boy, being almost completely in the wrong direction. When the stone finally struck the trees Daniel clapped and laughed but a second later he screamed and turned away from some sound that only he could hear, holding his hands to his ears. He ran back to the path, and towards the farm. Martin chased after him, caught him and hugged him reassuringly.

'What is it? What is it?'

'Monster . . .' the boy whispered, shaking. 'Heard monster . . . Black Dog . . . crunching bone . . .'

'It's only a story,' Martin assured him, wrapping arms around the trembling lad. 'Nothing's going to hurt you. It's just a bit of fun.'

'I know! I know!' Daniel crowed triumphantly. 'Joke! Joke!'

And he squirmed away from his father, giggling and screeching, stumbling over a rock as he celebrated his trickery.

Martin chased after him, wrestling him to the ground. 'Why you little . . . you little *monster!* . . . I'll teach you to pretend that there's *monsters* in them there woods . . .'

The boy laughed hysterically as his father's fingers engaged with ribs and soft belly, tickling powerfully through the heavy winter clothing.

Then suddenly Daniel glanced away. 'Look at Mummy.'

Martin followed the glance. Rebecca was standing facing Broceliande, a hunched figure, arms tight around her chest.

'Something wrong. Mummy shadow wrong,' Daniel whispered.

Martin sat up, holding the boy. 'What's up, Beck?' he said to himself, disturbed by the dark figure, the motionless, living statue of the woman, everything about her suggesting that she was in distress.

And then he looked at Daniel, at the way the boy was staring at the distant figure. He moved an open palm across Daniel's gaze but the eyes never flickered, the pupils remained fully dilated as usual.

'What's Mummy doing?' he asked cautiously.

'Listening. Big dog,' Daniel replied.

'Can you see her?'

'I hear shadow,' came the quiet reply. 'Mummy shadow. Mummy shadow frightened.'

Leading Daniel by the hand, Martin went over to Rebecca, and put his arms around her, kissing her quickly on her cold, right ear. 'What's up with Mummy shadow?' he whispered. 'What's upset you?'

'Mummy shadow?'

'Daniel's words. I think he feels the fact that you're upset. What's upset you?'

'For a second it was like being a kid again, seeing the ghosts. I thought I saw the Black Dog. Seriously, it seemed to hover in the woodland edge, up on its hind legs, watching me, like one of those bloody great big dogs from Grimm. Or was it Hans Andersen?'

'The soldier? The tinder box? That story?'

'That one. Yes. Each dog was bigger than the last, and had bigger eyes, like saucers. I saw the biggest. And it was so real. But it was so shadowy, everything is so shadowy . . . maybe I need a stronger prescription.'

She took off her silver-framed spectacles and peered at them. 'My sight's really going. I find it so hard to read these days.'

'Then it's the opticians for you, my girl,' Martin said with mock severity. 'As soon as they open after Christmas.'

He looked at the wood, frowning. 'But maybe you really saw what you saw.'

'New lakes, wolf-girls and wailing men. Why not Black Dogs?' Rebecca smiled and reached for Martin's hand. 'There's something changing in the forest . . .'

Daniel was tugging at his jacket, staring up at his father.

'Dog's gone, now,' he said.

It hadn't snowed at Christmas for years and Daniel was disappointed, having heard all about snow from the poem 'Night of Old Christmas'. As far as Martin was concerned, it was too damned cold anyway, but they spent Christmas Eve in traditional style, with Jacques and Suzanne. The priest came by for an hour or so, taking a little supper and several glasses of the spiced wine that every house would have in abundance.

Daniel ran around the warm kitchen, a bat with out-stretched wings, guided by sound, flawless in his neg-otiation of obstacles, such as the inebriated adults who sat around the wide table, the remains of Eve Goose spread before them. Christmas day itself was a day of fasting, not that anyone ever took much notice of that particular tradition.

'Night of Old Christmas! Night of Old Christmas!' Daniel chanted, as he realised Rebecca was trying to get him into his nightshirt, to put him to bed.

He was allowed to sit with the adults a while longer, warm, wrapped in a blanket. Martin read the long poem by the heir to the British throne, a parody of the Victorian classic by Clement Moore, watching the enthralled boy curled against his mother and feeling the shivers of his own childhood as some of the stanzas brought back memories of Christmas past . . .

'The Deep of the Winter was now in the past,
And the snow that had fallen looked fair set to last,
And deep in the heartwood a cairn of grey stones

Was shifting and stirring and full of strange groans
For down in the earth, all wrapped up and snug
Old Provider was waking, his mind in a fug.

The black dog was barking, away in the wood,
And the children were quarrelling, who had been good?
And whose head was forfeit, that dread time of dark
If the fish and the fowl should fall short of the mark
And the man in his rags, with his good gleaming eye
Should bring gifts for the three, but the fourth child
   should die?'

Before he went to bed, Daniel reached to the big bowl of chicken and trout that was put out for the Odinesque Old Provider. 'Feel plump enough?' Martin asked.

'I'm good!' Daniel said emphatically, adding, 'Is Old Provider . . . hungry?'

'Very hungry. But there's enough fish and fowl here to feed him, his dog, *and* his wailing daughter.'

'Why? Wailing?'

'Enough questions, young man. Daughters wail because daughters wail, and presents come at dawn, because that's the way it works.'

A simple way of saying he had no idea.

'Head in sack, slung on his back,' Daniel murmured, and shuddered, making a chilled sound as he curled into Martin's arms and was lifted from the cold flagstones of the porch.

'But you've been good. There'll be no head in a sack on the end of *my* bed tomorrow – *or* on Old Provider's back. Just lots of fun toys, and funny songs. But only if you sleep, now, and don't make any noise during the night . . .'

He used his foot to open the door to the stairs, and glanced back at the group around the table, where Father Gualzator was using a teaspoon to scoop the last of the mulled cider from the copper tureen into his glass.

'Do we have any more holy water?' Martin asked with a grin, and Rebecca grasped the signal, went to the wood stove and uncorked another flagon of the apple.

In his arms, Daniel murmured, 'Rest of my bones, under grey stones.'

'Why? Wailing? Uncle Jacques. Why?'

'Because she was Old Provider's eldest child and favourite child, but she wanted gifts without earning them, and she wanted gifts that he couldn't give. So he took away everything that she had, except her sorrow, and made her run blindly after the dog, to pick up every gift that fell from his sack, especially the heads that he gathered from the greedy and the evil and the pretenders, and you know how many pretenders there are among the children of the world, so his sack was full of heads with their tongues sticking out, and their eyes crossed, even some still with their fingers stuck up their noses. Sometimes he put the head in a flour sack and left it on Christmas Eve for the parent. But sometimes he put the head on a small tree, and if the child repented the tree grew into a new body and walked home on its roots. If the parents took the tree-child

back, they would have to cut a small piece of the skin, or bark, every year to offer to Old Provider with the fish and fowl. That's where we get the expression, a chip off the old block. You remember the song Auntie Suzanne and I taught you?'

> *'A chip off the block,*
> *I'll live a full clock.*
> *A splinter forgot*
> *I'll end full of rot.'*

'That's right. You do remember things well, young man. Well, sleep now, and in the morning we'll dance around the kitchen to Baloo's Song . . .'

'Saw Black Dog. Saw shadow.'

'You saw the Black Dog?'

'It's hungry. It wants Mummy.'

'Where did you see it?'

'It runs up the path. It eats shadows.'

'What do you mean, It wants Mummy?'

'Mummy shadow. Black Dog wants to eat Mummy shadow.'

Old Provider duly provided, and Christmas Day passed with pleasure, leftovers, and a long walk over the fields. There was no more talk of Black Dogs and Mummy shadows, and Martin's frisson of excitement when he had thought, for that instant, that Daniel had actually seen something was soon forgotten.

The songs from Disney's *Jungle Book* became

semi-permanent residents in the house until well into the Spring, when the weather, which until then had been abysmal, began to improve dramatically, heralding an early and warm summer and the opportunity for the family to spend time outside.

Resurrection Sunday was particularly fine, and Martin drove the family across to the megalithic site at Carnac, encouraging Daniel to touch the stones, describing the ranks of uprights, stretching miles towards the west.

Daniel made it clear that he wished to hear the sea, and they drove to a small bay and descended the steep path to the red sand. Here, Rebecca sat on the rocks peering gloomily through her thick lenses at the shifting ocean. Martin searched for fossils, and Daniel wandered in circles, laughing and shouting.

And it was here, about half an hour after they'd come to the fresh air and salt spray, that Martin saw Daniel pursuing a broken-winged gull. The black-headed bird was weaving across the sand and Daniel was following the creature exactly, reaching for it. When it suddenly jumped, half flying for a few yards before descending again, the boy followed it with his gaze!

Martin walked stiffly towards his son, his heart thundering. 'Daniel?' Daniel looked round and grinned.

'What colour's the bird, Daniel?'

'Black and white,' the boy said. 'Broken wing.'

'Can you see it? Can you see the bird?'

'See it,' Daniel whispered. 'Bird shadow. Like Mummy shadow. Like Daddy shadow. See it.'

'My God! At last!'

He waved a hand in front of Daniel's eyes and the boy followed the movement, gaze bright, breath sweet as his father kissed him, joyfully, ecstatically. Then he looked towards the rocks. 'Mummy shadow crying.'

Rebecca's head in her hands. She was shuddering silently. Martin ran to her, sat next to her, lifted her chin to peer at the tears. 'Beck?'

'Christ, Martin. It gets worse. It keeps getting worse. I can feel it going. The world is shrinking. Oh Christ, everything is shrinking, everything's going dark, everything's starting to look like shadow.'

5

The boy played with his cars, running them across the stone floor using the small radio-control panel, his fingers working the switches confidently and accurately. He was getting tall for his age. He would soon be six, though he looked older, perhaps because he had grown fast in the last few years. He could not see colours, but he could see shades of grey. He was beginning to talk very coherently, almost gabbling, at times, as if catching up for lost conversations, though his conversation was self-centred, occasionally brutal, rarely questioning.

Martin felt very frightened of him.

It was hard, now, to deny that there was some close link between Daniel and Rebecca. He had dismissed

Flynn's letter, the slow stealing of song, as quackery: the Australian had put crazy ideas into the head of a vulnerable, suggestible woman. Now, though, he regretted that impatience. Now he was afraid.

Rebecca could not bear to spend time around her son, and Daniel had noticed this. Sometimes he expressed concern in an ordinary and childlike way: he cried for his mother. She spent an hour with him each evening, rubbing her eyes, squinting as he played, telling him stories in a voice that was becoming hushed, using words that seemed to sit thickly on her tongue. She complained of a permanent headache and constant tinnitus, the sound of surging waves in her hearing.

Each evening, when she could bear no more, she made an excuse and went to her room, the third bedroom, now converted to her study since music no longer meant anything to her. One day when Daniel ran up the stairs and pushed the door open, calling for Rebecca, Martin heard her scream abuse and throw a heavy book. Daniel scampered into the living room and hid below the cushions on the sofa, crying softly.

She was ashen-faced when she came to bed that night, skin glistening with dried tears. She stumbled to the bed and stared vaguely at Martin. She undressed slowly. He thought she was drunk, the way she tottered, the way she held her head as she unbuttoned her dress, awkwardly, loosely, then sat down heavily to peel off her stockings.

'Beck?'

'Blind,' she whispered and started to shake. She crawled under the covers, a naked, cold body, trembling like a frightened cat. She clung to Martin, sought his mouth with hers, held the kiss urgently, eyes closed.

'Love me. Now. Love me.'

'Beck . . .'

'Love me! Quickly!'

Her hands were on him, stroking, tugging. Her touch was icy and Martin shivered, feeling unaroused and frightened by this blind and passionate urgency. He eased her fingers from his body, pushed her down gently and moved across her, cradling her face as he kissed her softly, warming the freezing skin below him.

'Hold me now. Hold me gently,' he whispered.

As they loved, her breathing became calmer. Eyes closed, she gripped him with fierce fingers, nails drawing blood from his back, teeth clamping on his shoulder as she made quiet sounds, then whispered, 'Can't take this. Daniel. Can't take this. This is us. Can't take this away.'

'Oh Beck . . .'

'Don't stop. This is . . . Good. So good . . .'

Someone was running along the landing. Hot and quite breathless, Martin paused for a moment, listening to the heavy footfall.

The door to the bedroom was flung open. He twisted in alarm, staring at the tall figure that stood there, dark against the glowing nightlight.

Angrily, Martin shouted at the boy: 'Daniel! Back to bed. Now!'

'What are you doing? What are you doing?'

'Daniel! I said back to bed! Now!'

Rebecca began to cry. The boy stood obstinately in the doorway. Martin kicked the covers off and walked quickly and furiously to his son, his hand coming up to strike the lad, who watched him defiantly.

'Yes. Hit me. Hit me hard. Why not?'

The boy's face was a mask of anger and defiance. Naked, Martin dropped to a crouch and held Daniel by the shoulders.

'What are you doing? Why aren't you asleep?'

'I don't like what you're doing to mummy.'

'None of your business. Go back to bed. Go to sleep.'

Daniel glanced across his father's shoulder and grinned. Then he suddenly hugged Martin, whispering in his ear, 'He's wrong. He's wrong. I can have it all.'

'What the hell does that mean? Who's *he*?'

But already Daniel had turned and was scampering back along the landing, to his room, to his own bed.

Martin closed the bedroom door. There was no key for the lock and on a vague impulse he moved a chair and wedged it below the brass door-knob.

In bed again, Rebecca was propped on her elbow, staring into the distance.

'Where were we?' Martin asked gently. She shook her head. Then, as if with great effort, she said, 'Stay. Close. Keep him. Away.'

'Beck, what's wrong? You sound as if you're drunk.'

'Words. Effort. All gone. Going. Knew it. Would happen. Flynn right. Oh God . . .'

She fell back heavily, crying silently. Martin lay down below the covers and held her close to him for the rest of the night.

In the morning, Rebecca seemed almost her old perky self. She sat on the edge of the bed and peered around the room through her lenses.

'All grey,' she said matter-of-factly. 'No colour, now. Daniel has all colour now.'

She dressed easily and went downstairs. The boy was standing in the inglenook by the wood fire, leaning against the brick wall, hands in his pockets. As she bent to stoke up the embers he watched her silently. No words were exchanged. Martin watched this from the stairs, then came into the kitchen to make breakfast. Rebecca put on her coat and went to the back door.

'Where are you going?'

'Something,' she said and smiled, peering at him. 'To do,' she added. 'Alone.'

'Where's mummy going?' Daniel asked. 'I don't like mummy going off alone. What's she up to? Why doesn't she stay here and play with me?'

'What do you want for breakfast?'

'Anything and everything,' Daniel said loudly. 'I like lots of everything. Hot bread, eggs, melted cheese, oranges. Just give me everything.' Then: 'Where's Mummy going? She shouldn't leave the house.'

'Shut up. Sit down. Read a comic book. Eat when the food comes.'

'Don't be rude to me.'

'It's too early in the morning, Daniel. Shut up. Read. Wait for breakfast.'

'Where's mummy going?'

'Bugger mummy! Did you hear what I said? I've not slept a wink all night. Now be a kind and thoughtful son, and shut up, and wait for your eggs!'

'Two eggs. And fried bread and tomatoes. And bacon.'

'What are you, English? That's what the English eat.' He remembered quickly that there was an English boy attending the local school for a few weeks, and Daniel was fascinated by him. '*Very* unhealthy. You'll make do with what I give you.'

6

After he had taken Daniel to school, Martin went back to the house, but instead of working on his designs he prowled restlessly along the path, up to the church, then back again. All over Broceliande the flocks of starlings and sparrows were crowding the sky as they returned from the south to flow in great speckled floods about the canopy and the villages. The air was fresh, scented with new growth.

On impulse, Martin followed the forest road, and turned off along the track that took him to the old bosker's edgewood mansion.

He stood by the fence, looking first at the grizzled remains of last summer's catch. There were no new carcasses here, and there were streaks of green on the iron and oilskins on the hut. No smoke rose from the chimney, and the path to the door was fresh with yellow weeds.

'Conrad?'

Martin called, then called again, waiting hesitantly at the edge of the shack before stepping forward to pull back the oilskin door and peer into the foetid gloom.

'Conrad? Are you here? I'm looking for Rebecca.'

There was movement in the shafting light from the only window, a sudden shift of body mass below the piled furs on the bed. As his eyes accustomed to the gloom, and his nose to the stink in the place, Martin moved towards the farther end of the habitation. It was cold in here, the fire grey with ash, long dead.

'Conrad!' The old man's face became clear suddenly, pale against the yellow of the pillows. He was like a skull, his eyes fully sunken into the bone, his lips no more than thin lines defining the grinning face of death. In hands that were like white spiders he clutched the wooden panel of one of his pictures, hugging it to his breast through the blankets, as if holding a lover.

'My God. You need help. You need a doctor.'

'Do I?' the ghostly figure wheezed, and then made a sound that Martin was sure was a laugh. 'Isn't she beautiful? Oh Lord, how I would love to see her now.' He peered with difficulty at the smudged crayon drawing.

Martin gently teased the piece of wood from the trembling hands. He cradled it and stared at the crude drawing of the girl in full face. The colours were scratched where nails had probed and stroked the slim and smiling features of the long-gone girl.

'I dream of her all the time,' Conrad said. 'But it's such a long march home. I don't think I have the strength. *Do* I have the strength? Please tell me. I can't be sure unless you tell me.'

The bosker was leaning up from the bed, his face a frightening mask of need, of questioning, of seeking – his eyes blazed with urgency, his mouth trembled. Martin was shocked, deeply saddened. He had realised suddenly that he was present at the end of the woodsman's life.

Quietly he said, 'No, my friend. No you don't. You don't have the strength. I'm sorry.'

'There's no way home for me?'

'No. I'm sorry. I don't know what else to say.'

But as if he had heard some welcome words Conrad's breath hissed from his lungs in a pleasure of release, and he lay back, his watery gaze upon the dust that spiralled in the light from the window. His fingers again clawed across the crayon face.

'Thank you,' he said. 'I'd thought as much. But I tried. Oh Lord, I did try. Not one minute of one hour of any day in all of my life since I marched here, since I walked the circle here, not one moment have I abandoned her, and I think of her now, and God bless her, she has certainly done the good thing and sustained me, although I don't suppose she knows it. I am so tired, Martin. I hardly have the strength to lift an arm. But I must go and listen to the boats. That is where I belong, now. Will you take me to the lake? Please? You asked about Rebecca. She was here. Yes. Will you take me to the lake? I'll tell you about Rebecca as we go. Will you take me?'

'Of course. I'll get your clothes. I'd sooner take you to the infirmary.'

'No. Please don't. It's outside the circle, else I would have gone there years ago. It would make me happy to hear the travellers' boats again, to hear the water. Thank you anyway.'

Some hours later, by the lake, Conrad crawled into his crude shelter, padded up the furs and the pillow he'd brought with him and settled back to die. Martin built a wood fire and stacked a good amount of tinder in arm's reach, below the hide canopy. The lake was very still, very quiet, dragonflies humming among the rushes. There was a chill touch to the air, in this sheltered place, even though the sky was bright, luxuriant and calm.

Conrad's gaze never left the far wood, across the mere.

'There's a battle being fought. You should have gone away, as Eveline was keen to tell you. If you hadn't stayed, the battle could never have been joined.'

Martin cast the line again, a hook with a grub on the end of a willow rod, watching the small weight splash as it struck the surface of the lake. He was determined to catch a fish and give the old bosker a taste of fresh food.

'What battle?'

'The age-old battle,' Conrad wheezed, half laughing. 'You know how it goes: I want the power that you have.

I want to be strong though it will make you weak. Nothing has changed for thousands of years. Sometimes the battle is fought on whole landscapes, sometimes in the small kitchen of a warm and cosy house. Martin, you really should have gone away. Eveline knew what she was talking about. She was frightened for you, and for Rebecca, and all you have done by staying here is let the fight be fought again.'

'I don't understand—'

The weight was tugged, the line snagged. Martin jumped up and held the willow rod tightly, dragging it in against the pull, reaching out to wind the coarse line around his hand.

'Which fight?'

'The fight for magic,' Conrad murmured. 'Don't pull too hard.'

The fish struggled but was completely hooked. Silver and green thrashed on the scummy lake, eyes flashed angrily from jutting jaws. It was a pike.

'Greedy bastard!' Martin taunted from the shore. 'But you'll make food for three days.'

'It's quite a monster,' Conrad agreed excitedly, sitting up, grinning as the struggle continued. 'Let him have a little slack, give him a false sense of security. When he drags back he'll stop, hoping to be abandoned. Jerk the line and the hook'll fix deeper, right in the bone. He'll be lost then. You can let him die in the lake, or wind him in slowly, but not too fast. It's a strong line, but that fish has a kick like a mule, and a mule can break a line like this.'

'*Who's* fighting for magic? I don't understand.'

'Of course you don't. You're on the outside. The battle is not between Rebecca and Daniel – it's between enchanter and enchanter . . .'

Martin was stunned into silence for a moment, hearing the words, half understanding them, not quite ready to accept the deeper, stronger truth. Eventually he said, almost disbelievingly, 'Do you mean Merlin? You really think it's Merlin doing this?'

'He's trapped, across the lake,' Conrad said quietly, pointing vaguely to the distant shore where the trees crowded and the crows flew. 'His prison lies across the lake, just on the other side. When the lake came back into existence, it brought him close again. The woman too. Vivien! The screaming man, the wily enchantress. With the old enchanter's knowledge as the prize! I don't know how the strategy is working. All I know – don't pull so hard!' he snapped, as Martin's line was tugged. 'You'll lose him, and I want to taste this monster. Better . . . better! Ease him in, just ease him in . . .'

'All you know?'

'All I know is that *Broceliande* – the two warring lovers – is in your son and in your sister.'

'She's not my sister. No blood link at all.'

'Whatever she is. In Rebecca. Your mother sensed the possession all those years ago, when your brother died. I'm sure of it. That's why she sent you both away. But you came back, and now the wood has Rebecca, and her son. The power has them both. She came here, God knows why. Rebecca. She came here to the lake, then she came to my lodge and sat with me. She's blind, you know. And nine parts deaf, now.'

'I know.'

'She's lost song, she's lost story, she's losing language. It's all going into the boy. Or rather, to the traveller inside the boy.'

'To Vivien?'

'To Vivien.' The pike thrashed suddenly, then was still. Frightened by the ideas that the bosker had put in his head, tired of the struggle out on the lake, Martin jerked the line angrily. The fish – it was two feet long, and gleamed purple as it broke the surface – rose into the air then fell back, but a second jerk on the line, the line cutting into his skin now and drawing blood, that second jerk snared the beast and it fell quiet.

He wound it in, cut the hook out of its mouth, cut off its head and tail. He gutted the monster, scraped the scales and pushed two pieces of willow through the carcase, propping it over the fire on a crude spit.

'How do I stop it?'

'The fight? You can't. It's too late. You were a fool. You were warned.' And he added quietly, 'There's no way home for you either.'

'That doesn't help.'

'Nothing can help.'

'I don't believe that. There's a transference going on. Language, sight, song . . . the boy is taking it from Rebecca. Or is he? Is it possible that Rebecca is just reacting in an hysterical way?'

'She sees shadows, now,' Conrad said. 'Only shadows.

She hears only first words, hears only the oldest songs, the shadow songs. She's lost the first part of the fight. Daniel has drawn her out, he caught her unawares. Now she has a chance, though. This is only the middle game. Do you play chess? She has by no means lost. Leave them alone, leave them to end the struggle, one of them will win, one of them will be whole, nothing you can do will help shift the balance. So don't start choosing. You'll be left with one of them, and one only. If you interfere, you risk losing them both.'

I don't believe what I'm hearing! Oh God, this can't be real . . .

'There's something I don't understand, though,' Conrad went on in a hushed, weary voice. 'If the woman we think of as Vivien tricked and trapped the old enchanter, all those centuries ago – why is she still here? Why does he taunt her? Something must have gone wrong.'

Martin was hardly listening. He stared out across the blue lake at the heart of Broceliande, where the moans of a dying man could sometimes be heard, and the cries of a woman, and from which shore came silent boats, and ghostly travellers, escaping whatever evil lay at the heart of the wood.

I don't believe it! Merlin and Vivien still playing their tricks, their games . . . and in the process a family is destroyed?

But he *did* believe it. All his life he had believed it. All his life he had accepted that people moved up the path, to vanish below the hill where the church – even as a ruin – had tolled its bells of calling, and mourning, and feasting: bronze-ringing that signalled the changing of the quarters of the year, when the fires were burned in different ways, and the offerings were made in different ways, and the people of the land came to dance and talk and drink and remember.

Of course he believed it. But what was happening now was something beyond his experience.

I can't choose between them! Don't ask me to choose between them!

'I think we should go back to the edge of the wood.'

Conrad sighed and snuggled down among the skins, below the protecting umbrella of oilskin. The lake glimmered in the setting sun. It was close to dusk. The pike had been picked clean, the uneaten flesh wrapped carefully.

'I'll stay here, I think. A boat will be coming for me shortly.'

'A boat?'

As Martin understood the old man's point he felt again a moment of intense grief. 'I don't want you to die.'

'I'm already dead,' Conrad breathed, and chuckled through his parchment lips. 'Do you know the way back? Can you find the way back?'

'I think so.'

'Too bad if you can't. There's no way of drawing you a map!'

The bosker smiled again, then closed his eyes, drawing the skins around his neck as he lay by the lapping waters.

'Goodbye, Martin.'

'Do I just leave you here?'

'I won't be here for long. The boat's already on the lake.'

Martin stood and peered across the water. A wake was spreading, as if a water bird were swimming, but Martin could see no creature there.

He put more wood on the fire, throwing the bony remains of the pike into the reeds. When he looked back, Conrad's eyes were closed, his mouth gaping. There was no movement below the furs. He was probably dead.

Martin made the sign of the Cross and Wheel on his chest, then followed the path, away from the lake, through the crowding trees, running back to the hunting lodge, then the edgewood, and at last to the path and his own house.

7

It was early afternoon, now. He had spent too long in the forest and it had been difficult to find his way back to the edge. He had felt crowded and crushed. At times he had imagined himself followed, which had been a disorientating experience.

As he ran to the house to pick up his car – he was late for Daniel, who had to be fetched from school – he heard the terrible screaming from the kitchen, and for a second was stunned into immobility. Then Rebecca's terror resolved clearly and he broke into a breathless run, almost flinging himself through the door.

Rebecca was standing in the middle of the room, which was in chaos. She had thrown the table over, kicked the chairs, broken plates, cups and picture glass. Her hands were bloody, her face smeared with red streaks. Her hair was awry, her long dress torn and stained. She was turning where she stood, and screaming, and shaking her head, battering at her eyes with the raw horrors of her fingers.

Martin grabbed her and forced her still. 'I'm here! I'm here! Beck, what's happened? What's happened?'

'Shadows!' she wailed, then collapsed against him, weeping openly, clutching him in an embrace that said *never let me go!*

'What *about* shadows?'

'All round. Everywhere. Watching. Laughing.'

'Come on . . . let's get you cleaned up.'

He urged her upstairs. She stumbled, felt blindly, whispered, 'I can't see. Anymore. All gone. Shadows only.' In the bathroom he tended to the cuts on her hands, then undressed her and helped her into a warm bath. She lay back, her plastered fingers playing on his as he washed her, stroked her, comforting her as much as he could.

'Please,' she said quietly, through the steam and the heat. 'Don't. Let. Daniel. Home . . . *Please* . . .'

Even as she spoke, downstairs the back door was flung open. Outside, the sound of a departing car told Martin that one of the other parents had brought their son home.

The boy pounded up the stairs, came straight to the bathroom, bursting in to stand there, face glowing, breathing hard. 'Got a lift from Thierry's dad. Why weren't you there? What's up with Mummy? I'm hungry. Can I have some bread? It's all messy downstairs. Have you been fighting? Why weren't you *there?*'

'Go downstairs and straighten the table and the chairs. I'll get you a sandwich in a minute.'

Daniel stepped quickly to the side of the bath and looked at the pinkish water, at the rigid, naked body of his mother, her hands wrapped firmly, tensely around Martin's. She stared blindly at the ceiling.

The boy said, 'I love you, Mummy. Don't be hurt. I really do love you. I always did.'

Rebecca turned her head to the tiled wall, slipping slightly in the water. 'Away!' she hissed.

Daniel grinned at his father. 'I think I'm in the way. Shall I close the door?'

And with a suggestive chuckle he ran to the landing, pulling the bathroom door shut behind him.

Downstairs, the sound of noisy rearranging was testimony to Daniel's efforts to tidy up after his mother's period of hysterics. Martin led Rebecca to the bedroom, insisting she get under the covers. She was shaking, a terrified creature, confronting darkness saved for shadows – and no shadows that were cast by the warm and familiar sun. She had few words, now. She struggled to speak, resorting to a scrawled note as Martin sat on the bed, close to tears himself.

She wrote: *ask Jac and Suz to have the boy. Ask priest to visit.*

'You're going to stay with Uncle Jacques for a few days.'

'Why?' Daniel asked. He was sitting at the table, staring defiantly as ever, his face that of a ten-year-old, though only six summer suns had warmed his lanky body. He had cut a chunk from a stale baguette, toasted it and spread it with brie. He chewed slowly, arms folded on the table, eyes fixed firmly on his father. 'Why?' he repeated.

'Because I said so. Mummy isn't well and I need to look after her, and it will be easier if you stay with Uncle Jacques.'

Daniel shrugged. 'All right. When do I go?'

'When you've finished your sandwich. Pack some clothes and I'll drive you over.'

The boy did as he was told. He appeared downstairs, a small case in one hand, his New York Yankees windcheater opened to expose a Spookbusters T-shirt. Martin knelt down and pinched the boy's cheek. 'You don't mind, do you? It's only for a while, to help mummy get better.'

'I don't mind,' Daniel said, then dropped the case and flung his arms around Martin. He was fighting back tears, and when Martin pulled away slightly he could see how the boy's lip trembled.

'It's not for ever.'

'Are you sure?'

'Of *course*!'

'Mummy doesn't love me. She told me.'

'Nonsense. Mummy loves you very much. *When* did she tell you?'

'In a dream. She's frightened of me. She thinks I'm trying to hurt her.'

'She's very ill, Daniel. And I really want to do everything I can to get her better. But part of her being ill is that she behaves strangely, she says things she doesn't mean. I want you to go and stay with Uncle Jacques and Aunt Suzanne, and behave yourself, and do what you're told, and in a few days you'll come back here.'

And in his head, as he spoke these words, a voice whispered, *you liar. You liar. You're terrified of what is happening. You suspect your son. Conrad's words have frightened the life out of you. You liar . . . liar . . .*

Martin left the priest and Rebecca alone, the woman sitting huddled by the window, apparently staring out across Broceliande, the man, in jeans and track-suit top, standing behind her, talking quietly.

Later he came down and accepted a mug of coffee. 'She's made her peace,' he said. 'I hadn't realised her spirit was still so strong.'

'Is that why she wanted to talk to you? To make her confession?'

Father Gualzator nodded, staring into the mug. 'What are you going to do?'

The question unleashed in Martin the full burden of helplessness. What to do? What *could* he do?

'I have no idea. Specialists . . . speech therapists . . . psychologists . . . opticians . . . Rebecca says she can only see shadows, not even shadows of objects that are real. Like a kid round here, dancing through the people on the path, but they were never terrifying. She's terrified of these shadows.'

'There's something else,' the priest said, frowning. 'Her language—'

'Almost gone . . . ?'

'Almost completely gone, I think. I believe she has clung to these last few words to make her peace with God and the hill. Now, she has begun to speak strange words. Literally, strange words, but familiar. I can't be sure . . . I wrote some down . . .'

He came over to Martin and showed him the page of his notebook. He had scrawled Rebecca's murmured phrases phonetically.

'It's gibberish,' Martin said.

'I don't think so. There are constructions here that have familiarity. Look: iambathaguz. That sounds like *Mabathagus*, a particularly unpleasant entity from mythology, a sorcerer.'

'Never heard of him.'

'Of course you haven't. All you do is use your eyes to read. You don't use your eyes to *remember*. But then who am I to criticise? Here's something else: jingux. In Basque, that's almost the word for God, although not God as the church and the hill would understand it. Jinx.

'I think a lot of the rest of this is a deeper peace being made, but there is so much, she is speaking so much, and keeps laughing, as if triumphantly. I don't understand it. Not at all. But this fascinates me. I'm going to go south for a while, to find an old friend, someone who has a wider eye, an older eye than mine, someone who might see a little deeper into this, er . . .' he hesitated, searching for the word.

'Gibberish?'

'It's not gibberish, Martin. It's pain. Look after Rebecca. She's terrified.'

'I know she is. I'll look after her with all my heart.'

8

Almost as soon as the priest had departed for Basque country Martin took Rebecca to Paris, to her appointment with a specialist, André Benvenista, at the National Institute for Parapsychology. Suzanne accompanied them, while Jacques took care of Daniel.

The meeting, the observation on Rebecca, was unsatisfactory and distressing.

She lay in a room overlooking the Seine, her scalp covered with a fine tracery of electrodes and sensors. It was a bright day, and Paris, at least, was alive with activity.

Martin sat quietly by the window, watching the technicians about their business, aware of strange patterns on black video screens, outlines in three dimensions of the brain of the silent, shadowed woman. Colour flickered in the infra-red as she was tested – reds, blues, starbursts of yellow. Martin thought of turbulent or boiling water.

Everything was recorded and later he was shown the findings, understanding nothing. He watched the screens. Bursts of activity in the frontal lobe triggered sequential activities in the temporal lobe, limbic system and brain-stem. This was as it should have been. But he listened, uncomprehending, as he was shown a 'furious' echo from the limbic system, an 'after-event' that spread rapidly back, insidiously setting off activity in other regions of the neuro-cortex, a pattern of response that was meaningless to the psychologists who watched.

This 'event' occurred when Rebecca spoke words in the strange tongue that Martin had listened to in the deep of the night. But each time she spoke in what Father Gualzator had suggested was some form of early Basque, a normal speech pattern could be observed, though once, when she was whispering at random, she suddenly murmured in the deep-of-night sounds again and set up what Benvenista called a 'standing field of bio-electric activity', a split-second in which her whole brain was illuminated, as if awakened at once, a terrible shock that caused her to gasp, sit bolt upright from where she lay, to stare and froth, a fit of tremendous power, but a moment only, a moment of ancient memory too strong for her sheltered twentieth-century mind to cope with.

Immediately after this there was nothing but darkness on the screen, but she whispered 'Martin . . .' and a small glow appeared, a flicker of light, a guttering candle, a calm flame in the Stygian darkness that was the web within her skull.

Finally, she spoke words in the sequence of lisps and glottal sounds that was the deep-of-night language, and there was no signal at all from the language centre of her cortex, only from the motor area, showing nothing more than that her tongue was moving. She spoke words from a darkness so deep that it no longer registered. Over and over these odd sounds whispered, yet among them came the name 'Martin', and when 'Martin' was sounded there was that comforting flash from the frontal lobe, but thereafter, just the gloom of visual silence until she was stopped and brought back to whatever consciousness she could experience through touch and sound and shadow.

'To put it simply,' Benvenista said, 'it's as if her learned language has been scraped away, exposing older forms, primitive forms – like a city, destroyed to expose the hill where the first settlers camped in prehistoric times. The core of our language is embedded – we build upon that core as we grow and experience communication. But the core of Rebecca's language no longer registers. It is either still there, but has been hidden somehow; or it has been destroyed.

'But there are no tumours, no areas of necrosis, no

fibrous masses, no signs of a stroke, no abnormalities. Everything in physiological and anatomical terms is healthy. And it's the same with the visual cortex: show her a shadow and it registers. But the shadows she sees – at least, that she indicates she sees – do not show – except, of course, in the motor cortex as she follows the ghost with her eyes.'

'But you think her language might still be there? All of her senses? Somewhere – just hidden?'

Benvenista spread his hands and shrugged as he stared out at the bright day. 'In the absence of damage, I can't imagine an alternative.'

Martin almost said, *what if someone had stolen her words, her songs, her dreams*, but he refrained from speaking. Across the room, Rebecca was making incoherent sounds and staring in the direction of the voices.

Although Benvenista would have liked to keep Rebecca longer, she was signalling with her body, with her crude speech, that she did not wish to stay. Martin drove them all back to the farm by Broceliande and spent an hour ringing around for a full-time, live-in nurse. He eventually found someone to take the position as from the next day.

Suzanne stayed the night, but Rebecca, once in her room and seated by the window facing the forest, was relaxed. She could perform most bodily functions without assistance, but gave no indication of being aware of either Martin or the older woman.

Two days later, Father Gualzator returned.

Martin was walking along the path with Daniel, holding the boy's hand, talking to him gently. Daniel's behaviour at school that day had been disruptive, and Martin had been advised to take him home. He was coming down with flu, perhaps, was the diplomatic suggestion. As Martin had entered the classroom to take his son home there had been an almost tangible tension. Daniel was by the window, at a desk on his own, illuminated by the pale sun. The rest of the class whispered and wrote in exercise books. Daniel came quickly over to his father, and the teacher, a fair-haired man in his late twenties, smiled reassuringly as he closed the door behind Martin.

'I'm sure it's just a temporary upset,' he said.

As Martin led Daniel down the corridor, behind him the classroom erupted into the sound of baying, barking and cheering, only subdued after thirty seconds of the teacher's shouting.

On the path, Daniel suddenly stopped, clutching Martin's hand more tightly. He was listening against the light wind. 'It's the priest,' he said. 'He's hiding something.'

Martin scanned the land around, the dark wood, the hill with the sun setting, the scatter of houses. After a few minutes he saw the wobbling figure of Father Gualzator, approaching them on his ancient bicycle.

Smiling broadly, breathing hard, the priest dismounted. He was wearing his track-suit and a Redskins baseball cap. His smile, as he greeted Daniel, was transparently fixed, but he dropped to a crouch and embraced the boy.

'How are you getting on with Uncle Jacques?'

'All right. I miss Mummy, though.'

'I'm sure you do.'

'Uncle Jacques watches football all the time, and his computer can't play good games.'

'Oh dear. That is a tragedy. But he has a lot of books, doesn't he?'

'I suppose so.'

'Would you like to have a wobble on the bike? It's a bit big for you, but it's good exercise. Too bloody good,' he added with a smile at Martin, taking a deep breath. 'I'm out of condition.'

Daniel had grabbed the bicycle and was racing it away towards the church, hidden from view over the nearest hill. As he cycled furiously, he called back, 'I can hear everything you say!'

Martin shouted, 'Did you hear what I just said, then?'

Ringing the bell, Daniel called back, 'You didn't *say* anything.'

The boy was in the distance. 'How much is two and two?' Martin said in a normal voice. The bike skidded to a halt. Daniel laughed. He rang the bicycle bell four times then began to pedal furiously, riding perilously close to the ditch by the path.

Father Gualzator pulled a face. 'He has *very* good hearing, your son. Conrad had the same facility. Must be something to do with the air round here.' He gave Martin a meaningful glance. The priest, too, was aware of Conrad's encounters with the ghosts, and with his belief that Merlin was behind the new phenomena around Broceliande.

'Daniel's a very talented young man,' Martin said. 'As

soon as Rebecca is better we'll all be going on a long holiday. Somewhere hot, with lots of sea and sand.'

Daniel had vanished. The two men stopped and stared at each other for a moment, the unspoken words between them signalling their unease with the boy, with the idea of being listened to. Then the priest shrugged, as if to say, 'What else can we do?'

Martin said, 'So. Did your Old Eye help at all?'

'Only a little. Let's go to the house, I'd like Rebecca to be with us when I tell you what I've learned. At least, what I *think* I've learned.'

Outside the farmhouse, the priest's bicycle was propped against the fence. Rebecca was at the window, a pale face in dark dress, staring out across the forest. She didn't move when the gate rattled shut. Martin stared at her in sorrow, standing on the driveway until a second face behind her resolved into Suzanne, who waved at him.

Inside the house, Daniel was playing a computer game in his room. Martin stood behind him for a few minutes, watching the way the boy manipulated the two 'mouse' controls, determining the three-dimensional action of the two mediaeval armies as they engaged on the wide landscape. It always astonished Martin how so much information, so much awareness of what was off-screen, could be held in the mind of a child playing these complex interactives.

'I'm staying home, now,' Daniel said quietly,

suddenly. Martin squeezed the boy's shoulder and was surprised when Daniel looked up at him, moist-eyed.

'That's what I want too,' he said. 'A nurse will look after Mummy. I'll look after you. Uncle Jacques will be sorry to see you go, though.'

'No he won't.'

Ignoring the bitter words, Martin went to Rebecca. Father Gualzator was sitting with her, holding her hand. He had two sheets of paper on his knee.

Martin kissed Rebecca's pale cheeks, then brushed her lips with his, eliciting a response, a desperate hug, a shuddering embrace that lasted for minutes. Then slowly Rebecca relaxed, again becoming blank-expressioned and almost limp.

The priest mouthed the words written on the sheets of paper.

I am in hell now. So is the other.

The fire was put out. The swan drowned in ice waters.

The bronze thorn pricked as it was intended. The blood was quick. Love was quick.

Martin. Martin. The stag danced by falling water. Enchantment killed me. The god/ghost behind the mask is in the stone. ('That refers to "Mabathagus", I mentioned him before.') The stone covers the pit. The pit consumes the bones. (But) the shadow ones are on the path.

Love you. Love you.

The hemp knot is twisted twice. She has no breath. The trickster is tricked.

I am in hell. Let me out.

The ghost has been drawn from me. Martin. Martin.
Help me.
Let me out.
I am in hell.
Let me out.

There was the sound of breaking glass, of smashed machinery. Martin leapt from where he was sitting, by the silent, staring Rebecca, by the frowning priest. He ran along the landing to the room where Daniel had been playing.

As he opened the door, the boy pushed past him, screaming as he ran to his mother. The VDU screen was smashed, the keyboard broken in half, the mirror in the room broken too, and all the shelves emptied of their toys and books. Daniel had thrown a fit of rage. Now he was screaming incoherently at the priest. Martin reached for him and dragged him away. Rebecca sat quite motionless, undisturbed, unperturbed.

The boy suddenly stiffened. He was white with rage. His eyes seemed to stare from his head, popping from below the lids. The breath in his lungs was hoarse and animal. Martin felt his skin tingle with an odd electricity.

'What happened, Daniel?' he asked quietly.

The boy fled past him, thumping down the stairs. Chasing him, Martin was only able to stand by the back door and see his son, hair flying, racing into the dense edgewood of Broceliande. Where Daniel had leapt over the fence, a bloody shred of his torn jeans hung limp and sickly.

Upstairs, for a brief and wonderful moment, Rebecca laughed; but it was just the rattle of a dying ghost.

The boy had vanished into the woods. Martin wanted to follow him, but he was frightened, he realised, frightened of the alienness, the anger, the incomprehensibility of the behaviour of the lad.

'Daniel,' he whispered. 'Whatever is happening, whatever rage is in you, you *are* my son. Rebecca's son too. Don't abandon us.'

Did Daniel hear? Was that movement in the edge-wood, that shift of branches, the rustle of leaves?

In a state of emotional limbo, Martin returned to Rebecca. She was asleep, now, fully clothed, but covered with a thin blanket. The nurse said that the drowse had come quite naturally, as if the woman had been exhausted and just curled up for forty winks.

Downstairs again, Martin read through the meaningless words.

'Let me out. Let me out,' he quoted. 'A genie in a bottle?'

'There are two voices here,' the priest said, taking the sheets. 'There's the old voice, with its odd references – swans, stags, stone gods; and the phrase "let me out". And there's Rebecca's last message to you. Here, where it says the ghost has been drawn from me; and the use of your name, and the sentiment of love. And "help me". That's Rebecca. The other voice is what's inside her, the traveller, and the language is a lost one, and the references are to lost events. At least, that's the conclusion of my Old Eye in the mountains; but even so it was only an intuitive guess on her part. The language Rebecca whispered to me is older than the painted caves. Even to an Old Eye, it's like trying to reconstruct a burned city from the charred remains of its foundations.'

'Everyone who talks to me talks of ruined cities,' Martin said, staring at the forest.

Father Gualzator walked down the drive to where Daniel had thrown his bicycle. He picked it up and checked the tyres, then rang the bell. He was distracted and unhappy and before he cycled back to the church and the hill he walked back to Martin and took the man's hands in his, staring down, not meeting eyes. 'This will sound cruel,' he whispered. 'And don't assume it's true. But I don't think you can get *both* of them back.'

'Oh Christ! That's what Conrad said to me. But I can't accept it.'

'You may have to. The old bosker may have been touched, but he was touched by charm, not madness. I don't think Daniel and Rebecca can ever be together. The one so dead, the other so alive . . . but they're both of them ghosts, Martin. I don't know where you go from here.'

'Exorcism. That's all I can think of. Exorcise them.'

'Bronzebell, Book and Nightfire?' The priest shook his head. 'The travellers in your family are too old to be intimidated by the Church and the Hill. The exorcism needed in this case isn't something I can accomplish.'

For half an hour Martin walked briskly to and fro along the edge of the forest, calling for Daniel. The light was going, and a storm was coming from the west. The breeze was cold and beginning to stiffen.

He went quickly back to the house, called Jacques, then another neighbour, and when both told him that they'd seen nothing of the boy, he fetched his torch and overcoat and went out again.

It was beginning to rain as he reached the first of the old bosker's lodges, the ramshackle iron and wooden hut. The heads of the hunted foxes had vanished from their stakes, but the hanged line of squirrels turned and twisted in the wet wind, as did the torn oilskin over the door.

Daniel was sitting on the bed, a shadowy figure. He blinked as Martin flashed the torch in his face, but kept staring at the light. He was leaning against the wall, below the remaining pictures of Conrad's childhood sweetheart. His arms were limp by his sides, his gaze quite expressionless, save for his narrowed eyes.

'Stop shining it in my face.'

'Sorry.'

Martin set the torch's light to fluorescent. The stark glow illuminated the boy's pale features and set sharp shadows around the room. Martin sat down in the old man's chair.

'Why did you break your computer?'

'I don't know. Just felt like it.'

'Why are you upset?'

'I'm angry. Not upset. Angry.'

'Why don't you come home, Daniel? I'll make supper, we'll look after Mummy.'

'Leave me alone.'

'You can't stay here all night. The storm is going to be fierce . . .'

As if to illustrate his words, the whole structure shook and shuddered, the oilskin billowing as the rain and wind swirled and gusted.

'I need the storm. I need the darkness. I like the darkness. It helps me think.'

'Daniel . . .'

'Not Daniel!'

'Not Daniel?'

The boy stared through the white light. A smile touched his lips; he was otherwise limp, propped against the rough wall like a doll.

'Leave me alone.'

'Who are you? What do you want?'

'I've got what I want. Most of it. He thought he could starve me at birth, but I've taken what I want, and now he can't see anything but the shadows of lost forests. He's *skogan*. He can't hear anything but stone songs. He can't make any sound except running water . . .' Daniel laughed hoarsely, then looked away. 'Leave me alone. I have to think.'

'Let Daniel go. I want him home.'

'Too late. The boy doesn't want to go home.'

'But I want him to come home, and I'll take him home, and you too unless you release him.'

Daniel sniggered, his eyes closed as if with deep weariness. The storm raged through the forest, wind swirling through the eaves, sending skins and paper flapping in the cold shack.

'Don't threaten me,' Daniel said. 'I'm here for the duration. He's kept something back from me. He always keeps something back from me . . .'

Martin felt that the reference was not to the boy, but to the 'he' who travelled inside Rebecca. 'I intend to get it. But how? How?'

And suddenly, uncontrollably, Martin leapt at the limp human figure on the bed. The surge of rage had surfaced unbidden, and took him unawares. He just knew that he *hated* the traveller, that he was incensed at the so-calm dismissal of the human life in which it was a passenger. As he struck at the face, and squeezed at the neck, he was aware that it was his son's body that he was assaulting; but it was not Daniel who was the object of his attack. It was the enchantress inside him, who screamed, and laughed through her choking throat, used strong fingers to bend back Martin's, then kicked him powerfully, sending him hurtling back across the shack.

Daniel sat up straight, rubbing his neck, weeping from his left eye where Martin's first blow had landed, taunting. 'Daddy, Daddy, child abuser!'

'Get out of my son!'

'I *am* your son, you fool! This is how I was born. The body's just the shell. *Your* body's just a shell. We're all *travellers*, as you so quaintly call it. Now go away! I'm stronger than you by far.'

And Martin left, staggering back through the driving rain, leaving his son behind him in the darkened ruin, leaving his life behind.

He was weeping as he entered the house. Suzanne was there, and she drew him into her bosom, holding him very tightly as the rain rattled the windows, and upstairs Rebecca shrieked and howled, her words incoherent, her footfall heavy as she stumbled about the room, the nurse trying to calm her, to ease her back to bed.

At about four in the morning, as the storm abated slightly, Martin woke from a deep, disturbed sleep. He was sprawled on a blanket, by the still-warm stove, using a cushion as a pillow. He became aware of someone crouching by him, a hand on his back, and he turned over quickly, looked up to see Rebecca, dimly lit by the night-light in the hall. She was wet around the eyes and lips, feeling blindly in the dark. When he reached for her she grasped for him and twisted below him, murmuring sounds.

'Oh Beck! Beck . . . you shouldn't be up . . .'

'Ssssh!' she breathed, and he drew back.

'Can you understand me, Beck?'

She had opened her dressing gown. He placed his hands on her breasts and she closed her blind eyes, covering his hands with hers, holding him hard. He leant down and kissed her and at the back of her throat she started to sing, her legs jerking violently, meaning-lessly until Martin realised what she was trying to do. He reached down and undressed quickly, desperate to keep the kiss, desperate not to lose her.

Moments later, as she reached down to draw him deeply home, he felt a great fatigue. It was an irresistible drowsiness, and though he fought against it, he was helpless in its grasp; and making love he fell asleep, his last thought a silent plea for wakefulness.

In the morning she was gone. He woke, cold, half naked, to find the nurse in a panic.

'She's gone. Oh my God, she's gone!'

Quickly covering himself, Martin stood, blinking the sleep from his eyes, rubbing them furiously. *She put a spell on me!*

'Where? Gone?'

'I don't know. I don't know. The door was open. I only woke a few moments ago . . .'

'Call Jacques. The number's in the book. And the priest. Tell them that Rebecca has gone walkabout, and I need them to help search for her.'

Outside, in the grey dawn, the forest of Broceliande shimmered with the rain from the night's storm. It seemed to have grown, to have become heavier, to have leaned towards the farm, to have consumed a little of the path. The air was fresh. The milk-cart was rattling past. Up on the hill, the church was a black tower against the spiralling clouds.

'She's dead,' Martin whispered. He couldn't find tears. He remembered her touch from the middle of the night, the feel of her lips, the warmth of her sex, the touch that said how much she needed him, the touch that had said goodbye.

'She's dead . . .'

And he knew she would be at the lake. He walked indoors again and found his coat and rubber boots. He fetched a rake from the shed. The nurse watched him. He felt very calm. He felt dead.

'Where are you going? Where are you going to look?'

'She's in the lake,' he said. 'Tell Jacques. She's in the lake.'

'What lake?'

'The lake in Broceliande, by Conrad's grave. The lake in the heart of the forest.'

'Will he know which lake you mean?'

'Just tell him to follow the path.'

'If you're sure of this, then go. Now. Hurry!'

He walked down the path. After the storm, the wood was quite still. It was as if the world had ceased to breathe. He was cold inside, he might have been floating through the trees, not walking. The memory of the kiss, the memory of her body, these things were gentle pleasures, memories of a lost life that walked with him, accompanied him calmly down the path, past the bosker's cabin, through the silent forest of Broceliande.

And yet, as he passed Conrad's hunting place, the frame of wicker, the wooden igloo with its rough skins, a voice said, 'Hurry!' and he began to run.

And by the time he came to the lakeside, to flounder in the mud among the rushes, he was screaming for his lover – as if a spell had broken and suddenly there was hope after all. As if the drowned were not yet dead, and the water could be brought out through their mouths, their eyes, all the passages of their bodies, and the spirit returned to the flesh.

As he thrashed in the cold water, so the birds rose in flocks, to wheel about the lake, dark shapes in the dawn, circling and watching like hungry crows over the battle-fields of old, waiting for the spoils.

When he saw her he screamed. As he approached he stumbled, aware of the two shapes floating in the deeper water.

He rose with a howl, soaking from head to foot, the rake held like a weapon, waved angrily above his head. The rats that had been feeding swam away. The dawn breeze caught the spill of hair. The bodies, interlocked by arms, turned slowly as the waves began to break against them. Martin staggered through the lake, then swam to reach them, drawing them by the feet, drawing them back to the shore, back to the mud.

They were alike, so alike. They were asleep, their arms entwined, their hair entwined, their faces white and almost smiling. In death the travellers had left them, no doubt. The peace of lives released in death touched each closed eye, the corners of each wide, perfect mouth.

Martin kissed them both, and hugged them, standing in the lake, the wind chilling his body. Then he dragged them through the reeds and to the dry earth where the wood began, and when Jacques arrived, hours later, astonished by the sight of the lake, he found his nephew on his knees between the dead, holding their hands in his against his chest, as if the three were praying.

'Turn them over! Get the water out of them! Turn them *over*, man.'

'They've *been* turned over. Let them rest at last.'

PART THREE

The Vision of Magic

How from the rosy lips of life and love
Flash'd the bare-grinning skeleton of death!

From *Idylls of the King*

Opening the Tomb

'Martin! Martin! There are people on the path. Your people!'

The words, shouted from outside, seemed like a dream at first, but with the constant hammering at the door, and the rattle of dirt on the window, he soon came awake, stretching out on the floor, groaning as his deadened limbs came back to life. He was fully clothed and his mouth felt sour and dry.

Again, the boy's voice, 'Martin. Martin! Hurry!'

He peered out into the brightening dawn. It was Richard, the Lordez's eldest child, a familiar and cheery youth who kept his pony in Martin's field. The boy saw the man and beckoned, then pointed to where Clarisse, his sister, was cautiously circling an invisible spot on the path, astonished by what she was seeing.

He went downstairs and drank copiously from the water bottle, then walked outside, shivering with the chill.

Richard called to him. The boy, fourteen now, was frightened, or perhaps apprehensive.

'What is it? What have you seen?'

'People on the path,' Richard said, his voice a whisper, his pale eyes wide. '*Your* people.'

'My people?'

'It's Daniel. And Rebecca. They're walking up to the hill.'

It took a moment for the meaning of the words to register. Then Martin was running, gaining speed, all sleep gone, all alcohol drained from a mind that was suddenly racing. Rebecca? Daniel? And as he ran he murmured, 'Rebecca . . . ?' and his voice began to rise in volume until he screamed, literally screamed, 'Rebecca!'

He reached the suddenly startled girl and gripped her by the shoulders. 'Where? Where is she? Where's Rebecca?'

Clarisse looked terrified, trying to pull away from the unshaven man, her eyes a window into combined terrors.

'Where is she?' Martin shouted, shaking her. 'Where is she?'

'You're inside her,' Clarisse whispered and her face twisted into a sob. 'Please – let me go.'

He released the girl. She scampered away, then stood with her brother, slightly hunched, watching the path.

Martin turned, his arms outstretched. He could feel nothing. But he danced on the path, turning, turning, remembering Seb, desperate to touch the dead.

'Beck. Oh God, Beck. Are you here?' And loudly to the children, eyes still closed, 'Where is she? Am I still inside her?'

Clarisse's voice was a howl of sadness, 'No. You've danced in front of her. Just stand still.'

Martin stood on the path, eyes closed, trying to feel. There was the scent of dawn, and a gentle breeze. He could hear the girl making noises, like a kitten, frightened. She was crouching, now, her brother with her, watching the man as he embraced the empty path.

'She's passing through you again,' Richard called, and Martin closed his arms around his body, trying to hold the ghost.

'What about Daniel? How does he look?'

They walked together up the path. The children described what they could see, and Martin tried to remember how it had been when he had been a child. Rebecca was walking slowly. She was dressed as she had been dressed when he had dragged her from the lake. Daniel was looking back, looking worried. Why was there always one person on the path who looked back, as if haunted, as if hunted?

They came to the church and Martin began to cry. He could feel nothing! He ran to the frightened children, grabbed at Clarisse. 'Dance inside her. Please! Dance inside Rebecca. Tell me what you hear, tell me what you feel!'

'It's too dangerous,' Richard said, but he hesitated. The girl shuddered, gripped by Martin's hands. Her eyes filled and flowed, but she remained silent, blinking nervously.

Martin was desperate. 'Please? Clarisse, will you?'

'*Dangerous!*' Richard said earnestly. 'Our parents always told us – not inside people we know!'

Screaming, not hearing those odd words *not inside the people we know*, Martin implored the girl. 'Dance inside her! I must know how she feels! For Christ's sake, do it! Clarisse – do it! Please! For me!'

The girl burst into tears, but nodded. 'Look after me,' she wailed as she tugged free and ran in pursuit of the invisible people on the path. Richard stared icily at the man, terrified. His sister's sobs turned to screams of fear as she slowed to enter the ghosts, looking back.

And at that moment Martin realised what he had done. He raced after the girl, grabbed her, swung her round and hugged her as she cried out and sank down with relief. 'I'm sorry. Clarisse, I'm so sorry. I was forgetting how dangerous it is. I'm so confused, so frightened. I'm so sorry, love. Of course you mustn't dance inside her.'

Richard suddenly screamed, 'Be careful! Clarisse! Watch out—'

The girl's eyes had widened and she smiled. Somewhere, a long way away, the sound of someone running . . .

Martin held the girl, noticing how she seemed to melt, how her eyes glowed. Richard was running towards them.

'Get out! Get out!'

They were inside the people! Rebecca and Daniel were passing through them!

Martin dragged the girl to the side. Richard thumped him hard on the back, a small man, furious. 'You let them into her! You shouldn't have done that!'

'I didn't know. I thought they were ahead of me. I

can't see them, Richard. I can't see them. Only you can see them. Christ, I want to *see* them! Where are they now?'

The boy hesitated, fury calming, then he looked towards the hedge around the cemetery. 'Passing through. Rebecca is looking back at you. Do you think she knows you're here? Did she feel something?'

'I don't know.'

'Did you feel anything?'

'Nothing.'

They both looked at Clarisse.

'Sis? Did you feel anything?'

'Let me out,' the girl said quietly. 'So close, now. So near. Let me out!'

'Who's saying this?'

'The old man. The old man in Rebecca. Let me out. I'm nearly out. Let me out!'

'I don't understand.'

But all Clarisse would say was, 'Stuck in the shaft. Trapped in the tree. Let me out. Let me free!'

Her brother Richard took her home. A few hundred yards down the path the huddled pair broke into a run, holding hands, racing against the rising of the sun to return to their house.

Martin swung on the iron gate, imagining the way that Rebecca and Daniel were now descending below the hill, to pass through their own gate into a world beyond his understanding.

Let me out? Trapped in the tree. Trapped in the shaft . . .

I'm nearly out. Let me out . . .

And Martin remembered Sebastian's drawings, made years ago, shortly before the boy had died.

It took him two hours to find the faded paper, the scrawled sketches that Sebastian had made. Eveline had kept them safe, of course, as she had kept everything that her sons and daughter had drawn and written. They had been locked in one of many boxes, and the boxes stacked in orderly array within the attic. It was volume and security that made the task of discovery so difficult, but at last, from the filed and ordered memories of his mother, Martin found the sketches of the 'vases', the odd drawings that his brother had produced shortly before his death.

By the time he reached the church, Matutinus was underway, the priest, in his black robe, singing the words-of-morning to a congregation of two (the Delbondes, who never missed Matutinus). Candle smoke filled the church. Martin sat quietly at the back, and when the Delbondes scurried out, ready for breakfast, Father Gualzator snuffed the candles and came quickly down the aisle.

'I was watching you. I saw everything. This morning.'

'Richard and Clarisse?'

The older man nodded, taking the papers from Martin's hand as if already he had intuited their content.

'My old eye didn't fill in the figures, but the children could see the ghosts of Rebecca and Daniel. And I heard the old man's voice: Let me out.'

'You heard it as an old man's voice? It was the girl who was speaking.'

The priest laughed drily. 'Old eyes do see, old ears do hear. It was an old man, speaking through the girl. He's trapped, like the genie in the bottle. Except that he's close to getting free. He's been close to getting free for nearly two hundred years, now. These sketches are fascinating. They confirm something I've half suspected since I came to Broceliande. Come into the vestry.'

'I wish you'd shown me these before. Look here . . .'

Father Gualzator produced a box file, opening it to reveal yellowed parchment, vellum, torn pages from note books, schoolbooks, even the blue tint of quality writing paper from earlier in the century. He spread the sheaf of paper on the table. On all of them were sketched, in childish hand, bottles and vases, all with bits of tree and bone inside them, each stoppered with little hats, or caps, consisting of round blobs.

But they weren't vases. They were shafts into the earth, and the stoppers were:

'Stones. These are votive shafts, dug deeply into the ground and capped with stone cairns. Do you see? The image was confusing for the children who glimpsed them from the ghosts, and they've always drawn jars, or vases. But they're shafts. It's a familiar device from pre-history, running on into late Celtic times. The shafts were filled with bones, stones, trees, whatever, and there is no reason why a shaft in one area of the world should necessarily function in the same way as a shaft from another. But they are clearly an attempt to commune with the earth, perhaps to mollify the earth. Sebastian, like all the other children whose drawings I've managed to accumulate, has shown a shaft with a tree inside it. That was very common. The deepest shaft I know was dug about two hundred years before Christ, and was one hundred and forty feet deep, and very narrow. A whole tree had been thrown down it, plus pottery and bones, a dog, a stag, some bits and pieces of gold and bronze. Right at the bottom, below everything, was the corpse of a child, a deformed child, mind you, its skull neatly divided by a single blow.'

Martin leafed through the drawings. The similarities were astonishing. Each of these had been drawn by a child after dancing through the people on the path. Yet the oldest was from the early eighteen hundreds. The proportions were so much the same. The lopped off tree, its branches cut, all showed the same number of stubs: six, six for the stubs of a dismembered male human body.

'Then this is the evil at the heart of the wood. Conrad knew it. He told me, just days ago. Merlin *is* trapped in the heart of Broceliande. His grave is there. Just across the lake, according to Conrad. It's always been there, hidden from prying eyes, but no longer hidden, I think. We can get to it. We can dig him up!'

Father Gualzator smiled and leaned on the table. 'This is the *pain* at the heart of the wood. And yes, it's Merlin, or whatever it is that we've come to call Merlin. A vague memory of the killing in ancient times has survived as a legend of Merlin trapped in a tree, in a shaft of air, accessible only to Vivien. But it's an *earth* shaft. And probably very deep. And he, or it, is down there. And it wants to be let out. It's been creeping out for ages. It's been trying to tell us where it's buried. That sounds dangerous to me.'

Martin let the priest's words flow into and over him. All he could think was: perhaps he can help. If I let him out, perhaps he can bring back Rebecca. Perhaps he can give life again to Daniel. There is old magic in song, as Rebecca discovered. I must try. I must try . . .

But he couldn't do it on his own.

Martin watched as the priest filed the drawings, adding Sebastian's own sketches to the collection.

'I'm going to dig him up.'

Father Gualzator shrugged, frowning. 'Most of me wants to counsel against such an act. It should have occurred to you that you stand to release not just Merlin, but to revive Merlin's tormentor again. They're both down there, although how and why Vivien was trapped is beyond me. Something went wrong, all that time ago. She has been a vengeful and violent spirit for two thousand years, striking from the grave – possessing, using, destroying . . .'

'Nevertheless . . .'

Martin hesitated. The priest was in a cold sweat, his hands shaking as he tied the ribbon on the box-file.

'Will you help me?'

'I suppose so. I'll try. I'll help until I can't. Then you'll have to forgive me, but I'll not help if I feel the people in this parish are threatened. Do you understand that?'

Martin understood and said so.

They moved through the woodland for hours, following the path by Conrad's first home, by his hunting lodge, dragging the canoe on its makeshift sled, lowering it down the rock faces, hauling it across the marshy ground, around the giant oaks, through the sun-bright glades, shifting their packs as they sweated on the path. Breathless and hot in the humidity of Broceliande, the priest in physical distress despite his fitness, they listened for the sound of the lake.

The canoe could carry two. Martin had driven to Bordeaux to buy it. It was made of fibreglass and was styled like the canoes of the North American Indians. It should easily transport them across the lake, from home-shore, to heart-shore.

Towards the end of the day they were moving still, dragging the long canoe along the path, but at dusk, just as the sun was blinking out of sight above the trees, they found the quiet water and the old bosker's ruined fishing lodge. The body of Conrad lay there, drawn deeply into its skins. The cross above the grave where Martin and his uncle had buried Rebecca and Daniel was dark in the tree line. Father Gualzator went and blessed the hump of earth before coming back and watching the mist rise on the water.

'Did you wrap them in linen?'

'Very carefully.'

'In one piece, I hope—'

'I'm no butcher.'

'Good. We should stay overnight here, I think. Cross the lake at dawn.'

Martin hauled the canoe to the reeds, pushing it half across the mud so that it was taken by the lake. He heaved the two packs into the middle of the craft, then came back for the shovels and the winch.

'No. Let's cross now. I'm impatient to go, impatient to be there.'

Without a further word, the priest clambered into the prow of the canoe, picking up one of the paddles. Martin pushed the boat afloat, splashing through the muddy shallows, then flinging himself aboard. The mist parted before them, even as the sun dropped from view and the whole lake, the whole wood, became grey and silent.

It took less than fifteen minutes to float, rowing gently, to the farther shore, pulling the boat onto the bank and turning it over, to make a crude shelter for the rest of the night, close to the thin trail they could see leading inwards.

The stone cairn had spread under its own weight and, of course, the weight of time. Perhaps it had once been as high as the man whose dismembered corpse, represented in blue-stone, now probed obscenely from the spill of boulders, earth and weeds. The cairn, now, was no more than a hump, half-filling the curious glade with its eight confining oaks, its single stone, a piece of grey stone, fallen, resting heavily against the broadest of the spreading trees. There was room, in this clearing, to sit, to camp. The flowers were yellow, the thistles high, the branches draped with old, old rags. The canopy was heavy, but left a clear space to the sky and the light, as the day began, gleamed on the blue torso of the stone statue.

'Are you feeling fit?'

Father Gualzator grinned as he rolled up his shirt-sleeves, responding to Martin's question with a shrug. 'Soon find out. Statue first?'

They scrabbled the stones away from the broken statue. The eyes in the sharply carved face stared blindly; the mouth gaped as if in death. It was made of green and white marble, and the skin of the naked form was covered with tiny marks, a complete tattoo of designs and symbols which the priest examined with fascination.

'Everything, from cuneiform . . . see? Here, the little wedges . . . to ogham, over here, over most of it. These are a sort of rune, these . . . only the Lord knows. Interesting man, below, our Merlin.'

Together they managed to prop the statue against the leaning grey-stone. By day's end they had cleared the cairn to expose the stone slab that covered the shaft and fixed up the winch, which made the tree sigh as weight was taken. The stone slab was a foot thick, and the metal hook could hardly grip it, but as the last of the dark birds returned to their nests, and Father Gualzator's small fire, with its jug of coffee, began to signal the end of the first day's work, so Martin got the stone to rise, exposing the compacted earth below. The priest came to lend a hand and they pushed the slab away from the shaft. It fell heavily. The earth felt as cold as ice.

'Come out, come out, wherever you are,' Martin whispered, digging his fingers into the hard soil.

But the genie below remained quiet.

In the morning, Martin discovered the priest sitting shivering, terrified, cold and puffy-eyed. The man had not slept during the night, or rather, he had fallen asleep, only to be woken by the sound of terrible screaming.

'Whilst you slept, I saw the murder. She used an axe and a great knife. He was a small man, young, dark-haired, dark-bearded, trim and tidy, like a prince. He lay motionless, as if helpless, as she hacked off his limbs, then blinded him. I have never seen such fury, such triumphant fury. This woman, like death in a white and green robe, raced into the wildwood, came back with a tall thin tree and lopped off its branches. She sharpened the point of the tree and drove it through the body in the glade until a full four feet extended from the skull. She made a pit, the air around her was filled with spinning earth, and into that pit she flung the body.

'And then she screamed, and the vision faded, save for the sound of fury and despair.

'When the screaming passed away there was an hour or more of silence, but there was movement here, movement I can't understand. Even my Old Eye wasn't sufficient to show the process by which the people came to be on the path. But they came, I know it. The wood, while you slept, became alive with activity. I heard children's voices, I think I counted seven in all, and a man's voice intoning in a lost language. At last a man appeared, the ghostly white image of a man, who seemed at first bemused by the glade, then behaved as if he had been struck, holding his eyes, his head. For a while he had walked normally, despite his ethereal thinness. Now he began to flow, that sublimely delicate movement which you will remember from your childhood visions and which I can still see at times. He left the glade towards the lake. I followed him along the trail. He became immersed in the fog that sits on the water, but flowed away from this glade, across to the path by Rebecca's grave.

'After he had gone I couldn't sleep, and about two hours ago I began to be tormented by a voice, and by the feeling of pain in my ears and eyes, as if fingers were gouging at me. I'm not wanted here, Martin. Whatever lies in the shaft, it doesn't want me here. I don't belong, and it will not let me stay.'

Martin comforted the older man. The glade was dew-wet, webbed with silk, quite silent. He pushed wood onto the fire and set light to a wax block, pouring coffee grounds into the jug, with water, and setting it to heat in the flames that crackled from the wood.

'I need you to help me dig. When the digging's done, then go, by all means. But please stay till then. I need you to help with the digging. If you get attacked again, refer them to me.'

The priest laughed, pushing his hair back and shaking the moisture from his hand. 'Don't take on—'

'More than I can handle? I'll try not to. Just stay. This

thing wants to be let free. It will understand that I need you to help that process.'

'You're very confident, all of a sudden.'

'I'm desperate,' Martin said with a glance across the glade. 'I've got less than thirty days to bring them back—'

'Forty days before the spirit leaves the corpse? That's Church-lore. We're outside those rules, now.'

'Maybe. Maybe not. How can I tell? All I know is, I want them back, father. I want them back.'

'I know you do, Martin. And I'm sure they want to come back. But you are aware, of course . . .'

'What? Aware of what?'

'That they can never come inside the hill again. They can never come inside the church.'

'Yes. Of course. Of course I'm aware of that. The sacrament must come to them. I know that.'

'As long as you do remember. It's the first time I've been faced with such a possibility. It will be very hard to deny Daniel. I don't relish the thought. But of course I'll stay and dig. When the digging's done, though, please let me go.'

'When the digging's done, I may not have any choice in the matter.'

Six feet into the shaft Martin's shovel struck against wood, a thick cut of oak, a round sliced from a wide tree. It was sealing the shaft below. He scraped the black soil from one small arc, then an arc on the opposite side. The lid was six feet in diameter and the winch should lift it

165

easily. The wooden platform was set upon more earth, from the dead sound it emitted when struck by iron.

With the winch hook in place, Martin gouged the earth from the rim of the wheel, then ascended to the grove to assist with the hauling. The wheel came up, an undecorated piece of oak, and the stony soil below was revealed, as was the pointed tip of the tree that was buried there.

As he dug down, so he found the evidence of offerings, from fragments of pale red terracotta figures to carved wooden animals and bits of metal. Gold flashed, a thin crest with holes for a chain; then silver, beaten into the now battered shape of a boar with long legs and a delicate filigree of spines along its back.

The tree was a tall, thin hawthorn, its limbs lopped short.

His own length below its tip, Martin found the broken skull of the man impaled upon it, the jaw broken where the thrust of the trunk had carried it through the mouth. He passed the skull to the priest, then excavated as much of the skeleton as he could, noticing as the bones were brought to light how all of them were delicately carved with just the same signs and symbols, runes and letters as the skin of the statue. When at last he had found the long bones of the leg, and the yellowed game tiles that might have been the feet and toes, he tied the winch hook to the tree and clambered out of the shaft.

'Bring her up!'

The tree came out of the grave. Father Gualzator had dug a hole in the clearing to receive it and they planted it anew, then arranged the bones at its base, with the bits and pieces of gold, silver, stone and wood that had been resurrected during the excavation.

It was late, again, and the grove stank of mud and fresh earth. The priest gathered up his pack and Martin went with him to the lake, helping him to the canoe.

'I'll go home and wash, then come back with a second boat. It's by far the easiest way. I don't mind waiting for you, by Conrad's grave, but you might be some time and I have the hill to think of, the church and all.'

'If I need you, I'll tie a white flag by this landing place.'

'If you remember . . .'

'Don't cross unless you see me, or see the flag.'

'We'll see. Goodbye, Martin. I'll be praying for you. To Old Provider . . .'

'Thanks for your help.'

He watched the priest paddle away, soon lost by distance and vapour.

He returned to the grove and sat by the open shaft for a while, smelling the earthy stink of time. Then he crawled to his shelter and blew fire into the embers below the pot of coffee.

Merlin

The bottle had been uncorked, the genie loosed.

In the dead hours of the morning the darkness around Martin became filled with the sound of children. If there was a moon it was hidden behind the heavy overcasting of clouds, and only the dull glow of embers gave a touch of light in the gloom. He sat up and listened to the dancing in the grove, the laughter, the language, the curiosity of these creatures who explored him from another realm.

He sensed a particular excitement in the grove of trees, and watched the tall thorn, and caught glimpses of the bones that he had arranged about the tree. If his ear was tweaked, it could easily have been a breeze, an insect or his imagination. He had long lost the sight of the ghosts that were shed from this place, but he was delighted that he could hear them.

At length, they withdrew into the forest, although the sudden flight of herons, away towards the lake, and the sudden splash of wings on water as a duck was disturbed suggested to Martin that something, someone, had gone that way.

Then with dawn came the feeling of being breathed upon, closely scrutinised. As light turned the canopy to a series of stark branches, the grey stone to a wraithed figure leaning against a tree, as dawn brought the sense of old sight to this grove, so the smell of stale breath, the presence of an old man in front of him, grew more strongly.

'I know you're there,' Martin whispered to the grove.

The sour breath was still heavy in the air, the almost-sound of breathing, as if a man crouched before him, trying to keep as quiet as was possible.

'I know you're here,' Martin repeated. 'I need your help.'

The presence went away.

An altar bell was ringing, a thin tinkling sound but quite insistent, coming from the direction of the lake. Martin stirred from sleep – he had been two days here, now – and trotted through the forest to the reedy shore.

The priest was there in the larger canoe, but he had hauled across a kayak, which was pushed into the mud. 'It seemed like a good idea,' he said from the water. 'And I've brought you more coffee, some fresh bread, cheese, various things. Here. Catch!'

He flung a rucksack which Martin caught easily. There was the clink of full, glass bottles. 'Thanks.'

'Has he come?' Father Gualzator asked, wobbling unsteadily on the lake.

'Yes. I think so. But he doesn't want to talk. He hasn't talked yet, anyway. I'm going to stay on.'

'For your information,' the priest called finally as he rowed the heavy canoe away, back to the village, 'the body of the old bosker is no longer in its shelter. I don't know what that means, exactly, but there is no sign of an animal having dragged it away.'

The dead body of the woodsman, Conrad, came across the lake in the late afternoon. It was slumped forward in the canoe, an oilskin over its shoulders and lowered head like a shroud. The corpse was not rowing. The thin craft glided silently on the grey water, pulled by unseen hands, and by the time it reached the rushbed, Martin was back in the grove, huddled and apprehensive.

Whatever he had expected to see next, the thin, youthful, naked man who walked quickly among the trees and came across to him did not meet that expectation. And yet, for a moment as the vibrant figure stooped to touch his eyes, Martin saw the grimace of the fleshy skull, the faded eyes, the yellowing flesh of the old bosker. It was a glimpse only, and it was a reflection of the dead man that would haunt him through the days, when the light was just so, perhaps when the enchanter's glamour faded for a second.

The traveller in the corpse said, 'I don't know how much you loved this man, and if it disturbs you to see him like this, then say so. I can change its look.'

'No. No . . . I'm not disturbed.'

'The body of the woman was more tempting to use, but I think you would have been more disturbed . . .'

'Yes,' Martin murmured, watching as Conrad walked easily to the bones, squatted and rumbled among them. 'Conrad?'

'Not Conrad. The harder you try to see him, the more you'll see the decay. Concentrate on the conversation and the . . . what do you call it? Glamour? Charm? The charm will help. It's a simple magic, but I'm still quite weak.'

Martin shivered with a growing understanding. 'From the way you speak I suppose you must be . . .' he glanced at the shaft. 'Are you the spirit from the tomb? Are you . . . Merlin?'

Conrad seemed to be amused, but all he said was, 'Thank you for releasing me.' He looked round sharply, saying softly, 'Why *did* you release me, I wonder? No doubt you expect something in return.'

'I don't expect anything. I have a hope, a dream, that's all.'

The 'glamorous' body was crouching, again facing Martin, Conrad aglow with life, despite his years, holding in his hands the yellowed skull that Martin had lifted from the pit. Gaze met gaze, curious, searching, considered.

Then Merlin smiled, glancing away to where the path led to the lake. 'The drowned woman. The drowned boy.'

'Her name was Rebecca. She was adopted by my

parents when she was thirteen or so. We loathed each other as children. At first. Then . . . didn't. No-one ever knew, but we were each other's first lovers. We came to love each other very deeply when my mother died. We had a child, Daniel. They both died by drowning a few days ago. It had been a terrible few years. Daniel literally drained her, took all her sense and senses. I found them in the lake, on the other side of the lake.'

After a long while of curious watching and thinking, Merlin rose and walked to the pit, where for two thousand years he had been entombed. The robust flesh of the glamour was like a halo around the racked and shrivelled corpse, and Martin remembered Conrad's tale of Rebecca, wolf-shadowed and shimmering.

Merlin said, 'And you believe I was a part of this?'

'Yes. It's all I can think of. The man in whose body you are travelling thought so too. Some part of you was in Rebecca. You fought against an enchantress who travelled in my son. The battle was fought to the death. You both lost. But I implore you, since I've found you, if you can do it, bring them back to me.'

'How?'

'Rebecca *sang* to her dead lover. He'd been drowned. The water left him and he recovered. That singing magic was a part of you, wasn't it? If she could do it, you can do it. Sing them back to me . . . both of them!'

Merlin turned quickly, frowning. He moved back to the fire, head low. 'But what you don't understand, when you ask something so reasonable, is how much damage would be caused. There would be a great deal of damage done! I don't think so. I don't think it would be wise to help you.'

'I beg you. If it's possible . . .'

'But the damage. Singing magic, as you call it, is very powerful. It has always been the hardest magic to control. I repeat – I don't think it would be wise to help you.' He shook his head, crouching and prodding at the flames with a small stick. After a moment he smiled, still staring at the fire, and whispered, 'It was the hardest magic to deny the woman, I remember. She wanted it so much!'

'The woman?' Martin echoed. 'Vivien?'

Merlin glanced up at the name, thoughtful for a second, then amused. 'Vivien. Yes. Vivyana . . . ivanyavok . . . evunna . . . evye . . . The name has always been attached to her, always means the same thing.'

'The Lady of the Lake? As in the Arthurian Romances?'

Again the man had to think, then seemed to comprehend some connection or other. '*Vision of magic*,' he said. 'Her name approximates to that: the vision of magic. But the word that stands *behind* her name was often used to mean whirlpool, or sucking waters. Yes. She was often associated with lakes. But The Vision of Magic goes closer to the heart.'

'Is there more than one Vivien, then?' Martin asked.

Merlin laughed, genuinely amused, now. The sparks flew from the fire as he prodded the embers. 'It depends what you mean. Is there more than one of you? Apparently not. And yet there's a line inside you that connects you with the past and the future, a line running from your fathers to your sons, your mothers to your daughters. All different from you. All of them you, though, just as you are all of them. But each of you is short lived. For the likes of Vivien and myself, the line runs along a path that is *outside* ourselves. It is the path that changes, not the spirit. We live a lot longer than you. Why are you frowning?'

'Your words: lines, paths: it's the language that Rebecca used. It brings back memories.'

'The land is criss-crossed with lines, paths, channels and hollowings. The people who live among those lines are crossed and criss-crossed also. I am not unaware of Rebecca . . .'

Hope surged furious: 'Then can you bring her back? You travelled in her, you were there when she died. Can you bring her back? Can you help me bring back Daniel?'

'I don't know. I've been trapped a long time. When you say I travelled in her . . .' Merlin shook his head. 'You're right, yet you're wrong. You don't really understand.'

Martin collapsed forward, tears surfacing, despair in control again. 'How do I make it *clear* to you? I had a life. Now I'm in hell. I loved a damaged boy. I watched him get better. I loved him more. I watched my lovely Beck decline. I couldn't love her more, I just felt helpless. Then I realised . . . Not Beck, not Daniel . . . not them at all.' He raised his head and stared at the impassive corpse. 'You! You and your own tormentor! You fucked with my life! You used us for your games!'

'They were not games . . .'

'I don't care! How can I care? I had a *life*. You and your tormentor took that life from me, took it from the two people I loved, left them dead, drowned in the lake.'

He had started to cry, missing Rebecca so much, missing the sweet boy, terrified of what was happening, aware that he was in a cold glade talking to a dead man, aware that his hope was no more than a dream, that waking dream to which one clutches, not wanting it to go away, holding on for fear of the coming light, because for a moment, just for a moment, there is a little hope.

After a while he ceased to cry. He was shivering. The fire had burned low. He looked up, rubbing hands against his eyes, and the cowled form of the young-old man was there, head low as if thinking.

'Help me . . .' Martin whispered. 'If I can have them back . . . help me . . .'

'How long are you prepared to wait?' the woodsman asked quietly. 'Two thousand years?'

Martin's hopes had risen, but he collapsed again when he heard those taunting words. *Two thousand years?* 'No,' he said. 'You know I can't.'

'Two hundred, then.'

'You're playing games. You know I can't.'

'Twenty years? Can you wait that long?'

'That's the worst of all! That's like being in hell. No. I can't wait twenty years. I love them. I want them *now*, not when I'm a husk.'

Merlin laughed below the cowl, but it was a sinister echo of despair and frustration. 'Then twenty days.'

Martin sat up quickly. 'Twenty days?'

'Time enough to talk to you. Time enough to warn you. Time enough to decide what I can do for you. You *did* let me out. But you're asking something very damaging. I have to think. I have dreams too. I have needs. You find it hell to wait twenty years, yet I've waited two thousand.'

'You live longer.'

'I die more slowly. Anger has time to flourish. But you *did* let me out . . . but where is Vivien? In the boy still? Or has she found another place? What to do? Which one to help? What to do with you . . . ?'

Martin said nothing, waiting desperately.

'We'll begin tomorrow. I think I'll talk to you. I think I'll tell you something about the path, and something of the magic that Vivien lusts for. We'll begin tomorrow. We have twenty days. But at the moment, the shadow is going from the wood.'

It seemed that Merlin drew for his strength upon that time of change in the forest when the sun was descending, leaving behind a swirl of its own power, which circulated freely and randomly for a while and was a source of energy. Soon after, the earth took control again, and at that moment Merlin could not exercise his will. The 'window of opportunity' – an expression that Martin had learned as a child from watching the various shuttle launches into space – varied according to the brightness of the day, the conditions of the atmosphere. Magic was in this way barometric, and Merlin's ability to coat the corpse of the old bosker with glamour, and then use it to communicate, was severely limited.

'We'll begin tomorrow.'

Vivien

Shortly before dusk of the following day, glamour came back to the stiff and shrouded corpse of Conrad, and Merlin came from below the tree to the fire, where Martin huddled, cold and afraid, his thoughts drifting between his need for Rebecca and his son and the clear reluctance of this ghost to help him in their resurrection, and the spiritual presence of Merlin himself, a fearful effigy which he had accepted and to whose whim he was now committed.

For a while Martin sat within the hard and shining gaze of the old woodsman; then Merlin whispered, 'Listen . . .'

The path that passes through Broceliande is circular, stretching from this western coast a vast distance to mountains in the east, in the very depths of the land. It winds its way through valleys to the south of here, through caves, then east along the sun-baked coast of an inland sea. North of the far mountains it cuts through dense forests, lakes and rivers. Much of it is now drowned below the ocean. But when the path was first walked, the land in those places was above the sea. Time and the pull and tug of the moon simply changed things. The path is still there below the ocean, but it takes a special concentration to walk it.

It was neither I, nor the woman of magic vision that you call Vivien, who first walked the path, although I have an inkling as to the nature of that long forgotten traveller. I came later, much later, although I am earlier than the legends with which you associate me.

My first encounter with Vivien was where the path passes among the lakes and blue forests of the north, in a place of grey and white swans, red wolves and reindeer. The insects in those forests were a trial to any voyager. The lakes were so cold that in each and every one of them a hundred human bodies floated, half-way down, dead yet still alive, suspended from the process of living by the ice. The magic men of the region, the shamans, swum among them naked, feeding on the faint echoes of memory in the drowned, learning past truths to aid their own journeys to the underworld. They surfaced for air at regular intervals, screaming with the cold, then plunged again, almost dancing with the slowly turning bodies in the deep.

On the surface of the lakes, the swans glided, and Vivien swam among them. She had a light fledge of black feathers on her arms and the red and blue shapes of an owl and a salmon on her breasts and belly. She was a child at the edge of womanhood and otherwise quite pale.

As this sprightly juvenile swam and dived among the feeding swans, playing with their shapes – adopting their shapes – amusing herself with the inner and outer forms of the peaceful birds, I knew at once that the girl was an enchantress.

She was so young, though, that her power was unfocused. She was like a baby, clutching at new things, half inclined to destroy, only gradually discovering the need to be gentle. The mosquitoes which swarmed about me, drawn by the scent of the reindeer on my body and the aroma of the hawk on my head, were a tribulation to me. Yet she, with the swiftest of movements of her left hand and clutching a small talisman of nothing more than birch twigs shaped as a circle and a cross, banished the voracious creatures from her pale skin, crouching in the reeds, preening her feathered arms with a long, white comb.

She knew I was watching, of course. No doubt she'd been aware of my stink from the moment I left the birch forest to walk along the rushy shore, looking for a place to fish.

Like a cat, her head kept turning up to sniff the air. She watched me by sound not sight, but I'm familiar enough with the glance of light on the keen eye that tells that sight has been briefly employed. Oh yes, she was aware of me, and I was wearing the skins of the beast, bird and fish, so she knew I was kin with the Vision of Magic. But as the grizzled men of the villages floundered in the ice waters, listening for the tunes that would guide them to the past, so in me she had detected a different breed of conjuror.

Her interest was as pointed as the breasts on which she gently splashed cold water, as bright as the light on her long black hair. I moved slowly through the tall rushes and like a trout swimming in shallow water I was alert, fully aware of the taste of the fly, but half aware of the bait, of the trap, of the hook.

As if to further tease and entice me, this pristine, nubile creature flew suddenly above the reeds, the action of the flight like that of a dragonfly. It was a brief flight, high above the lake, a short dance in the air with outstretched wings. Whatever charm she had used, however, wore off quickly and with a slight cry, the sound of irritation, she plunged from the height into the mud, where she floundered and spluttered, her wings now filthy.

But it had been a moment of exceptional magic, and charm in every sense, a waif-like body, pale and slender, perfect and unbroken, hovering, then swooping above the blue lake, slim legs kicking in the action, a moment of control – the wile in the woman – then the moment of chaos – the impetuosity of the girl.

She was proud and angry as I hauled her from the mud. She didn't resist, despite the indignity of the moment, which told me instantly that this had in part been designed for me.

Almost at once she was laughing. Her hands were over me, parting the folds and creases of my furs and skins, looking for the skin within the skin, finding first the rank, torn wool of my vest, then the marks, scars and tattoos of my trade. But made curious by these patterns her fingers tried to read them, like a blind man reading the marks and gnarls in hardened clay of the Babylonians.

'They mean nothing to me!' she cried aghast, then covered the slip. 'They're fascinating,' she added, with transparent caution.

'Fascinating?'

'What do they mean? What do they do? Where do they help you travel?'

'Marks of my birth, signs of my tribe, nothing more,' I said, but she tugged the thin hair of my beard.

'Liar!'

'Prove it.'

'I will.'

It was a tease, and there was a smile on her face. And anyway, I was young then. You may not be aware of it, but there is a bone in every human body which, when broken, begins the passage of time. For most of you, this bone is broken in the womb and soon dissolved. Rarely, it remains unbroken for centuries without end. My bone in those years was unbroken, although I was certainly cautious of too much vigour, too much of the hunt. My beard was black, my hair strong, the muscles in my body like whales below the grey sea, firm and powerful. They had to be – it was just as well – since I was travelling great distances, and existing on precious little, save for fish.

It is always the fish that betrays us.

The trout, splendid in so many ways, can never learn to tell when there is a hook inside the juicy fly. And the trout is the great weakness of all hunters. It is itself a hunter of superb prowess, but it is incapable of swimming anywhere other than into the flow of the river. It feasts blindly and voraciously through that flow, only to die, surprised, on a sharpened bone.

At some time in our lives we all will be caught. And young though she was, when I first met her, I am certain that Vivien was aware of this simple, ageless truth.

I was about to say more to her when one of the shamans ran naked and screaming from the lake. Wild, frenzied, and blue as if starved of air, he shivered past us, his hands encasing the grey, winter buds of his sex. He danced and cried, a man older than his years, patterned on his arms for flight, I noticed, but not yet on his face for travel through the earth, nor on his legs for the great running, the hound running.

He saw me, and saw my furs, and came bounding over to me, huddling inside the reindeer skin, so physically strong that I couldn't detach his icy hands from my flesh, where they sought my heat, and so the two of us fell struggling and yelling into the mud, the one in search of warmth, the other in a desperate escape from cold fingers.

Now it was Vivien's turn to laugh, and she hauled us up. The shaman, bereft at this moment of any power worth his drum, began to flog the warmth into his body with a handful of rushes, running back to the village and the long lodge, where the fires burned continually.

This, it turned out, was also Vivien's village. The raven-feathered girl dressed herself in a simple woollen skirt, a bright blue shirt and wolfskin overcoat, then led me to her home.

It was here, choking on the smoke from the fires on

which fish and small game were being cooked, that Vivien demonstrated her second piece of magic, an entrancing act again, and one which was a sinister portent for the future, although I was not aware of this at the time. It was simply an interesting piece of magic. But I should certainly have understood the significance of the performance, and that I failed to do so, I am still convinced, is because she had put her first hidden charm on me.

The longhouse was crowded, mothers and fathers grouped around the fires, each watched over by a *loki*, a heavy tree whose animal faces grinned across the room. There was the constant sound of laughter and raised voices, and of song, accompanied by reed pipes and small drums.

The shaman who had so frigidly and irritatingly fled the lake waters, and the memories of drowned men, paid particular attention to me for a while. He brought me soup, then the raw cheeks of salmon, and flat cakes of bread in which the resinous and delicious taste of birch was abundant.

He talked nonsensically of his experiences in the lake, and showed me drums and stretched skins that reflected his visits through what he called the 'swan's neck', visits to the places where the shape-changers lived. Everything in this land of lakes and forests was defined by animals, and each journey described as a voyage: to higher worlds through the gullet or crop of a bird, to hidden forest worlds through the heart or gut of the reindeer; to worlds below the water by passage through the gills of a pike. It occurred to me in a moment of humour to ask if the longer the bowel the more difficult the journey, but to the *Pohola* it made no difference. In any event, the food tasted wonderful, despite the fact that recently each limb or cheek or sausage had been the channel to another realm.

Vivien had been conspicuous by her absence for some time. There was an air of apprehension and humour in the longhouse, and I was aware that an entertainment was being prepared for me. These people, the Pohola, were of a generous nature, if inclined to melancholy (their songs and stories were remorselessly depressing, a fact I attribute to the harshness of the land and the extent of darkness that subdues their spirits).

Vivien entered suddenly, causing the smoke to swirl. She was wearing a dress of white wool, which flowed about her as she turned, her feathered arms extended. Her face was painted black, but like a bird. Behind her, six small girls from the village entered quickly, all equally simply dressed, and each with the severed wings of swans tied to their arms, which they flapped awkwardly. Their hair, waist length and amber, flowed as they twirled and laughed. They were not normally permitted in this lodge, and were both nervous and thrilled to be within the fish-smoke.

My friend, the shaman, laughed noisily, pointing and making comments that I couldn't interpret. The mothers clapped, the fathers smoked, watching the small dance, watching me for my reaction.

By *their* reaction to what followed I can only assume that they had seen no such event before. It happened like this:

The seven dancers formed into a circle, wings out-stretched and touching, dancing slowly round the fire. People moved back where they sat, towards the walls, throwing cushions and rugs between them in a wonderful display of relaxation. I was pushed back too, and only just rescued my bowl of salmon cheeks. These were a rare treat for me and I intended to eat until I could eat no more.

Then Vivien moved into the ring, her steps and movements timed to the steady chant of her companions, who still danced as they giggled, firelight making them glow.

To my astonishment, Vivien lifted her skirts and crouched down suddenly on the fire, throwing back her head and screaming. Smoke billowed from below her dress and somewhere someone cried, 'She's burning. Stop her!'

But at the same moment she flung herself aside with a high-pitched laugh. Instantly the air was filled with a ghostly shape, a huge translucent apparition that towered to the rafters, filled the centre of the lodge, a swirl of white, a touch of amber, that at once *hardened* and became a swan of vast proportion, a bird whose wings, when stretched, filled the longhouse from end to end.

And now it beat those wings and screeched. The movement threw the people hard against the turf walls of the lodge. The swan's neck, thick and powerful, thrashed a boat's length this way and that, its huge head sweeping over us, the beak opened to emit its pain, a mouth that could have swallowed a child.

Wings struck against the rafters, and the rafters broke,

the thatch fell, the turf crumbled. Fires went out, wooden pillars cracked as the beak struck; the whole place was mayhem. Everyone was screaming as the beast struggled to escape the confines of the house.

It was tied by a tether to its leg. It fought against the tie, and I felt tugged myself, as if responding in sympathy. As the beast struggled and flexed, so did I. I caught a glimpse of the girl. She was watching me from behind the biggest of the wooden *loki*, the huge totem that guarded the centre of the lodge. She was grinning, she was out of control. She had terrified the people. I knew then that she, like me, was a stranger here.

The swan suddenly broke through the roof. It beat its wings frantically, shedding feathers, breaking feathers, straining its massive neck towards the sky. As it started to rise, the wind catching its wings, so the tether tightened, and the unseen loop around my foot tightened too.

The wretched girl! She had conjured not just this apparition of the swan, but a link between the swan and me, tied by our feet, tethered by magic!

The swan flew and I was dragged across the floor, as if carried by those spirits of the hearth called *fyjulga*. I had an instant only to reach for my bone knife and 'cut' the cord, falling back upon the cold embers of the fire that Vivien herself had extinguished earlier, when she had used its flame for the magic to make this apparition. The girl laughed, then fled. Starlight shone, and the swan died, somewhere out among the blue lakes. It was a creature fabricated by a young, fierce mind; it died a quick and cold, wet death, but that is appropriate.

There was a cut on my ankle, no less deep than if real wolf-gut had gouged into me. The blood flowed and I bound the wound carefully.

Angry though I was, all I could think of was the girl's laugh of surprise that her trick had worked, the glint in her eyes and the sudden apprehension that followed as she knew that she would be punished for causing the longhouse rafters to be broken.

And if indeed she were punished, then no doubt the sting of the wet birch branch sharpened and heightened her power. I don't know. I could think of nothing from then until the moment, early in the first spring dawn, when I slipped away along the path at dawn, nothing but the girl and the way she had tested me, and teased me.

Yes. I wanted her fingers on my body again.

Yes, I wanted her to read me, though she would have understood nothing.

And yes, I was determined that it would never happen. I knew that if she touched me, now, I would be dead before too long.

She may have conjured a giant swan, and dazzled guileless eyes. I was more aware that she had squatted down and smothered a blazing fire without harm, using the searing heat for magic!

As if exhausted by this recollection of an event so long in his past, Merlin sank down inside the cowl and fell silent. Martin stoked the fire and sparks swirled among the spreading oaks, to dim and die below the black but star-bright void of the night sky.

Abruptly, the grim figure sat up and drew a wheezing breath, which Martin thought might have been a chuckle. Merlin whispered, 'It all comes back to me. I can see that time again as clearly as a fish can see the fly—'

When I left those tribal lands in the far north, Vivien followed me. I'd known she would. Since she was young she was trapped in the place by her own inexperience, but at length she learned of the existence of the path, and she used her skills to enter the long walk, the movement around the path that is endless, that is its own world. By the time she took her first faltering step – no doubt aided by the wings of birds, her favourite manifestation – lifetimes had passed, and I was in the land of the Pretini, which you probably know as Albion, or Logres – the place has many names. My bone had still not broken, but the fire that she had extinguished during that simple illusion among the Pohola burned within me, forming a link across the ages.

I constantly dreamed of fire. She burned into me from the years lost.

She ran like a wolf across the land. She swam across the ocean. She slept in caves and moved through the sap in the trees. She came close to me, then found her form again, a powerful woman, now, still seeking to understand the marks upon my body.

The truth is that there is a great attraction in the moment of touching. The moment she touched my painted, patterned flesh, the moment that she felt the carved bones *below* that flesh, she was not just intrigued, she was seduced. The shaman with his cold hands suffered a similar seduction, but was easy to deny. Vivien was wilier by far, and had the talent of time, the ability to play her strategy across more than a single lifetime's span.

She knew that she had touched power, touched secrets that could be of great use to her. She intuited that having touched my power she could either have it, or live in its shadow, but that we could not share it. How could we?

If Vivien was to have my skills, she would have to wear my skin. She would have to age by wearing my own age; all beauty would have to be sacrificed to wear the scarred skin of an older man.

Her exuberance, her youth, prevented her from pursuing this until the bone in her body broke. She was clever enough to hold the break, so that though the years passed for her, she aged slowly. As I remained a wolf, seasoned, skilled and always lean, she aged steadily; but she had her charms, and her wings, and there is nothing so youthful as the first flight of a bird at the breaking of dawn.

Old, then, yet still young, Vivien pursued me for the secrets in my flesh.

To confuse her, I created a shadow of myself and sent it back along the path, back to the northlands, travelling towards the sunrise.

It was my intention to meet the shadow again as our

paths crossed, and take it back, but I never found it. It still wanders somewhere; perhaps it was seduced from the path, perhaps it faded. It's hard to know these things, although I have heard of a land bridge in the far east, where the ice makes a thick bridge between this and another world, so perhaps it strayed further than I realised. It was a small shadow, possessing small magic. More charm than substance, you understand, and though its life should have been long, it would have been at the whim of all creatures.

Nevertheless, the trick worked at first and I was not aware of Vivien again until after I had stayed for many years in the forests of the Caledon.

One day I sniffed her presence. The air in those mountains is very clear. I have always believed smell to be a form of substance, invisible to the eye, continually shed like skin from the body. I knew she was in the land, though still distant, and I packed my things and walked south.

In any case, it was time to leave the Caledon. There was very little of interest in the forests, although the game was good, the game is always good. I had been there for far too long and I was tired of the cold, tired of the flight of gulls, which could take me out across the wide sea but show me only rocks. The ocean to the west is a forbidding place. If there is a magic beyond it, it defied my eyes to see it.

I rested for a few years or so in the land of the Parisii, near a large town called Eboracum. The distress of dogs, one day at dusk, told me that they had smelled the small enchantress and again I fled.

I passed time in high hills, in deep woods, and confronted passing horsemen, often solitary princes or low
kings, seeking this, seeking that, the mind of the warrior king in those days was singularly triumphant, and
discovering the lost arms and armour of forgotten heroes
was all they seemed concerned with.

In each act of confrontation there was a moment – the
moment of surprise, as they saw this wild and hairy
man screaming at them from the tree – when their
thoughts spilled out like sun through a sudden break in
clouds. I fed upon these fears and thoughts, and in this
way kept abreast of change as I slowly travelled south.

At some point I sent a second shadow north along the
path, but this time the trick failed. She found it and
turned it round, and I let it pass me by. She pursued
me, then, with energy, running through her lives with
the agility of a cat. And in time her persistence was
rewarded.

Our paths crossed in the fort of Caerleon, one bitter
autumn evening, when the cattle and sheep were being
drawn back behind the high walls as the light faded, and
the fires lit to show the land. There was a raiding party
on its way and the stronghold's warlord, Peredur, was to
make a chariot charge against them. Fire and fury was
all about me as I stood within the gate and watched the
nightland, the confusion and fear of imminent battle.
The air was filled with prayers and charms. The blood
in the horsemen and the farmers was a sour stench in
every corner where they crouched, drinking deeply,
waiting for the onslaught.

Vivien came running through the heavy gates just as

they were being closed, her red cape flowing, the cowl back from her long hair and pale, beautiful face. She saw me and ran to me, breathless. 'Got you! At last.'

She tugged my beard and frowned, then smiled. 'Still black, still strong. It isn't fair. You look no different now than then. Are you using charm? Do you need charm?'

I replied as ambiguously as possible. 'I use charm occasionally. I never *need* to use it. And you?'

'I use it!' she said directly, staring at me as if daring me to comment. 'Oh yes. I use charm.' Then more immediate concerns occurred to her. 'Where do I get food? I need water. Will we die? There's no need for us to die, my feathered arms can carry us both. I'm so glad to see you again. It's been a long hunt. But where do I get food?'

'I'll take you.'

And she fell against me, no longer the enchantress, simply a refugee, exhausted and in need. I led her through the fires and cattle to the heart of the fort. I had pitched my tent here, above a hidden well. This bubbled briefly through the ground and satisfied her need.

Her performance on arrival at the stronghold, her behaviour, I am certain was not a guile, simply the last defiance of her long journey in search of me.

The enemy had built no fires, their warriors scattered in discreet bands from the river to the higher land, north of the fort. Their tactic, clearly, was to invite a night attack. Almost certainly there was a larger band waiting to fire the gates and pillage the stronghold.

I counselled the warlord as to this, but found that his

own seers, by reference to their local augurs, had perceived the same eventuality. They could not, however, locate the bigger army, a task I attended to with as much phony ritual and simple illusion as possible (I was earning my keep, you understand) and discovered them hiding in the overhang of the river bank, a force of horsemen some sixty strong. I could see as well that most of them had come by boat, and that they were unused to the stolen horses with which they had been supplied.

They would be ferocious, then, from the land of the Eriu, probably, but they would have the disadvantage of the night, unfamiliar trails and restless steeds.

This was the sort of language the warlord of Caerleon understood. He divided his horsemen at once, carefully allocating them to two attacking forces.

The lightning raid on the group of men by the river left them shattered. The horses were driven off – twenty recaptured and led back to the fort – and skirmishing along the woodland edge left honours even and the dead paired-up.

The hostiles licked their wounds and marched northwards at dawn, seeking smaller prey. Vivien taunted them for a while with ravens, which she was adept at summoning, while in the fort there was a feeling of the feast and celebration.

But Peredur was furious.

In his eyes he had treated the raiders with honour, he had paired-up the dead, he had won the skirmish. The fact that the Eriu had stayed in his land was an insult to his name.

Grimly, then, he picked his ten best warriors. They put on black cloaks, black armour, black helmets, armed themselves with feathered spears, knives, but no shields. At dawn they rode from the fort in silence, eleven against forty.

Later, near dusk, seven of them returned, Peredur leading the bloody troop, two heads slung by their hair across the neck of his horse, forty sword hands tied to the spears, the four dead knights tied to their flagging mounts.

He sent boats to the twenty Eriu who had survived the second battle and who were now by the river again, to take them home.

For seven months or more, well into the winter, which was fortunately mild, Peredur strengthened the ramparts of the fortress, a tremendous task, filthy and exhausting, but one undertaken with great enthusiasm by the people who sheltered on the hill.

Such was Peredur's command and authority that only the sourness of the ale was ever complained about, a fault which he addressed at once by sending a raiding party across the wide river to the islands in the marshes, where apples and honey were produced in abundance.

He was a great man, this one, and in the presence of great men, magic is enhanced. As such I was able to move the heavy tree trunks used in the re-construction, and even aid the transport of new gates, heavy blocks of blue-stone that would eventually be hauled down and used as grave markers.

Peredur affected my magic more than any other man. I put wings on his shabby little horses, or so it must have seemed to his knights, since they were able to ride at the canter for half a day and the horses were as fresh at dusk as at dawn. In this way Peredur patrolled the land to the east as far as Camulodunum and north beyond the seven totems that marked the edge of Eboracum. This was a vast distance for any man to be recognised by name and to have the pattern on his sword known too.

Peredur was truly the offspring of the wolf.

Behind the new walls, the warlord built new houses, as if to say this is my final place; this place will endure.

He enlarged the forges and the bakeries and built new grain stores. He described the house that he wished to construct for me where my tent was pitched, but I refused, tempting though it was. But as if he needed to demonstrate his gratitude, he surrounded the tent with a wicker fence – which made it hard to walk out by night, since he'd included only a single gate. But his need was stronger than my irritation, and Vivien and I inhabited a skin house on a birch frame, behind a wall of willow.

We had wanted to be left alone, but we became a place of homage. We were plagued with effigies in straw, with limbs in coarse clay or bread, with painted wood and feather charms. These things accumulated, slung and strung to the wicker, thrown into the tent, buried just around the edge. At night we would gather them in, but by the morning there were twenty more. Some had power, and these we acknowledged and responded to. Most were simple dreams, and we discarded them as quickly as we could, taking them by the sackful to the deep woods at the bottom of the hills. Vivien dug a shaft there, faster than I have ever seen – I found nothing ominous in this at the time – and plugged it with stone in such a way that we could open it at leisure to deposit more of these charms.

I imagine the shaft is there today, rank and sour with hopeless dreams.

If the scouring of that pit did not disturb me, Vivien's water magic did.

I had never shown her how to conjure water from the earth – this is a strong magic, and must be carefully applied – but she must have watched me from afar, or spied through the eyes of a bird. I caught her out when I saw her at the forge, bringing water in a bucket. I fled at once to the tent and felt the ground. It was damp. The filling cup was wet as well.

She had found out how to tap the source!

But what was she doing at the forge? I feared the worst, and devised charms against iron, bronze and tin. I was already protected, by my nature, against bone and wood, but in any case these substances were not easily controlled by fire, only subject to its heat.

Discreetly, I watched her. She was fussing at the bellows, shaking her head at the ironworker: not right; not that way, this way. Do it again. And again.

At length a small shape appeared from the coals. Vivien watched as the ironworker tempered it in the water from our well. Steam billowed and she saw me, smiling quickly, perhaps with embarrassment, or guilt. She reached into the bucket and brought the cooling object to me. It was not iron at all, but bronze, bright as the sun. It was in the shape of three leaves of the May tree, with four berries and a single thorn. I could not believe this exquisite work to be the handicraft of the man who worked the forge, but the talisman was so enchanting that I took it and turned it.

The thicket itself could not have produced as perfect a twig in such perfect detail.

'What is it for?' I asked Vivien. She laughed and kissed my cheek and chin.

'It's for you.'

'What does it do?'

'It shines,' she said, still amused.

'What does it give me?'

'Shining!'

'What does it take from me?'

'Nothing but darkness. A touch of darkness.'

'But I like darkness. I need it. I *walk* with dreams and darkness. I thought you knew that.'

'It doesn't touch the shadow. It's not a *taking* thing. It's a *shining* thing. Like you.'

'Why are you giving it to me?'

'Because I love you, idiot. Because we complement each other.'

'You spied on me to learn how to make the water rise.'

'Not at all. I thought about the water, and how it might rise by magic. I constructed the magic myself. I didn't spy on you. That would have been wrong. You either tell me, teach me, or leave me to my own devices. Don't be jealous.'

She punched my chest, hard! and walked past me

back to the tent. The thorn was sharp – I was careful not to draw blood. The shining leaves felt soft, the bronze soft. When the sheen of the metal bloomed, when the leaves began to green, they would be powerful indeed.

I reciprocated the gift almost at once. We went away from the fortress and found a place of isolation, high on the hill, with a view, further to the south of Lyonesse and the ocean that was consuming it.

'I hate to see the world drowned,' she said one day.

'Why? What makes you sad?'

'When it drowns it dies.'

I knew, then, that for all her charm, all her skills, she was simply a chancer, that is to say, a dabbler, without true insight. She thought that as Lyonesse drowned, it was gone. She had no understanding that as it drowned here so it was surfacing, reshaped, regenerated in another place. She could not feel that connection through the hard places of the earth. She saw only the sea and the rock, and the battle that was fought between them.

By now she was intimate with my body, and I with hers. She could feel the patterned bones below my flesh, but had no understanding at all of their meaning. Truly, I felt my age, even though I was younger than her. The bone in her body cracked further, on occasion, and the skull in the beauty grinned at me as she tossed about me on the summer heath, wild hair flying. Sometimes I slowed time so that I could watch that raven hair flow dreamily against the white of cloud and the intense blue of sky.

The day came when she caught me at my tricks and broke the charm, leaning down to bite my lip, murmuring, 'Pay attention, you old trout! This is costing me!'

Her words were a shock to me. She leaned back against my knees, disappointed, rather frightened, trying to squeeze the unsqueezable.

'You've gone.'

'Not for ever. What do you mean – costing you?'

She glanced away, then pulled away, curling her body against my thighs, her dress drawn over her shoulder, her fingers and lips gently caressing the disappointing member.

'I'm not as strong as you,' she said. 'I want the pleasure, but I have to guard against the consequences. I want to give you pleasure too—' she phrased it precisely in this way '—but you don't seem bothered by the consequences. I'm using magic, when all I want to do is use my body. You seem uncaring.'

How deftly she had covered the slip. Did she really think I hadn't noticed those inadvertent, angry words?

This is costing me.

Of course it was! She was trying to work herself below my skin, to draw out my skills. Realising the slip, she had covered quickly with concerns about childbirth.

But it was a wonderful lie. And she was a wonderful lover.

For all my skills, I am as blind as any other man to the way that others see us. Vivien was ageing, aged, and because I was experienced with time she seemed as luscious to me, as we loved in various private groves in Albion, as the black-feathered swan-girl of the Northlands who had aroused me by the lake. But to those around us, she was older than me, a woman in her prime, and I was still a man in firm, wisp-bearded youth. Talented, yes, but still, by appearance, a son. Our liaison, the congress of which was often heard and seen, was not hailed with the same enthusiasm when otherwise the first sign of the White May was celebrated.

The time came, then, to leave this land, this chieftain, to follow further round the path, the long path. I mentioned it before. I was progressing south, and almost at the place on the loop of tracks and ridges that marked my own beginning.

There was an ocean to cross. Lyonesse was gone. Boats would be needed.

A greater difficulty was that I was loved by Peredur. He had, in that naïvete that comes with power, depended upon me because I was dependable. He was not threatened by betrayal, simply with withdrawal. It shook him deeply, but like the man of stone he was, he turned to stone for his thanks and his parting kiss.

'You can't leave! How will I move rocks without you?'

'Try ropes.'

'All very well to say that, but how will I test the ropes without you?'

'Stretch them between horses.'

'And the necks of horses? How can I possibly test the necks of horses without you?'

'Do what you do best. Ride them. Ride them till they drop. Some will never drop.'

He laughed. 'If I ever find such a horse I'll *marry* it. And when it dies I'll follow it to the cairn! You can't leave. How will I remember you?'

'On a stone, tall and grey. Nothing else. Not if you really care for me.'

'Don't insult me. I don't carve rock for pleasure! Far too much hard work. That's why I employ the likes of you,' he added with a mischievous smile. 'Where will I put this stone? *Should* I make it.'

'Somewhere where not even your horses can find it.'

'In the heart of the forest, then.'

'Yes. And near falling water. That's where my own heart will be.'

'I forbid you to go.'

'Have you ever tried to hold a shadow?'

'But our shadows are always on the road. It just takes sun and fire to see them.'

'Exactly. I was here before, I'll be here again. Endlessly.'

'But I shan't see you, shall I?'

'If you pass your eyes on wisely, who knows?'

How could I explain the endless, ageless circulation of time and the path?

How could I explain to him that I not only had generations of trail *ahead* of me, but unfinished business in past cycles that I would constantly – that is to say, every four generations or so – return to? His life was a function of birth, fighting, lovemaking and death. Mine was all of these things too, but without end, without end.

I simply kissed him. I promised him that I would remember him, and this is the end of this particular conversation, because I have done what I promised to do. I've remembered him.

Peredur was a great man, but that is all he was when it comes down to it. A man. And of importance. Like a stone broken into pieces he has become known to you in many forms, by many names.

It would dismay you to know what a simple man of strength and weakness, wisdom and humility, lies at the core of your romances.

Slow Ghosts

The long day, the longest he had ever lived, was almost ended, and Martin left his vigil at the lakeside – his long watch, across the water, over the graves of those he loved – to return through the forest to the ancient grove of trees which breathed with the life of an old enchanter, a broken stone, known by many names, but to Broceliande as Merlin—

As dusk grew close, the body in the cowl sat up, and without a word beckoned Martin to the fire. 'And so . . .'

With Vivien at the helm, the sail in my hands, we crossed by boat to the coast of Gaul, gaining the beach at Uxorum, north and west of here. I picked up the path to the south without much difficulty.

Within a few days we had reached Broceliande and Vivien became anxious. The forest was then as deep and entangled as it is now, and she felt herself cut off from some of her magic. Nevertheless, she hugged me close and followed in. She could tell, I imagine, that my own powers were closer to the surface, sustained by the wildwood. She imagined they would now be easier to draw out.

When we came to the waterfall we bathed in the deep pool, cleaned our clothes and built a shelter below the overhang. Vivien hunted in the deeper glades for a few hours, quite successfully as it turned out, and I found enough clay to make the vessels and pots in which to cook, consume and store our sparse supplies.

I had always liked this place, with its misting air, the strong, relentless fall of crystal, icy water, the crowding oaks. I had been here twice before, although no trace remained of those much earlier visits apart, perhaps, from a mark or two on stones, but the grey lichen was so thick it was hard to tell. Everything, otherwise, was the same, these sons-of-the-trees that had previously sheltered me being no less immense, no less embracing.

I was relaxed enough, secure enough in this place, to instruct Vivien in the essential nature of the magic that I carried. This is not to say I told her how to *work* that magic, but if she had talent (and I knew she did) then in due course – the passage of many generations – she could work it out for herself.

I quickly created a garden for her, a joyous place, full of song and wonder, fixed at its centre by proud ruins of hard-packed earth and heavy wood, in which she played and danced, delighted with the labyrinth of cold passages and high, rotting turrets. She was aware that I had drawn on memories of a city from antiquity, burned and sacked on the southern shore, a place of wonder that had long ago fallen to a siege by many hundreds of single-sailed ships. She was fascinated by the story.

'I want those ships!' she cried, standing in the ruins, green-daubed, slim and nude, feathered arms outstretched, eyes closed. 'Send them for me! Send them to fetch me. A sea full of ships, all for the love of me!'

And always, as she indulged in such fantasy, she ended with laughter and a wild dance in the wildwood.

Now I talked to her about the seven things that I could control, to a degree at least. All magic, you should understand, is developed from seven essential powers, call them talents. Different minds approach them in different ways, so there are no fixed rules. The first and oldest is the power of song, which is inborn in all of us, but only shaped by exceptional minds. You already know something about this talent, you've heard of its most dangerous usage. Song can create life and landscape. But there is a terrible price to pay. Vivien hungered for this knowledge, but I dazzled her away from it.

Secondly, there is the moving of stones by the power of the flow of hidden water. This did not interest Vivien at all. She could not see how such talent gives control over the shape of the land.

She was entranced, however by the third power, that of flying to and from the hinterlands of the Otherworld. It is impossible to enter the Otherworld completely, but the hinterlands are many, varied, and often quite accommodating.

The fourth power is connecting the parts of beasts, both hard and soft.

The fifth is an understanding of the human spirit as

sustenance for mind and body. There are four guardians associated with this power, but they are too complex to describe, let alone explain.

Sixthly, the movement of awareness between the hard and soft forms of life; a dog to a stone, for example; a tree to a fawn. This is a very useful talent.

The greatest talent of all is this: to control, to contain and to employ the vision, hearing and dreams of children.

When a child is born it moves through the seasons at the same rate as everyone around it. But to the child, time is slow. Only in adulthood does the time *inside* catch up with time *outside*. To harness the time of children is to control time as much as it can ever be controlled. It is a form of *imaginative* time. If there are forces beyond our understanding governing time, and I feel there must be, they are less in control when exercising their reach through a child.

Vivien, ageing steadily, slowly, still beautiful, still childlike, was using that very talent to stay as fresh, as keen, as quick as the lamb. She knew, however, that she must learn how to carve the knowledge of the child onto her bones if she was to step fully aside from time, and only I could supply her with that knowledge. Since I refused to give the knowledge to her she resorted to seduction, playing upon my need to rest, drawing out those shadows within me that are least circumspect, most guileless, despite their talents.

*

She addressed each shadow with a display, a vision, that enraptured me, enchanted me.

A song caused the water in the fall to pour in the opposite direction, exposing channels and passages in the rock from which odd, slow melodies cooed and wailed. This was a simple illusion – her talents were largely confined to illusion – but it suggested things to me that I had not thought of. In this way she entranced me. I have always been nervous of song, its power is deep, and yet is common; I have never been fully comfortable with the song in magic, but for a year or so after this illusion I played with melody, and harmony, and effected change upon nature. I came closer to the first song, although that is well guarded. It would take a greater mind than mine to go so far, so deep into the first songs.

She teased me and tickled me by bringing stones which cracked open, egg-like, to release lifeforms that are not bound by parents or offspring. Things that spring unbidden from the dark are fated only to amuse and die, since reproduction, as you or I would understand it, is not part of the life that exists within them.

She came to me in animal forms. She was especially exquisite as a vixen, dancing for me, leaping high to snatch bright birds in her crushing jaws. Somehow she could entwine herself with the language of animals – no illusion there! – and our conversations were fascinating. Animals have no greater sense of themselves, they run and live by certain stinks, by sight and by the deeper urges. But they have memory – although it is short lived – and with Vivien, as fox or fawn, as stoat or boar, I was able to hear those echoes of the animal mind, and gained a sense of how close they are to the Otherworlds. They occupy hinterlands that are denied to men. The animal realm is greater than instinct, but confusing. Vivien brought that confusion to vivid life, and for a while, through her illusions, through her visions of magic, I ran with creatures, *as* creatures, that until then had been denied to me.

She used charm to transform herself into the strangest, wildest, most alluring of creatures. She showed me, by illusion, how it would seem to live in fast time, then in slow time. She fashioned the earth into dolls and made them dance. I had seen nothing like this. It was pointless, in its way, but it was so amusing. I had taken magic seriously. I had long since forgotten how to *enjoy* the gift.

Eventually she took me home, a vision in the night of the remote past.

The man who danced wore the skin of a chamois around his shoulders and the broken horns upon his head. His face was painted and pierced with the features and feathers of an owl. The water-filled member of a horse, tied with leather about his hips, slapped at his legs like an obscene growth. His tail, stiff below the short cloak, was horse-hair. Clattering stones were tied around his ankles. His body was a swirl of painted blue and red as he danced before me by the water, half visible in the mist and spray, illuminated by a fire that cast his shadow on the trees. Sometimes he was upright, sometimes on all four legs, like the creature that possessed him.

His song was simple. He called to me to remember him from my birth in the deep caves, the animal caves. He called to me to paint again, as once before I had painted the smooth surfaces of the hidden stone, deep below the mountain. He called to me to dip my fingers in the cold, coloured pastes, to daub, to design, to reflect the life of creatures on the sensuous curves of the cold, moist rock, in the caverns, among the hands of my ancestors.

Vivien had seen my earliest memory! I was shocked, surprised; yet still entranced. She had drawn from me my first sights as a child, the Ghost Animal, come to greet me, and in so doing she had managed to go deep into my bones.

I think I knew then, as the sorcerer danced, as he had danced at my birth, I think then that I knew she would have me, she would kill me. She would tease me apart as a weaver teases apart the coarse wool fibres of a fleece.

To know that you are lost, yet to know that you have time to hide yourself, is a time of great pain. Around you, everything is normal, everything a joy. The anticipation of the moment of death is a voice that laughs from behind your head.

Vivien was laughing at me, even as she hunted for me, cooked the game, ate with gusto, ravished me with her body, and whispered in a way that meant: I need you.

She plotted the culling of my magic.

I planned its safe dissemination.

It was the final Vision of Magic that taught me the lesson I should have learned long before.

At the edge of Broceliande, in the west, is a wide clearing, ringed by twelve great oaks, tall trees on which have always been hung the trophies from the combats fought within its space. For as long as I can remember, warriors and champions have come to ring o'trees field to fight for honour, or for kings. Such a tournament was occurring there now.

Vivien came running through the forest. She had heard the squeal of horses and the rattle of wicker chariots. She came to fetch me and we returned to the forest's edge, coming to the clearing between the broad oaks, and standing back, behind the crouching forms of the defeated knights.

In the bright sun, seven chariots remained. They were circling the field, light wicker with small wheels, each pulled by two breathless horses, some grey, some black, one magnificent pair of whites. A charioteer in each, breech-clouted and grey-cloaked, spattered with blood, tugged and turned the restless team. The knight behind each of them was naked but for leather shoes and a sparkling torque around the neck. These grim-faced men, their hair spiked with white clay, their beards stiffened like quills, carried spears and small, curved swords. Each chariot had its shield, tall and thin, decorated with the clan totem, but these were not for protection. They were the trophy.

In the trees around hung battered shields, and broken spears. Two heads, still dripping, were slung in dishonour from one bough. The smell of the dead was upsetting the horses.

They attacked, each chariot facing left, picking its

prey, then charging. It was chaos and terrifying, for they were all enemies, and there was no strategy, no sides taken. It was bloody mayhem.

A chariot turned over, and the shield was taken, a naked man limping from the field, crying with disappointment.

'I've seen this before,' I said to Vivien. 'Many times.'

'Watch,' she whispered, then ran a short way forward, glancing back with a mischievous smile, crouching low, staring out across the field.

The light suddenly changed, the sound of horses changed, the earth at the edge of the field began to shake with a different hoofbeat.

As the chariots withdrew to the edge of the field, to circle again, so, to my astonishment, they transformed. No chariots, now, nor small ponies, but horses of gigantic stature, draped in coloured cloth, their faces bright with metal. Armoured men rode them, turning and charging these huge stallions, tugging on leather reins that were draped with flags. Long, loose hair flowed around hard, beardless faces; metal rattled, and the swords that caught the daylight were long and straight. With much snorting from the steeds and screaming from the warriors, a savage attack occurred across the field, but this time in two armies, each of about eight. Metal balls, hideously spiked, clanged off long shields painted in bright colours, striking designs in gold, red and green.

When a man fell or was struck from the saddle he threw away his sword and stood quite still as his vanquisher plucked the shield from his horse or from his arms, then tossed it below the trees. Here, as in the time of the chariots, a boy scampered with the trophy into the branches to tie it, hanging it, triumphantly.

Where had these warriors come from? What transformation had occurred? Tall tents were pitched between the great oaks. Fires burned. Spears of great length, and plumed, iron helmets, hideously featured, were propped on poles.

As fast as the transformation had occurred it had gone, and once again the chariots rattled, small ponies whinnied. Naked warriors, gleaming with sweat and blood, slashed, stabbed and struck in chaos.

Vivien was watching me hungrily.

And I realised with a moment of shock that I had opened my mind to her as easily as the minds of those knights whom I had surprised in the wilder woods of the north!

She had tricked me! She was breathless with the effort of her charm, but she was delighted too. Did she think I couldn't see what she had done? She asked me, 'What did you think of that?'

'How did you do it?'

'I saw it in a dream,' she said. 'I made the dream come back from then to now. It was to amuse you, nothing more. The next time you pass by this field, the next time you walk round the path, those horsemen will be here too.'

The long-to-come! She had touched the long-to-come. Not just the long-gone, then. Her fledgling power could reach through time in both directions.

But more importantly, she had crept into me through

the gaping mouth of my mask. I had been as vulnerable in that moment of astonishing vision as was a charioteer to a stray blow intended for the knight he carried.

I was lost. Instinct told me that. When the Ghost Animal, my life-guide, had danced for me, stepping out of my first mind, stepping out of the long-gone, I had known I was lost. What needed to be saved was the magic I contained. Vivien must not have it.

I spent a season thinking. I defined Broceliande by my restless pacing. I hid the lake to stop her drawing power from it. It was a risky thing to do, because of course it drew attention to the fact that I was making changes.

I blamed age and confusion for the act: too many water sources were interfering with my own vision, and quite soon, within a hundred years or so, I would have to start the next phase of my journey round the path.

Did she believe me? It's hard to tell. Her own mask was now firmly set. Have you ever looked into someone's eyes and seen not the loving heart but ice? Like the great ice that controls the land in the far north, that ice in the eye is a wall, a barrier, too cold to live beyond, too cold to cross, too slippery to even try to climb.

I had to get rid of my magic. I needed to hide it, to detach it from me. But I needed to hide it in such a way that I could gather it in later. The only answer was to turn it into shadow and send it on the path. I decided to send it south, travelling down the right side of the long trail, keeping its right side outermost to the ring. My intention was that I would then return north, retracing my journey – my life lived backwards – to meet the entities at some point along the way.

Vivien, I knew, would be looking for some escape to the north. She would be watching for me to turn in my tracks. She saw me as an animal, and knew the ways of clever beasts.

I knew that she would suspect the creation of shadows. I counted on her not expecting the creation of children.

It takes time and a great deal of concentration to fabricate even a single *infantasm*. I drew on the long-gone and that part of the long-to-come that I could reach. My difficulty was that Vivien's business, concerned mainly with providing for us, seeking the herbs, earths and waters that would enhance her own powers, did not take her away from the waterfall for very long. Even though I fashioned a Castle of enchanting visions for her, a place to explore, to stimulate her intellect, I was lucky if I had a full day to myself. I therefore chose my moments carefully.

I created seven children to carry my seven powers. I shall not concern you with the process of drawing the bones from the wood, the flesh from the wormy soil, the skin from leaves, the bloom from flowers, the blood from water, the bowels and other internals from killed animals – hares for the essence and spirit, of course, polecats for durability, boars for aggression, birds for most other things.

Finding flowers that were not illusion-born was the hardest task, since flowers are a rare presence in the season, whereas leaves only shrink from us in the time of Deep, or winter. But my time in the northern waste-lands, where Jack Frost has been created to serve the needs of the reindeer people, had taught me how to control frost and ice to maintain the bloom of life, like those crushed insects in amber shards, which when released sing briefly yet exquisitely about a time in the long-gone that not even I can comprehend. To decipher those fleeting songs will take a greater power than mine.

Flowers could be kept vibrant as long as ice could be kept hard, and I found a way of keeping ice even in the sun. It was a simple trick, but Vivien did not know it.

And in this way I hid my magic.

Song went into the first of the *infantasms*, who was a boy from the beginning of the world, because song, as you know, came before words. He chattered from the bough of an old oak for the first few hours following his creation, but at last I drew him to my breast, and soothed him. He would have been about five years old. The flowers and leaves that formed his skin were hard to smooth down, but after a while they blended with the earth. He looked a little patchy; he was an odd mixture of colours. His fragrance was confusing, but then so is song. It comes from very deep. I sent him into the forest, protected by a simple charm. He would hide for a while, then walk south, and in due course, after many generations, we would meet on the path again, and I would take him back.

I decided to hide stone-moving in a girl, since I was certain that this would confuse Vivien, and in any case, the frustrating of people's expectations is something in which I delight. It is a simple form of control, but can be quite effective. I shaped the girl from the long-gone, from my memory of a place where the rock, below baking deserts, is vastly hollowed to make a labyrinth of tunnels, all designed to conceal the body of a king or queen. Vivien, of course, had touched upon this magic, when she'd made the shaft, but she had only scraped a single shard of knowledge and there was a great deal left for her to win. And so it continued.

Whenever I could, I summoned a child from the past or future, from different lands along the path, gave them body, gave them substance, gave them spirit, gave them charm, then carved my secrets on their bones. One after the other they went into the wood to hide, awaiting their chance to escape the forest and travel southwards on the path, that long walk through the valleys, along the shores of the sea, then through the mountains, the journey that would eventually re-unite them with me, their source.

Seven in all, shapechangers all, I sent them on their way, and soon there was a *hollowing* inside of me, a sublime yet painful vacancy, as much to do with the scouring of my magic as with the sense of vulnerability that now possessed me.

I had kept a few charms back, of course, and just as well.

Vivien, a vision of the huntress, soon after dragged a fawn into the clearing by the falls, her bloody knife held between her teeth. Quickly, she opened and emptied the creature, then dug shallow pits for the storage of excess meat before butchering the animal.

She was naked, she always hunted naked, and as she crouched to her work – inviting, vibrant flesh working on the sweet, dead haunch – my raven spread its wings.

'Aha!' she said, noticing my hungry stare, the flush on my skin. She grinned, putting down the knife, coming to me first to preen and then to pluck my feathers.

The mist was in her hair and on her skin as she flew above me, her voice loud, her grip strong as she hunted me to the finish.

Stretched out upon me, listening to the fall of water, she said, 'I enjoyed that. But I have to finish off the beast.'

'The beast *is* finished. Believe me!'

'The beast we'll eat!' she laughed. But at once I saw the shadow, the hint of understanding. She had sensed something wrong. She had touched the *hollowing* inside of me.

She was suddenly cold. 'I have to joint the kill. I shouldn't have taken it. It's too much for our needs. But what could I do? Old Provider should have created smaller deer. If I kill, I kill for a month. You can't simply kill a *tenth* of the beast!'

She was wrong about that, but I kept the knowledge to myself. 'I'm hungry.'

'So am I. Lie back and let the moisture cool you.' She stroked my languid flesh, relaxing me, then hardened her grip, staring carefully into my right eye as I squirmed with the sudden shock.

'There's something wrong.'

'There's nothing wrong.'

'Are you quite certain?'

'I'm quite certain that I'm tired. I'm quite certain that I'm hungry, that you're hurting me. What else do you feel is wrong?'

'You weren't as close. You didn't feel as close. But perhaps I'm being foolish.'

'I'll make up the fire, then.'

She looked down at me, still holding me in her hand as a cook would hold the heart of a slaughtered pig, looking closely, looking for signs of the worm.

'I don't know that I believe you,' she whispered.

She rose to her feet suddenly and jumped, legs tucked against her chest, into the icy waters of the pool below the fall. Seconds later she had scampered out, screaming with the cold, laughing, signifying her understanding that the action had been foolish, yet had been wonderful to her senses. She had banished her suspicions.

'Make that unholy fire! Quickly! *Quickly*!'

The children were all gone. It had taken several years, but the last had left the forest and they were alone, now, pursuing for a while their own lives, their own adventures.

I was vulnerable. I felt my age. I took to dreaming, which is to say, to flying, and became the haunter of battlefields, spying from above, or from the past at the strange ways into the Otherworlds. I was not recognised. I learned nothing I didn't know already.

Dreaming, I became weak. Weakened, Vivien saw her chance to take what she did not yet know was lost to her.

Quickly, quickly, then, she made her preparations.

I was in the sky, in cold but brilliant sun, aware that the first snows of this Deep were gathering to the east. Below me, five men had gathered by a lake and the lake waters swirled about the centre. Something was rising, either summoned by these men, or coming to attack them. They seemed quite nonchalant, crouching with their horses, and I circled lower, casting an inadvertent shadow.

I had been seen in that moment, and sling-shot was loosed to drive me off, but these travellers in the long-gone (yes, I liked to fly into the past as much as hunt the present) were less interested in a falcon than in the *hollowing* that was opening before them, the way through the water to a deeper place than the scrubby land around them.

Who they were is of no relevance; if you must know, they were five brothers, Kyrdu's sons; they were in many ways the scourge of the long-gone, they were adventurers, mercenaries, sorcerers by acquisition. Their stories – their adventure was immense – may have been remembered after them. Somehow, though, I doubt it. They went too far. If you're interested I can tell you another time.

What is important is that as I watched them, I felt my right wing crack, as if twisted by invisible fingers, and knew at once that my death had come.

I found the right winds and swooped, looped, glided and struggled back to Broceliande. I came above the falls and saw Vivien above my dreaming body. She was dressed in green, her black hair flying as she raised the axe and struggled with her task.

I dropped upon her, clawed and scrabbled in her hair until she backed away, allowing me to come back home.

It was too late, of course. Dismembered, spitted on her special thorn, I could do nothing as she danced her swirling dance, nine times round my corpse, throwing up the earth, holding it there, using the magic she had stolen from me, burrowing into the cold-earth home, then gathering stones and slices of fallen trees to make the traps.

She had not yet reached below my flesh to steal the magic; she was not yet aware that my bones were smooth again.

She danced through Broceliande. I could still hear, through my dislocated pain, the way she laughed.

'Fool!' she called me. She shouted it loudly.

She swam in the cold waters, climbed trees to their precarious tips, chased down game with her bare hands, tearing the swirling fabric of her green dress as she haunted the wildwood in her ecstasy.

Bloody, muddied and triumphant, she came back to where I lay.

'Fool,' she whispered tenderly, then kissed my dry

lips, touching my eyes with raw-skinned fingers before, in the last act of her imprisonment of me, she put them out.

'What have you done? Where has it gone?'

The words, screeched like the scald-crow, were as sweet to my ears as song.

I had few charms left, but I had kept one back, a special gift.

I had been dreaming by the waterfall when she'd killed me, but my bed was a grey rock, and I shaped this, now, into the precise form of my broken, severed body. And on its mossy skin I carved the signs and runes of all the magic that I knew, but in a garbled form, sufficient to understand with the right wit, with time, with imagination, but certain to be incomprehensible to the lovely woman, the sinister woman, who had been a joy in my life – truly, the best of companions, the best of lovers; who can blame her for her more primal needs? – but a lovely woman who must now come to hell with me.

'Where has it gone? Where has it gone?' she shrieked.

I would have answered her, had I been able.

In her earlier moment of frenzied triumph, pursuing an older magic, she had devoured my tongue.

She threw me, head down, into the shaft she had fashioned in the manner of those shafts designed to conjoin with the Otherworld. She found – I have no idea from where – amulets and metal shards that would bind me to the earth; chalices and clay jugs that had once been buried with the dead; moonshards in silver, some in crystal, that would keep me forever in the shadow.

She let the earth fall back from its wildly spinning column, burying me. As it fell, she sealed the shaft at the four prime points with rounds of oak (she had learned *well*), then topped it with stones, topped these with the statue, whose nature and secrets had defeated her; and this she covered with earth, sprinkling the dirt with seed so that it would grow green.

Grow green and keep me down!

> Then, in one moment, she put forth the charm
> Of woven paces and of waving hands,
> And in the hollow oak he lay as dead,
> And lost to life and use and name and fame.

I wonder how long she embraced the statue, exploring its marks, working her fingers into every line and every shape and every crook and cranny of that broken stone, a lover sifting the cold ash of dead passion for some longed-for, warming ember?

The writing is tantalising because like a maze carved into the heart of a mountain it keeps on *almost* coming home, but never quite. And once she had engaged with those tantalising signs, once the first clues and hints of hidden power had embraced her fingers and her eyes, she was trapped, her spirit trapped, she was bound to me, tied by need, by greed, by a magic that was unfurling more slowly than the winter storm can level a snow-capped hill.

Each of us, then, was trapped by the other, and

perhaps we both deserved the fate. If I had truly wished to keep the woman away from me, I could have done so. Lust, intrigue, the need to control her vibrancy, all these things perhaps had made me evil, and I can say this now because I have paid the price, and so has she. Eventually, because that bone was broken at her birth, her flesh succumbed to time. Her bones, still smooth, lie at the bottom of the pool, by the waterfall.

As for the broken man himself, murdered that cruel time in the long-gone, I began to dream again. It was all I had power to do.

The damage was too great. I had nothing left to do but wait.

Vivien, for the time she lived, was as tied to Broceliande as was I. My children, carrying my magic, rounded the path time and time again, passing through the forest. Vivien was aware of them, but not of what they meant.

Yet somehow, as they walked through this old place, close to the murderous shaft, they sent off shadows, little echoes, shaped by experience, memories of the murder, raised by the pain that still survives within this grove. I was helpless to stop this process by which slow ghosts began to walk the path, moving southwards in the wake of my seven children, my eternal children.

Each ghost was a restless creature, a fragment of magic, magical to the short-lived children of Broceliande, and you danced within them, age after age, and shadow magic was yours for a while, odd powers, small talents, a moment of control, lost to each of you when the child in your heart was lost.

The ghosts moved south, then east, then north and west, following the path; echoes dogging the tracks of hidden wisdom. And time and time again they passed this place, my life in circles, never-ending circles.

> Then crying 'I have made his glory mine,'
> And shrieking out 'O fool!' the harlot leapt
> Adown the forest, and the thicket closed behind
>   her . . .
> And the forest echo'd . . . 'fool.'

PART FOUR

The Spirit-Echo's Promise

When shall we meet again, sweetheart
When shall we meet again?
When the bright thorn leaves on broken trees
Are green and spring up again,
Are green and spring up again.

The Unquiet Grave (folksong, variant)

The Spirit-Echo's Promise

A heavy mist was rising in the glade; it began to obscure the leaning stone, the shaft, the cowled shape of Conrad, who was whispering in a voice that was becoming hoarse and faint.

Martin prodded the fire, placed wood on it, shivered with a sudden cold. He realised he was becoming drowsy, a striking, irresistible tiredness that he recalled from his last night with Rebecca.

Merlin was watching him darkly. 'If it isn't already clear to you, let me make it clear; I have very little of my old skill left. Having put my talents outside of me, in the children, it will take time to gather them in again.'

'Did you travel in Rebecca? The priest thinks you did. You've been escaping the grave-shaft for centuries, he said . . .'

'The prison has been weakening, certainly. I could tell. It occurs periodically when the second shadow I released along the path to deceive Vivien – the one that failed – passes through Broceliande. As it does so it draws me up, it draws her out, it gives us a brief fling at life, a fling at each other, it gives me an opportunity to taunt her . . .'

'Costing the lives of families!' Martin shouted angrily. 'Costing the lives of children . . . My family, my child!'

The hooded figure lowered its head. Martin fought against the weariness that was draining all strength from his limbs.

Merlin said, 'When we use a human body, it certainly dies. It becomes a spirit on the path itself—'

'Always looking back. Always frightened.'

'They are all frightened. My children too. I *made* them frightened. I made them cautious.'

He hesitated, thinking, then went on, 'Oddly, a spirit-echo of Vivien must have stayed in Rebecca after that incident in her youth which the woodsman witnessed; when she murdered your brother. Later, when she was carrying Daniel, the echo slipped through to the child, and Vivien had a second chance.

'But before Vivien was born again in the boy, I dreamed of Rebecca coming to the lakeside. I was as free as I would get, a shadow moving among shadows, not really free at all, but able to move away from the shaft. And Rebecca called to me, though of course, it wasn't Rebecca calling. It was the enticement of the Vision of Magic. Your son was inside her, but all I could sense was *Vivien*. I was on the path for a while, a brief freedom, a spirit-echo only, and Rebecca was a warm shell for that dreaming spirit, and I passed into her. It would only be for days . . .

'Once inside, realising the danger in her womb, I took away all of Vivien's senses, all the senses in the boy Rebecca carried. It seems Vivien was stronger than I'd guessed. From what you say, she won them back.'

'That was a cruel thing to do. The act against the boy.'

'So it transpires. As I said, I *was* in a dream.'

'So will I be soon. So I'll ask you again – before I fall asleep: bring them back to me. Please! Can you bring them back to me? Or has all of this been nothing more than an opportunity for you to excuse yourself through story?'

The face in the glamour-mask round Conrad twisted with indignation, but Merlin said, 'When I referred to damage, when you first brought me out of the shaft, I meant the damage to your family.'

'Christ! They can't be more damaged than they are!'

Merlin nodded kindly. 'In the way *you* think, I suppose that's true. But to bring them back risks bringing back the enchantress. And besides, the singing magic has gone. I told you this before. I am almost powerless. I can perform a few simple tricks. This body only seems alive because of glamour, and I'm quite sure that you don't want *that* for your wife and son.'

'No,' Martin said quietly, frightened by the thought.

'I can't help you. I can give you illusion. Of comfort perhaps. I don't think . . . I don't think I can do more. You seem very tired. Go to sleep. I shan't harm you.'

Martin struggled against the charm that was closing

down his mind. He thrust his hand into the fire, the pain bringing brief life to his cry.

'No! I won't sleep! I *can't*.'

'You must.'

Merlin's grasp on his wrist was irresistible and his fingers were taken from the dying flames.

'Give me some hope, then. Just give me a little hope . . .'

'Hope?'

Martin stared hard into Merlin's eyes, and the corpse-grimace of Conrad showed for a moment. 'All I can give you is a vision. A small vision – of how it might end.'

'Anything.'

'Then go to sleep.'

Martin sank down into the cold mist by the guttering fire and half closed his eyes. As he began to dream, he was aware that Conrad had risen to his feet and was looking thoughtfully, almost curiously towards the lake.

* * *

An altar bell was ringing.

'Martin!' came the cry. (Again! . . . he had been half-aware of being called for some minutes.)

It was very cold. He sat up and stared around him, at the empty glade, the long-dead fire, the moisture on the grass, the scattered stones of the cairn, the trees. *Where was Rebecca?*

Again, the tinkling of the bell from the lake, and the

priest's call. Martin looked at his hands, suddenly shocked to see the shallow scars, the still-sore cuts and patterns. As he stood inside clothes that were damp and rank, so he felt the pain of cuts from neck to groin. He looked quickly to the tree where the bones of Merlin lay. The yellow shards were scattered, fox-struck, batted and played with as the marrow was found to have long been sucked away. Of Conrad, of the corpse, there was no sign.

Something was wrong. *That damned bell!* And the priest sounded frightened as he called. And the silence . . .

And the beard on his face.

Martin touched the thick stubble. It was wet with dew, an abrasive beard, now, a week's growth perhaps.

Where was the waterfall?

He was hungry, his hands shaking. He called, 'Rebecca? Daniel?'

His trousers were saturated with his own urine. Around him, where he had been curled up, were the remains of bread, some rinds of cheese, the picked bones of a chicken, a china flagon that might have contained cider or water.

And the dream broke! Rebecca wasn't here – she'd never been here – just a dream, just as Merlin had promised, but nothing more . . .

'Rebecca!' he cried aloud, then let his disappointment surface in tears, hugging his body, rocking where he sat as the anguish came through, and the brief touch with his family was taken away from him by the cold dawn, by cold reality.

When the despair had quietened, he left the grove of Merlin's tomb and followed the path to the lake. Father Gualzator saw him and stopped ringing the small, brass bell.

'I was worried about you,' the priest called from the canoe. The boat drifted sideways on the still water, just beyond the rushes. The man frowned, peering hard.

'Martin?'

'I saw her. I saw them both . . .'

'Who?'

'Rebecca. And Daniel.' The dream flowed through his mind again. He stared into the distance, remembering. 'I ran for so long, Father. It was such a wilderness – nothing but forest, and rivers. I ran across hills, I ran through caves, I felt the strength of a hound in my legs, I kept running. I was so lost, but I kept running – I could hear them, ahead of me, always just ahead of me. And then I found them, by a pool below a fall of water from the high rocks. They were crouching, drinking with cupped hands. For a while they didn't see me. I stood across the pool and watched them. Then I called to them and they seemed to hear me. I was very tired and I lay down by the pool and watched them. Rebecca lit a torch. It burned green. She waded through the pool towards me, apprehensive and curious as to who I might be. And then she said my name. The fire burned green and she leaned down to kiss me—

'She kissed me. And for a moment I was home. I had come home . . .'

*   *   *

'Martin!'

The priest's voice was harsh in the stillness of the new day. Martin looked at the man and frowned. 'Father . . . ?'

'Is that you, Martin?'

'Of course it's me.'

Father Gualzator seemed unsure, his face reflecting his confusion, his uncertainty. 'I've brought you what you asked for. Dressings for wounds, antiseptic, plasters, some more food.'

What I asked for?

'When did I ask for this?'

'Two days ago. You came to the church. Don't you remember?'

'No. I fell asleep by the grave shaft. I'm cut all over. Christ, I'm cut from head to foot . . .'

The stinging began to be unbearable and he tugged at his shirt, feeling it peel away from his skin, wincing as shallow but raw wounds opened. And as he collapsed through weakness and distress, the priest shouted distantly, 'By the Good God! What have you done to yourself?' and rowed through the rushes, to make the shore.

He bathed Martin's naked body with stinging antiseptic, then brewed a pot of coffee and insisted he eat the bread and coarse pâté he'd brought from the village.

'These are marks similar to those on the statue we excavated. You've mutilated yourself, copying the old man you say you saw.'

'When did I tell you about the old man?' Martin whispered. 'Christ! It hurts.'

'I should have brought fresh clothes. I'm sorry. You made me very nervous when you came from the forest. I haven't been thinking.'

'I don't remember . . .' Martin whispered. He tugged his jacket round his shoulders, pulled on the reeking trousers, the muddy shoes. 'Where's Conrad?'

'In his grave,' Father Gualzator said, grimly, pointedly. 'Where he belongs.'

'Rebecca? Daniel?'

'Back at the house. Where you brought them. You don't even remember that?'

Back at the house?

'Are they . . . oh God . . . Are they . . . ?'

'Are they what?' the priest prompted.

Martin grabbed at the man's jacket. 'How are they?'

Father Gualzator closed his eyes for a second, his head dropping as he realised Martin's misunderstanding.

'Drowned. They're drowned. You resurrected them and brought them back to the house. I'd assumed you wanted to see them properly to their cold-earth homes.'

'No!'

Shocked by the violence of the scream from the bleeding man, the priest stepped quickly back, stumbling and falling in the shallows among the rushes. As he picked himself up he was staring at Martin with a strange expression – part fear, part anger.

'I should have guessed! It's so obvious, now.'

'What is?'

'Who are you? Or do I even need to ask?'

'I don't understand.'

The priest laughed sourly. 'What have you done with Martin?'

'What do you mean by that? What do you *mean*, what have I done with Martin? Don't you recognise me? *I'm* Martin. You fool! It's only a beard. Only some cuts. I haven't changed.'

'No!' Father Gualzator was defiant as he brushed water and mud from his jeans. 'I *don't* recognise you. And Martin wouldn't call me *fool*.'

Martin watched the older man, felt the cuts on his body sting as his muscular response to the priest's attack made the skin part painfully. *What had he just said?*

'I'm sorry, Father. I don't know where that came from. I'm very confused, that's all. I can't remember coming to the church, asking for bandages . . .'

'Of course you can!' Father Gualzator growled, smiling grimly. 'It doesn't matter. What are you going to do with him? Don't look so uncomprehending, you don't fool me for an instant. My eyes are too old! Are you going to kill Martin like you killed Daniel?'

'I don't remember coming to the church,' Martin said weakly. *What was happening?*

'*Martin* doesn't, I'm quite prepared to believe that. But *you* do. And you killed Daniel . . . If I'm not mistaken. Stop pretending! *I know who you are.*'

Merlin allowed a quick smile on Martin's face, then whispered, 'Go back,' and Martin, still confused, retreated to listen from within as the priest and the resurrected sorcerer confronted each other by the lake.

*

Merlin said, 'I stopped the enchantress. I had to. In the boy she would have had fresh life. She would have been very damaging. She had learned many things – mostly illusion, but certainly some things more than that – but for all she had learned, she never learned the suppression of desire, or need, or of the senses. She never learned control, and that frightens me now as much as it frightened me then. Which is why, I suppose – it's so long ago, now, I've had so much time to make my excuses – which is why I let her destroy me. It was the only way to destroy her.'

Father Gualzator formed mud into a ball, murmuring words from the *Bronzebell*, *Book* and *Nightfire*, drawing on the forest to make a weapon that might *hurt* this raw and resurrected spirit, stalking up the bank towards the stooped body of his friend, the hiding place of evil.

'And now it's Martin's turn. Is it?' he challenged. 'Another life taken. Another death. And I'm helpless, I know it.' He hefted the mud ball pointedly, he tried to show that he understood its small significance, its possible power, its restraining power. 'But I'll stop you if I can . . . believe me.'

'I do believe you,' Merlin said. 'And I don't believe you're as helpless as you claim.' He frowned at the lump of faith-blessed mud, then shook his head. 'Although I'm not quite sure I'm right about that. Then again, I'm not sure about very much at all. I'm too new to the world. What I *am* sure about is that Martin let me out.

You were there to help him, I seem to remember, but I didn't want you around. Martin let me out, then asked for my help. I'm free in one way, of course, and relieved to be so. In another, I don't quite know what to do, where to go. I'm new to the world. I don't recognise it.'

'Let him go!'

'No. When Martin let me out, he asked for my help, and there was no fear in the request, no expectation of agreement, and no fear of retribution. I was surprised by that. I tried to warn him of the damage, the possible damage, but he seemed certain that it was a risk he would take, and who am I, who have I ever been, to argue against a man who is prepared to take a risk? What other function do I have? Why else was I born on the path? I can give you the small magic that can arm you against an unknown enemy. I don't *make* things happen, I can simply help in older, different ways.'

'Let him go!'

'Martin asked for my help, and he convinced me to help him. But I can't help him unless I travel in him. For a while at least.'

'And how long is "a while"?'

'In fact I'm nearly finished. I'll give him back to you quite soon. But if you want to help your friend, you should go to the church and watch him safely beyond the hill. And you should not interfere. He has a journey to make.'

'Where are you sending him?'

'To fetch back the singing magic . . .'

The priest shuffled uneasily by the lake, his gaze on

239

the body of Martin, his ears attuned to the words, so civilised, so calculated, the words of a man dead two thousand years.

'The singing magic? Who stole it?'

'Nobody stole it. I let it go. An echo of it was captured by Rebecca. She used it once, she never lost it. If Martin can catch up with Rebecca he can find the singing magic, he can use the singing magic, he can do with it what he likes, and the consequences will all be his, because I'm still not sure what has happened to the enchantress. But he has a chance. It's a risk he must take.'

Puzzled, Father Gualzator looked back across the lake, back to the village, to the farm, beyond the excavated graves. To Merlin he said, 'Rebecca's body is in the farmhouse. Daniel's too.'

'But only the bodies, only the flesh and bones. Martin saw them on the path. The essential part of them still lives, still walks the circle. He only has to catch them. He has to dance inside them. He tried it once, a few days ago. But he wasn't looking. You know how important it is to *look*. They passed right through him! He missed the chance.'

'How long, then? How long will it take for Martin to find the singing magic?'

'Six months, six years, six thousand years . . . It depends on how you look at it. He'll catch up with them eventually, and they'll come back to Broceliande, and life will go on for them.'

For a moment Father Gualzator was silent, his white, lined face showing grief, a desperate sense of loss. When he spoke, his words were scarcely audible. 'But I'll not necessarily see them. No-one here, no-one who loves them, none of us may see them again.'

And Merlin laughed. He was thinking of the long-gone, of the warlord Peredur, a brave man, a shining man, who had expressed the same wish that all things he could imagine should happen in the short, futile span of a single human life.

'That depends how well you pass on your eyes. With such Old Eyes as yours, Father, with such *long* sight – you should know that very well.'

'I suppose I do,' the priest said, all resistance going. 'I suppose I always have.'

Merlin came down the bank and took the ball of mud from Father Gualzator's hands. Without comment, without rebuke, without expression, he tossed the simple weapon out across the lake, then took the priest's muddy hands in his, embracing them with his fingers.

'Then why are you fighting me?'

'I don't know. Because I'm frightened . . .'

'Frightened of what?'

'The way you play with people – with their lives. And deaths.'

'Better to play with them than let them limp through time, warm home to cold home, birth to grave, no twists on the path. Don't you agree?'

Father Gualzator twisted away from the other man. 'No! How can I? It goes against everything that the church believes in—'

'And the hill?'

'The hill too. The path is not straight, but it goes forward. It was never meant for us to play tricks with the path.'

'How do you know?'

The priest was shivering as he stared from the water's edge at Martin, his friend, at Merlin, enchanting him.

'I don't, of course.'

'Of course you don't. You've forgotten how to play with toys. A toy is lifeless, but you give it life – you make it do things it could never do on its own.'

'Our lives aren't toys!'

Merlin laughed. 'Of course they are! And like toys, you can keep them to look at, or you can twist them and torment them, and give them the *illusion* of life. But one thing's for sure, Father. All toys wear out no matter how well you look after them. *Dance* them while you can. It's the only thing to do with toys. *Surely* you agree.'

Suddenly weary, Father Gualzator looked away across the lake.

'Yes . . . somewhere inside of me . . . I suppose I do. I do agree.'

Merlin laughed quietly. 'Then I'll say goodbye. And I'll let Martin go in pursuit of his Vision of Magic. And as for you, Father. Hurry home. There's a storm coming from the west.'

'A storm?' The priest looked up, looked round. 'Are you sure? The winds seem quite still.'

'Ah,' Merlin said with quiet humour, 'but you don't know the wildwoods of Broceliande as well as I do.'

'No. I suppose I don't.'

'Go home. Go back to the hill. There's nothing more, now, nothing that you can do that will make a difference. Go home.'

Other Tales:

Scarrowfell

I

In the darkness, in the world of nightmares, she sang a little song. In her small room, behind the drawn curtains, her voice was tiny, frightened, murmuring in her sleep:

> Oh dear mother what a fool I've been . . .
> Three young fellows . . . came courting me . . .
> Two were blind . . . the other couldn't see . . .
> Oh dear mother what a fool I've been . . .

Tuneless, timeless, endlessly repeated through the night, soon the nightmare grew worse and she tossed below the bedclothes, and called out for her mother, louder and louder, *Mother! Mother!* until she sat up, gasping for breath and screaming.

'Hush, child. I'm here. I'm beside you. Quiet now. Go back to sleep.'

'I'm frightened, I'm frightened. I had a terrible dream . . .'

Her mother hugged her, sitting on the bed, rocking back and forward, wiping the sweat and the fear from her face. 'Hush . . . hush, now. It was just a dream . . .'

'The blind man,' she whispered, and shook as she thought of it so that her mother's grip grew firmer, more reassuring. 'The blind man. He's coming again . . .'

'Just a dream, child. There's nothing to be frightened of. Close your eyes and go back to sleep, now. Sleep, child . . . sleep. There. That's better.'

Still she sang, her voice very small, very faint as she drifted into sleep again. '*Three young fellows . . . came courting me . . . one was blind . . . one was grim . . . one had creatures following him . . .*'

'Hush, child . . .'

Waking with a scream: 'Don't let him take me!'

2

None of the children in the village really knew one festival day from another. They were *told* what to wear, and *told* what to do, and *told* what to eat, and when the formalities were over they would rush away to their secret camp, in the shadow of the old church.

Lord's Eve was different, however. Lord's Eve was the best of the festivals. Even if you didn't know that a particular day would be Lord's Eve day, the signs of it were in the village.

Ginny knew the signs by heart. Mr Box, at the Red Hart, would spend a day cursing as he tried to erect a tarpaulin in the beer garden of his public house. Here, the ox would be slaughtered and roasted, and the dancers would rest. At the other end of the village Mr Ellis, who ran the Bush and Briar, would put empty firkins outside his premises for use as seats. The village always filled with strangers during the dancing festivals, and those strangers drank a lot of beer.

The church was made ready too. Mr and Mrs Morton, usually never to be seen out of their Sunday best, would dress in overalls and invade the cold church with brooms, brushes and buckets. Mr Ashcroft, the priest, would garner late summer flowers, and mow and trim the graveyard. This was a dangerous time for the children, since he would come perilously close to their camp, which lay just beyond the iron gate that led from the churchyard. Here, between the church and the earth walls of the old Saxon fort – in whose ring the village had been built – was a tree-filled ditch, and the children's camp had been made there. The small clearing was close to the path which led from the church, through the earth wall and out onto the farmland beyond.

There were other signs of the coming festival day, however, signs from outside the small community. First, the village always seemed to be in shadow. Yet distantly, beyond the cloud cover, the land seemed to glow with eerie light. Ginny would stand on the high wall by the church, looking through the crowded trees that covered the ring of earthworks, staring to where the late summer sun was setting its fire on Whitley Nook and Middleburn. Movement on the high valley walls above these villages was just the movement of clouds, and the fields seemed to flow with brightness.

The wind always blew from Whitley Nook towards Ginny's own village, Scarrowfell. And on that wind, the day before the festival of Lord's Eve, you could always hear the music of the dancers as they wended their way along the riverside, through and round the underwood, stopping at each village to collect more dancers, more musicians (more hangovers) ready for the final triumph at Scarrowfell itself.

The music drifted in and out of hearing, a hint of a violin, the distant clatter of sticks, the faint jingle of the small bells with which the dancers decked out their clothes. When the wind gusted, whole phrases of the jaunty music could be heard, a rhythmic sound, with the voices of the dancers clearly audible as they sang the words of the folk songs.

Ginny, precariously balanced on the top of the wall, would jig with those brief rhythms, hair blowing in the wind, one hand holding on to the dry bark of an ash branch.

The dancers were coming; all the Oozers and the Pikers and the Thackers, coming to join the village's Scarrowmen; and it was therefore the day of Lord's Eve: the birds would flock and wheel in the skies, and flee along the valley too. And sure enough, as she looked up into the dark sky over Scarrowfell, the birds were there, thousands of them, making streaming, spiral patterns in the gloom. Their calling was inaudible. But after a while they streaked north, away from the bells, away from the sticks, away from the calling of the Oozers.

Kevin Symonds came racing round the grey-walled church, glanced up and saw Ginny and made frantic beckoning motions. 'Gargoyle!' he hissed, and Ginny almost shouted as she lost her balance before jumping down from the wall. 'Gargoyle' was their name for Mr Ashcroft, the priest. A second after they had squeezed beyond the iron gate and into the cover of the scrub the old man appeared. But he was busy placing rillygills – knots of flowers and wheat stalks – on each gravestone and didn't notice the panting children just beyond the cleared ground, where the thorn and ash thicket was so dense.

Ginny led the way into the clear space among the trees in the ditch. She stepped up the shallow earth slope to peer away into the field beyond, and the circle of tall elms that grew at its centre. A scruffy brown mare – probably one of Mr Box's drays – was kicking and stamping across the field, a white foal stumbling behind it. She was so intent on watching the foal that she didn't notice Mr Box himself, emerging from the ring of trees. He was dressed in his filthy blue apron but walked briskly across the field towards the church, his gaze fixed on the ground. Every few paces he stopped and fiddled with something on the grass. He never looked up, walked through the gap in the earthworks – the old gateway – and passed, by doing so, within arm's reach of where Ginny and Kevin breathlessly crouched. He walked straight ahead, stopped at the iron gate, inspected it, then moved off around the perimeter of the church, out of sight and out of mind.

'They've got the ox on the spit already,' Kevin said,

his eyes bright, his lips wet with anticipation. 'It's the biggest ever. There's going to be at least two slices each.'

'Yuck!' said Ginny, feeling sick at the thought of the grey, greasy meat.

'And they've started the bonfire. You've got to come and see it. It's going to be huge! My mother said it's going to be the biggest yet.'

'I usually scrub potatoes for fire-baking,' Ginny said. 'But I haven't been asked this year.'

'Sounds as if you've been lucky,' Kevin said. 'It's going to be a really big day. The biggest ever. It's *very* special.'

Ginny whispered, 'My mother's been behaving strangely. And I've had a nightmare . . .'

Kevin watched her, but when no further information or explanation seemed to be forthcoming he said, '*My* mother says this is the most special Lord's Eve of them all. An old man's coming back to the village.'

'What old man?'

'His name's Cyric, or something. He left a long time ago, but he's coming back and everybody's very excited. They've been trying to get him to come back for ages, but he's only just agreed. That's what Mum says, anyway.'

'What's so special about him?'

Kevin wasn't sure. 'She said he's a war hero, or something.'

'Ugh!' Ginny wrinkled her nose in distaste. 'He's probably going to be all scarred'

'Or blind!' Kevin agreed, and Ginny's face turned white.

A third child wriggled through the iron gate and

skidded into the depression between the earth walls, dabbing at his face where he had scratched himself on a thorn.

'The tower!' Mick Ferguson whispered excitedly, ignoring his graze. 'While old Gargoyle is busy placing the rillygills.'

They moved cautiously back to the churchyard, then crawled towards the porch on their bellies, screened from the priest by the high earth mounds over each grave. Ducking behind the memorial stones – but not touching them – they at last found sanctuary in the freshly polished, gloomy interior. Despite the cloud-cover, light was bright from the stained-glass windows. The altar, with its flowers, looked somehow different from normal. The Mortons were cleaning the font, over in the side chapel; a bucket of well-water stood by ready to fill the bowl. They were talking as they worked and didn't hear the furtive movement of the three children.

Kevin led the way up the spiralling, footworn steps and out onto the cone-shaped roof of the church's tower. They averted their eyes from the grotesque stone figure that guarded the doorway, although Kevin reached out and touched its muzzle as he always did.

'For luck,' he said. 'My mother says the stone likes affection as much as the rest of us. If it doesn't get attention it'll prowl the village at night and choose someone to kill.'

'Shut *up*,' Ginny said emphatically, watching the monster from the corner of her eye.

Michael laughed. 'Don't be such a scaredy-hare,' he

said and reached out to jingle the small bell that hung around her neck. Her ghost bell.

'It's a small bell and that's a big stone demon,' Ginny pointed out nervously. Why was she so apprehensive this time, she wondered? She had often been up here and had never doubted that the stone creature, like all demons, could not attack the faithful, and that bells, books and candles were protection enough from the devil's minions.

The nightmare had upset her. She remembered Mary Whitelock's nightmare a few years before – almost the same dream, confided in the gang as they had feasted on stolen pie in their camp. She had not really liked Mary. All the same, when she had suddenly disappeared, after the festival, Ginny had felt very confused . . .

No! Put the thought from your mind, she told herself sternly. And brazenly she turned and stared at the medieval monstrosity that sat watching the door to the church below. And she laughed, because it was only frightening when you *imagined* how awful it was. In fact, it looked faintly ludicrous, with its gaping V-shaped mouth and lolling tongue, and its pointed ears, and skull cheeks, and its one great staring eye . . . and one gouged socket . . .

Below them, the village was a bustle of activity. In the small square in front of the church the bonfire was rising to truly monumental heights. Other children were helping to heap the faggots and broken furniture onto the pile. A large stake in its centre was being used to hold the bulk of wood in place.

Away from where this fire would blaze, a large area was being roped off for the dancing. The gate from the church had already been decked with wild roses and lilies. The Gargoyle himself always led the congregation from the Lord's Eve service out to the festivities in the village. Ginny giggled at the remembered sight of him, dark cassock held up to his knees, white bony legs kicking and hopping along with the Oozers and the local Scarrowmen, a single bell on each ankle making him look as silly as she always thought he was.

At the far end of the village, the road from Whitley Nook cut through the south wall of the old earth fort and snaked between the cluster of tiled cottages where Ginny herself lived. Here, two small fires had been set alight, one on each side of the old track. The smoke was shattered by the wind from the valley. On the church tower the three children enjoyed the smell of the burning wood.

And as they listened they heard the music of the dancers, even now winding their way between Middleburn and Whitley Nook.

They would be here tomorrow. Sunlight picked out the white of their costumes, miles distant; and the flash of swords flung high in the air.

The Oozers were coming. The Thackers were coming. The wild dance was coming.

3

She awoke with a shock, screaming out, then becoming instantly silent as she stared at the empty room and the bright daylight creeping in above the heavy curtains of her room.

What time was it? Her head was full of music, the jangle of bells, the beating of the skin drums, the clash and thud of the wooden hobby poles. But now, outside, all was silent.

She swung her legs from the bed, then began to shiver as unpleasant echoes of that haunting song, the nightmare song, came back to her.

She found that she could not resist muttering the words that stalked her sleeping hours. It was as if she had to repeat the sinister refrain before her body would allow her to move again, to become a child again . . .

'Oh dear mother . . . three young men . . . two were blind . . . the third couldn't see . . . oh mother, oh mother . . . grim-eyed courtiers . . . blind men dancing . . . creatures followed him, creatures dancing . . .'

The church bell rang out, a low repeated toll, five strikes and then a sixth strike, a moment delayed from the rest.

Five strikes for the Lord, and one for the fire! It couldn't be that time. It couldn't! Why hadn't mother come in to wake her?

Ginny ran to the curtains and pulled them back, staring out into the deserted street, crawling up onto the window ledge so that she could lean through the top window and stare up towards the square.

It was full of motionless figures. And distantly she could hear the chanting of the congregation. The Lord's Eve service had already started. Started! The procession had already passed the house, and she had been aware of it only in her half sleep!

She screeched with indignation, fleeing from her bedroom into the small sitting room. By the dock on the mantelpiece she learned that it was after midday. She had slept . . . she had slept fifteen hours!

She grabbed her clothes, pulled them on, not bothering with her hair but making a token effort to polish her shoes. It was Lord's Eve. She *had* to be smart today. She couldn't find her bell necklace. She had on a flowered dress and red shoes. She pulled a pink woollen cardigan over her shoulders, grabbed at her frilly hat, stared at it, then tossed it behind the hat rack . . . and fled from the house.

She ran up the road to the church square, following the path that, earlier, the column of dancers must have taken. She felt tears in her eyes, tears of dismay, and anger, and irritation. Every year she watched the procession from her garden. *Every year!* Why hadn't mother *woken* her?

She loved the procession, the ranks of dancers in their white coats and black hats, the ribbons, the flowers, the bells tied to ankle, knee and elbow, the men on the hobby horses, the fools with their pigs' bladders on sticks, the women in their swirling skirts, the Thackers, the Pikermen, the Oozers, the black-faced Scarrowmen . . . all of them came through the smouldering fires at the south gate, each turning and making the sign of peace before jigging and hopping on along the road, keeping time to the beat of the drum, the melancholy whine of the violin, the sad chords of the accordion, the trill of the whistles.

And she had missed it! She had slept! She had remained in the world of nightmares, where the shadowy blind pursued her . . .

As she ran she *screamed* her frustration!

She stopped at the edge of the square, catching her breath, looking for Kevin, or Mick, or any others of the small gang that had their camp in the earthen walls of the old fort. She couldn't see them. She cast her gaze over the ranks of silent dancers. They were spread out across the square, lines of men and women facing the lych-gate and the open door of the church. They stood in absolute silence. They hardly seemed to breathe. Sometimes, as she brushed past one of them, working her way towards the church where Gargoyle's voice was an irritating drone in the distance, sometimes a tambourine would rattle, or an accordion would sigh a weary note. The man holding it would glance and smile at her, but she knew better than to disturb the Scarrowmen when the voice was speaking from the church.

She passed under the rose and lily gate, ducked her head and made the sign of peace, then scampered into the porch and edged towards the gloomy, crowded interior.

The priest was at the end of his sermon, the usual boring sermon for the feast day.

'We have made a pledge,' Mr Ashcroft was intoning. 'A pledge of belief in a life after death, a pledge of belief in a God which is greater than humankind itself . . .'

She could see Kevin, standing and fidgeting between

his parents, four pews forward in the church. Of Michael there was no sign. And where was mother? At the front, almost certainly . . .

'We believe in the resurrection of the Dead, and in a time of atonement. We have made a pledge with those who have died before us, a pledge that we will be reunited with them in the greater Glory of our Lord.'

'*Kevin!*' Ginny hissed. Kevin fidgeted. The priest droned on.

'We have pledged all of this, and we believe all of this. Our time in the physical realm is a time of trial, a time of testing, a testing of our honour and our belief, a belief that those who have gone are not gone at all, but merely waiting to be rejoined with us . . .'

'*Kevin!*' she called again. '*Kevin!*'

Her voice carried too loudly. Kevin glanced round and went white. His mother glanced round too, then jerked his attention back to the service, using a lock of his curly hair as her means. His cry was audible to the Gargoyle himself, who hesitated before concluding,

'This is the brightness behind the feast of the Lord's Eve. Think not of the Death, but of the Life our Lord will bring us.'

Where was her mother?

Before she could think further someone's hand tugged at her shoulder, pulling her back towards the porch of the church. She protested and glanced up, and the solemn face of Mr Box stared down at her. 'Go outside, Ginny,' he said. 'Go outside, now.'

Inside, the congregation had begun to recite the Lord's Prayer.

He pushed her towards the rose gate, beyond which the Oozers and Scarrowmen waited for the service to end. She walked forlornly towards them, and as she passed the man who stood closest to her she struck at his tambourine. The tambours jangled loudly in the still, summer square.

The man didn't move. She stood and stared defiantly at him, then struck his tambourine again.

'Why don't you *dance*?' she shrieked at him. When he ignored her, she shouted again. 'Why don't you make *music*? Make *music*! Dance in the square! Dance!' Her voice was a shrill cry.

4

There was no twilight. Late afternoon became dark night in a few minutes and a torch was put to the fire, which flared dramatically and silenced all activity. Glowing embers streamed into a starless sky and the village square became choking with the sweet smell of burning wood. The last smells of the roasted ox were banished and in the grounds of the Red Lion the skeleton of the beast was hacked apart. A few pence each for the bones with their meaty fragments. In front of the Bush and Briar Mr Ellis swept up a hundredweight of broken glass. Mick Ferguson led a gang of children, chasing an empty barrel down the street, towards the south gate where the fires still smouldered.

For a while the dancing had ceased. People thronged

about the fire. Voices were raised in the public houses as dancers and tourists alike struggled to get in fresh orders for ale. A sort of controlled chaos ruled the day, and in the centre of it: the fire, its light picking out stark details on the grey church and the muddy green in the square. Beyond the sheer rise of the church tower, all was darkness, although men in white shirts and black hats walked through the lych-gate and rounded the church, talking quietly, dispersing as they re-emerged into the square. Here, they again picked up sticks, or tambourines, or other instruments of music and mock war.

Ginny wandered among them.

She could not find her mother.

And she knew that something was wrong, very wrong indeed.

It came as scant reassurance when a bearded youth called to the Morrismen again, and twelve sturdy men, all of them strangers to Scarrowfell, jangled their way from the Bush and Briar to the dancing square. There was laughter, tomfoolery with the cudgels they carried, and the whining practice notes of the accordion. Then they filed into a formation, jiggled and rang their legs, laughed once more and began to hop to the rhythm of a dance called the *Cuckoo's Nest*. A man in a baggy, flowery dress and with a big frilly bonnet on his head sang the rude words. The singer was a source of great amusement since he sported a bushy, ginger beard. He wore an apron over the frock and every so often lifted the pinny to expose a long red balloon strapped between his legs. It had eyes and eyelashes painted on its tip. The audience roared each time he did this.

As Ginny moved through the fair towards the new focus of activity, Mick Ferguson approached her, grinned, and went into his Hunchback of Notre Dame routine, stooping forward, limping in an exaggerated fashion and crying, 'The bells. The bells. The jingling bells . . .'

'Mick . . .' Ginny began, but he had already flashed her a nervous grin and bolted off into the confusing movement of the crowds, running towards the fire and finally disappearing into the gloom beyond.

Ginny watched him go. Mick, she thought . . . Mick . . . why?

What was going on?

She walked towards the dancers and the bearded singer and Kevin turned round nervously and nodded to her. The man sang:

'Some like a girl who is pretty in the face.
And some like a girl who is slender in the waist . . .'

'I missed the procession,' Ginny said. 'I wasn't woken up.'

Kevin stared at her, looking unhappy. He said, 'My mother told me not to talk to you . . .'

She waited, but Kevin had decided that discretion was the better part of cowardice.

'Why not?' she asked, disturbed by the statement.

'You're being denied,' the boy murmured.

Ginny was shocked. 'Why am I being denied? Why me?'

262

Kevin shrugged. Then a strange look came into his eyes, a horrible look, a man's look, arrogant, sneering.

The man in the hideous dress sang:

'But give me a girl who will wriggle and will twist

Each time I slap my hand upon her cuckoo's nest . . .'

Kevin backed away from Ginny, making 'cuckoo' sounds.

'It's a *rude* song,' Ginny said.

Kevin taunted, '*You're* a cuckoo. *You're* a cuckoo . . .'

'I don't know what it means,' Ginny said, bewildered.

'Cuckoo, cuckoo, cuckoo,' Kevin mocked, then jabbed her in the groin. He cackled horribly then raced away towards the blazing bonfire. Ginny had tears in her eyes, but her anger was so intense that the tears dried. She glared at the singer, still not completely aware of what was going on except that she knew the song was rude because of the guffaws of the adult men in the watching circle. After a moment she slipped away towards the church.

She stood within the lych-gate watching the flickering of the fire, the highlit faces of the crowds, the restless movement, the jigging and hopping . . . hearing the laughter, and the music, and the distant wind that was fanning the fire and making the flames bend violently and dangerously towards the south. And she wondered where, in all this chaos, her mother might have been.

Mother had been so supportive to her, so gentle, so kind. During the nights when the nightmare had been a terrible presence in the house by the old road, where Ginny had lived since her real parents had died in the fire, during those terrible nights the Mother had been so comforting. Ginny had come to think of her as her own mother, and all grief, all sadness had faded fast.

Where *was* the Mother? Where *was* she?

She saw Mr Box, walking slowly through the crowds, a baked potato in one hand and a glass of beer in the other. She ran to him and tugged at his jacket. He nearly choked on his potato and glanced round urgently, but soon her voice reached him and, although he frowned, he stooped down towards her. He threw the remnants of his potato away and placed his glass upon the ground.

'Hello Ginny . . .' He sounded anxious.

'Mr Box. Have you seen mother?'

Again he looked uncomfortable. His kindly face was a mask of worry. His moustache twitched. 'You see . . . she's getting the reception ready.'

'What reception?' Ginny asked.

'Why, for Cyric, of course. The war hero. The man who's coming back to us. He's finally agreed to return to the village. He was supposed to have come three years ago, but he couldn't make it.'

'I don't care about him,' she said. 'Where's mother?'

Mr Box placed a comforting hand on her shoulder and shook his head. 'Can't you just play, child? It's what you're supposed to do. I'm just a pub landlord. I'm not part of the Organisers. You shouldn't even . . . you shouldn't even be *talking* to me.'

'I'm being denied,' she whispered.

'Yes,' he said sadly.

'Where's mother?' Ginny demanded.

'An important man is coming back to the village,' Mr Box said. 'A great hero. It's a great honour for us . . .

and . . .' He hesitated before adding, in a quiet voice, 'And what he's bringing with him is going to make this village more secure . . .'

'What *is* he bringing?' Ginny asked.

'A certain knowledge,' Mr Box said, then shrugged. 'It's all I know. Like all the villages around here, we've had to fight to keep out the invader, and it's a hard fight. We've all been waiting a long time for this night, Ginny. A very long time. We made a pledge to this man. A long time ago, when he fought to save the village. Tonight we're honouring that pledge. All of us have a part to play . . .'

Ginny frowned. 'Me too?' she asked, and was astonished to see large tears roll down each of Mr Box's cheeks.

'Of course you too, Ginny,' he whispered, and seemed to choke on the words. 'I'm surprised that you don't know. I always thought the children knew. But the way these things work . . . the rules . . .' He shook his head again. 'I'm not privileged to know.'

'But why is everybody being so horrible to me?' Ginny said.

'Who's everybody?'

'Mick,' she said. 'And Kevin. He called me a cuckoo . . .'

Mr Box smiled. 'They're just teasing you. They've been told something of what will happen this evening and they're jealous.'

He straightened up and took a deep breath. Ginny watched him, his words sinking in slowly. She said, 'Do you mean what will happen to *me* this evening?'

He nodded. 'You've been *chosen*,' he whispered to her. 'When your parents were killed, the Mother was sent to you to prepare you. Your role tonight is a very special one. Ginny, that's all I know. Now go and play, child. Please . . .'

He looked suddenly away from her, towards the dancers. Ginny followed his gaze. Five men, two of whom she recognised, were watching them. One of them shook his head slightly and Mr Box's touch on Ginny's shoulder went away. A woman walked towards them, her dress covered with real flowers, her face like stone. Mr Box pushed Ginny away roughly. As she scampered for safety she could hear the sound of the woman's blows to Mr Box's cheek.

5

The fire burned. Long after it should have been a glowing pile of embers, it was still burning. Long after they should have been exhausted, the Scarrowmen danced. The night air was chill, heavy with smoke, bright with drifting sparks. It echoed to the jingle of bells and the clatter of cudgels. Voices drifted on the wind; there was laughter; and round and round the Morrismen danced.

Soon they had formed into a great circle, stretched around the fire and jigging fast and furious to the strident, endless rhythm of drums and violin. All the village danced, and the strangers too, men and women in anoraks and sweaters, and children in woolly hats, and teenagers in jeans and leather jackets, all of them mixed up with the white-and-black clothed Oozers, Pikers, Thackers and the rest.

Round the burning fire, stumbling and tottering, shrieking with mirth as a whole segment of the ring tumbled in the mud. Round and round.

The bells, the hammering of sticks, the whine of the violin, the Jack Tar sound of the accordion.

And at ten o'clock the whole wild dance stopped.

Silence.

The men reached down and took the bells from their legs, cast them into the fire. The cudgels, too, were thrown onto the flames. The violins were shattered on the ground, the fragments tossed into the conflagration.

The accordions wept music as they were slung onto the pyre.

Flowers out of hair. Bonnets from heads. Rose and lily were stripped off the lych-gate. The air filled suddenly with a sharp, aromatic scent . . . of herbs, woodland herbs.

In the silence Ginny walked towards the church, darted through the gate into the darkness of the grave-yard . . . Round between the long mounds to the iron gate . . .

Kevin was there. He ran towards her, his eyes wide, wild. 'He's coming!' he hissed, breathlessly.

'What's going on?' she whispered.

'Where are you going?' he said.

'To the camp. I'm frightened. They've stopped dancing. They're burning their instruments. This happened three years ago when Mary . . . when . . . you know . . .'

'Why are you so frightened?' Kevin asked. His eyes were bright from the distant glow of the bonfire. 'What are you running from, Ginny? Tell me. Tell me. We're friends . . .'

'Something is wrong,' she sobbed. She found herself clutching at the boy's arms. 'Everybody is being so horrible to me. *You* were horrible to me. What have I done? What have I done?'

He shook his head. The flames made his dark eyes gleam. She had her back to the square. Suddenly he looked beyond her. Then he smiled. He looked at her.

'Goodbye, Ginny,' he whispered.

She turned. Kevin darted past her and into the great mob of masked men who stood around her. They had come upon her so quietly that she had not heard a thing. Their faces were like black pigs. Eyes gleamed, mouths grinned. They wore white and black . . . the Scarrows.

Unexpectedly, Kevin began to whine. Ginny thought he was being punished for being out of bounds. She listened, and then for one second . . . just one second . . . all was stillness, all was silence, anticipation. Then she reacted as any sensible child would react in the situation.

She opened her mouth and screamed. The sound had barely echoed in the night air when a hand clamped firmly across her face, a great hand, strong, stifling her cry. She struggled and pulled away, turned and kicked until she realised it was the Mother that she fought against. She was no longer wearing her rowan beads, or her iron charm. She seemed naked without them. Her dress was green and she held Ginny firmly still. 'Hold quiet, child. Your time is soon.'

The iron gate was open. Ginny peered through it, into the darkness, through the grassy walls of the old fort and towards the circle of great elms.

There was a light there, and the light was coming closer. And ahead of that light there was a wind, a breeze, ice cold, tinged with a smell that was part sweat, part rot, and unpleasant in the extreme. She grimaced and tried to back away, but the Mother's hands held her fast. She glanced over her shoulder, towards the square, and felt her body tremble as the Scarrows stared beyond her, into the void of night.

Two of the Scarrows held tall, hazel poles, each wrapped round with strands of ivy and mistletoe. They stepped forward and held the poles to form a gateway between them. Ginny watched all of this and shivered. And she felt sick when she saw Kevin held by others of the Scarrows. The boy was terrified. He seemed to be pleading with Ginny, but what could she do? His own mother stood close to him, weeping silently.

The wind gusted suddenly and the first of the shadows passed over so quickly that she was hardly aware of its transit. It appeared out of nowhere, part darkness, part chill, a tall shape that didn't so much walk as *flow* through the iron gate. Looking at that shadow was like looking into a depthless world of dark; it shimmered, it hazed, it flickered, it moved, an uncertain balance between that world and the real world. Only as it passed between the hazel poles held by the Scarrows, and then into the world beyond, did it take on a form that could be called . . . ghostly.

Distantly the priest's voice intoned a greeting. Ginny heard him say, 'Welcome back to *Scarugfell*. Our pledge is fulfilled. Your life begins again.'

A second shadow followed the first, this one smaller, and with its darkness and its chill came the sound of keening, like a child's crying. It was distant, though, and uncertain. As Ginny watched, it took its shadowy form beyond the Scarrows and into the village.

As each of them had passed over, so the Scarrowmen closed ranks again, but distantly, close to the fire in the square, an unearthly howling, a nightmare wind, seemed to greet each new arrival. What happened to the spirits then, Ginny couldn't tell, or care.

Her mother's hand touched her face, then her shoulder, forced her round again to watch the iron gate. The Mother whispered, 'Those two were his kin. They too died for our village a long time ago. But Cyric is coming now . . .'

The shadow that moved beyond the gate was like nothing Ginny could ever have imagined. She couldn't tell whether it was animal or man. It was immense. It swayed as it moved, and it seemed to approach through the darkness in a ponderous, dragging way. Its outlines were blurred, shadow against darkness, void against the glimmering light among the trees. It seemed to have branches and tendrils reaching from its head. It made a sound that was like the rumble of water in a hidden well.

It seemed to fill her vision. It occupied all of space. Its breath stank. Its single eye gleamed with firelight.

One was blind . . . one was grim . . .

It seemed to be laughing at her as it peered down from beyond the trees and the earth walls that surrounded the church.

It pushed something forward, a shadow, a man, nudged it through the iron gate. Ginny wanted to scream as she caught glimpses, within that shadow, of the dislocated jaw, the empty sockets, the crawling flesh. The ragged thing limped toward her, hands raised, bony fingers stretched out, skull face open and inviting . . . inviting the kiss that Ginny knew, now, would end her life.

'No!' she shouted, and struggled frantically in the Mother's grip. The Mother seemed angry. 'Even now it mocks us!' she said, then shouted, 'Give the Life for the Death. Give it now!'

Behind Ginny, Kevin suddenly screamed. Then he was running towards the iron gate, sobbing and shouting, drawn by invisible hands.

'Don't let him take me! Don't let him take me!' he cried.

He passed the hideous figure and entered the world beyond the gate. He was snatched into the air, blown into darkness like a leaf whipped by a storm wind. He had vanished in an instant.

The great shadow turned away into the night and began to seep back towards the circle of elms. The Mother's hands on Ginny's shoulders pushed her forwards, towards the ghastly embrace.

The shadow corpse stopped moving. Its arms dropped. The gaping eyes watched nothing and nowhere. A sound issued from its bones. 'Is she the one? Is she my kin?'

Mother's voice answered loudly that she was indeed the one. She was indeed Cyric's kin.

The shadow seemed to turn its head to watch Ginny. It looked down at her, then reached up and pulled the tatters of a hood about its head. The hood hid the features. The whole creature seemed to melt, to descend, to shrink. Ginny heard the Mother say, 'Fifteen hundred years in the dark. Your life saved our village. Our pledge to bring you back is honoured. Welcome, Cyric.'

Something wriggled below the tatters of the hood. The Mother said, 'Go forward, child. Take the hare. *Take him!*'

Ginny hesitated. She glanced round. The Scarrows seemed to be smiling behind their masks. Two other children, both girls, stood there. Each was holding a struggling hare. Her Mother made frantic motions to her. 'Come on, Ginny. The fear is ended, now. The day of denial is over. Only you can touch the hare. You're the kin. Cyric has chosen you. Take it quickly. Bring him over. Bring him back.'

Ginny stumbled forward, reached below the stinking rags and found the terrified animal. As she raised the brown hare to her breast she felt the flow of the past, the voice, the wisdom, the spirit of the man who had passed back over, the promise to him kept, fifteen hundred years after he had lain down his life for the safety of *Scarugfell*, also known as the *Place of the Mother*.

Cyric was home. The great hunter was home. Ginny had him, now, and *he* had her, and she would become great and wise, and Cyric would speak the wisdom of the Dark through her lips. The hare would die in time, but Cyric and Ginny would share a human life until the human body itself passed away.

And Ginny felt a great glow of joy as the images of that ancient land, its forts, its hills, its tracks, its forest shrines, flooded into her mind. She heard the hounds, the horses, the larks, she felt the cold wind, smelled the great woods.

Yes. Yes. She had been born for this. Her parents had been sacrificed to free her and the Mother had kept her ready for the moment. The nightmare had been Cyric making contact as the Father had brought him to the edge of the dark world.

The Father! The Father had watched over her, as all in the village had often said he would. It had been the Father she had seen, a rare glimpse of the Lord who always brought the returning Dead to the place of the Lord's Eve.

Cyric had come a long, long way home. It had taken time to make the Lord release him and allow Cyric's knowledge of the dark world back to the village, to help Scarrowfell, and the villages like it keep the eyes and minds of the invader muddled and confused. And then Cyric, too, had waited . . . until Ginny was of age. His kin. His chosen vehicle.

Ginny, his new protector, cradled the animal. The hare twitched in her grasp. Its eyes were full of rejoicing.

She felt a moment's sadness, then, for poor, betrayed

Kevin, but it passed. And as she left the place of the gate she joined willingly in reciting the Lord's prayer, her voice high, enthusiastic among the nimble of the crowd.

Our Father, who art in the Forest
Horned One is Thy name.
Thy Kingdom is the Wood, Thy Will is the Blood
In the Glade, as it is in the Village.
Give us this day our Kiss of Earth
And forgive us our Malefactions.
Destroy those who Malefact against us
And lead us to the Otherworld.
For Thine is the Kingdom of the Shadow, Thine is
the Power and the Glory. Thou art the Stag which
ruts with us, and We are the Earth beneath thy feet.
Drocha Nemeton.

Thorn

for John Murry

At sundown, when the masons and guild carpenters finished their work for the day and trudged wearily back to their village lodgings, Thomas Wyatt remained behind in the half-completed church and listened to the voice of the stone man, calling to him.

The whispered sound was urgent, insistent: 'Hurry! Hurry! I *must* be finished before the others. *Hurry!*'

Thomas, hiding in the darkness below the gallery, felt sure that the ghostly cry could be heard for miles around. But the Watchman, John Tagworthy, was almost completely deaf, now, and the priest was too involved with his own holy rituals to be aware of the way his church was being stolen.

Thomas could hear the priest. He was circling the new church twice, as he always did at sundown, a small, smoking censer in one hand, a book in the other. He walked from right to left. Demons, and the sprites of the old earth, flew before him, birds and bats in the darkening sky. The priest, like all the men who worked on the church – except for Thomas himself – was a stranger to the area. He had long hair and a dark, trimmed beard, an unusual look for a monk.

He talked always about the supreme holiness of the place where his church was being built. He kept a close eye on the work of the craftsmen. He prayed to the north and the south, and constantly was to be seen kneeling at the very apex of the mound, as if exorcising the ancient spirits buried below.

This was Dancing Hill. Before the stone church there had been a wooden church, and some said that Saint Peter himself had raised the first timbers. And hadn't Joseph, bearing the Grail of Christ, rested on this very spot, and driven out the demons of the earth mound?

But it was Dancing Hill. And sometimes it was referred to by its older name, *Ynys Calidryv*, isle of the old fires. There were other names, too, forgotten now.

'Hurry!' called the stone man from his hidden niche. Thomas felt the cold walls vibrate with the voice of the spectre. He shivered as he felt the power of the earth returning to the carved ragstone pillars, to the neatly positioned blocks. Always at night.

The Watchman's fire crackled and flared in the lee of the south wall. The priest walked away down the hill to the village, stopping just once to stare back at the half-constructed shell of the first stone church in the area. Then he was gone.

Thomas stepped from the darkness and stood, staring up through the empty roof to the clouds and the sky, and the gleaming light that was Jupiter. His heart was beating fast, but a great relief touched his limbs and his mind. And as always, he smiled, then closed his eyes for a moment. He thought of what he was doing. He thought of Beth, of what she would say if she knew his secret work; sweet Beth; with no children to comfort her she was now more alone than ever. But it would not be for much longer. The face was nearly finished . . .

'Hurry!'

A few more nights. A few more hours working in darkness, and all the Watchman's best efforts to guard the church would have been in vain.

The church would have been stolen. Thomas would have been the thief!

He moved through the gloom, now, to where a wooden ladder lay against the side wall. He placed the ladder against the high gallery – the leper's gallery – and climbed it. He drew the ladder up behind him and stepped across the debris of wood, stone and leather to the farthest, tightest corner of the place. Bare faces of the coarse ragstone watched the silent church. No mortar joined the stones. Their weight held them secure. They supported nothing but themselves.

At Thomas's muscular insistence, one of them moved, came away from the others.

With twilight gone, but night not yet fully descended, there was enough grey light for him to see the face that was carved there. He stared at the leafy beard, the narrowed, slanting eyes, the wide, flaring nostrils. He saw how the cheeks would look, how the hair would become spiky, how he would include the white and red berries of witch-thorn upon the twigs that clustered round the face . . .

Thomas stared at Thorn, and Thorn watched him by

return, a cold smile on cold stone lips. Voices whispered in a sound realm that was neither in the church, nor in another world, but somewhere between the two, a shadowland of voice, movement and memory.

'I must be finished before the others,' the stone man whispered.

'You shall be,' said the mason, selecting chisel and hammer from his leather bag. 'Be patient.'

'I must be finished before the magic ones!' Thorn insisted, and Thomas sighed in irritation.

'You *shall* be finished before the magic ones. No-one has agreed upon the design of their faces, yet.'

The 'magic ones' were what Thomas called the Apostles. The twelve statues were temporarily in place above the altar, bodies completed but faces still smoothly blank.

'To control them I must be here first,' Thorn said.

'I've already opened your eyes. You can see how the other faces are incomplete.'

'Open them better,' said Thorn.

'Very well.'

Thomas reached out to the stone face. He touched the lips, the nose, the eyes. He knew every prominence, every rill, every chisel-mark. The grains of the stone were like pebbles beneath his touch. He could feel the hard-stone intrusion below the right eye, where the rag would not chisel well. There was a hardness, too, in the crown of Thorns, a blemish in the soft rock that would have to be shaped carefully to avoid cracking the whole design. As his fingers ran across the thorn man's lips, cold, old breath tickled him, the woodland man breathing from his time in the long past. As Thomas touched the eyes he felt the eyeballs move, impatient to see better.

I am in a wood grave, and a thousand years lie between us, Thorn had said. *Hurry, hurry. Bring me back.*

In the deepening darkness, working by touch alone, Thomas chiselled the face, bringing back the life of the lost god. The sound of his work was a sequence of shrill notes, stone music in the still church. John Tagworthy, the Watchman, outside by his fire, would be unaware of them. He might see a tallow candle by its glow upon the clouds, he might smell a fart from the distant castle on a still summer's night, but the noises of man and nature had long since ceased to bother his senses.

'Thomas! Thomas Wyatt! Where in God's Name *are* you?'

The voice, hailing him from below, so shocked Thomas that he dropped his chisel, and in desperately trying to catch the tool he cut himself. He stayed silent for a long moment, cursing Jupiter and the sudden band of bright stars for their light. The church was a place of shadows against darkness. As he peered at the north arch he thought he could see a man's shape, but it was only an unfinished timber. He reached for the heavy stone block that would cover the stone face, and as he did so the voice came again.

'God take your gizzard, Thomas Wyatt. It's Simon. Miller's son Simon!'

Thomas crept to the gallery's edge and peered over. The movement drew attention to him. Simon's pale features turned to look at him. 'I heard you working. What are you working on?'

'Nothing,' Thomas lied. 'Practising my craft on good stone with good tools.'

'Show me the face, Thomas,' said the younger man, and Thomas felt the blood drain from his head. *How had he known?* Simon was twenty years old, married for three years and still, like Thomas himself, childless. He was a freeman of course; he worked in his father's mill, but spent a lot of his time in the fields, both his family's strips and the land belonging to the Castle. His great ambition, though, was to be a Guildsman, and masonry was his aspiration.

'What face?'

'Send down the ladder,' Simon urged, and reluctantly Thomas let the wood scaffold down. The miller clambered up to the gallery, breathing hard. He smelled of garlic. He looked eagerly about in the gloom. 'Show me the green man.'

'Explain what you mean.'

'Come on, Thomas! Everybody knows you're shaping the Lord of Wood. I want to see him. I want to know how he looks.'

Thomas could hardly speak. His heart alternately stopped and raced. Simon's words were like stab wounds. *Everybody knew! How could everybody know?*

Thorn had spoken to him, and to him alone. He had sworn the mason to silence and secrecy. For thirty days Thomas Wyatt had risked not just a flogging, but almost certain hanging for blasphemy, risked his life for the secret realm. Everybody *knew*?

'If everybody knows, why haven't I been stopped?'

'I don't mean *everybody*,' Simon said, as he felt blindly along the cold walls for a sign of Thomas's work. 'I mean the village. It's spoken in whispers. You're a hero, Thomas. We know what you're doing, and for whom. It's exciting; it's *right*. I've danced with them at the forest cross. I've carried the fire. I *know* how much power remains here. I may take God's name in oath – but that's safe to do. He has no power over me, or any of us. He doesn't belong on Dancing Hill. Don't *worry*, Thomas. We're your friends . . . Ah!'

Simon had found the loose stone. It was heavy and he grunted loudly as he took its weight, letting it down carefully to the floor. His breathing grew soft as he reached for the stone face. But Thomas could see how the young man drew back, fingers extended yet not touching the precious icon.

'There's magic in this, Thomas,' Simon said in awe.

'There's skill – working by night, working with fear – there's skill enough, I'll say that.'

'There's magic in the face,' Simon repeated. 'It's drawing power from the earth below. It's tapping the Dancing Well. There's water in the eyes, Thomas. The dampness of the old well. The face is brilliant.'

He straggled with the covering stone and replaced it. 'I wish it had been me. I wish the green man had chosen me. What an honour, Thomas. Truly.'

Thomas Wyatt watched his friend in astonishment. Was this *really* Simon the miller's son? Was this the young man who had carried the Cross every Resurrection

Sunday for ten years? Simon Miller! *I've danced with them at the forest cross.*

'Who have you danced with at the crossroads, Simon?'

'*You* know,' Simon whispered. 'It's alive, Thomas. It's all alive. It's here, around us. It never went away. The Lord of Wood showed us . . .'

'Thorn? Is that who you mean?'

'*Him!*' Simon pointed towards the hidden niche. 'He's been here for years. He came the moment the monks decided to build the church. He came to save us, Thomas. And you're helping. I envy you . . .'

Simon climbed down the ladder. He was a furtive night shape, darting to the high arch where an oak door would soon be fitted, and out across the mud-churned hill, back round the forest, to where the village was a dark place, sleeping.

Thomas followed him down, placing the ladder back against the wall. But on the open hill, almost in sight of the Watchman's fire, he looked to the north, across the forest, to where the ridgeway was a high band of darkness against the pale grey glow of the clouds. Below the ridgeway a fire burned. He knew that he was looking at the forest cross, where the stone road of the Romans crossed the disused track between Woodhurst and Biddenden. He had played there as a child, despite being told never *ever* to follow the broken stone road.

There was a clearing at the deserted crossroads, and years ago he, and Simon Miller's elder brother Wat, had often found the cold remains of fire and feasts. Outlaws, of course, and the secret baggage trains of the Saxon Knights who journeyed the hidden forest trails. Any other reason for the use of the place would have been unthinkable. Why, there was even an old gibbet, where forest justice was seen to be done . . .

With a shiver he remembered the time when he had come to the clearing and seen the swollen, greyish corpse of a man swinging from that blackened wood. Dark birds had been perched upon its shoulders. The face had had no eyes, no nose, no flesh at all, and the sight of the dead villain had stopped him from ever going back again.

Now, a fire burned at the forest cross. A fire like the fire of thirty nights ago, when Thorn had sent the girl for him . . .

He had woken to the sound of his name being called from outside. His wife, Beth, slept soundly on, turning slightly on the palliasse. It had been a warm night. He had tugged on his britches, and drawn a linen shirt over his shoulders. Stepping outside he had disturbed a hen, which clucked angrily and stalked to another nesting place.

The girl was dressed in dark garments. Her head was covered by a shawl. She was young, though, and the hand that reached for his was soft and pale.

'Who are you?' he said, drawing back. She had tugged at him. His reluctance to go with her was partly fear, partly concern that Beth would see him.

'Iagus goroth! Fiatha! *Fiatha!*' Her words were strange to Thomas. They were *like* the hidden language, but were not of the same tongue.

'Who *are* you?' he insisted, and the girl sighed, still holding his hand. At last she pointed to her bosom. Her eyes were bright beneath the covering of the shawl. Her hair was long and he sensed it to be red, like fire. 'Anuth!' she said. She pointed distantly. 'Thorn. You come with Thorn. With Anuth. Me. *Come.* Thomas. Thomas to Thorn. *Fiatha!*'

She dragged at his hand and he began to run. The grip on his fingers relaxed. She ran ahead of him, skirts swirling, body hunched. He tripped in the darkness, but she seemed able to see every low-hanging branch and proud beechwood root on the track. They entered the wood. He concentrated on her fleeing shape, calling, occasionally, for her to slow down. Each time he went sprawling she came back, making clicking sounds with her mouth, impatient, anxious. She helped him to his feet but immediately took off into the forest depths, heedless of risk to life and limb.

All at once he heard voices, a rhythmic beating, the crackle of fire . . . and the gentle sound of running water. She had brought him to the river. It wound through the forest, and then across downland, towards the Avon.

Through the trees he saw the fire. Anuth took his hand and pulled him, not to the bright glade, but towards the stream. As he walked he stared at the flames. Dark, human shapes passed before the fire. They seemed to be dancing. The heavy rhythm was like the striking of one bone against another. The voices were singing. The language was familiar to him, but incomprehensible.

Anuth dragged him past the firelit glade. He came to

284

the river, and she slipped away. Surprised, he turned, hissing her name; but she had vanished. He looked back at the water, where starlight, and the light of a quarter moon, made the surface seem alive. There was a thick-trunked thorn tree growing from the water's edge. The thorn tree trembled and shifted in the evening wind.

The thorn tree grew before the startled figure of Thomas Wyatt. It rose, it straightened, it stretched. Arms, legs, the gleam of moonlight on eyes and teeth.

'Welcome, Thomas,' said the thorn tree.

He took a step backwards, frightened by the apparition.

'Welcome where?'

In front of him, Thorn laughed. The man's voice rasped, like a child with consumption. 'Look around you, Thomas. Tell me what you see.'

'Darkness. Woodland. A river, stars. Night. Cold night.'

'Take a breath, Thomas. What do you smell?'

'That same night. The river. Leaves and dew. The fire, I can smell the fire. And autumn. All the smells of autumn.'

'When did you last see and smell these things?'

Thomas, confused by the strange midnight encounter, shivered in his clothing. 'Last night. I've always seen and smelled them.'

'Then welcome to a place you know well. Welcome to the always place. Welcome to an autumn night, something that this land has always known, and will always enjoy.'

'But who are you?'

'I have been known by many names.' He came close to the trembling man. His hawthorn crown, with its strange horns, was like a broken tree against the clouds. His beard of leaves and long grass rustled as he spoke. His body quivered where the night breeze touched the clothing of nature that wound around his torso. 'Do you believe in God, Thomas?'

'He died for us. His son. On the Cross. He is the Almighty . . .'

Thorn raised his arms. He held them sideways. He was a great cross in the cold night, and his crown of thorns was a beast's antlers. Old fears, forgotten shudders, plagued the villager, Thomas Wyatt. Ancestral cries mocked him. Memories of fire whispered words in the hidden language, confused his mind.

'I am the Cross of God,' said Thorn. 'Touch the wood, touch the sharp thorns . . .'

Thomas reached out. His actions were not his own. His fingers touched the cold flesh of the man's stomach. He felt the ridged muscle in the crossbeam, the bloody points of the thorns that rose from the man's head. He nervously brushed the gnarled wood of the thighs, and the proud branch that rose between them, hot to his fingers, nature's passion, never dying.

'What do you want of me?' Thomas asked quietly.

The cross became a man again. 'To make my image in the new shrine. To make that shrine my own. To make it as mine forever, no matter what manner of worship is performed within its walls . . .'

Thomas stared at the Lord of Wood.

'Tell me what I must do . . .'

286

Everybody knew, Simon had said. Everybody in the village. It was spoken in whispers. Thomas was a hero. Everybody knew. Everybody but Thomas Wyatt.

'Why have they kept it from me?' he murmured to the night. He had huddled up inside his jacket, and folded his body into the tight shelter of a wall bastion. The encounter with Simon had shaken him badly.

From here he could see north to Biddenden across the gloomy shapelessness of the forest. The Castle, and the clustered villages of its demesne, were behind him. He saw only stars, pale clouds, and the flicker of fire, where strange worship occurred.

Why did the fire, in this midnight forest, call to him so much? Why was there such comfort in the thought of the warm glow from the piled branches, and the noisy prattle, and laughter, of those who clustered in its shadowy light? He had danced about a fire often enough: on May eve, at the passing of the day of All Hallows. But those fires were in the village bounds. His soul fluttered, a delighted bird, at the thought of the woodland fire. The smell of autumn, the touch of night's dew, the closeness to the souls of tree and plant; timeless eyes would watch the dancers. They were a shared life with the forest.

Why had he been kept in isolation? *Everybody knew.* The villagers who carried the bleeding, dying Christ through the streets on Resurrection Sunday – were they now carrying images of boar and stag and hare about the fire? He – Thomas – was a hero. They spoke of him in whispers. Everybody knew of his work. When had *they* been taken back to the beliefs of old? Had Thorn appeared to each of them as well?

Why didn't he *share* the new belief with them? It was the same belief. He used his craft; they danced for the gods.

As if he were of the same cold stone-stuff upon which he worked, the others kept him distant, watched him from afar. Did Beth know? Thomas shivered. The hours passed. He could feel the gibbet rope around his neck. Only one word out of place, one voice overheard – one whisper to the wrong man, and Thomas Wyatt would be a grey thing, slung by its neck, prey for dark birds. Eyes, nose, the flesh of the face. Every feature that he pecked for Thorn with hammer and chisel would be pecked from him by hard, wet beaks.

From the position of the moon, Thomas realised he had been sitting by the church for several hours. John the Watchman had not walked past. Now that he thought of it, Thomas could hear the man's snoring, coming as if from a far place.

Thomas eased himself to his feet. He lifted his bag gently to his shoulder, over-cautious about the ring and strike of iron tools within the leather. But as he walked towards the path he heard movement in the church. The Watchman snored distantly.

It must be Simon, the miller's son, Thomas thought, back for another look at the face of the woodland god.

Irritated, and still confused, Thomas stepped into the church again, and looked towards the gallery. The ladder was against the balcony. He could hear the stone being moved. There was a time of silence, then the stone was put back. A figure moved to the ladder and began to descend.

Thomas watched in astonishment. He stepped into greater darkness as the priest looked round, then hauled the ladder back to its storage place. All Thomas heard was the sound of the priest's laughter. The man passed through the gloom, long robe swirling through the dust and debris.

Even the priest knew! And that made no sense at all. Thomas slept restlessly, listening to the soft breathing of his wife. Several times the urge to wake her, to speak to her, made him whisper her name and shake her shoulders. But she slumbered on. At sunrise they were up together, but he was so tired he could hardly speak. They ate hard bread, moistened with cold, thin gruel. Thomas tipped the last of their ale into a clay mug. The drink was more meaty than the gruel, but he swallowed the sour liquid and felt its warming tingle.

'The last of the ale,' he said ruefully, tapping the barrel.

'You've been too busy to brew,' Beth said from the table. 'And I'm not skilled.' She was wrapped in a heavy wool cloak. The fire was a dead place in the middle of the small room. Grey ash drifted in the light from the roof hole.

'But no *ale*!' He banged his cup on the barrel in frustration. Beth looked up at him, surprised by his anger.

'We can get ale from the miller. We've done it before

and repaid him from our own brewing. It's not the end of the world.'

'I've had no time to brew,' Thomas said, watching Beth through hooded, rimmed eyes. 'I've been working on something of importance. I expect you know what.'

She shrugged. 'Why would I know? You never talk about it.' Her pale face was sweet. She was as pretty now as when he had married her; fuller in body, yes, and wider in the ways of life. That they were childless had not affected her spirit. She had allowed the wise women to dose her with herbs and bitter spices, to take her to strange stones, and stranger foreigners; she had been seen by apothecaries and doctors, and Thomas had worked in their fields to pay them. And of course, they had prayed. Now Thomas felt too old to care about children. Life was good with Beth, and their sadness had drawn them closer than most couples he knew.

'Everybody knows what I'm working on,' he said bitterly.

'Well, I don't,' she replied. 'But I'd like to . . .'

Perhaps he had been unfair to her. Perhaps she too was kept apart from the village's shared knowledge. He lied to her. 'You must not say a word to anyone. But I'm working on the face of Jesus.'

Beth was delighted. 'Oh Thomas! That's wonderful. I'm so proud of you.' She came round to him and hugged him. Outside, Master mason Tobias Craven called out his name, among others, and he trudged up to the church on Dancing Hill.

*

290

His work was uneven and lazy that day. The chisel slipped, the stone splintered, the hammer caught his thumb twice. He was distracted and deeply concerned by what he had seen the night before. When the priest came to the church, to walk among the bustle of activity and inspect the day's progress, Thomas watched him carefully, hoping for some sign of recognition. But the man just smiled, and nodded, then carried the small light of Christ to the altar, and said silent prayers for an hour or more.

At sundown, Thomas felt his body shaking. When the priest called the craftsmen – Thomas included – into the vestry for wine, Thomas stood by the door, staring at the dark features of the Man of God. The priest, handing him his cup, merely said, 'God be with you, Thomas.' It was what he always said.

Tobias Craven came over to him. His face was grey with dust, his clothing heavy with dirt. His dialect was difficult for Thomas to understand, and Thomas was suspicious of the gesture anyway. Would he now discover that the foreigners, too, knew of the face of the woodland deity, half completed behind its door of stone?

'Your work is good, Thomas. Not today, perhaps, but usually. I've watched you.'

'Thank you.'

'At first I was reluctant to allow you to work as a mason among us. It was at the priest's insistence: one local man to work in every craft. It seemed a superstitious idea to me. But now I'm glad. I approve. It's an enlightened gesture, I realise, to allow local men, not of Guilds, to display their skills. And your skill is remarkable.'

Thomas swallowed hard. 'To be a Guildsman would be a great honour.'

Master Tobias looked crestfallen. 'Aye, but alas. I wish I had seen your work when you were twenty, not thirty. But I can write a note for you, to get you better work in the area.'

'Thank you,' Thomas said again.

'Have you travelled, Thomas?'

'Only to Glastonbury. I made a pilgrimage in the third year of my marriage.'

'Glastonbury,' Master Tobias repeated, smiling. 'Now that is a fine Abbey. I've seen it just once. Myself, I worked at York, and at Carlisle, on the Minsters. I was not a Master, of course. But that was cherished work. Now I'm a Guild Master, building tiny churches in remote places. But it gives fulfilment to the soul, and one day I shall die and be buried in the shadow of a place I have built myself. There is satisfaction in the thought.'

'May that not be for many years.'

'Thank you, Thomas.' Tobias drained his cup. 'And now, from God's work to nature's work—'

Thomas paled. Did he mean woodland worship? The Master mason winked at him.

'A good night's sleep!'

When the others had gone, Thomas slipped out of the sheltering woodland and made his way back to the church. The Watchman was fussing with his fire.

There was less cloud this evening and the land, though murky, was quite visible for many miles around.

Inside the church, Thomas looked up at the gallery. Uncertainty made him hesitate, then he shook his head. 'Until I understand better . . .' he murmured, and made to turn for home.

'Thomas!' Thorn called. 'Hurry, Thomas.'

Strange green light played off the stone of the church. It darted around him, like will-o'-the-wisp. Fingers prodded him forward, but when he turned there was nothing but shadow.

Again, Thorn called to him.

With a sigh, Thomas placed the ladder against the gallery and climbed up to the half-finished face. Thorn smiled at him. The narrow eyes sparkled with moisture. The leaves and twigs that formed his hair and beard seemed to rustle. The stone strained to move.

'Hurry, Thomas. Open my eyes better.'

'I'm frightened,' the man said. 'Too many people know what I'm doing.'

'Carve me. Shape my face. I must be here before the others. *Hurry!*'

The lips of the forest god twitched with the ghostly figure's anguish. Thomas reached out to the cold stone and felt its stillness. It was just a carving. It had no life. He imagined the voice. It was just a man who told him to make the carving, a man dressed in woodland disguise. Until he knew he was safe, he would not risk discovery. He climbed back down the ladder. Thorn called to him, but Thomas ignored the cry.

At his house a warm fire burned in the middle of the

room, and an iron pot of thick vegetable broth steamed above it. There was fresh ale from the miller, and Beth was pleased to see him home so early. She stitched old clothes, seated on a low stool, close to the wood fire. Thomas ate, then drank ale, leaning on the table, his mason's tools spread out before him. The ale was strong and soon went to his head. He felt dizzy, sublimely detached from his body. The warmth, the sensation of drunkenness, his full stomach, all of these things made him drowsy, and slowly his head sank to his arms . . .

A cold blast of air on his neck half roused him. His name was being called. At first he thought it was Beth, but soon, as he surfaced from pleasant oblivion, he recognised the rasping voice of Thorn.

The fire burned high, fanned by the draught from the open door. Beth still sat on her stool, but was motionless and silent, staring at the flames. He spoke her name, but she didn't respond. Thorn called to him again and he looked out at the dark night. He felt a sudden chill of fear. He gathered his tools into his bag and stepped from the house.

Thorn stood in the dark street, a tall figure, his horns of wood black against the sky. There was a strong smell of earth about him. He moved towards Thomas, leaf-clothes rustling.

'The work is unfinished, Thomas.'

'I'm afraid for my life. Too many people know what I'm doing.'

'Only the finishing of the face matters. Your fear is of no consequence. You agreed to work for me. You must go to the church. Now.'

'But if I'm caught!'

'Then another will be found. Go back to the work, Thomas. Open my eyes properly. It *must* be done.'

He turned from Thorn and sighed. There was something wrong with Beth and it worried him, but the persuasive power of the night figure was too strong to counter, and he began to walk wearily towards the church. Soon the village was invisible behind him. Soon the church was a sharp relief against the night sky. The Watchman's fire burned high, and the autumn night was sweet with the smell of woodsmoke. The Watchman himself seemed to be dancing, or so Thomas thought at first. He strained to see better and soon realised that John had fallen asleep and set light to his clothing. He was brushing and beating at his leggings, his grunts of alarm like the evening call of a boar.

The moment's humour passed and a sudden anger took Thomas. Thorn's words were like sharp stab wounds to his pride: his fear was of no consequence. Only the work of carving mattered. He would be caught and it would be of no consequence. He would swing, slowly strangling, from the castle gallows and it would be of no consequence. Another would be found!

'No!' he said aloud. 'No. I will *not* work for Thorn tonight. Tonight is *my* night. Damn Thorn. Damn the face. Tomorrow I will open its eyes, but not now.'

And with a last glance at the Watchman, who had extinguished the fire and settled down again, he turned back to the village.

*

But as he approached his house, aware of the glow of the fire through the small window, his anger changed to a sudden dread. He began to feel sick. He wanted to cry out, to alert the village. A voice in his head urged him to turn and go back to the night wood. His house, once so welcoming, threatened him deeply. It seemed surrounded by an aura, detached from the real world.

He walked slowly to the small window. He could hear the crackle and spit of the flames. Wood smoke was sweet in the air. Somewhere, at the village bounds, two dogs barked.

The feeling of apprehension in him grew, a strangling weed that made him dizzy. But he looked through the window. And he did not faint, nor cry out, at what he saw within, though a part of his spirit, part of his life, flew away from him then, abandoning him, making him wither and age; making him die a little.

Thorn stood with his back to the fire. His mask of autumn leaves and spiky wood was bright and eerie – dark hair curled from beneath the mask. His arms were wound around with creeper and twine, and twigs of oak, elm and lime were laced upon this binding. Save for these few fragments of nature's clothing he was naked. The black hair on his body gave him the appearance of a burned oak stump, gnarled and weathered by the years. His manhood was a smooth, dark branch, cut to the length of firewood.

Beth was on her knees before him, her weight taken on her elbows. Her skirts were on the floor beside her. The yellow flames cast a flickering glow upon her plump, pale flesh, and Thomas half closed his eyes in despair. He managed to stifle his scream of anguish, but he could not stop himself from watching.

And he uttered no sound, despite the pain, as Thorn dropped down upon the waiting woman.

As he ran to the church the Watchman woke, then stood up, picking up his heavy staff. Thomas Wyatt knocked him down, then drew a flaming wood brand from the brazier. Tool-bag on his shoulder he entered the church, and held the fire high. The ladder was against the balcony. Pale features peered down at him and the ladder began to move. But Simon, the miller's son, was not quite quick enough. Casting the burning wood aside, Thomas leapt for the scaffold and began to ascend.

'I was just looking, Thomas,' Simon cried, then tried to fling the ladder back. Thomas clutched at the balcony, then hauled himself to safety. He said no word to Simon, who backed against the wall where the loose stone was fitted.

'You mustn't touch him, Thomas!'

In the darkness, Simon's eyes were gleaming orbs of fear. Thomas took him by the shoulders and flung him to the balcony, then used a stone to strike him.

'No, Thomas! No!'

The younger man had toppled over the balcony. He held on for dear life, fingers straining to hold his weight.

'Tricked!' screamed Thomas. 'All a trick! Duped! Cuckolded! All of you knew. All of you *knew*!'

'No, Thomas. In the Name of God, it wasn't like that!'

His hammer was heavy. He swung it high. Simon's left hand vanished and the man's scream of pain was deafening. 'She had no other way!' he cried hysterically. 'No, Thomas! No! She chose it! She *chose* it! Thorn's gift to you both.'

The hammer swung. Crushed fingers left bloody marks upon the balcony. Simon crashed to the floor below and was still.

'All of you knew!' Thomas Wyatt cried. He wrenched the loose stone away. Thorn watched him from the blackness through his half-opened eyes. Thomas could see every feature, every line. The mouth stretched in a mocking grin. The eyes narrowed, the nostrils flared.

'Fool. Fool!' whispered the stone man. 'But you cannot stop me now.'

Thomas slapped his hand against the face. The blow stung his flesh. He reached for his chisel, placed the sharp tool against one of the narrow eyes.

'NO!' screeched Thorn. His face twisted and turned. The stone of the church shuddered and groaned. Thomas hesitated. A green glow came from the features of the deity. The eyes were wide with fear, the lips drawn back below the mask. Thomas raised his hammer.

'NO!' screamed the head again. Arms reached from the wall. The light expanded. Thomas backed off, terrified by the spectre which had appeared there, a ghastly green version of Thorn himself, a creature half ghost, half stone, tied to the wall of the church, but reaching out from the cold rock, reaching for Thomas Wyatt, reaching to kill him.

Thomas raised the chisel, raised the hammer. He ran

back to the face of Thorn and with a single, vicious blow, drove a gouging furrow through the right eye.

The church shuddered. A block of stone fell from the high wall, striking Thomas on the shoulder. The whole balcony vibrated with Thorn's pain and anger.

Again he struck. The left eye cracked, a great split in the stone. Dampness oozed from the wound. The scream from the wall was deafening. Below the balcony, yellow light glimmered. The Watchman, staring up to where Thomas performed his deed of vengeance.

Then a crack appeared down the whole side of the church. The entire gallery where Thomas had worked dropped by a man's height, and Thomas was flung to the balcony. He struggled to keep his balance, then went over the wall, scrabbling at the air. Thorn's stone-scream was a nightmare sound. Air was cool on the mason's skin. A stone pedestal broke his fall. Broke his back.

The village woke to the sound of the priest's terrible scream. He stumbled from the mason's house, hands clutching at his eyes, trying to staunch the flow of blood. He scrabbled at the wood mask, stripping away the thorn, the oak, the crisp brown leaves, exposing dark hair, a thin dark beard.

The priest – Thorn's priest – turned blind eyes to the church. Naked, he began to stagger and stumble towards the hill. Behind him, the villagers followed, torches burning in the night.

Thomas lay across the marble pillar, a few feet from

the ground. There was no sensation in his body, though his lungs expanded to draw air into his chest. He lay like a sacrificial victim, arms above his head, legs limp. The Watchman circled him in silence. The church was still.

Soon the priest approached him, hands stretched out before him. The pierced orbs of his eyes glistened as he leaned close to Thomas Wyatt.

'Are you dying, then?'

'I died a few minutes ago,' Thomas whispered. The priest's hands on his face were gentle. Blood dripped from the savaged eyes.

'Another will come,' Thorn said. 'There are many of us. The work will be completed. No church will stand that is not a shrine to the true faith. The spirit of Christ will find few havens in England.'

'Beth . . .' Thomas whispered. He could feel the bird of life struggling to escape him. The Watchman's torch was already dimming.

Thorn raised Thomas's head, a finger across the dry lips. 'You should not have seen,' said the priest. 'It was a gift for a gift. Our skills, the way of ritual, of fertility, for your skill with stone. Another will come to replace me. Another will be found to finish your work. But there will be no child for you, now. No child for Beth.'

'What have I done?' Thomas whispered. 'By all that's holy, what have I done?'

From above him, from a thousand miles away, came the ring of chisel on stone.

'Hurry,' he heard Thorn call into the night. 'Hurry!'

Earth and Stone

The sunshine is a glorious birth;
But yet I know, where'er I go,
That there hath passed away a glory from the earth.

Wordsworth, *Intimations of Immortality*

Carrying loudly across the rolling grasslands the *crack* of transmission was almost indistinguishable from that *crack* which follows the splitting of the great boulders, the megaliths of the tomb-builders who had lived in this land for seven hundred years. The man, riding on a stocky, black horse, appeared as if out of nowhere. He was well wrapped in skins and fur leggings, and wore his hair in tight, shoulder-length plaits. His beard and moustaches were curled and stiff with some reddish paste. His saddlebags were anachronistic in this third millennium before Christ, but were at least fashioned crudely out of leather; their geometrical bulkiness was unavoidable since the equipment they contained was essential for the man's ultimate return to his own age. Like the horse, the leather bags and what they contained would be destroyed as soon as they had served their purpose. Of that there was no doubt in the man's mind at all; but his conviction was for the wrong reason. He had no intention of ever returning to his own time. He was going to remain here, among the people of the Boyne valley with whom he had become so involved – in an academic sense – during the short span of his life.

His name was John Farrel. He was nearly thirty years old and in this time of earth and stone he expected to be able to live another ten years.

As he came through the transmission field he turned his horse and peered into the blur that was the future. It started to fade and the last air of another time leaked five thousand years into its past, bringing with it a sour smell – the smell of machines, of artificial scent, of synthetic clothes; the odour, the stench, of successful adaptation.

Cold winds, the winter's last voice before the sudden warmth of spring, carried the smell of the future away, dispersed it across a land wider than Farrel had ever known. Machine, perfume, plastic, drained into the earth, were sucked down and away, lost from the grassy crispness of this age of rock and blood.

Farrel rode up the small hillock that lay immediately in front of the transmission field, turned again as he reached the summit, and peered down into the valley. The river Boyne wound across the landscape, a silver thread meandering eccentrically between the low hills until it passed out of view. Farrel's mind's eye felt, for a moment, the lack of the sprawl of red brick dwellings that would one day supersede those ragged forestlands of the wider curve. For a moment he thought he saw a car flashing along a main road: sunlight on speeding chrome. The illusion was just the gleam of fragmentary sunlight on the spread wings of a gull, riding the winds above the river, back to the sea.

Where the transmission field was slowly dissolving the river was a blur, the land a green haze that came more and more into focus. Wind caught Farrel's hair, cooled the sweat on his cheeks and made him blink. The grass beneath him seemed to whisper; the wind itself talked in an incoherent murmur. It droned, distantly. Grey clouds swept across the pale sun and shadows fled across the valley, were chased away by brightness. The transmission field finally faded and was gone.

For a moment, then, Farrel imagined he saw a woman's face, round and ageing; blonde hair perfectly styled, but eye-shadow blurred and smeared with tears and bitter, bitter anger. *Why you? Why you? Why you?*

Her remembered words were only the gusting winds and the animal sounds of his horse, restless and anxious to be given free rein across this wild land.

How loud the silence after hysteria, he thought. He had not known how haunting another's heartbreak could be. *You'll never come back! Don't lie to me, you'll never come back. I know you too well, John. This is your way out, your means of escape. My God, you must really hate me. You must really hate us all!*

Last words, lost in the roar of street traffic. The stairs had trembled beneath him. The outer door had slammed, an explosion finishing them forever.

I'm here now. I'm here. I got away from them, from all of them, and they think – most of them think – that I'm going back when my job is done. But I'm not! I'm not going back! I'm here and I got away from everything, and I'm not going back!

The ghosts of the future faded, then, following the transmission field forward across the centuries. The land about Farrel came sharply into focus. His mind cleared. He breathed deeply, and though for a second he felt the urge to cry, he stifled that urge and looked around him, staring at the unadulterated landscape.

Small mounds were scattered in clusters down the hillside and concentrated along the river itself (thus being nearer to the river goddess, or so Burton had implied in his last transmission). The oldest tumulus was possibly no more than two hundred years of age. The youngest? Farrel searched among them: four hundred yards away there was a mound, perhaps twice his height, perhaps fifty feet in diameter. It had a kerb of grey stones which separated the dull greenness of the hillside from the dark earth mound, not yet fully covered with its own field of grass. A grave, perhaps no more than half a year old; new, with the cremated remains inside it still heavy with the smell of burning.

He felt dizzy with excitement as he associated this new tomb with the low grassy bump that it would become during the next five thousand years, a tomb so crumbled and weathered that only the discovery of its fractured kerb-stones would identify it. A handful of carbon fragments, preserved in a natural cist between two of the chamber stones and identified as human remains, would raise a thousand questions in the minds of those who were fascinated by this enigmatic neolithic culture. And a year ago those splinters of charred bone might have been alive, walking this very countryside.

A flight of starlings wheeled above his head, spiralling at the mercy of the winds. A lone magpie darted among them until the starlings turned on it, and then the bigger bird dropped away down the hill to vanish against the sheen of the river. The shrill bird song was a brief symphony of panic and Farrel reined his horse around so that he could look towards the distant forest and the rolling downs of what would one day be his home county.

From behind a low, rain- and wind-smoothed boulder, a boy was watching him.

FIRST TRANSMISSION — SECOND DAY

I have arrived in early spring, and as far as I can determine, seven months later than anticipated rather than five months early. I don't blame Burton for not being here to meet me. He must have rapidly become tired of hanging about, especially with something 'fantastic' in the offing. Whatever was about to happen that so excited him, there is no sign, now, of either him or the Tuthanach themselves. Correction: a single Tuthanach . . . a boy. This is the strange boy that Burton mentioned in his last transmission, and he is the only human life I have seen in these first few hours, apart from some invisible activity (in the form of smoke) from the direction of the hill of Tara. The boy was not overly curious about the horse, and has shown no interest in its disappearance. He ate some of its meat today and never commented on what must surely have been an unusual flavour. I'm very grateful to everyone who made me bring the horse, by the way. I'd never have caught any of the wild life, and I had to travel a good two miles to find a satisfactory hiding place. The village – I suppose I should say *crog Tutha* – is deserted and shows distinct signs of weathering. I confess that I am somewhat puzzled. The burial mound of Coffey's site K, by the way, is very new, something that Burton failed to report. I had a frightening thought earlier: could Burton be buried there? There is no sign yet of tombs on sites L or B, but there are so many others that are not detectable at all by the twenty-first century that I don't know where to begin. Burton hinted as much, didn't he? I wonder why he didn't go into specifics? The tumulus at site J is already well weathered, which suggests our dating was a little out – say by four hundred years? And as Burton reported, the site of the giant Newgrange mound is still barren. I actually came out of the transmission field on the very spot the great tumulus will occupy. I didn't realise it for quite a while, and then it made me feel very strange. Further details will follow in my second transmission. For the moment, since my fingers are aching: signing off.

For the first two nights Farrel and the boy slept in the spacious shelter afforded by a deep rock overhang and the entwined branches and roots of several stubby elms that surrounded the cave. By the third day Farrel's interest in the unexpectedly deserted crog began to outweigh his reluctance to actually camp in the decaying village. He remained uneasy. What if the Tuthanach returned during the night and took exception to a stranger setting himself down in their tents? Burton's report had not indicated that this particular Boyne people was in any way warlike or violent, but this period of the neolithic was a time of great movement, populations succeeding populations, and axe and spear-head used for drastic and final ends. The megalithic tomb-builders of Brittany, especially, were familiar with this part of the Irish coast. In their massive coracles they hugged the south coast of England until the confused currents around Land's End swept them round the Scillies and up into the warm flow of the Irish Sea. From there they up-oared and the shallow seas carried them automatically to the Irish coast north of Dublin, along just those picturesque beaches that had seen the original settlers putting into shore, seven or eight hundred years before.

In one of his transmissions, Burton had given a single, brief account of a small 'rock-stealing' party that had raided a crog further south, near Fourknocks (crog-Ceinarc). The raiders had killed and been killed, not by the Ceinarc, but by wolves.

Wolves were what Farrel feared most. In his own time wolf packs were quite timid and easily scared. In this age, however, their behaviour was altogether different – they were fierce, persistent and deadly. Better, he thought, to believe in the non-hostility of the Tuthanach than risk the teeth of such wolf packs. Provided he kept clear of the rocks and stones in the territory of crog-Tutha, and in no way 'stole' them by carving his own soul spirit upon them, he imagined he would be safe.

He explained his plan to the boy, whose name was Ennik-tig-en'cruig (Tig-never touch woman-never touch earth). The boy put a hand to his testicles and inclined his head to the right. Uncertainty? Yes, Farrel realised – a shrug, but a shrug overlain with anxiety.

'Would this Tig's people kill us if they returned?' he asked, hoping he had said what he meant to say . . . (Man-woman this Tig and this Farrel on the wind – tomorrow, more tomorrow man-woman close to this Tig this Farrel?)

Tig darted to the entrance of the overhang, peered out across the windy downs, looked up to where the branches of the elms waved and weaved across the drifting clouds. He spat violently upwards, came back to Farrel grinning.

'Death (– wind –) has no room for this Tig. If this Farrel stranger will be my friend (– lover? – earth-turner? –) death will spit at this Farrel too.'

'Did death make room for that Burton?'

Tig sat upright and stared deeply into Farrel's eyes. For two days the boy had declined any knowledge of Burton, pretending (obviously pretending) not to understand. Now Farrel pushed his advantage home.

'Does this Tig want this Farrel stranger as a friend? Then this Tig must tell this Farrel where that Burton lives or dies.'

Tig curled up into a ball, burying his head beneath his

arms. He wailed loudly. Farrel was about to ask again when Tig spoke:

'That man-stranger Burton is touching earth. All Tuthanach are touching earth. Not this Tig. Not this Tig. Not this Tig.'

Farrel considered this carefully, not wishing to distress Tig to the point where the boy would leave. He knew that 'touching earth' was something immensely important to the Tuthanach, and he knew that Tig was forbidden his birthright of touching. He could not touch women, he could not touch earth. No love, no involvement with the land. No children for Tig, and no spring harvest as the result of his love for the earth. Poor Tig, denied the two most wonderful consummations of this early agricultural age. But why?

'Where does that Burton touch earth?' he asked.

The boy looked blank.

'Where?' pressed Farrel.

Tig again crawled to the cave entrance and spat into the wind. 'This Tig is just a beast!' he yelled. 'That man-stranger Burton said this Tig is just a beast!'

And with a loud and painful shriek he vanished, running across the downs, a small skin-clad figure, clay-dyed hair sticking stiffly outwards, fat-greased body shimmering in the weak sunlight.

THIRD TRANSMISSION — FIFTH DAY

Still no sign of the boy who ran off three days ago when I questioned him about Burton. I suspect Burton upset

309

him in some way, possibly as simply as calling him names. Burton is 'touching earth' apparently, but I have a suspicion that he is dead and touching it from a few feet under. I hope I'm wrong. But Tig – the boy – has said that *all* his people are touching earth. What can it mean? I see few of the expected signs of agriculture in the area. My hunch is that they are either farming at some distance from the crog, or raiding other neolithic settlements. Time will tell. I confess that I am worried, however. There is no sign of any equipment or any message or record discs of Burton's. I shall continue to search for such things and also for Burton, whether or not he is alive.

I am now encamped in the crog itself. A pack of dogs terrorises me, but they are sufficiently diffident at times that I suspect they belong to the village. They have one useful function – they help keep the wolves at bay. I have seen wolves prowling through the cemetery, near the river. They seem to scent something and occasionally excavate a shallow trench in the earth, but always they leave in apparent panic. They also prowl around the skin wall of the crog, but the bones and shrivelled carcasses of their own kind that hang suspended from tree limbs have some effect of discouraging their entry. The dogs chase them off which concludes the process, but they always return. I am not myself safe from the obviously starving mongrels that are sometimes my guardians. If only Tig were here, he might be able to control them.

My HQ is the largest hut, possibly the headman's house. The inner walls are daubed with eccentric symbols that are identical to the rock carvings in and around the many tumuli. These paintings are absent from other huts, and I may well be in the local shaman's hide-out.

I keep saying 'hut'. I should say tents. The material is deer skin, sewn together with leather thongs. No evidence of weaving, though mats, door edges and light-holes through the tents have been made out of leather threads interlinked in suspiciously familiar ways. Wig-wam style, four or five shaped wooden poles hold the tent upright. Each tent has a fence of carved bone points standing around it, and in the centre of the crog is a group of four low tents, skin stretched over bowed wooden frames making four rooms not high enough to stand in. These have been separated from the rest of the community by a deep ditch. Carved boulders, showing circle patterns, stand both sides of a single earth bridge across the ditch. Is it a sacred enclosure? An empty grain store? I don't know. I've explored the tents thoroughly and there is nothing in them save for a few polished stone beads, some maul-shaped pendants, spirally carved, and a skin cloth containing five amphibolite pestle-hammers, unused I think. Maybe you can work it out. (Ironic, isn't it . . . I'd normally jump to all sorts of conclusions!)

Imagination is the worst enemy still – I'd thought that particular frustration would have stayed behind when I left the future. Ah well. Incidentally – the ditch is probably that small enclosure between the trees at strip-site 20. We're in that sort of area, as I said in my second transmission. Other features along that strip are not in evidence, and may well not be neolithic. I am fairly convinced that this is the Newgrange settlement. There are no other communities in the area, and this one settlement will probably be responsible for all three major tumuli, even though several miles separate them. There's nothing but small burials on the Newgrange site as yet. I wonder when building will begin?

Artifacts? Thousands of drilled stones, pendants, axe and arrow heads; several bows, very short, very limited range; slings, leather of course – two tents used for pottery and some marvellous Carrow-keel pots all lined up ready for firing in small clay and stone kilns. Most of the weapons and stones are clustered inside the skin wall – ready for action? The skin wall itself is two layers of hide, suspended from wooden poles. Human heads have been sewn between the two layers and the outer skins have been drilled with holes so that the dead eyes look out. Although some of the heads are fairly recently severed (both sexes) I can't see Burton's. Hope still flickers.

Head hunting seems to have started even earlier than the pre-Celts, unless these are sacrifices. But no carvings of heads, so perhaps it's just a small part of the culture at the moment.

God, where *are* they all?

It's a marvellous spring. I've never seen so many birds in my life, and the insects!

At dawn of the day following his third transmission, sudden activity among the already noisy lark population of the deserted tents on the western side of the crog brought Farrel running. He recognised the darting grey shape as Tig and called to him. The boy furtively crept out from his hiding place and stared at Farrel, lips slack, eyes dull.

'Glad to see you,' called the man. Tig smiled and slapped his hands together.

'This Tig hungry.'

'This Farrel hungry too. Can this Tig use a sling?' He waved a leather sling he had been practising with. The boy rushed forward, lips wet, eyes wide, snatched the weapon and lovingly caressed the leather. He stared up at Farrel.

'Lark or hare?'

'Which is the tastiest?'

Tig grinned, slapped his stomach, then dropped to his knees and kissed the soil. Jumping to his feet again he ran off out of sight behind the wall of skins, and ultimately out of earshot down a tree-capped slope. He returned after half an hour, blood on his knees, dirt on his face, but carrying two fat white-chested hares. Farrel started a fire in the small outside hearth that seemed to serve as a fire-pit to all the tents in the vicinity. As the wood fire crackled and browned the pungent flesh, Tig threw tiny chips of stone onto the embers. Retrieving one of the fragments Farrel saw it had been scratched with zigzag lines. The patterning, which he recognised as a standard rock-carving of the Boyne Valley area, suggested flame and Tig confirmed this. We take fire from the earth, he explained, so we must make the earth complete again with a small soul-carving.

'But this Farrel didn't carve this. Nor did this Tig. Is that the way it is done?'

Tig immediately became worried. He crawled away from the fire and sat distantly, staring at the smoke. Farrel drew out his mock bone knife, scratched a zigzagging line on the same piece of stone, and cast it onto the flames. Tig grinned and came back to the pit.

'This Tig can't carve. This Tig can't touch earth, or carve soul. But this Farrel is a good soul-carver.' He pointed up into the air and Farrel noticed the smoke rising straight up since the wind had suddenly dropped. He didn't understand the significance, but soon forgot to question it as the meat cooked through. The fats sizzled loudly as they fell on the flame and rich odours brought both man and boy crowding to the tiny spit, eyes aglow with anticipation.

'Ee-Tig, cranno argak ee-eikBurton en-en na-ig?' *You knew Burton?* (This Tig eye-felt wind-felt that Burton man-stranger?)

Tig spat a small bone onto the dying fire. He eyed Farrel suspiciously for a moment, then rose up on his haunches and passed wind noisily. He seemed to find the offensive action very funny. Farrel laughed too, rose up and repeated the action. Tig opened his mouth wide and shrieked with laughter. Farrel repeated his question and Tig spat onto the fire. The saliva hissed and steamed and Tig laughed. Farrel asked for the third time.

'Kok.' *Yes.*

'Ee-eikBurton 'g-cruig tarn baag?' *Is Burton dead and buried?* (That Burton eats earth, skin cold?)

Tig hesitated. Then his hand touched his genitals, his head inclined. He didn't know, but he was uneasy.

'Ee-eikBurton pa-cruig pronok dag?' *Is he alive?* (That Burton kisses earth, urine warm?)

Tig said he didn't know.

'Ee-Tig ganaag ee-Farrel olo ee-eikBurton ee-Farrel ka'en ka-en?' *Are you afraid of me because you think I was Burton's friend?* (This Tig afraid of this Farrel because that Burton this Farrel were not not-strangers?)

'Kok.'

'Ee-Farrel cranno orgak ee-eikBurton. Ee-Farrel en-Burton, 'n nik Farrel.' *I knew him but I didn't like him. I have a woman.* (This Farrel eye-felt wind-felt that Burton. This Farrel not touch/never touch that Burton. This Farrel close/touch woman Farrel.)

What would she think, he wondered, of being used as a sex object to a twelve-year-old moron? Joke. How many thousands of years would it be for the joke to be appreciated? To the Tuthanach, to all the Boyne peoples, denial of friendship to a man had to be coupled with a declaration of friendship with a woman. It seemed so unrealistically simple to believe that a man with a woman whose sexual appetite was high would not have a close male friend . . . (*nik*, woman, implied a sexually aggressive woman; a woman or man without any such desires was called *crum-kii* – stone legs.) It was a bizarre piece of nonsense and yet it appeased. Like the beast that presents its hindquarters to an attacker – submission. The name of the game.

Tig was much happier. He clapped his hands together repeatedly, pausing only to chew a ragged nail on his left index finger.

'Ee-Tig en-Burton. Ee-eikBurton en-Tig. Ee-Tig tarn ee-eikBurton baag na-yit.' *I didn't like Burton either, and he didn't like me. But I killed him some time ago.* (This Tig never touch that Burton. That Burton never touch this Tig. This Tig skin Burton cold several yesterday.)

'A-Tig tarn ee-eikBurton baag?' *You killed him?*

'Ee-Tig . . .' eyes downcast, voice lowering. 'Ka-kok.' *I hope so/I wish to do so/I think so.* Which was it? Farrel felt infuriated with himself. What *had* Tig said?

'Orga-mak ee-eikBurton m'rog?' *Where is Burton's body?* (In all the wind Burton's head?)

'Ee-Tig-ee-Farrel Tig cranno na'yok.' *I'll show you now.* (This Tig this Farrel Tig eye feel high sun.)

FOURTH TRANSMISSION – SIXTH DAY

The simplicity of the language is deceptive, I'm sure. I talk easily with Tig, but have an uncomfortable feeling that he is misunderstanding me in subtle ways. Nevertheless one thing seems sure – Burton is in trouble, and possibly dead, killed at the hands of the backward boy who is now so important to me (while he is in the crog the dogs don't come near). Everyone who should be here is 'touching earth'. You might dispense with that as something unimportant – tilling the ground somewhere? Planting seeds? Nothing of the sort.

Tig led the way across the hills, some miles from the river. The forest is patchy across the downs, never really managing to take a dominant hold on the land – trees in great dense clusters hang to the tops of some hills and the valleys of others so that as one walks across the country there appear to be bald knolls poking through the foliage on all sides. Tig himself is inordinately afraid of the woods and skirts them with such deliberation that I feel some dark memory must be lying within his poor, backward skull.

After about an hour we waded across a small stream and ran swiftly (Tig covering his head with his hands and wailing all the time) through a thinly populated woodland, emerging on the rising slope of one such bald hill that I had seen earlier. Boulders probed through the soil which was perhaps not deep enough to support the tree life. There were shallow carvings on many of the boulders and Tig touched some of these reverently. Most noticeable about this hill, and most puzzling – and indeed, most alarming – was the profusion of small earth mounds, overgrown with a sparse layer of grass and invisible from any substantial distance. Tig ran among these mounds, the highest of which was no more than four or five inches from the ground and vaguely cross-shaped, and eventually found a resting position on one of the least carved boulders. His stiffly crouched figure seemed overwhelmed by fear and regret, his hair sticking out from his head like some bizarre thorn growth, his thin limbs smeared with dirt and crusted with his own faeces. He stared at me with an expression of total confusion and I tried to put him at his ease but he turned half away from me and began to vocalise an imitation of the lark song that echoed around us from the vast early spring population.

I asked him about Burton and he merely clapped his hands together and shrilled all the louder.

You will have the picture – I appeared to be standing in a wide and irregularly laid-out cemetery. Crouching over the nearest mound I excavated a little of the earth away. A few inches below the surface my fingernails raked flesh and came away bloody!

I can't explain it but I panicked completely. Some terrible dread crept into my whole body, some inexplicable fear of what I was witnessing. I left Tig sitting there singing with the larks and starlings and ran back to the crog. I shook for hours and failed to sleep that night. The blood beneath my nails clotted and blackened and when I tried to wash it away it wouldn't come. In my frantic efforts to clean the stain I tore one of my nails right back to the quick and that sudden, appalling pain brought me back to my senses. I can't explain it. My reaction was panic. Something external possessed me for an instant and I was psychologically unready for the power of it. There is something in the ground of that hill, and I don't just mean a body.

I shall return tomorrow and report again.

Farrel left the crog at dawn. The grass was wet underfoot, and across the valley a heavy mist hung silent and sombre. The birds seemed quieter today and what song he heard was often drowned by the murmur of the trees and the disturbing crying of the wind.

Strange, he thought, how mist seems to tangle itself in the forest, hanging in the branches like cotton.

He made his way back towards the strange cemetery on the hill, stopping occasionally to listen to the stillness, hoping to hear Tig crashing towards him, or calling him. When he emerged onto the hillside the mist had lifted and he could see, from the top of the knoll, the river Boyne and the scattered tumuli of the Tuthanach. He could see the hills where, in the next few years, work would begin on the massive sheer-fronted mounds of Newgrange. Who or what, he wondered, would be honoured by that vast structure? And who or what would be honoured by the second and third giant tumuli, built to the east and west of Newgrange at almost the same time (and not centuries earlier as the dating techniques of Farrel's time had suggested).

Of Tig there was no sign. The larks began to sing quite suddenly and sunlight pierced the early morning clouds, setting the forest alive with light and colour. As if – reflected Farrel – some force of night and cold had suddenly gone. Normal service being resumed . . .

Where he had dug in the soil of one of the human burial places yesterday, there was now no sign of interference. The earth was smooth and quite firmly packed. Tig, probably, had repaired the damage.

Farrel wasted no time in excavating down to the flesh again. He felt a cold unease as he cleared the soil from the naked back of the Tuthanach male, that same surge of panic, but today he controlled it. He scooped the earth out of the narrow trench until the man's body lay exposed from head to buttocks. Face down in the mud the man looked dead; his skin was cold and pale grey, the pallor of death. His arms were outstretched on either side and Farrel, on impulse, dug the soil away from one limb to discover the fingers, clenched firm into the earth as if gripping.

Turning the man's head over Farrel felt a jolt of disgust, a fleeting nausea. Open mouthed, open eyed, the earth was everywhere. It fell from the pale lips, a huge bolus of soil, dry, wormy. It fell from his nostrils and from his ears – it packed across his eyeballs, under the lids, like some obscene blindness.

Surely the man was dead; but the flesh was firm – cold, yet not in that rigidity associated with recent death, nor the moving liquefaction associated with decay. Easing the body down again Farrel put his ear to the naked back, listened for the heart.

For a long time he heard nothing. Minutes passed and he felt sure the heart was dead. Then . . .

A single powerful beat. Unmistakable!

Over the course of half an hour Farrel ascertained that the buried man's heart was beating once every four minutes, a powerful, unnaturally sustained contraction, as if the organ were forcing round some viscous fluid and not the easy liquid blood it was used to . . .

An unnerving thought occurred to Farrel and for a second he was ready to cut a vein in the man's hand – but, quite irrationally, fear of what he would find dripping from the body held him back until he recollected the blood under his fingernails and felt a strange relief.

He stood above the body, staring down at the un-dead corpse, then let his gaze wander across the countryside. The spring breeze irritated his scalp by catching the clay-stiffened strands of his hair and bending them at its will. As he stood on the knoll he grew irritated with his make-up and wished he could be clothed in denim shorts and a loose cotton shirt instead of being wrapped in skin that smelled of its previous owner and attracted flies.

Everything, bar this cemetery, was so normal.

The tumuli, the crog, the weapons and pottery, the hunting, the language – it was all just what he had expected, a new stone age colony, conscious of religion, of its ancestry, its future and its agriculture, a colony just a few generations into its life in this green and bountiful land. Further north and south were other communities. Farrel had seen the signs of them, and had read reports about them from previous expeditions to this time. Some were larger than the Tuthanach, some already showing different cultural styles. They all seemed to mix and mingle together (so Tig said) to exchange ideas, to form joint hunting trips during the winter, to compare art forms and techniques of etching them into the rock. They were basically agricultural and peaceful. They feared the Moaning Ones from the earth, and the rock stealers from across the sea, some miles to the east. But for the most part they lived without fear, growing and maturing, becoming ready to accept the new Age of Bronze, still some eight hundred years in their future, at a time when the peacefulness of this country would be shattered by the new sounds of metal clashing with metal.

All those settlements had mixed together and had welcomed Burton – so he had reported – during his first four days in the valley. He had not told them from where he came (his arrival site, like Farrel's) for if the Ceinarc and the Tagda were passively afraid of the Moaning Ones and the Breton raiders, they held a healthy and active hostility for one other thing – crog-Tutha, and the insane settlers from beyond the forest. They would not float their coracles through the wide bend of the Boyne that took them round the foot of the Tuthanach hills, with their scattered mounds and shrieking women. It was a fearsome area, and one where no man could go and return unpossessed.

Reading the reports five thousand years away, Farrel had at first thought this to be a typical piece of forest-fearing, with the settlement on the wrong side of that forest being linked to those same dark forces. He had dismissed them aloud.

Now he realised he shouldn't have dismissed them at all.

There was something wholly unnatural about the people of crog-Tutha. He had travelled more than five thousand years through time and expected surprises – but he had not anticipated being so totally mystified. This was not the simple life of a primitive people – it was something out of the dark corners of the super-natural!

No-one up-time would believe him, he was sure of that.

. . . and as I filled the grave back in, Tig appeared at the edge of the wood. He ran up the hill and crouched over the mound, watching fascinated as I covered the body of the Tuthanach. I get the feeling that Tig, when he vanishes, is never far away. I always have an acutely uncomfortable feeling of being watched, and I suspect that wherever I go Tig is never far behind. What do I represent to him, I wonder? He is afraid of me still, and still refuses to show me where Burton is buried (if indeed he *is* buried). There are too many mounds on the knoll to excavate them all on an off-chance, so I really do need the boy to open up a little more.

I sat for an hour or so, on a boulder, looking across the forest to where the great crog on Tara was in evidence as a winding spiral of black smoke. The encampment there, Tig tells me, is surrounded by a wooden post-fence and seems to be more hostile than the other crogs. He says they are raising earthworks behind the wooden walls; does that suggest the first dun is being raised on the site? Fascinating. I have no idea how Tig knows this. Tara lies four days to the south. Would he wander that far?

While I watched Tara Tig sat quietly, chewing moodily on the remnants of one of those hares. I didn't ask him about Burton, or about anything. I hoped he would tell me of his own accord. His eyes suddenly grew wide and the bone dropped from his fingers. He was looking up at the knoll and I turned to see what had scared him.

It gave me quite a turn too, and I don't blame Tig for scampering off.

One of the graves was moving, as if the body it contained was trying to force its way out. As if . . . ? First the man's hands poked through the ground, the fingers bloody and dirty. Then the earth fell away from where his head was raising up and his whole body followed. He stood upright, black with dirt, and earth fell from his ears and mouth. He spat violently and shook more vigorously, brushing soil from his chest and arms. I hid behind the boulder and watched as the strange apparition turned slowly round, looking upwards into the sky through eyes still caked with dirt. He was sexually aroused and the skin of his penis was lacerated and dripping blood profusely. I have the uncomfortable feeling that he had been copulating with the earth.

Several minutes of brushing and shaking exposed his skin again, cleared his eyes and nostrils and he seemed to get his bearings. He swept back his hair, which showed yellow through the mud, and ran off down the knoll, leaping the mounds and entering the woodlands with loud shrieks and painful crashes.

I followed him to a small stream, a tributary of the Boyne, and watched him crouching in the flow, washing and splashing, and emptying his bowels of a phenomenal amount of soil. He warbled bird song and laughed in abrupt, almost humourless bursts. He seemed to wash himself for hours, but finally crawled up onto the bank and sat quietly for a while, obviously sensing and enjoying the scenery around him. Then he rose to his feet, waded the stream, and vanished towards the crog.

That all occurred a few minutes ago and it means I shall not return there myself. I'm too puzzled and too frightened if you must know. I have my transmission equipment with me, but medication and field-link pack are still in the crog, which means I'm trapped here for a while, and must be careful not to injure myself.

When Farrel arrived back at the knoll Tig was crouched over one of the mounds, the only one to show a good grassy overlay, and poking at it. He saw Farrel approaching and ran away, leapt onto a boulder and slapped his hands together.

Farrel stared at him for a moment, then at the grave, and an icy unease crept into his mind. Oh no, he thought. Oh God, this is the moment.

The boy gibbered something incoherent.

Farrel asked, 'Ee-eikBurton 'n cruig pad-cruig?' *Is Burton buried here?* . . . (Touching earth, feet on earth?)

'Don't know.'

Farrel sensed the lie. He dropped to his knees and scrabbled at the soil and after a moment he found himself staring at black hair, the back of Burton's head. 'Thank God,' cried Farrel, and grinned at the boy.

What should he do though? It might be dangerous to move the man – the best thing would be to leave Burton alone until the strange process had finished and he resurrected himself in the 'natural' way.

But Farrel found he could not resist examining his colleague in the same way as he had examined the

Tuthanach earlier. He scraped back the earth from Burton's head and shoulders.

A funny smell.

For a moment his hands hesitated; he stared silently and motionlessly at the body beneath him. The skin was grey, cold – that was, by all accounts, normal. But there was something wrong, something indefinable, something not quite right.

He reached down and turned Burton's head sideways. Earth poured from empty sockets, worms fell from the gaping, toothy mouth. Where skin remained it was taut and shrunken. Putrefaction rose from the rotting brains through the holes in the skull, driving Farrel to his feet with a terrible cry.

Sweeping back the earth from the torso he found the thigh bone fragment that had been driven into Burton's heart as he lay there, thrusting through the rib cage from behind, ripping skin and flesh and cracking bone. The clenched fists of his colleague took on a new significance. He had died in agony.

For a moment Farrel screamed abuse at Tig for what he had done, then his anger drained away. There was something in the boy's eyes, something in his expression . . . Farrel felt instantly terrified. He reached out towards Tig and shook his head.

'I'm sorry, Tig. Burton called you a beast . . . I understand . . .'

'Not once. Many times,' said Tig. 'I hated Burton. I gave Burton everything he had earned.'

Tentatively Farrel touched the boy's shoulder and when Tig did not flinch he secured the grip and smiled.

'Burton was not my friend . . . but he was known to me and he was important to me. I was upset to see him dead. Forgive me, Tig. I didn't mean what I said.'

'I didn't understand what you said.'

Farrel, guiltily, realised he had shouted in English. He laughed quietly, almost thankfully. He wouldn't have wanted the boy to hear what he had called him. He needed sleep too much and the boy was potentially very lethal.

He walked back to Burton's body and covered it over. A few feet away another mound began to move and Farrel and Tig ran out of sight and watched.

SIXTH TRANSMISSION – EIGHTH DAY

Burton is dead. Tig killed him, perhaps some months ago. I am terrified of Tig now and don't dare question him further about Burton. If only I knew where Burton's equipment was hidden. Tig knows, I'm sure of it. He has hidden it. I pray that in the same way that he indicated Burton's grave to me (uncompromisingly) he will lead me to Burton's records. Burton understood what I have been watching, he must have done – he participated.

Meanwhile I am back in the cave and Tig, now, is in full control. I sleep fitfully and in snatches – terrified of him striking when my defences are down. I woke, last night, to find him crouching over me, peering at my sleeping face. I dare not ask him to refrain from startling me like this. My head hurts and my heart is in pain, as if

327

in anticipation of a long-bone shaft being driven through it.

I can't get my field-link equipment. The crog is active again. Over the last day many Tuthanach have risen from the earth and returned to their homes – men, women, children, they return with bountiful energy and begin to lead a life no different from the Ceinarc or the Tagda – what *were* they doing in the earth? What have they gained? What was the purpose of it all?

SEVENTH TRANSMISSION – TENTH DAY

The trickle of Tuthanach returning to their crog has ceased. They are all home. I remain in the cave, uncertain, insecure. Tig hunts on my behalf, but no longer eats with me. He has become very affectionate, but behind the kindness is a repressed anger that I truly fear. Sometimes he stands in the cave entrance and shrieks with laughter. The garble of words he yells refers to Burton and to me, and I hear 'stone legs' and 'twisting head', two favourite Tuthanach insults. He invariably ends his tirade of abuse by defecating in the cave mouth and elaborately holding his nose and backing away. And a few hours later he brings me a hare or a brace of fat doves, some gift, some appeasement for his show of fury. A bizarre boy and not – I now realise – backward at all, but in some way insane. Listen to me! Do I understand the meaning of my own words any more? What do I mean – *insane?* Is my behaviour sane? Tig is more than just a boy. I suspect he was chosen for his role – Tig-never-touch-woman-never-touch-earth; the only Tuthanach not to touch earth in the strange way I have described . . . why? Why Tig? Or should I ask, why *one Tuthanach*? What was he watching for? What are they asking of him now? What role does he fill?

Tig seems aware of some finality in his role. On his most recent visit he came with a large chunk of meat – deer, I think. Tears filled his eyes as he passed the joint to me and accepted a small portion back. We ate in silence. As he chewed he watched me, and tears flooded down his cheeks. 'Farrel, my friend, my dear friend,' he said, over and over. The warmth was immense. The Tuthanach have no way of expressing magnificent friendship and he struggled to voice his feelings and I eventually had to stop him. I had understood. 'Farrel and Tig are the only ones not to touch earth,' he said. 'Tig can't, but Farrel . . .'

Time and time again he began that sentence, staring at me. Each time he said it I was filled with his intensity, and with my own anxiety. The thought is terrifying, truly terrifying.

Then the anger from the boy, the shrieking. He raced out into the dusk and vanished swiftly. I face another night alone, more than half afraid to close my eyes . . . not just Tig, though that is certainly a part of it, but the past . . . my past. I am haunted by memories and faces; they fill my dreams, and I can sense my own time in everything I smell or see here. It is insecurity that makes me rue the warmth of civilisation, and I shall not bend to any great desire to return; but it hurts, sometimes. Sometimes it really hurts.

Three days after the seventh transmission two Tutha-nach males came to the cave and crouched in its en-trance watching Farrel. They were both middle-aged, dark-haired, and their skin was decorated with green and blue dye: circles around their eyes, lines across their cheeks, elaborate patterns on their breasts and bellies. They looked angry. Farrel remained quite still, trying to hide his fear.

Then Tig came slipping into the cave, boisterous and noisy as ever. Farrel tried to piece together something from the boy's excited gabble, but all he could make out were words for 'woman' and the insult 'stone legs'.

A tension grew in the pit of Farrel's stomach and wild thoughts filled his mind. What was Tig up to?

The next thing he knew he was being chased from the cave by the two men. Tig grinned at him, and winked elaborately. 'Soul curers,' he said, pointing to them. 'Make soul good for this Farrel. Make this Farrel's soul ready for earth.' And he patted his loins.

Farrel felt terrified.

They took him to the crog and led him inside the skin wall, past the fire pit and to a smaller circle of skins around which were grouped several women and chil-dren. He was led to a small tent and pushed to the ground. Making no attempt to speak to him, nor demon-strating any puzzlement over him, the men left. After a while one of the younger women got up and walked across to him.

By that time, realising that his sexual need was far more intense than he had admitted to himself for the last few days, Farrel was lost in thoughts of his past.

He saw the Tuthanach woman through a blur of remembered faces, saturated bodies and irritatingly noisy beds. He smelled her through an imagined veil of perfumes, cigarette smoke and the salty and erotic smell of sweat. He felt pain as he remembered these things, a real pain, unlocalised. The woman had crouched before him, her wool skirt drawn up above her knees so that she displayed her white and grossly fat thighs to Farrel's casual gaze. He tried not to think too hard about what he saw.

Then she extended her hand and cocked her head to one side, smiling broadly, letting him see that only two of her teeth were missing.

Farrel took her hand, pressed the cool, firm fingers and noticed how the woman's palm was sweating like his. The past surged into his mind, agony:

A girl he had known for years as a friend. He had been taking his leave of her small, two-roomed apartment, conscious that his wife would start to worry soon. With his usual calculated shyness he had reached out and shaken her hand again, playing at being nervous. 'I don't like all this hand shaking,' she had said, in a way that made him realise that she had wanted to say it on previous occasions. 'I'd much rather have a cuddle.' So he'd cuddled her, and she hadn't let him draw away. She was tall and lean and felt awkward against his stocky, muscular body. But it had been a long moment, and a good one.

He realised he was excited and the Tuthanach woman was pleased. Her breath was sour as she leaned across him, her left hand gripping him gently between the legs; she kissed each cheek and then the tip of his nose. Then she rose and tugged him to his feet, pulled him into the tent and slipped off her clothes.

She picked up a stone chip, artificially smoothed by all appearances, and made marks on it with a piece of flint. Farrel watched her as he undressed. Her breasts were full and plump at the ends, flat and sac-like where they grew from her body. He hated that. She smelled of animal grease and smoke (as did he) and of something else, something pungent and sexual and offensive. Spitting on the stone she grinned at Farrel and passed it to him, indicating that he should do the same. As he spat he saw the crude phallus she'd drawn on the rock. With her thumb she rubbed the spittle into the sandstone, and laughed as she lay back on the skin-covered floor. She patted her belly with the fragment. She still said nothing.

As Farrel climbed onto her recumbent body and tried to find her he noticed that she popped the stone into her mouth and swallowed it.

They made love for about ten minutes. At the end of it she was obviously disappointed, and Farrel for no reason that he could identify felt like crying.

EIGHTH TRANSMISSION – FIFTEENTH DAY

It has begun. Newgrange, I mean – the building has begun. Yesterday I crept around the crog and went to

332

the hills overlooking the Boyne, where the cemetery is located. There was much activity down by the river, men and women gathering water-rolled granite boulders for the facing of the mound; they carry these, one per person, in a great chain up the hillside and the piles grow large. Earth is being excavated from several sites ready for the tumulus. Several small tombs on the site have been demolished for the earth and rock they can offer. The past no longer matters. Only the great tumulus seems to concern them now. The first massive ortho-stats have been dragged to the site, and an artist is working on what can only be the small lintel that will lie above the passage entrance. The work, especially the art, will take many months. The air is filled with the sharp sounds of repeated picking blows as symbols and designs are carved on the dressed rocks, ready for in-corporation into the tomb. The speed with which they work is fantastic, but the job they face is enormous. Who will be buried here? Who will be honoured?

I walked closer to the activity, managing to remain undetected behind some trees, and watched the artists at work. Imagine my surprise when I discovered Tig direct-ing the symbol-carving operations! Some thirty men, all old, all frail, were crouched beside or above their slabs and each worked on specifications laid down by the darting, probing, shouting form of the boy.

I watched fascinated for a while, until the sun, beating bright and hot upon my naked back, drove me away to a shadier place. Tig must have caught sight of me because, as I crept down the hill towards the slopes rising to the unbuilt mound of Knowth, he came racing after me, calling my name.

'It will be a huge mound,' he said, breathing heavily. 'A great temple.'

'A temple to who, Tig?'

But he just laughed and slapped his hands together. 'They have all forgotten the symbols of the earth, and the wind, and fire and water,' he babbled happily. 'This is why I was left behind, to remember, to teach them . . .' He was obviously delighted about it. 'Soon this Tig shall no longer be Tig-never-touch-woman.'

'Will this Tig touch earth?' I asked him.

He fell moody, but brightened suddenly and grinned. 'This Tig never touch earth always . . . but this Farrel . . . this Farrel will touch earth soon . . . this Farrel will understand and learn the symbols.'

'This Tig might kill me,' I said carefully. 'Like he killed that Burton.'

He slapped his genitals repeatedly, not hard, but apparently quite painfully for he winced visibly. 'If this Tig kills this Farrel may legs turn to stone.'

And at that moment . . . I felt the compulsion, the fascination to discover, the intrigue, filling me like some uncontrollable ecstasy, like a psychological magnet pulling me down towards the earth. Tig danced happily about . . . had he seen my possession? He ran off, then, shouting back over his shoulder, 'This Farrel knows where to go.'

I am torn between desire to know, and fear of knowing. I keep seeing Burton's rotted corpse, lying there, denied that same knowledge by a thin shaft of bone and a vengeful child. But I also remember the pull of the earth, the feel of magic and glory, the glimpse (for glimpse is what it was) of some great power lying beneath the grass . . .

I will have to make my choice soon.

Farrel knew where to go all right. He thought about the knoll and its now empty burden of graves, and as the night wore on and a heavy rain began to drum across the countryside, sending icy rivulets across the uneven rock floor of his cave, so the knoll, dark and invisible in the night, seemed to beckon to him. Tig writhed before him, a boy at the mercy, the whim, of forces dying, but still far greater than any that man had ever conceived of, either now or in Farrel's own time, far in the future. And yet, perhaps that was wrong – perhaps the people of this time *had* conceived of the sons and daughters of the earth who somehow, inexplicably, were directing the destiny of the Tuthanach. Perhaps it was only with time and greater self awareness that man came to forget the spirits and guardians of all that he surveyed, the rock and stones, the trees and winds, the earth, the vast earth, mother . . .

She called to him and Farrel responded with fear. They had been with him for some time, directing his thoughts, but their touch was tenuous, uneasy. Farrel drew back into his cave and covered his head, blocked his ears and eyes and tried not to see or hear or feel what was coming to him: he tried not to think of it, but he could not empty his mind of their presence.

He screamed, confused and terrified by the strangeness of the contact. Dark-eyed, shivering with cold and terror, he cowered in his cave until morning, and dawnlight, and peace again.

He ran across the storm-threatened land, pacing heavily on the saturated turf, waiting for the next cloudburst. Tig scampered towards him and he felt a great sense of relief.

The boy saw his fear and laughed, jumped high in the air, then clapped his hands together in glee.

'What does it mean?' cried Farrel.

Tig-never-touch-woman-never-touch-earth dropped to his haunches and plunged his fingers between the tightly knotted grass mat.

'This Farrel is being prepared to touch earth,' he said. 'Don't be afraid.'

'But this Farrel *is* afraid. This Farrel is terrified!'

'There is no need to be,' said Tig, suddenly less childish. He watched Farrel through bright, deep brown eyes. Grease and paint were smeared about his cheeks and chin, a meaningless mosaic of colour and half formed design. The wind blew suddenly strong and Tig shivered. He rose to his feet and glanced up, rapping his thin arms around his naked torso. Farrel too hunched up and followed the boy's gaze into the heavens, where dark clouds and lancing sunlight played confusing chase games across the valley.

'What is going to happen to this Farrel?' asked the man.

Tig smiled, almost patronisingly. 'Wonderful things.'

'What is underneath the grass? What is hidden there?'

'This Farrel will soon know. Fear is unnecessary. This Farrel will lose nothing he has not already lost.'

Farrel stared at him, feeling suddenly old, suddenly alien.

'What has this Farrel lost?'

Tig grinned. 'His past, his people, his dreams, his strange images. This Tig never understood them, never understood the words. This has always been between us. When this Farrel has touched the earth they will be gone. We will build the temple together: we will build our dreams and our people together.'

'It sounds magnificent,' said Farrel. 'But this Farrel is still afraid.'

Tig laughed again. 'Afraid of the earth?' He scuffed the ground with his bare feet. 'Afraid of clouds? Afraid of sun?'

'Afraid of . . .' He stopped, unsure. 'This Farrel doesn't know what of.'

Tig slapped his hands together, shook his head. 'This Farrel should go back to the cave. Wait there. When you are called, go to them. Go to them.'

Unquestioningly, resigned to his bizarre fate, Farrel turned and walked back to the overhang.

By dusk it was raining again.

She called to him and again Farrel responded. He was still afraid, but Tig's words, his reassuring attitude, helped him overwhelm that fear and put it from his mind.

He walked through the driving rain, the clay in his

hair running into his eyes and mouth, giving him a foretaste of the great oral consumation to come. He swallowed the clay, tasted its texture, wept as he ran through the rain, through the moaning woods. Behind him, high on a hill, torch light burned beneath a skin shelter where an artist worked on stone late into the night, anxious to express the earth symbols that he had relearned from the one boy who had not forgotten. He was an artist who added his soul to the rock and the rock to the temple . . . a temple to the earth gods, Woman in the Hill, Dying Father Thunder, those who inhabited the boulders and the wind, the clouds, and the running mud, the grassy turf of uncountable acres of virgin earth.

Through the night and the rain Farrel ran, until he found himself, without thinking, on the knoll that rose above the woods, the great source of earth energy that he had tapped so briefly, so frighteningly, several days before. And here he lay down on the ground, in the trench left by one of the Tuthanach, and stretched out his arms—

Gripped the mother's flesh—

Penetrated the mother's fertile womb, ejaculated with the ecstasy of contact—

Ate her breast, drank the cold and grainy milk of her glands, felt it flood into his body, through the apertures of his prostrate corpse, driving the substances of his canals before it, replacing his warmth with its own loving cold. Earth closed over his back, the rain filtering through ran down his skin, drained deep into the tissues of the soil below. His lungs filled with mud – he

breathed deeply and after a moment his heart stopped, his breathing stopped . . . suspended, touching the
earth.

Almost immediately they were there, rising out of the
deep rock, flowing through the earth and the pores of the
soil, entering Farrel's body through the tips of finger and
penis, down the earth bridge that extended along the
convolutions of his gut. He was consumed by them,
consumed them for his own part, welcomed them and
heard their dying greeting, the words that had flowed
through the minds of the Tuthanach during the weeks
previous . . .

I am earth, Farrel, I am the earth, I am of earth, the earth
is within me and without me, I am soil and rock,
diamond and jade, ruby and clay, mica and quartz, I am
the litter of the dead who live in crystalline echo in the
sediments of sea and lake, I am ground, I am woman
who suckles the infant flesh of man and beast, I am
womb and anus, mouth and nose and ear of the great
world lover, I am cave and tunnel, bridge and haven, I
am the sand that sucks, the field that flourishes, I am
root and clay, I am life pre-carnate, I am dirt, who has
been called Nooma and Shaan, and is Tutha and Cein,
and will be Ga-Tum-Dug and Nisaba, I will be Geshtin
and Tammuz and my branches will be earth against the
sky and all will be one, I will be Faunus and I will
be Consus, I will be Pellervoinen and Tapio, I will be
Luonnotar who floats on white water and touches the
wind, I will be Asia and Asia-Bussu, Lug and Jesus, I will

339

be coal and ore and I have existed since a time of desolation and of thunder and of sterility – you, Farrel, who know all these things should know also that this is the moment of our great dying, the breath of wind passing out of the body of earth and into the memory of man . . .

A second voice: I am wind, who has been called God-singer by the Kalokki who were the first men, and is called Tag and Feng-po, and Huaillapenyi, I am breath and life, I am death, the rising odour of decay, I am storm and rage, light and dark, I am thunder and fear, I am the changing seasons of time, I am the urger of seas and the calmer of wings, I will be remembered as Taranis and Wotan, Thor and Zephyrus and Ga-oh and Hino and my thunder shall be heard until the final fire, but you, Farrel, who knows all these things, should know also that this is the moment of our great sorrow, where we abandon our domain and enter the minds of men, for only in the minds of man can we continue to survive . . .

And others, then, crowding in, jostling to be heard: I am fire who is Tinedia, who will be Svarogich and Sun and Steropes . . . I am water who is Uisceg . . . I am sky . . . I am serpent . . . All these Farrel heard and consumed, and then they fell away, back into the rock, up into the wind, leaving just a fragment of each god, a morsel of each great being, settling in his crowded mind.

He rose from the earth, shaking his body and feeling

the dirt and clay fall from his limbs and his mouth and his eyes. The day was cold; he was conscious of rain, of heavy cloud, of a dullness about the saturated countryside: he loved this. Some greater or lesser part of him was aware that a full two seasons must have passed while he lay in his intimate embrace with the earth. From this same greater or lesser part of him came an alien thought, a last tearful cry from his dead future; *truly a great and noble glory will have gone by my time of glass and steel.*

The new born child turned to regard the virgin land. Rain beat against him, washed him. He opened his mouth to drink it and his laughter joined the gentle sounds of the natural world.

I've found life, at last, at last . . .

The great gods were still there, he thought, as he blinked rain away and stared at the greenness all around him. They were dying, now, committing their great suicide, surviving only in the Tuthanach and their children, and their grandchildren, and so on until they were spread everywhere . . . this they were doing as a gesture of acquiescence to man, but just by staring through the rain, through the unspoiled distance, the man called Farrel could see those gods, could feel them and smell them and hear them.

As he ran down the knoll he could sense them, too, in the brightness of his mind. They were with him by inheritance when he came here, and now they had come direct and he was ecstatic at the greater awareness they had brought him of so many things . . . over the centuries their presence would dilute and become weak and perhaps they had not reckoned on that.

There was plenty of time for them to explore him and understand how things would be. As far as Farrel was concerned there were more important things to do than worry over a day and an age when he would be dust and ashes.

He was a part of the earth, now, a man of the earth, a Tuthanach. His people were building a temple to the earth, and he knew how magnificent that temple would be, for he had seen it. He would mark the rocks of the temple with his soul, raise the walls of the temple with his sweat, and fill the temple with his ecstasy. He ran faster across the rain-soaked land until he could hear the sounds of the stone being carved.

The earth went with him.

The Bone Forest

Time past and time future
Allow but a little consciousness.

T.S. Eliot

I

The sound of his sons' excited shouting woke Huxley abruptly at three in the morning. His breath frosting in the freezing room, he shivered his way into his dressing gown, tugged on slippers, and walked darkly and swiftly to the boys' room.

'What the devil – ?'

They were standing at the window, two small, excited shapes, their breath misting the glass. Steven turned and said excitedly, 'A snow woman. In the garden. We saw a snow woman!'

Rubbing the glass for clarity, Huxley peered down at the thick snow that covered the lawn and gardens, and extended, without break, into the field and to the nearby wood. He could just see the fence, a thin dark line in the moongrey landscape. The night was still, heavy with the muffling silence of the snow. He could see clearly enough that a set of deep tracks led from the gate, towards the house, then round to the side.

'What do you mean? A snow woman?'

'All white,' Christian breathed. 'She stopped and looked at us. She had a sack on her shoulder, like Father Christmas.'

Huxley smiled and ruffled the boy's hair. 'You think she's bringing presents?'

'Hope so,' said Steven. In the dark room his eyes glittered. He had just turned eight years old, a precocious and energetic child, and Huxley was conscious of the extent to which he neglected the lad. Steven was forever soliciting instruction, or games, or walks, but there was so much to do, and Huxley rarely had time for frivolity.

The wood. There was so much to map. So much to discover . . .

He found the torch and went down to the back door, opening it wide (pushing against the drifted snow) and shining the beam across the silent yards. Steven huddled by him. His elder brother Christian had returned to bed, cold, teeth chattering.

'What did she look like, this woman? Was she young? Old?'

'Not very old,' Steven whispered. He was holding on to his father's dressing gown. 'I think she was looking for somewhere to sleep. She was going towards, the sheds.'

'Dressed in white. Not very old. Carrying a bag. Did she wave at you?'

'She smiled. I think . . .'

By the light of the torch he could see the tracks. He listened hard but there was no sound. Nothing in the chicken hut was being disturbed. He closed the back door, looked out of the front, shining the torch around the wide drive and the garages.

Bolting the door closed he chased his son up to bed, then tucked himself down below the covers, taking ages to get the circulation back into his frozen hands and feet. Jennifer slept soundly next to him, a hunched, curled lump below the eiderdown.

Not even wild horses could wake her when the weather was as cold as this.

4 JANUARY 1935

What had woken the boys? Did she call to them? They say not. They were aware of her in some secret way. Steven especially is attuned to the woodland. And it is he who has called this latest visitor from the edge 'Snow Woman'. It may be that she is nothing more than a traveller, using the shelter of Oak Lodge as she makes her way towards Shadoxhurst, or Grimley, one of the towns around. But I am increasingly aware that the wood sheds its mythagos in the night, and that they journey into the unreal world of our reality, before decaying and fading, like the leaf and woodland matter that they are. There have been too many glimpses of these creatures, and insufficient contact. But in the spring, with Wynne-Jones, I shall make the longest journey yet. If we can succeed in passing the Wolf Glen and entering more deeply, then with luck we should begin to make a firmer contact with the products of our own 'mythago-genesis'.

He closed the book and locked it with the small key he kept hidden in his desk, then stood and stretched, yawning fiercely as he tried to wake up a little more. A tall, lean man of forty-five, he was inclined to stoop, especially when writing, and he suffered agonies of back pain. He took little exercise, apart from the long treks into Ryhope Wood, and, as happened every winter, he was allowing himself to become unkempt. His hair was long, hanging over his collar slightly, and with its burden of grey in the oak brown, he was beginning to look older than he was, especially now that he had a winter's growth of grizzled beard (to be removed before he started teaching again, in a week's time).

The diary in which he had just written was not his regular journal, the scientific record of his discoveries and experiments with Wynne-Jones. This was a more private book in which he was keeping a log of 'uncertainties'. He didn't want Steven or Christian reading accounts of his study of *them*. Nor Jennifer. Nor did he want his dreams read, but the dreams he recorded, after visiting the wood, were sometimes so appalling that even he had difficulty in confronting them. These were private thoughts, a private record, for analysis in quieter times.

He kept this second log hidden behind the bookcase where his journals were shelved. He placed the book there now, then tugged on his Wellington boots and overcoat. It was just after dawn, seven thirty or so, and he was aware of two things: the odd silence of the day outside (no clamour from the chicken house), and the second set of tracks through the snow.

These led back, almost in parallel with the first. He could see, now, as he followed them at a distance, that a coat or cloak had trailed between the prints. The right step dragged slightly, as if the woman had been limping.

At the gate, which opened to a track and then a field, there was a crush of snow where the visitor had climbed over and fallen, or struggled upright. Beyond the gate the tracks led down towards the winter wood, and Huxley stood there for a while, staring at the tall, black trees, and the dense infill of bright green holly. Even in winter Ryhope Wood was impossible to enter. Even in winter it was not possible to see inwards more than fifty yards. Even in winter it could work its magic, and dissolve perception in an instant, spinning the visitor round and confusing him utterly.

There was such wonder in there. So much to learn. So much to find. So much 'legend' still living. He had only just begun!

Steven appeared in the doorway, wrapped up warmly in muffler, school overcoat and boots. He sank in snow up to his knees and had to wade with great difficulty towards his father, his cheeks red, his face alive with pleasure.

'You're up early,' Huxley called to his son. Steven bent down and scooped up a snowball. He flung it and missed, laughing, and Huxley thought about returning fire, but was too intrigued by what he might find in the chicken hut. He was aware of the look of disappointment on Steven's face, but blanked it.

Steven followed him at a distance.

There was no sound from the ramshackle chicken house. This was unnerving.

When he opened the door he smelled death at once, and half gagged. He was used to the smell of a fox-attacked hut, but often the scent of the fox itself was the odour that was most prominent. There was only the smell of raw meat, now, and he stepped into the slaughterhouse and his mind failed to comprehend what he could see.

Whoever had been here had made a bed of the chickens. There had been twenty birds and they had been torn into fragments, and the fragments, featherside up, had been spread about to make a mattress.

The heads had been threaded onto a length of primitive flax, which was looped across the hut from one shelf to another.

A small patch of burning, with charred bones, told of the fire and the meal that 'Snow Woman' had created for herself.

Expecting mayhem, finding such order in the slaughter, such ritual, Huxley backed out of the hut and closed the door, puzzled and perturbed. The sound of such slaughter should have been deafening. He had heard nothing. And yet he had lain awake for most of the night, after the boys had disturbed him.

The chickens had made no sound as they'd died, and the smoke from the fire had not reached the house.

Aware that Steven was standing by him, looking anxiously at the chicken house, Huxley led the boy away, hand on his shoulder.

'Are they all right?'

'A fox,' Huxley said bluntly, and felt a moment's irritation as he realised that his tone was callous. 'It's sad, but it happens.'

Steven had not failed to understand the meaning of his father's words. He looked shocked and pained. 'Are they *all* dead? Like in the story?'

'They're all dead. Old Foxy's got them all.' Huxley rested a comforting hand on the boy's shoulder. 'We'll go to the farm later and buy some more, shall we? I'm sorry, Steve. Who'd be a chicken, eh?'

The boy was disconsolate, but remained obedient, looking back over his shoulder, but stepping away through the snow at his father's urging, to walk down to the gate again.

There were tears in his son's eyes as Huxley rounded up a snowball and tossed it in a shallow curve. The snowball impacted on the lad's shoulder, and after a moment of sad blankness, Steven grinned, and threw a snowball back.

Christian was up at the bedroom window, banging on the glass, calling something that Huxley couldn't hear. Probably: wait for me!

It was then that Huxley found the 'gift', if gift it was. It was by the gate, a piece of rough cloth wrapped around two inch-long twigs of wood and a yellowing bone from some small creature, a fox, perhaps a small dog. The pieces had holes bored through them. The package had sunk slightly into the snow, but he spotted it, rescued it, and opened it before the boy's fascinated gaze.

'She *did* leave you a present,' Huxley said to his son. 'Not much of one. But it must be a lucky charm. Do you think?'

'Don't know,' Steven said, but he reached for the cloth and its contents and clutched them into his grasp, rubbing his fingers over the three objects. He looked more puzzled than disappointed. Huxley teased the gift back for one moment in order to examine the shards carefully. The wood looked like thorn, that smooth, thin bark. The bone was a neck vertebra.

'Look after these little things, won't you, Steve?'

'Yes.'

'I expect there's a magic word to say with them. It'll come to you suddenly . . .'

He straightened up and started to walk indoors. Jennifer appeared in the kitchen door, a sleepy, pretty figure, arms wrapped tightly around her against the cold. 'What's all the activity?"

'That old Drummer Fox,' said Steven gloomily. Jennifer woke up fast. 'Oh no! A fox? Really?'

' 'Fraid so,' Huxley said quietly. 'Got the lot.'

As Jennifer led the frozen boy inside to breakfast, Huxley turned again and watched Ryhope Wood. A sudden flight of crows, loud in the still air, drew his attention to the stand of holly close to the ruined gate where the sticklebrook entered the wood. This was his way into the deeper zones of the woodland, and he fancied he saw movement there, now, but it was too far away to be sure.

Two pieces of twig and a bone were small payment for twenty chickens. But whoever had been here, last night, had wanted Huxley to know that they had visited. There was, he felt, an unsubtle invitation in the shadowy encounter.

2

Ryhope Wood is unquestionably a stand of *primordial forest*, a fragment of the wildwood which developed after the last Ice Age, and which – using a power which remains obscure – has erected its own defences against destruction. It is impossible to enter too far. I can at last penetrate further than the eerie glade in which a *shrine to horses* is to be found. I am not the only visitor to this site of worship, but of course my fellow 'worshippers' come from *inside* the wood, from the zones and hidden world that I cannot reach.

I have coined the word *mythago* to describe these creatures of forgotten legend. This is from 'myth imago', or the *image of the myth*. They are formed, these varied heroes of old, from the unheard, unseen communication between our common human *unconscious* and the vibrant, almost tangible sylvan mind of the wood itself. The wood watches, it listens, and it draws out our dreams . . .

After the thaw came a time of rain, a monotonous and seemingly endless downpour that lasted for days, and depressed not just the land around Oak Lodge, but the life within that land, so that everything moved slowly, and sullenly, and seemed devoid of spirit. But when the rain eased, when the last storm cloud passed away to the east, a fresh and vibrant spring set new colour to the wood and the fields, and as if coming out of hibernation, Edward Wynne-Jones made a new appearance on the scene, driving to the Huxleys' from Oxford, and arriving in enthusiastic mood one afternoon in early April.

Wynne-Jones was also in his forties and lectured, and researched, in historical anthropology at Oxford University. He was a fussy man, with odd and irritating habits, the most obvious and annoying of which was his smoking of a prodigious pipe, a calabash that belched reeking smoke from its bowl, and did little to improve the aura around the smoker. With his weasel looks, a certain sourness of expression that Jennifer Huxley had at once taken against, and which did nothing to relax the children of the house, he seemed incongruous as he sat, puffing on the 'billy', as it had been nicknamed by the Huxley boys, and holding forth in lecturer's tones about his ideas.

He caused a strain in Oak Lodge, and Huxley was always glad to be able to shunt his compatriot and valued fellow, researcher into the haven of the study, at the farther end of the house. Here, with the french windows opened, they could converse about mythagos, Ryhope Wood, and the processes of the unconscious mind that were at work in the sylvan realm beyond the field.

A map was spread out over the desk, and Wynne-Jones pored over the details, stabbing with his pipe handle as he made points, brushing at the pencil-covered paper. They had detected several 'zones' in the wood, areas where the wood's character changed, where the dominant tree form was different and where the season felt different from that which existed on the ontside of the stand. The Oak-Ash Zone was particularly intriguing, and there was a Thorn Zone, a winding, spiralling forest of tangled blackthorn that ran close to a river, but which kept that water source hidden from view.

It would be Wynne-Jones's task, this trip, to try to break through the thorn and photograph the river.

Huxley would strike deeply into the wood from the Horse Shrine which both men had discovered two years before.

They assessed their route, and listed provisions necessary.

Then Huxley displayed the artefacts he had gathered over the winter months, while Wynne-Jones had been in Oxford.

'Not a great haul. These are the most recent,' he indicated the wood and bone from the gate, 'left by the first mythago to actually enter the garden. She returned—'

'She?'

'The boys say it was a female figure. They called her Snow Woman. She slaughtered the chickens – in silence, I might add – stayed the night in the coop, then returned to the wood. I followed the trail: she had emerged and returned at the same point. I have no idea what her purpose was, unless it was to make a tentative contact.'

'But nothing since?'

'Nothing.'

'Do you have any sense of her status as a "heroine"? What legend she represents?'

'None at all.'

Other finds included a head-piece of rusted, battered iron, a circlet wound round with briar, the thorns trimmed on the inside, and a gorgeous, luxuriantly coloured amulet, the stones not precious, the metal work merely filigreed with gold on a bronze plate. But it was unlike anything that Huxley could find listed or depicted in the pages of his books of previous finds and ancient treasures. It had been suspended from the branch of a beech, two hundred yards inwards, just before the first barrier in the wood where orientation was affected. Wynne-Jones handled the amulet appreciatively.

'A talisman, I'd say. Magic.'

'You think everything's a talisman,' Huxley laughed. 'But on this occasion I'm inclined to agree. But who would have worn this, do you think?'

He placed the cold, crushed circlet on his head. It fitted well, uncomfortably so, and he removed it at once.

Wynne-Jones did not volunteer an opinion.

'And figures?' the younger man prompted after a while. 'Encounters?'

'Apart from Snow Woman, and I didn't see her . . . just the Crow Ghost, as I call him . . . the feathers are mostly black, but I noticed this time that his face is painted and that he *sings*. I'm intrigued by that aspect of him. But he's just as aggressive as before, and so *fast* in his movement through the wood. So, the Crow Ghost, Who else . . . let me think . . . oh yes, the wretched "Robin Hood" form, of course. This one seemed advanced, perhaps thirteenth century.'

'Lincoln Green?' Wynne-Jones said.

'Mud brown, but with some fancy weavework on arms and breast. Slightly bearded. Very large in build. Took the usual shot at me, before merging—'

He placed a broken arrow on the table. The head was a thin point of steel, flanged. The shaft was ash, the flights goosefeather, no decoration. 'The "Hoods" and "Green Jacks" worry me. They've already shot me once. One day one of them is going to strike me in the heart. And the way they just appear—'

He used the word 'merge' deliberately. It was as if the forms of the Hunter – the Robin Hoods, or Jack o' the Greens – *oozed* from the trees, then slipped back into them, merging with the bark and the hardwood and becoming invisible. Too frightened to investigate further, because of the threat to his life, Huxley had no idea whether he was dealing with a phenomenon of the supernatural, or superb camouflage.

'And of the Urscumug?'

Huxley laughed dryly. But it was less of a joke, these

days, more a fixation, a belief, bordering on the obsessive. The first hero, the primal form, ancient, probably malevolent. Huxley had heard *references* to it, found *signs* of it, but he could not get deeply enough into Ryhope Wood to come close to it – to see it. He was convinced it was there, however. *Urscumug*. The almost incomprehensible hero of the first spoken legends, held in the common unconscious of all humankind and almost certainly being generated in Ryhope Wood, somewhere in the glades of this primal, unspoiled stretch of forest.

The Urscumug. The beginning.

But Huxley was beginning to think that he was fated *never* to engage with it.

Standing by the open windows, watching the woodland across the neat garden, with its trimmed cherry trees and clipped hedges, he felt suddenly very old. It was a sensation that had begun to concern him: all his adult life he had felt like a man in his thirties, but it had been a vigorous feeling; now that he was in his middle forties he felt stooped, sagging, a fatigue that he had expected to encounter in his sixties, not for many many years. And it was a feeling of being too old to *see*, to see the wood for what it was, to see out of the corner of his eyes – those frustrating, tantalising glimpses of movement, of creatures, of colour, of the *ancient* that hovered at peripheral vision, and which vanished when he turned towards them.

The boys, though. They seemed to see *everything*.

'Have you brought the bridges?'

Wynne-Jones unpacked the odd electrical equipment,

the headsets with their terminals, wires and odd face-pieces that formed electric linkages across the brain. The voltage was low, but effective. After an hour of electrical stimulation, 'peripheral view awareness' perked up remarkably. And it was in the peripheral vision that glimpses of mythagos were mainly to be experienced: Huxley called them the 'pre-mythago' form, and imagined these to be gradually emerging memories of the past, the passage of memory from mind to wood.

Huxley picked up the apparatus. 'We are old, Father Edward, we are too old. Oh God for youth again, for that far sight . . . The boys see so much. And so often with full fore-vision.'

'What could they see if we enhanced them, I wonder?' Wynne-Jones said softly.

Huxley was alarmed. This was the second time that the Oxford man had suggested experimenting on Steven and Christian, and whilst the idea tantalised Huxley, he felt a strong, moral repellence at the notion. 'No. It wouldn't be fair.'

'With their consent?'

'We may be damaging ourselves, Edward. I couldn't inflict that risk on my boys. Besides, Jennifer would have something to say about it. She'd forbid it outright.'

'But with the *boys'* consent? Steven especially. You said he was a dreamer. You said he could call the wood.'

'He doesn't know he's doing it. He dreams, yes. Neither boy knows what we know. They just know we go exploring, not that time runs differently, not that we encounter dangers. They don't even know about the mythagos. They think they see "gypsies". Tramps.'

But Wynne-Jones wrestled with the idea of enhancing Steven's perception of the wood. 'One experiment. One low voltage, high colour stimulation. It surely would do no harm . . .'

Huxley shook his head, staring hard at the other man. 'It would be wrong. It's wrong to even think about it. Fascinating though the results would be, Edward – I *must* say no. Please don't insist any more. Set the equipment up for ourselves. We'll enter the wood the first moment after dawn.'

'Very well.'

'One other thing,' Huxley added, as the scientist busied himself. 'In case anything should ever happen to me – and I'm disturbed by being shot at by the Merry Man, the Hood figure – in case something unfortunate should occur, I keep a second journal. It's in a wall safe behind these books. You are the only other person who knows about it, and I shall trust you to secure it, should it become necessary, and to use it without revealing it. I don't want Jennifer to know what it contains.'

'And what *does* it contain?'

'Things I can't account for. Dreams, feelings, experiences that seem less related to me than they do to . . .' he searched for appropriate words. 'To the animal realm.'

Huxley knew that he was frowning hard, and that his mood had become dark. Wynne-Jones sat quietly, watching his friend, clearly not comprehending the depth of despair and fear that Huxley was trying to impart without detail. He said only, 'In the wood . . . in parts of the wood . . . I have been very disturbed – As if a more primordial aspect of my behaviour had been let out, dusted off, and set loose.'

'Good God, man, you sound like that character of Stevenson's.'

'Mr Hyde and Mr Jekyll?' Huxley laughed.

'*Dr* Jekyll, I believe.'

'Whatever. I remember reading that whimsy at school. It hadn't occurred to me to see any connection, but yes, my dreams certainly reflect a more violent and instinctual creature man I'm accustomed to greeting every morning in the shaving mirror.'

'And these observations and records are in the second journal?'

'Yes. And accounts, too, of what the boys are experiencing. I really don't want them to know that I've been watching them. But if our ideas about the mythago-genesis of heroes in the wood are right, then all of us in this house, even you, Edward, are having an effect upon the process. At any one time, the phenomena we witness might be the product of one of five minds. And then there are the farm hands, and the people at the Manor. Our moods, our personalities, shape the manifestations—'

'You've begun to agree with me, then. I made this point a year ago.'

'I *do* agree with you. That Hood form . . . it was strange. It echoed a mind different to my own. Yes. I do agree with you. And this is an area we should study more assiduously, and more vigorously. So let's prepare.'

'I shall say nothing about the second journal.'

'I trust you.'

'I still think we should talk about Steven, and enhancing his perception.'

'If we talk about it, let's talk about it after this excursion.'

'I agree.'

Relieved, Huxley reached into his desk drawer for his watch, a small, brass-encased mechanism that showed date as well as time of day. 'Let's get ourselves ready,' he said, and Wynne-Jones grunted his agreement.

3

'Your son is watching you,' Wynne-Jones said quietly, as they walked away from the house, still shivering in the crisp and fresh dawn. All around them the world was coming alive. The light was sharp to the east, and the wood was dark, shadowy, yet becoming distinct with that peculiar clarity which accompanies the first light of a new day.

Huxley stopped and shrugged his pack from his shoulders, turning to look back at the house.

Sure enough, Steven was pressed against the window of his bedroom, a small, anxious shape, mouthing words and waving.

Huxley stepped a few paces back, and cupped his ear.

Chickens clattered close by, and the old dog growled and worried in the hedges. Rooks called loudly, and their flight, in and among the branches of Ryhope Wood, made the day seem somehow more desolate and silent than it was.

Steven pulled the sash window up.

'Where are you going?' he called down, and Huxley said, 'Exploring.'

'Can I come?'

'Scientific research, Steve. We'll only be gone today.'

'Take me with you?'

'I can't. I'm sorry, lad. I'll be back tonight and tell you all about it.'

'Can't I come?'

The dawn seemed to lengthen, and the early spring cold made his breath frost as he stood and stared at the anxious, pale-faced boy in the window, high in the house. 'I'll be back tonight. We have some readings to take, some mapping, some samples to take . . . I'll tell you all about it later.'

'You went away for three days last time. We were worried . . .'

'One day only, Steve. Now be a good boy.'

As he hefted his pack onto his back again, he saw Jennifer standing in the doorway, her face glistening with tears. 'I'll be back tonight,' he said to her.

'No you won't,' she whispered, and turned into the house, closing the kitchen door behind her.

4

. . . poor Jennifer is already deeply depressed by my behaviour. Cannot explain it to her, though I dearly want to. Do not want the children involved in this, and it worries me that they have now twice seen a mythago. I have invented magic forest creatures – stories for them. Hope they will associate what they see with products of their own imaginations. But must be careful.

There is a time before wakening, an instant only, when the real and the unreal play games with the sleeper, when everything is right, yet nothing is real. In this moment of surfacing from the sleep of days, Huxley sensed the flow of water, and the passing of riders, the shouts and curses of a troop on the move, and the anguish and excitement of pursuit.

Something bigger than a man was moving through the wood, following the pack of men that ran before its lumbering assault.

And there was a woman, too, who came to the river, and touched her hand to the face of the sleeping/waking man. She dropped a twig and a bone on him, then left with a laugh and swirl of perfumed body, the sweat of her skin and her soul, sour and sexual in the nostrils of the recumbent form that slowly . . .

Came to waking . . .

Came alive, again.

Huxley sat up and began to choke. He was frozen, and icy water ran from his face.

He was deafened by the sound of the river, and his sense of smell was offended by the stink of his own faeces, cool and firm, accumulated in the loose cotton of his underclothes.

'Dear God! What's happened to me . . . ?'

He cleaned himself quickly, crouching in the river, gasping with the cold. From previous experience he knew to bring a change of clothing and he searched gratefully in his pack, now, finding the gardening trousers and a thick, cotton shirt.

He fumbled with shaking fingers for his watch and closed his eyes as he saw that it had been four days since he had reached this place, dazed and confused, and lain down on the shore with his head on his arms.

Four days asleep!

'Edward! Edward . . . ?'

His voice, a loud, urgent cry, was lost in the rush and swirl of this river; he was about to shout again, when the first piece of memory returned, and he realised that Wynne-Jones was long gone. They had parted days before, the Oxford man to find, if he could, the river beyond the thornwoods, Huxley himself to document the edges of the zones that were Ryhope Wood's first true level of defence.

How perverse, then, that Huxley should find himself by the expanded flow of the tiny sticklebrook. Had Wynne-Jones been here too? He could see no sign of the other man.

There were the ashes of a small fire, away from the

water, in the shelter of a grey sarsen, whose mossy green stump seemed almost to thrust from the tangle of root and ragged earth. Huxley had seen enough failed fires, built by Wynne-Jones, to notice that this was not of the other man's making.

He gathered his things together. Starving, he wolfed down a bar of chocolate from his pack.

Memory raced back, and the disorientation resulting from his sudden waking after another of the long dreams began to fade.

He stared hard at the patch of thorn through which he had entered this place. He fixed, in his mind, the image of the woman who had caressed him as he slept in a half slumber, semi-aware of her presence, but unable to rise beyond the semi-conscious state. Not young, not old, filthy, sexual, warm . . . she had pressed her mouth to his and her tongue had been a sharp, wet presence against his own. Her laughter was low. Had he put a hand on her leg? He had the sensation of less than firm flesh, the broad smoothness of a thigh below his fingers and palm, but this might have been his dream.

Who, then, had the riders been? And that creature that had stalked them across the river?

'Urscumug,' he murmured as he checked for spoor. There were no tracks, beyond the shallow imprint of an unshod horse.

'Urscumug . . . ?'

He was not sure. He remembered a previous encounter.

The Urscumug has formed in my mind in the clearest form I have ever seen him . . . face smeared with white clay . . . hair a mass of stiff and spiky points . . . so old, this primary image, that he is fading from the human mind . . . Wynne-Jones thinks Urscumug may predate even the neolithic . . .

He wanted his journal. He scrawled notes in the rough pad he carried with him, but the pad was wet, and writing was difficult. Around him the wood was vibrant, shifting, watching. He felt intensely ill at ease, and after a few minutes shrugged on the pack and began to retrace his steps, away from the river.

Half a day later he had reached the Wolf Glen, the shallow valley, with its open sky, where he and Wynne-Jones had separated several days before. This was an eerie place, with its smell of sharp pine, its constant, cool breeze, and the sound of wolves in the darkness. Huxley had seen the creatures several times, fleet shadows in the dense underbrush, rising onto their hind limbs to peer around, their faces half human, of course, for these creatures were no ordinary wolves.

They moved in threes, not in packs; and never – as far as he could see – in solitary. Their barking resolved into language, though of course the language was incomprehensible to the Englishman. Huxley carried a pistol, and two flares, well wrapped in oilskin, but ready to be lit if the wolves came too close.

But in the three visits he had made to the Wolf Glen, the beasts had shown curiosity, irritation, and then a lack of interest. They had approached, gabbled at him, then slunk away, running half on hind limbs, to hunt beyond the edge of the conifer forest, beyond the low defining ridge of the Wolf Glen itself.

If Wynne-Jones had returned here he would have left the prearranged mark on one of the tall stones at the top of the Glen. No such mark was in evidence. Huxley used chalk to create his own message, gathered the necessary wood for a fire, later in the day, and went exploring.

At dusk, still Wynne-Jones had not returned. Huxley called for him, his voice echoing in the Glen, carrying on the wind. No hail or hello came back, and a night passed.

In the morning Huxley decided that he could wait no longer. He had no real idea of the passage of time, this far into Ryhope Wood, but imagined that he had now been absent the better part of a day and a night, longer than he had intended. He had a precise idea of how distorted time became as far in as the Horse Shrine, but he had never tested the relativity of these deeper zones. A sudden anguish made him strike hard along the poor trails, cutting through deep mossy dells, drawn always outwards to the edge.

It was always easier to leave the wood than to enter it.

He was exhausted by the time he reached the area of the Horse Shrine. He was hungry, too. He had brought insufficient supplies. And his hunger was increased by the sudden smell of burning meat.

He dropped to a crouch, peering ahead through the tangle of briar and holly, seeking the clearing with its odd temple. There was movement there. Wynne-Jones, perhaps? Had his colleague come straight to this place, to wait for Huxley? Was he roasting him a pigeon, as he waited, with a flagon of chilled local cider to accompany it? Huxley smiled at himself, laughed at the way his baser drives began to fantasise for him. He walked cautiously through the trees, and peered into the glade.

Whoever had been there had heard him. They had backed away, hugging the shadows and the greenery on the opposite side. Huxley was sufficiently attuned to the sounds, smells and shifting of the wood to be aware of the human-like presence that stared back at him.

Between them, close to the bizarre shrine, a fire burned and a bird, plucked and spitted, was blackening slowly.

5

The Horse Shrine, in its oak glade, is my main point of contact with the mythic creatures of the wood. The trees here are overpoweringly immense organisms, storm-damaged and twisted. The trunks are hollow, their bark overrun with massive ropes of ivy. Their huge, heavy branches reach out across the clearing and form a roof; when the sun is bright, and the summer is silent, to enter the glade is like entering a cathedral. The greying bones of the odd statues that fill the shrine reflect the changing shades of green and are entrancing and enticing to the eye; the horse that is central to the shrine seems to move; it is a massive structure, twice the height of a man, bones strapped together to form gigantic legs, fragments of skull shaped and wedged to create a monstrous head. It could be some dinosaur, reconstructed out of madness by an impressionist. Shapeless but essentially manlike structures stand guard beside it, again all longbone and skull, lashed together with thick strips of leather, impaled by wood, some of which is returning to leaf. They seem to watch me as I crouch in the shifting, dancing luminosity of this eerie place.

Here I have seen human forms from the palaeolithic, the neolithic and the Age of Bronze. They come here and watch the greening of the spirit of the horse. To the earliest forms of Man, this silent respect is for a wild, untamed creature, a source of nourishment rather than burden. To later forms, it is a closer need that is reflected. Some visitors to the shrine leave brilliant trappings and harnessing, invocations to their primaeval form of Epona, or Diana, or any other *Goddess of the Steed*. These I have collected. Many of them are fascinating.

I have watched and recorded many of these visitors, but failed to communicate with any of them. All this now changed as I encountered the woman. She was in the glade, tending a small fire, and staring up at the decaying statues. Alarmed by my sudden arrival, she stood and drew back into the edgewood, watching me. The sun was high, and she was drenched in shadow and green light, blending with the background. The fire crackled slightly, and on the still air I could smell not just burning wood, but the charred smell of some meat or other.

I waited cautiously, also within the scrub that lined the glade. Soon she re-emerged into the cathedral, and crouched by the fire, spreading her skirts. She began to sing, rocking forwards in rhythm, prodding at the smouldering wood. She was very aware of me, glancing at me continually. I gained the impression that she was . . . disappointed. She frowned and shook her head.

Eventually she smiled, and there was an invitation to approach in that simple gesture. As I stepped through the tangled grass and fern of the glade, her lank hair fell forward. It was copper-hued, magnificent, but full of leaf-litter, nature's decoration. She occasionally pushed it back with her free hand, watching me through eyes that were enchanting. Her clothing was of wool, a skirt dyed a dull shade of brown, a faded green shawl. She wore a necklace of carved and painted shapes, bone talismans, I thought, and many of these were strikingly bright. Rolled beside her was a cloak, fur side hidden for a while. Then she unfurled the garment to fetch out a thin knife, and I saw white fur – fox fur, I think – and knew at once that this creature was the 'Snow Woman' that the boys had seen last Christmas.

We sat in silence for a while. She cooked and picked at the small bird she had snared, a wood pigeon, I believe. Around us, the dense wood seemed alive with eyes, but this is the life of Ryhope Wood, the sylvan-awareness drawing out human dreams and fashioning forgotten memories into living organisms. When I am in the oak and ash zones, deeper than the Horse Shrine, I can often *feel* the presence of the wood in my unconscious mind; images at the edge of vision seem to slip past me: out of mind, into the forest, to become shaped, then no doubt to return to haunt me.

Was this woman one of my own *mythagos*, I wondered?

She carried an ash stick, and when she had finished eating she lay this across her lap before flicking earth onto the smouldering wood of her fire. She smiled at me. There was grease on her lips and she licked at it. Below the grime she was truly lovely, and her smile, and her laughter, were enchanting. I mentioned my name and she grasped what I was trying to do, referring to herself in some incomprehensible tongue. Then, seeing my puzzlement, she held up the stick and pointed to herself. She was called Ash, then, but this reference meant nothing to me.

Who or what was she? What aspect of legend was embodied here? By sign and smile, by gesture, by the tracing of shapes in the air, by exaggerated communication with fingers, we began to understand each other. I showed her a rag effigy that I had gathered from near this shrine on the inward journey, and she stared at this bounty with puzzlement (at first) and then with an odd, searching look. When I dangled a bronze, leaf-like necklet – found by a stream – she touched the piece, then shook her head as if to say 'don't be so childish'. But when I showed her an ochre-painted amulet that I had found in the Horse Shrine itself, she exhaled sharply, looked at me with murderous, then pitying eyes. She would not touch the object and I ran it through my fingers, wondering what message reached from this crafted bone to the mind of the woman. The uneasiness lasted a little while, then – by sign – I asked her about herself.

She returned to me, a bird returning from a flight of fancy, a mind returning to the reality of a woodland glade. In a moment or two she seemed to understand that I was questioning her about her own history. She frowned, watching me as if wondering what to reveal. I noticed distinctly, but took no warning from the observation, that she looked afraid and angry suddenly.

Then, with the merest shrug, she reached into her rolled cloak and drew out two leather bags which she shook. One of them rattled, the sound of bone shards.

By gesture, she had made certain strange comments during the previous hour, and now she compounded my confusion. First she shook out the contents of the larger bag, dozens of short fragments of wood, strips of bark, some dark, some silver, some green, some mottled, all gouged with a small hole. I formed the idea that she had something, here, from every type of tree. With her eyes on the amulet that I had shown her, she picked out two of these pieces of wood, held them in her left hand. She sang something softly and the glade seemed to shiver. A coolish breeze whipped quickly through the foliage, then danced up and away; an elemental life-form, perhaps, summoned then dismissed.

From the second bag she poured out the bone, forty or fifty shards of ivory. From these she picked a single piece. Holding wood and bone in her hand she shook the three fragments, before threading a loop of thin, worn leather through the holes and passing the necklet to me. I accepted it, remembering, with no clear understanding, the gift she had left by the gate during the winter. I put the necklet on.

She sat back and replaced the rest of the wood and ivory into their respective bags. Then she stood and gathered her fox-fur cloak, and with a knowing smile, stepped out of the glade and into the silence and darkness of the forest. Her last gesture before departing was to rattle a tiny wrist-drum, a double sided cylinder of skin, beaten by small stones attached to thongs.

I had no idea what to do next. She had seemed to dismiss me, so I rose, intending to leave the glade and return to Oak Lodge.

6

Huxley got no further than the first overpowering oak. As he ducked below its heavy branch, heading towards the narrow track outwards, his world – the wood itself – turned inside out!

From the warm and musty odour of summer, suddenly the air was sharp and autumnal. The light from the foliage was stark, brilliant; the drowsy green luminosity had gone. Trees, dense and dark, rose straight and bleak around him. These were birches, not oaks; thickets of holly shimmered in the lancing silver light. He stumbled through this unknown world, scratched and torn in his panic to orientate himself. Above him, birds screeched and took to wing. A cold wind swept through the upper branches. Unfamiliar smells struck at random, damp leaf mould, pungent vegetation, then the crystal sharpness of autumn. The light from above was startling in its brightness, and if he glanced up, then looked around him, the trees showed as black pillars, without feature, almost formless.

He suddenly heard horses crashing through the forest, their lungs straining as they ran, their whinnying screams telling of the burden of pain and bruising inlicted by this tangled, ancient wood. Huxley glimpsed them as they struggled past, immense creatures, each impaled on its back with what he assumed quickly were the signs of *taming*: one carried flaring torches, spears with burning heads that had been stuck deeply through its thick skin; another was decorated with stems of corn or wheat; a third with tight bundles of greenery and thorn, blood seeping from where the sharpened stalks of some of these plants had been pushed too deep. The fourth carried in its flesh the slim, quivering shafts of a pale wood – *ash* perhaps – that were arrows, each trailing rags of the skin of creatures, the grey, white, brown and black of furry hides.

What had sounded like the frantic passage of a *herd* of these wonderful creatures was in fact the furious bolting of four horses only.

One came close enough to show Huxley the grey and bloodied hide of its flanks. This was the creature 'decorated' with burning and smouldering torches. It towered over him, its mane full, flowing and lank; it reeked richly of dung. The horse turned briefly to stare at him and its eyes were filled with a feral panic. Huxley pressed himself against one of the great birches, which shuddered as the beast kicked at the trunk, turning to expose huge, cracked teeth that were the colour of summer-ripened wheat; it moved on, then, working its way inwards, escaping its tormentors.

The tormentors, following close behind the horses, were humans, of course. And Huxley was soon to realise what Ash had done.

There were four men, dark haired and heavily cloaked. They moved through the forest, uttering shrill cries, or gruff barks, or resonating song fragments that increased in pitch until they became an ululating echo. Sometimes they screeched *words*, but these were frightening and alien sounds. Each of the men wore his hair in a different, elaborate plaited style. Each was bedecked with stone or bone or shells or wood. Each had a colour on his face: red, green, yellow, blue. They passed by Huxley, sometimes running, sometimes laughing, all of them torn by thorn and holly, the leaf and wood impaling their crude clothing, so that they seemed no less than extensions of the birch and thorn forest itself.

Crying out and celebrating their vigorous pursuit of horses!

It was, Huxley chose to think at that moment, their way of controlling the horses. How many myths of the *secret language* of horses had come down to modern times, he wondered briefly? Many, he imagined, and here were men who *knew* those secrets! He was watching an early herding, the horses pushed into the tangle of

374

the wood, the best way to trap them, in fact, a *wonderful* way to trap them, in a time before corrals or stables! Run the horse into the thicket, and the sheer difference in size between *chaser* and *chased* would have marked the difference between *eaten* and *eater*.

For he had no doubt at that moment – this being a pre-neolithic event – that these beasts were being herded for food, rather than as creatures of burden.

Striking at the underbrush with long, flint-edged sticks, the four men strode past. And the hindmost of them, looking as broad in his heavy furs as he was tall, turned suddenly to stare at the hooded intruder, green-grey light glittering in pale eyes. On his chest he wore an identical amulet to that which Huxley had found in the Horse Shrine. He touched it, almost nervously, a gesture of luck, perhaps, or courage.

His companions called to him, shrill sounds, almost musical in their rhythm and pitch, that sent birds whirring from the tree tops. He turned and was gone, consumed by the thickets of holly, and the confusing patterns of light and shade of the birchwood. Nervously, Huxley tugged the green hood of his oilskin lower over his face.

I followed, of course. Of course! I wished to see this ritual herding through to its final, awful conclusion. For I had now begun to imagine that a *sacrifice of horses* would be the outcome of the pursuit to which Ash, by her magic, had despatched me.

Yet, in substance I was wrong. It was not to be the

oddly bedecked stallions that were sent on to the after-life, encouraged there by flint and by flax rope. Not immediately, anyway. In the wide clearing, with its tall, crudely fashioned wood-gods, the horses were disturbed by the smells and the cries of extinguished life. The gathering of winter-clad men calmed the beasts. The glade in the birchwood echoed to the thumping of wood drums and the chanting of ancient hymns. There was laughter within the cacophony of sacrifice, and throughout all, the whooping cries of other herders, the music of magic, punctuating the confusion, serving to bring peace to the restless horses as they were held by their harnessings, and loaded with their first real burden.

Towards dusk, the horses were sent into the world again, running, slapped to encourage them, back along the broken tracks, towards the edge of the wood, wherever that lay. On their backs, tied firmly to cradles of wood, the horrific shapes of their pale riders watched the gloom, dulled eyes seeing darker worlds than even this darkening forest. The first to depart was a chalk-white corpse, grotesquely garrotted. Then a man, still living, swathed in thorns, screaming. After that, a ragged creature, stinking of blood and acrid smoke from the part-burned but newly skinned pelts that were wrapped around him.

Finally came a figure decked and dressed in rush and reed, so that only his arms were visible, extended on the crucifix-like frame that was tied about the giant horse. He was on fire; the blaze taking swiftly. Flame streamed into the night, shedding light and heat in eerie streamers as the great stallion galloped in panic towards me.

I thought I had moved quickly enough to take avoiding action, but before I knew it the beast had collided with me, one front leg striking me a blow to the side, then its shoulder pitching me down. I curled up to protect myself, but my body seemed to disobey and struggled to stand . . .

For one eerie moment I sensed I was *behind* the flaming figure, feeling the heat on my body, the wind and fire on my face, the rough movement of the horse below me.

The illusion lasted a second only before I was pitched backwards again, stunned and disorientated as I lay on the ground, stifled as if hands were pressing down on my mouth, neck and lungs.

I recovered swiftly.

I cannot record the full detail of what I saw in that clearing – so much has faded from memory, perhaps because of the blow from the stampeding horse. I am still shocked by the nature of the sacrifices and the awareness that the murdered men seemed *willing participants* in this early form of acknowledgement of the power *of the horse*.

Such wonderful creatures, and yet they would be both friend of Man and carrier of his destruction . . .

All of this was passing through my mind as a freezing night fell upon the primaeval world, and other thoughts too: by horse would come war, and plague, and the populations to overrun and overwhelm the food available from the land. By horse would come the fire that clears, and kills, and cleanses.

But this forest, this event, reflected something that had occurred *tens of thousands of years before the present!*

Was I witnessing one of the first true *intuitions* of early humankind? That the beast could be both friend and foe to a tribe that increasingly looked for control over nature itself? Sacrifice was made to new gods: the assuaging of fears. And it entertained me to think that later, much later, John the Divine would remember these early fears, and talk of the four horsemen, in fact describing his deep-rooted memories of an ancient understanding . . .

But with darkness came silence, and with the freezing silence of night came my helpless abandonment to sleep.

I awoke from the dream to the wet nuzzling of a dog. I was at the edge of Ryhope Wood – God alone knows how I had got there – in the scrub that overlooks the fields of the Manor House. The dog was a springer, being walked by an alarmed and determined woman, who strode away from what she presumably believed to be a tramp. She called for her hound, which bounded after her, not without a regretful and hungry glance towards me.

7

When he opened the back door to Oak Lodge, Jennifer screamed and dropped the mug of tea that she was holding. She looked at her husband through wide, frightened eyes, then collapsed back with relief against the table, laughing and brushing at the tea which had spilled over her dressing gown.

'I didn't realise you'd gone out again . . .'

Her words were meaningless, but he was too tired to think. He said, 'I must look terrible. I should bath at once.'

He was dog tired. He drank the fresh tea she made, and wolfed down a slice of buttered bread. Steven came and watched him as he undressed, stripping off his stinking clothes, drawing hot water from the tank to make a deep bath. Jennifer picked up the clothes, frowning as she watched her husband.

'Why did you put these on again?'

'Again? I don't know what you mean . . . I'm sorry . . . to have been away so long . . .'

He sank into the water, groaning and sighing with pleasure. Steven and Christian giggled on the landing outside. They had seen their father's naked body, something they had never witnessed before, and like all children this glimpse of the forbidden had amused and shocked them.

When he had washed himself, and dried off, he went to Jennifer and tried to explain. She was distant. He had already noted from the calendar that his absence, this time, had been two days. For himself, the passage of time had been much greater, but even so, Jennifer was rightly anguished, and had suffered an intense day of concern.

'I hadn't intended to be away so long.'

She had made him breakfast. She sat opposite him at the table in the dining room, and leafed through *The Times*. 'How could you get so dirty in so few hours?' she said, and he frowned as he forked slices of sausage into his mouth. Her words were confusing, but he himself was confused, now. He was oddly disorientated.

When he went to his study he found that his desk drawer had been disturbed. Angry, he almost confronted Jennifer, but decided against it. The key to his private journal was lying on the desk top. And yet the last time he had written in the journal he had – he was sure – replaced the key carefully in its hidden position, pressed to the underside of the desk top.

He wrote an official entry in his research journal, and then fetched the personal diary from its hiding place, entering an account of his encounter with Ash. His hand shook and he had to make many corrections to the text. When he had finished he blotted the ink dry, sat back, and turned back through the journal's pages.

He read through what he had written shortly before the last trip with Wynne-Jones.

And he suddenly realised that there were six additional lines to the text!

Six lines that he bad no recollection of writing at all.

'Good God, who's been at my journal?'

Again, he stopped himself going to Jennifer, or confronting the boys, but he was shocked, truly shocked. He bent over the pages, his hands shaking as he ran a finger word by word along the entry.

It was in his own handwriting. There was no question of it. His own handwriting, or a brilliant forgery thereof.

The entry was simple, and had about it that haste with which he was familiar, the scrawled notes that he managed when his encounters were intense, his life hectic, and his need to be in the wood more important than his need to keep a careful record of his discoveries.

She is not what she seems. Her name is Ash. Yes, You know that. It is a dark world for me. I will acknowledge terror. But there is
  I cannot be sure
  She is more dangerous, and she has done this. Edward is dead. No. Perhaps not. But it is a poss
  The time with the horses. I can't be sure. Something was watching

'I didn't write this. Dear God. Am I going mad? I *didn't* write this. Did I?'

Jennifer was reading and listening to the radio. He stood in the doorway, uncertain at first, his mind not clear. 'Has anyone been to my desk?' he asked at length.

Jennifer looked up. 'Apart from you yourself, no. Why?'

'Someone's tampered with my journal.'

'What do you mean "tampered" with it?'

'Written in it. Copying my own hand. Has anybody been here during my excursion?'

'Nobody. And I don't allow the boys into the study when you're not here. Perhaps you were sleepwalking last night.'

Now her words began to fidget him. 'How could I have done that? I didn't get home until dawn.'

'You came home at midnight,' she said, a smile touching her pale features. She closed the book, keeping a finger at the page. 'You went out again before dawn.'

'I didn't come back last night,' Huxley whispered. 'You must have been dreaming.'

She was silent for a long time, her breathing shallow. She looked at him solemnly. The smile had vanished, replaced by an expression of sadness and weariness. 'I wasn't dreaming. I was glad of you. I was in bed, quite asleep, when you woke me. I was disappointed to find you gone in the morning. I suppose I should have expected it . . .'

How long had he slept at the edge of the wood, before the woman and her dog had woken him? Had he indeed come home, unconscious, unaware, to spend an hour or two in bed, to write a confused and shattered message in his own journal, then to return to the woodland edge, to wait for dawn?

Suddenly alarmed, he began to wonder what other magic Ash had worked on him.

Where was Wynne-Jones? He had been gone over a week, now, and Huxley was increasingly disturbed, very concerned for his friend. Each day he ventured as far into the wood as the Horse Shrine, seeking a sign of the man, seeking, too, for Ash, but she had disappeared. Four days after returning home Huxley trekked more deeply, through a mile or so of intensely silent oakwood, emerging in unfamiliar terrain, not at the Wolf Glen at all.

Panicked, feeling himself to be losing touch with his own frail perception of the wood, he returned to Oak Lodge. He had been gone nearly twenty hours by his own reckoning, but only five hours had passed in the house, and Jennifer and the boys were not at home. His wife, no doubt, was in Grimley, or had perhaps taken the car to Gloucester for the day.

So it startled him to enter his study through the locked main door and to see his french windows opened wide, and the cat nestling in his leather chair. He shooed the animal away from the room, and examined the doors. There was no sign of them having been forced. No footprints. No sign of disturbance in the room. The study door had been locked from the outside.

When he opened his desk drawer he recoiled with shock from the bloody, fresh bone that lay there, on top of his papers. The bone was in part charred, a joint of some medium-sized animal, perhaps a pig, that had been partially cooked, so that raw and bleeding flesh remained at the bone itself. It was chewed, cracked and worried, as if a dog had been at it.

Gingerly, Huxley removed the offending item and placed it on a sheet of paper on the floor. The key to his private journal was not in its place, and shakily he fetched the opened book from its hole behind the shelves.

Bloody fingerprints accompanied the scrawled entry. This one was hastier than before, but unmistakably a copy of his own hand.

A form of dreaming. Moments of lucidity, but am functioning in unconscious.

No sign of WJ. Time has interfered.

These entries seem so controlled, the others. No recollection of writing them. I have so little time, and feel tug of woodland. Have linked somehow with sylvan time, and everything is inverted.

So hungry. So little chance to eat. I am covered with the blood of a fawn, hunted by a mythago. I grabbed part of carcase. Ate with ferocious need.

Pangs strong. Flesh! Satiation! Blood is on fire, and night is a peaceful time, and I can emerge more strongly. But no way of entering those moments when I am clearly myself.

So controlled, the other entries. Cannot remember writing them.

I am a ghost in my own body.

Huxley looked at his own hands, smelled the fingers. There was no blood in evidence, not under the nails, no sign of charcoal. He examined his clothes. There was mud on the trouser legs, but nothing that suggested he had torn and wrenched at a half-cooked carcase. He ran his tongue around his teeth. He checked his pillow in the bedroom.

If *he* had written this entry, if he himself had come into the study, in a moment of unconscious separation, eating the raw bone, he would surely have left some trace.

The words were odd, had an odd feel. It was as if

the writer genuinely believed that he *was* Huxley, and that Huxley's own entries in the journal were being made during times of unconscious calm. Reality, for the bloody-fingered journalist, was a time of 'lucidity'.

But Huxley, keeping a rational and clear mind now, was certain that two different men were entering notes in the private journal.

It astonished him, though, that the other writer knew about the key.

He picked up his pen and wrote:

Today I went in search of Wynne-Jones. I didn't sleep, and I am convinced that I remained alert and aware for the full twenty hours that I was away. I am concerned for Wynne-Jones. I fear he is lost, and it grieves me deeply to anticipate the fact that he might never return. In my absence, someone else is making entries in this journal. The entry above was not written by me. But I believe that whoever has entered this place believes themself to be George Huxley. You are not. But whoever you are, you should tell me more about yourself. And if you wish to know more about me, then simply ask. It would be preferable for you to show yourself, perhaps at the edgewood. I am quite used to strange encounters. We have much that we need to talk about.

He had just finished writing when the car pulled into the drive. Doors slammed and he heard the sound of Jennifer's voice, and Steven's. Jennifer sounded angry.

She came into the house and a few seconds later he heard Steven go into the garden and run down to the gate. He stood from his desk and watched the boy, and was disturbed by the way his son glanced suddenly towards him, frowned, seemed to stifle back a tear or two, then went to hide among the sheds.

'Why do you neglect the boy so much? It wouldn't hurt you to talk to him once in a while.'

Huxley was startled by Jennifer's calm, controlled, yet angry tones speaking to him from the entrance to his study. She was pale, her lips pinched, her eyes hollow with fatigue and irritation. She was dressed in a dark suit and had her hair tied back into a tight bun, exposing all of her narrow face.

She entered the room the moment he turned and crossed to the desk, opening the book that was there, touching the pens, shaking her head. When she saw the bone she grimaced and kicked at it.

'Another little trophy, George? Something to frame?'

'Why are you angry?'

'I'm not angry,' she said wearily. 'I'm upset. So's Steven.'

'I don't understand why.'

Her laugh was brief and sourly pointed. 'Of course you don't. Well, think back, George. You must have said something to him this morning. I've never known the boy in such a state. I took him to Shadoxhurst, to the toy shop and the tea shop. But what he really wants—' She bit her lip in exasperation, letting the statement lie uncompleted.

Huxley sighed, scratching his face as he watched and listened to something that simply wasn't possible.

'What time was this?'

'What time was what?'

'That . . . that I said something to Steven, to upset the boy . . .'

'Mid-morning.'

'Did you come and see me? Afterwards?'

'No.'

'Why not? Why didn't you come and see me?'

'You'd left the study. You'd gone back to the woods, no doubt. A-hunting and adventuring – down in dingly dell . . .' Again she looked at the grim and bloody souvenir. 'I was going to suggest tea, but I see you've eaten . . .'

Before he could speak further she had turned abruptly, taking off her suit jacket, and walked upstairs to freshen up.

'I wasn't here this morning,' Huxley said quietly, turning back to the garden, and stepping out into me dying sunlight. 'I wasn't here. So who *was*?'

Steven was sitting, slumped forward on the wall that bounded the rockery. He was reading a book, but hastily closed it when he heard his father approaching.

'Come to my study, Steve. There's something I want to show you.'

The boy followed in silence, tucking the book into his school blazer. Huxley thought it might have been a penny-dreadful western, but decided not to pursue the matter.

'I went deep into Ryhope Wood this morning,' he said, sitting down behind the desk and picking up his small pack. Steven stood on the other side, back to the window, hands by his sides. His face was a sad combination of uncertainty and distress, and Huxley felt like saying, 'Cheer up, lad,' but he refrained from doing so.

Instead he tipped out the small collection of oddities he had found at the Horse Shrine, and beyond: an iron torque, a small wooden idol, its face blank, its arms and legs just the stumps of twigs that had once grown from the central branch; a fragment of torn, green linen, found on a hawthorn bush.

Picking up the doll, Huxley said, 'I've often seen these talisman dolls, but never touched them. They usually hang in the trees. This one was on the ground and I felt it fair game.'

'Who hangs them in the trees?' Steven asked softly, his eyes, now, registering interest rather than sadness.

Huxley came close to telling the boy a little about the mythogenetic processes occurring within the wood, and the life forms that existed there. Instead he fell back on the old standby. 'Travelling folk. Tinkers. Romanies. Some of these bits and bobs might be years old, generations. All sorts of people have lived in and around the edge of our wood.'

The boy stepped forward and tentatively picked up

the wooden figure, holding it, turning it over, then grimly placing it down again.

Huxley said, 'Did I upset you this morning?'

Oddly, the boy shook his head.

'But you came to the study. You saw me . . . ?'

'I heard you shouting by the wood. I was frightened.'

'Why were you frightened?'

'I thought . . . I thought someone was attacking you . . .'

'*Was* someone attacking me?'

The boy's gaze dropped. He fidgeted, biting his lip, then looked up again, and there was fear in his eyes.

'It's all right, Steven. Just tell me what you saw . . .'

'You were all grey and green. You were very angry . . .'

'What do you mean, I was all grey and green?'

'Funny colours, like light on water. I couldn't see you properly. You were so fast. You were shouting. There was an awful smell of blood, like when Fonce kills the chickens.'

Alphonsus Jeffries, the farm manager for the Manor. Steven had been taken round the farm several times, and had witnessed the natural life of the domestic animals, and their unnatural death with knife and cleaver.

'Where were you when you saw this, did you say?'

'By the woods . . .' Steven whispered. His lips trembled and tears filled his eyes. Huxley remained seated, leaning forward, holding his son's gaze hard and firm. 'Grow up, boy. You've seen something very strange. I'm asking you about it. You want to be a scientist, don't you?'

Steven hesitated, then nodded.

'Then tell me everything. You were by the woods . . .'

'I thought you called me.'

'From the woods . . .'

'You called me.'

'And then?'

'I went over the field and you were all grey and green. You ran past me. I was frightened. I could hardly see you. Just a little bit. You were all grey and green. I was frightened . . .'

'How fast did I pass you?'

'Daddy . . . ? I'm frightened . . .'

'Be quiet, Steven. Stand still. Stop crying. How fast did I pass you?'

'Very fast. I couldn't see you.'

'Faster than our car?'

'I think so. You ran up to here. I followed you and heard you shouting.'

'What was I shouting?'

'Rude things.' The boy squirmed beneath his father's gaze. 'Rude things. About Mummy.'

Stunned and sickened, Huxley bit back the question he longed to ask, stood up from his desk and walked past the wan-faced lad, into the garden.

Rude things about Mummy . . .

'How do you know the man you saw was me?' he murmured.

Steven ran past him, distressed and suddenly angry. The boy turned sharply, eyes blazing, but said nothing.

Huxley said, 'Steven. The man you saw . . . whoever

it was – it only *looked* like me. Do you understand that? It wasn't me at all. It only *looked* like me.'

The answer was a growl, a shaking, feverish, feral growl, in which the words were dimly discernible from the furious face, the dark face of the boy as he backed slowly away, sinking into himself, lowering his body, eyes on his father. Angry.

'It . . . *was* . . . you . . . It . . . *was* . . . you . . .'

And then Steven had fled, running to the gate. He left the garden and crossed the field almost frantically, plunging into the nearby woods.

Huxley hesitated for a moment, half thinking that it would be better for the boy to calm down first before pursuing the matter further. But he was too intrigued by Steven's glimpse of the ghost.

He picked up one of Wynne-Jones's frontal-lobe bridges and trotted after his son.

9

As I had imagined he would, the boy became intrigued when I told him about the frontal-lobe bridges (I called them 'electrical crowns'). He was hovering in the edge-woods, shaking, by the time I reached him. I have never seen Steven so distressed, not even after he and Christian glimpsed the Twigling, and were given a great fright. I said that WJ and myself had been experimenting on seeing ghosts more clearly. Would he like to try one on? Oh the delight! I felt smaller than the smallest creature in so tricking Steven, but by now there was an overwhelming compulsion in me to know who or what this 'grey-green figure' had been.

As we returned to the house Steven glanced backwards and frowned. Was it the figure? I could see wind stirring the trees and scrubby bush that borders the denser zones of the wood, but no sign of human life. Can you see anything, I asked the boy, but after a moment he shook his head.

We returned to the study and after a few minutes I tentatively placed a crown on Steven's head. He was trembling with excitement, poor little lad. I should have remembered WJ's instructions of two years ago, when first he had started to tinker with this electrical device. Always use with a calm mind. We had had our greatest successes under such conditions, perking up the peripheral vision, sharpening the focus of the pre-mythago forms that could be glimpsed when within the swell and grasp of the sylvan net. It was wrong of me to go ahead with Steven without first checking the note-books. I have no excuse, just shame. The effect on the boy was devastating. I have learned a severe and sobering lesson.

10

Steven remembers nothing of the incident with the frontal bridge. It is as if the electrical surge that sent him into such hysteria has blanked the last five days from him. His most recent memory is of school, on Tuesday. He remembers eating his lunch, and walking to a class, and then nothing. He is happy again, and the fever has died down. He didn't wake last night, and has no memory of the grey-green man. I walked with him by the edge of the wood, then ventured in through the gate, down by the thin stream with its slippery banks. Inside the wood I sensed the pre-mythagos at once and asked Steven what he could see.

His answer: Funny things.

He smiled as he said this. I questioned him further, but that is all he would say. 'Funny things.' He looked quite blank when I asked him to look for the grey-green man.

I have destroyed something in him. I have warped him in some way. I am frightened by this since I do not understand even remotely what I have done. Wynne-Jones might know better, but he remains lost. And I cannot bring myself to explain in full just what I did to Steven. This act of cowardice will destroy me. But until I understand what has happened, who is writing in my journal, I must keep as free as possible of domestic difficulty. I am denying something in myself for the sake of a sanity that will collapse as soon as I am free of mystery. This is limbo!

Jennifer treats me harshly. I am spending as much time as I can with the two boys. But I must find Wynne-Jones. I must find out what has happened to bring this haunting upon myself.

So tired he could hardly walk, Huxley walked across the night field, glad of a moonglow behind clouds that showed him the stark outline of Oak Lodge. Using this as a marker he stepped slowly towards his home, the sickness in his stomach still a jarring pain and a nauseous surge. Whatever he had eaten, he should have been more careful.

This excursion had been short, again, but he had hoped to have returned before nightfall. As it was, he imagined dawn was just an hour or so away.

The sound of Jennifer's cry stopped him in his tracks. He listened carefully, close to the gate, and again he heard her voice, a slightly strangled, then increasingly intense evocation of pain. She was gasping, he realised. The sound of her voice stopped quite suddenly, and then there was a laugh. The sound was eerily loud in the night, in the still night, this solitude of sound and sensation that was so close to dawn.

'Oh my God. Jennifer . . . Jennifer!'

He began to walk more swiftly. An image of his wife being attacked in the night was insisting its superiority over the obvious.

The doors of his study were shattered abruptly. Glass crashed and the doors flung wide. Something moved with incredible speed across the lawns, through the trees, causing leaves and apples to fall. Whatever it was stopped suddenly close to the hedges, then crashed through them, passing Huxley like a storm wind.

And stopped. And moved in the moonlight.

Grey-green man . . . ?

There was nothing there. There was moon-shadow only. And yet Huxley could sense the outline of a man, a naked man, a man still hot from exertion, the smell of the man, the heat of the man, the pulse of heart and head, the shaking of the limbs of the man . . .

Grey-green . . .

'Come back. Come and talk.'

The garden was aflow with movement. Everything was bending, twisting, writhing in a wind that circled the motionless shadow. And the shadow moved, towards Huxley, then away, and there was no glimpse, no sight, no feeling of reality, just the sense of something that had watched him and had returned to the wood.

Huxley ran back to the broken gate, tripping on the shattered wood. He had not even heard the breaking of the gate, but he followed the wind with his ears and night vision, and saw the scrubwood thrash with life, then die again into the steadiness of night, as whatever it was passed through it and beyond, into the timeless realm of the wood.

'Jennifer . . . oh no . . .'

She was not in the room. The bed was still warm, disturbed and dishevelled in an obvious way. He walked quickly out onto the landing, then downstairs again, following the slightest of sounds to the smallest of rooms. She was seated on the toilet, and pulled the door shut abruptly as he opened it.

'George! Please! A *little* privacy . . .'

'Are you all right?'

'I'm very all right. But I thought you were going to have a heart attack.'

She laughed, then pulled the chain. When she emerged into the dark corridor she reached for him and put her arms around his neck. She seemed startled to discover him wearing his jacket. 'You've not got dressed again! Good *grief*, George. There really is very little hope for you.' She hesitated, half amused, half anguished. 'Well . . . perhaps there's *some* hope . . .' Her sudden kiss was deep, moist and passionate.

Her breath was strong, a sexual smell.

'I'm going back to bed. I rather hoped you'd be there too . . .'

'I have to think.'

In the darkness he couldn't see her face, but he sensed the smile, the weary smile. 'Yes, George. Of course. You go and think. Write in your journal.' She walked away from him, towards the stairs. 'There are fresh bones in the pantry should you get peckish.'

But her voice gave away her sadness. He heard the moment's crying, and intuited instantly and painfully that something she had thought renewed she now realised was not.

So he *had* been here again. The encounter in the garden, in the darkness . . . that *had* been the grey-green man. And he had seduced Jennifer!

Huxley drew the journal from its hiding place, and with shaking hands opened it, switching on the lamp.

*

The same? You and I? No. No! It feels wrong. I am no ghost.

Am I a ghost? Perhaps. Yes. When I read your words. Yes. Perhaps right.

I am confused. I live in brief moments, and the dreams are strong and powerful. I am dreaming a life. But I belong in Oak Lodge. When I am there I feel warmth. But the wood pulls me back. You are right. You other writer. I am your dream and I am free, but not free. Oh confused! And ill. Always so ill. The blood is so hot.

The dreams, the urging. I am such a hunter. I run them down and use my hands. I am plastered with detritus from the forest.

My son Steven. You have tampered with my son. This was wrong. Such fury in me. If I see you I fear to control my anger. Leave Steven alone. I am aware of him in the wood. He is here. Something has, or will happen, and he is everywhere. Something with happen to him. Do not interfere with him. An immense event is shaping around him, not yet happened, but already changing the wood, and time is recoiling and refashioning. I watch seasons in frantic change, in full, seconds-long flight. I hear sounds from all times. This is Ash's doing.

The horses, the time of horses. Something happened there, something small. Something to you/me to cause this you/me, this wild split. What happened? I see it only in dreams. I am too wild, too base, when I am free of dreams I am wild and running, the merest scent of blood is an enragement, the scent of flesh sends me surging, Jennifer is not safe from me, guard her guard her, even though you recognise that passion.

Find Ash and find where she sent you. Why did she send you there? The horse, the fire in that wood. All a dream.

Guard Jennifer from the ghost and the bloody obsessions of the ghost

I am so close to this earth, so much matter of rock and wood and silent night that lives, claws, crawls, devours, desires, surges and comes into all life that interferes and crosses paths and tracks

Kill me?

How?

Join again, return me to you. Ash. The key. The wood is tugging, a root around me. It draws me tight. The smell of must and rotten wood. The stink. Each a chain around me. Each a tug. I am a prisoner

Steven will be lost to us. He will never

But with this tantalising and terrifying half sentence, the entry ended.

12

What *had* happened in that living dream of the cold wood, and the running horses? He had been run down by one of the creatures. He had tried to see the face of the corpse on its back, but had failed. He had, when he thought about it clearly, felt himself torn spiritually apart: there had been that moment of wild riding, of moving with horse and cadaver through the trees . . .

Had that been the moment of division?

Had that been when Green-grey man had split from him?

He wrote in his journal:

To my shadow: What do you know of Ash? What do you remember of the moment when the horse collided with you in the birchwood glade? How shall I contact Ash again? Why do you think Wynne-Jones is dead? Why do you think Steven will be lost? What is the great event that you feel forming? Is there any way that we can talk? Or must we continue to correspond through the pages of this journal?

He placed the book behind the shelves, then went out into the rising dawn. Wisps of what looked like smoke, funnels of greyish smog, rose, from over Ryhope Wood. As the light increased, the odd vortices vanished. The last thing he saw before returning to the house was the shimmering movement of leaves and green, running, it seemed, for several yards along the edgewood. He could not quite focus upon it, although the sensation of movement was strongest when he looked away, catching it from the corner of his eye.

*

The new day was a Saturday and both boys were at home. By mid-morning the sound of their antics and play had begun to irritate Huxley as he tried to concentrate his mind – his tired mind – on thinking through the experience with Ash. He watched the boys from his study window. Christian, the more rumbustious of the two, was swinging from every branch he could find during a game of some form of chase. Steven seemed to become aware of his father, watching him, and froze for a moment, his face anxious. Only when Huxley moved away did he hear the sound of the game restart.

They are both afraid of me. No: they are both missing closeness with me. They hear their friends talk about fathers . . . they think of their father . . . I feel so helpless. I am not interested in them as boys, only in the men, the minds, the thoughts and explorations of deeper thought that they will become . . . they bore me . . .

The moment he had written these lines, he inked them through, so strongly, so savagely, that none would ever read this terrible and sickening moment of self honesty.

No. I am envious of them. They 'see' in a way that is beyond my ability. Their fantasy games include glimpses of pre-mythago forms that I would give *anything* to witness. They are attuned more deeply to the wood. I hear it in their stories, their fantasies, their games. But if they were too aware of what was happening, to them . . . might that not diminish their spontaneous 'seeing'? These thoughts seem irrational, and yet I feel that they must be kept in ignorance for their talents to be pure.

Later in the day the boys left the garden. The sudden cessation of their noise attracted Huxley and when he went to see where they'd gone he noticed them, distantly, tearing round the edge of the wood, in the direction of the railway tracks.

He knew where they'd be going, and out of curiosity followed them, taking his stick and his panama hat. The day was bright, if not hot, and there was a brisk, moist-smelling breeze, heralding rain later.

They had gone to the mill pond, of course. Christian was sitting on the old jetty, where the boat had once been tethered. The pond was wide, curving round between dense, overhanging trees, to end in a sprawling patch of rushes out of sight. The oaks at that far end were like a solid wall, great thick trunks, the spaces between them a clutter of willow and spreading holly. It was as if the wall had been deliberately built to stop the wood being entered at that point.

Once, there had been fish in abundance in this pool, but at some time in the twenties the life had faded. A pike or two still could be seen, gliding below the water. But there was little point in fishing, now, and the old boat was rapidly rotting.

Huxley had warned both boys *never* to take that boat

out, but he could see that Christian was contemplating such an act, as he dangled his feet in the water. Such a headstrong boy. So wilful.

Steven was beating through the reeds with a stick. No, not beating: cutting. He gathered a thick armful and carried them back around the pond's edge, and Huxley drew back into the concealing undergrowth.

The exchange of conversation between his sons confirmed that they were planning to make a reed boat, and float it on the pond.

He smiled, and was about to withdraw and walk silently back along the short path that led from open land to this pond, when he realised that the boys were alarmed.

Christian was running over the decaying piles of the boat-house, pointing into the thick woods. Steven followed him, and they dropped to a crouch, peering into the gloom.

From his lurking place, Huxley followed the direction of their interest. He realised that a wide, strange face was watching from high in the branches of a tree. He was reminded of the Cheshire Cat from Alice, and smiled. But the face wasn't smiling.

It withdrew abruptly from the light. Something crashed noisily to the ground, startling and scattering birds from the tree tops. It moved with great speed through the woodland, round the pondside, was silent for a moment, then crashed noisily into the deep wood, finally vanishing from earshot.

Huxley remained where he was. The excited lads passed by him, talking about the 'monkey face', and sharing the burden of reeds for the hull of their reed ship, which they intended to build in the woodshed. As soon as they were gone Huxley went round to the boathouse, and struck into the tangle of undergrowth behind. There was no path, and his trousers were snagged and torn by the screen of briar rose and blackberry bramble. He found that the simple barrier of this untamed wood would not allow him in, but after a while he found a patch of nettles, stamped them down, laid his jacket over them, and sat, screened from sight, surrounded by the heavy silence and air of the wood, watching through the shifting light for any further sign of 'monkey face', a mythago that he had not yet observed himself at quarters close enough for him to make a judgement upon its mythological nature.

It was a fruitless wait, and he returned to Oak Lodge a disappointed man. There were no further entries in his private journal, and he made a short entry in his research journal, defining the mythago as far as he was able. He asked Steven and Christian about their day, and teased their perception of the creature from them, affecting idle interest. But neither boy could add more to what he himself had seen, save to say that the face was wide, high-browed and painted. It was perhaps, then, an early manifestation of Cro-Magnon belief? Its appearance was too modern for it to be associated with the culture that had given rise to the man from Piltdown, the nature of whose belief systems constantly exercised Huxley's imagination and interest.

At eleven o'clock Jennifer announced that she was retiring for the night, and as she walked past him paused, held out her hand. 'Are you coming?'

It horrified Huxley to feel such shock, such fear of accepting his wife's invitation. A cold sweat tingled on his neck and hairline, and he said casually, 'I do need to read a little further.'

'I see,' she breathed with resignation, and went to bed.

How could he feel like this? He noticed that his hands were shaking. The intimacy that had characterised their first years together more by its regularity than its passion, had certainly, in recent years, changed to a self-conscious routine of tentative suggestion, almost unknowing touch, and brief encounter by darkness. And yet he had accepted this change for the worse – it always occurred to him that Jennifer might have been accepting the status with far less complacency – without really conscious thought. It had taken the sound of her pleasure to remind him of their early years, and to make him aware, now, of the avoidance that he had been practising.

He nearly cried as he thought of how much he had denied the closeness of their life that Jennifer so needed.

He stared hard at the ceiling, thinking of her in bed, thinking of holding her. And gradually he forced himself to his feet, and walked upstairs, and entered the bedroom where she slept softly, half exposed from below the summer sheet, her body faintly illuminated by moonlight from the bright summer night.

She was naked, he realised, and the shock made him

catch his breath. He was almost embarrassed to look at her, at the leg that lay outside the covers, the soft breast that was crushed in the bend of her arm, as she slept, her head turned half towards him.

He undressed and pulled on pyjamas. In bed beside her he watched her for a long time, long enough to bite all skin from the inside of his lower lip, so that he tasted blood, and his lip was sore.

He almost woke her once, his hand out to her, the fingers hovering just above her tousled hair.

But he didn't. He closed his eyes, sank a little lower, and thought of the primal mythological form of human-kind, his great quest: The Urscumug . . .

Somewhere in the woods, the creature lives. It must have formed many times. But it is deep. It is in the heart. How to find it? How to find? I must devise a way of calling it to the edge . . .

He was still thinking about his quest when he heard the sound of movement downstairs. It startled him at first, but then he lay quietly, listening hard.

Yes. It was in the study. There was a long time of silence, then again the sound of furniture being moved, drawers opened, cabinets opened as perhaps his souvenirs were examined.

Then a sudden sound on the stairs, someone coming up the stairs at great speed.

Again, silence.

It was on the landing. It moved along the landing to the door of the bedroom and again stopped; then the door was opened and something sped into the room, a fleet shadow crossing the floor to the window in an instant, and closing the curtains. A deeper darkness descended, but in the moment of dim light Huxley had seen the man shape, the deep shadow shape that was unquestionably a naked human male. The shoulders were broad, the body hard and lean, and the creature's member was distended and almost vertical. A strong odour filled the room, something of undergrowth, something of the sharp smell of an unwashed man.

Slowly Huxley sat up in bed. He sensed the movement of the figure, short darting movements that carried it from one side of the room to the other, then back again.

It was waiting for him to go!

In its last journal entry it had written 'protect Jennifer against me. Protect her against the ghost . . .'

'Go away,' Huxley breathed. 'I won't let you come near her. You told me not to . . .'

It raced up to him in the darkness and hovered there, its eyes dimly reflecting, showing how wide they were, how intense. It was hard to define shape; he sensed shadows shifting, a depthlessness to the figure, but yet it was solid. The heat and the smell that came off it were overpowering.

In a voice that sounded like the restless stirring of a breeze, it whispered 'journal'.

It had written in the journal!

It towered over him, and Jennifer suddenly stirred. 'George . . . ?'

She tossed her head slightly, and her arm extended towards him, but before the hand could touch him it was intercepted. The creature had her, and Huxley felt willed to leave the bed.

'Journal,' breathed the grey-green man, and there was the hint of a laugh, of a smile as the word was said for the second time.

'George?' Jennifer murmured, coming more awake.

His heart pounding, the sense of the grey-green man's mocking laughter teasing at his conscience, Huxley swung out of bed and left the room.

Half way down the stairs he heard Jennifer's cry of surprise as she woke fully. Then her sudden, splendid laugh.

He blocked his ears against the sounds that came next, and went into his study, tears streaming down his face as he fumbled behind the books for his private journal.

13

Will try to speak. But you move slowly, ghostly. Perhaps I am the same to you. I observe the house and Jenny, the boys, and they are real, although they seem to be a dream. But you are slow, the me part, the me factor, too ghostly, and it is hard to speak.

Steven is in the wood, Chris too. Something huge in the wood, some event, some rebirth or regeneration. I sense it. I hear it from mouths, from tales. I have been here so long, and the world of the mythago is my world.

This is puzzling. Why have you not been in the wood,

in the some way, in the same wood? Confused. My mind does not focus. But I have had encounters. You have not had the same encounters.

I can't answer about Steven. As a man, he will come here. Or as a boy and grow to a man. Somehow. It has to do with the Urscumaga. Pursuit. Quest. I cannot say more. I know NO more! Be gentle with Steven. Be careful of him. Be watchful. Love him. LOVE HIM!

Wynne-Jones was in the horse temple. You saw him. You MUST have seen. I think he was killed. He was trapped.

You should know this. Why not? Why do you not?

Perhaps you have forgotten. Perhaps some memory is stripped from you and exists in me. Memory in you is denied me. No. Not true. Your account of Ash is my account. Almost. You describe the amulet as dull. The amulet was bright. You say a green stone. Yes. You say a leather thong. No. Horse hair. Twined horse hair. Can you have made such a mistake?

I see now that you make no mention of Ash previously. Not my journal then, though so many entries are the same. Yes. Snow Woman, Steven's word, was the same as Ash. I remember her visit, that winter. But Wynne-Jones made contact in February. No mention in the journal of that. But I wrote an account. He understood the basic nature of Ash. But no mention in either journal. Yet it was written.

Are we the same?

Ash; She carries the memory of wood. She is the guardian of ancient forest and can summon from them and send to them. She uses the techniques of the shaman *to do this. By casting her charms of wood and bone she can create – and destroy, too, if she wishes – forests of lime and spruce, or oak and ash, or alder and beech. She can send hunters to find pigs, or stags, or bears, or horses.* Other things! *Forgotten creatures. Forgotten woods. Her skills are legion. She can send the curious to find curiosities. She can even send a* stealer of talismans *to find . . . well, what can I say to you?* To find a little humility, *perhaps. I am certain that she was telling me to leave alone things I did not understand.*

The hunters of the land have always believed in her, knowing that she can control all the woods of the world. In her mind, and in her skills, forests are waiting to be born, ancient forests are waiting for the return of the hunters. Through Ash there is a strange continuity. No matter what has been destroyed, it lives in her, and one day can be summoned back.

She sent us to the horse sacrifice for a reason.

We must ask: what reason?

I was riding the horse when it collided with the hooded man. I remember nearly falling. The horse was bolting. It had two bodies on its back. One alive (me) beginning to burn badly. One dead. The hooded man was struck. I fell, the horse ran on. Then I came home. But I am a ghost.

Find Ash! Return us to the horses! Something happened!

He had walked quietly to the landing, tiptoeing up the stairs, shaking badly, but with a rage, now, and not with fear. He stripped off his pyjamas and felt the cool touch of night air on his naked skin. Then he banged loudly on the banister.

As he expected, the door to his bedroom opened and something moved, with blurring speed, into the darkness.

Grey-green man stood at the far end of the landing, and Huxley sensed the way it watched, the way it suddenly grinned.

Jennifer was hissing, 'What *is* it?'

Huxley moved along the landing. Grey-green came at him and there was static in the air where they almost touched.

'Go to the study,' Huxley hissed stiffly. 'Wait for me . . .'

There was hesitation in the ghost, then that mocking smile again, and yet . . . it acceded to the instruction. It passed Huxley, and went downstairs, lurking in the grim darkness.

Jennifer ran out onto the landing, dragging her house-coat around her. There was no sound of disturbance from the boys' room, and Huxley was glad.

She sounded anxious.

'Is there someone in the house?'

'I don't know,' he said. 'I'd better look around.'

Her hand touched his bare back as she peered over the banister into the gloom below. She seemed slightly startled. 'You're so cool, now.'

And a lot flabbier, he thought to himself.

And Jennifer added, 'You smell fresher.'

'Fresher?'

'You needed a good bath. But you smell . . . cleaner, suddenly . . .'

'I'm sorry if I smelled strong before.'

'I quite liked it,' she said quietly, and Huxley closed his eyes for a moment.

'But perhaps it's the sheets,' Jennifer said. 'I'll change them first thing in the morning.'

'I'll investigate downstairs.'

The french windows were open, the study light off. Huxley switched on the desk lamp and peered down at the open page of the journal.

Grey-green man had scrawled the words: *then how do I get back? Must think. Will go to Horse Shrine and stay there. But the blood is hot. You must understand. I am not in control.*

This entry occurred below the response that Huxley had penned to his alter ego's earlier, substantial account of Ash, and his questions about the nature of their dual existence.

Huxley had written:

We are clearly not the same, but only similar. We are aspects of two versions of George Huxley. If I am incomplete then it is in a way that is different from the incompleteness of you. You seem to be the most isolated. Perhaps your existence in this world, my world, is wrong for you. Perhaps there is a part of me that is running, fearful and dying, in a world that is more familiar to you.

If I had no other reason for concluding these things it

411

is this: I have never called Jennifer 'Jenny'. Not ever. It is not possible for me to even contemplate writing that nickname. She is J. in my journals, or Jennifer. Never the shorter form.

Your Jennifer is not my Jennifer. I have let you loose upon the woman I love, and you have taught me one thing, about how callous I have become, and I accept that lesson. But you will not enter this house again, not beyond the study. If you do, I shall endeavour to destroy you, rather than help you. Even if it means losing Wynne-Jones forever, I shall certainly find a way to disseminate the bestial spirit that you are.

I should prefer to return you to the body from which you have gone missing: *my* body, albeit in another location, another time, some other space and time that has somehow become confused with my own world.

Yes, other things give away the fact that we are living parallel lives, closely linked, yet subtly different. I refer to the 'Urscumug', not 'Urscumaga'. You know more about Ash than I do. Wynne-Jones, in your world, has raced ahead of my own, pipe-reeking friend. The talisman most definitely was hung with leather, not horse hair. Clearly *I* am the hooded man over whom you ran, in your mad canter from the forest glade. My oilskin hood was torn, quite beyond repair!

And so you must propose a way for us to meet, to engage, to communicate.

But I repeat, you are not to enter my house beyond this desk.

If you doubt that I have the skill to destroy you, then look into your own bestial heart: remember what I/you have achieved in the past. Remember what happened to you/I in the Wolf Glen, when we discovered a certain magic of our own, destructive to mythagos!

And below this entry, Grey-green man had scrawled *then how do I get back?*

Huxley closed and concealed the journal. He walked out into the garden, and stepped carefully across the lawn to the bushes. The ground was wet with dew, the air scented with raw, rich night perfume of soil and leaf. Everything was very still.

Huxley stepped among the moist bushes of rhododendron and fuchsia. He pressed the wet leaves and flowers against his torso, and found, to his mild surprise, that he was excited by the touch of nature upon his dry, cool body. He rubbed leaves between his fingers, crushed fuchsia flowers, reached down and rubbed his hands over the dewy soil. He drew breath in through his nostrils, filling his lungs, and as he stood so he smeared his hands over his shoulders and belly . . .

A blur of night-lit movement, the earth vibrating, the undergrowth shaking, and Grey-green man was there, shimmering and shadowy, watching him.

They stood in silence, man and ghost, and then Huxley laughed. 'You frightened me once, but no longer. And yet, I feel sympathy for you, and will try to send you back. By doing that I believe I can release Wynne-Jones.'

Grey-green man took a slow step forward, reaching to Huxley.

Huxley stepped forward too, but ripped up a branch of bush, and swept it at the ghost.

'Go to the Horse Shrine! I'll meet you there to-morrow.'

Grey-green man didn't cower, but there was something about it, something less triumphant than before. It hovered, then withdrew, then turned (or so Huxley thought) to stare again at its alter ego. It seemed to be questioning.

Huxley squeezed sap from the torn branch and rubbed it on his face.

'She liked the smell,' he said, and Laughed as he tossed the branch aside, before turning and entering the house.

Locking the french windows behind him.

Jennifer was sitting up in bed, the covers round her knees. She stared at Huxley by lamplight, her face puzzled, anguished.

'I want you to tell me what's going on,' she said quietly, firmly. She was looking at him, staring at him, taking in his nakedness. He imagined he knew what she was thinking: he did not look like the body she had so recently felt against her. He was broader, chubbier, less fit.

'It will take some time.'

'Then take time.'

He climbed into bed beside her, and on a new and strong impulse turned towards her, putting his arm across her to turn out the lamp.

'I would like to kiss you first,' he said. 'And then 'I'll tell you everything.'

'One kiss, then. But I'm angry, George. And I want to know what's happening . . .'

14

The boys were at school. Huxley entered their room and stood, for a moment, surveying the truly appalling mess that the lads had left after a weekend of playing, pillow fighting, and reading. They had been making a model boat, and against their father's instructions had brought the model up to their bedroom. The floor, the surfaces, the bed itself, were covered with bits of reed.

He reached down and picked up several sheets of white paper with pencil drawings. They were the blueprints for the model: crude, but skilful, and he recognised Christian's imagination at work here. He was impressed. Plan view, side view, rear elevation, cross section . . .

Of the ship itself there was no sign. It was an ambitious project. They usually contented themselves with smaller, wooden models.

The room was quiet and he closed his eyes for a moment, summoning the imaginations at work here. He banished from his mind the smell of unwashed socks that instantly struck his consciousness. What he wanted was to feel the *fantasies* of the boys, their dreams, and in this room he might be able to touch the edge of those dreams.

It was an odd thought, and yet: he was convinced that one of the boys had created the Ash mythago.

He went through their drawers, where clothes were crushed and crumpled, apple-cores rotted, penny dreadfuls were concealed, and rock hard ends of sandwiches – made for midnight feasts – nestled side by side with pictures torn from magazines.

Eventually he found the fragments of wood and bone that Ash had left. They were still in their leather container. Huxley placed them on the desk, rolled them over the surface, remembered the time last winter when Snow Woman had left these items at the gate.

Then he went over to the bed and sat down, staring at the magic from across the room.

Why did you leave these pieces? Why? Why did you come to Oak Lodge? Why did you destroy the chickens? Why did you ensure that Steven would see you?

Why?

Steven and his passion for presents, his need for gifts. Had he created a mythago that was designed to fulfil that need in him?

Give me something. Bring me something. Bring me a gift. Give me something that makes me feel . . . wanted . . .

Was she Steven's mythago, then? Gift-bringing Ash. But what sort of gift was implied in two fragments of thorn, and a piece of wild cat?

Perhaps Steven was intended to wear them. Perhaps then he would journey, in the same way that Huxley had journeyed. These bits of wood represented a different forest, though.

Why did you come out of the wood? Why did you leave these fragments? Why the chickens? What did you hope to achieve?

He thought back to the time in the Horse Shrine. Ash had watched him closely and carefully for a long while, and perhaps there *had* been disappointment in her face? Was she expecting someone else?

She had been waiting for someone. She had been at the Horse Shrine since the winter, if the evidence of the waste spoils was to be believed. She had been trying to make contact with the Huxleys, and yet all she had done was send George Huxley on a nightmarish trip to a freezing wood, long in the past . . .

If she had wanted Steven, what had she wanted to do with him?

And if Wynne-Jones *had* been present in the same ancient mythago-realm – and the grey-green man suggested that perhaps he had – what had Ash wanted with *him*?

How had he come to play a part in the same ancient sequence?

Why had he played any part at all, if Ash had wanted *Steven* . . . ?

Huxley prowled the room, drinking in the disorder, tapping the imagination that reverberated here.

Steven and Ash . . . a shocking visitation to the henhouse . . . a bed of dead hens . . . *just like in the story* . . .

He went quickly to the window, staring down at the yard, the spring sunshine. He tried to replay the whole of that snow-deadened encounter, after Christmas.

What had Steven said to his mother? 'Got them all . . . just like in the story . . .'

What story?

Steven hadn't seen inside the shed, but Huxley had told him that all the hens had been killed. A fox had done it, he said, and Steven had seemed to accept that statement, despite the fact that Ash had clearly been to the henhouse herself.

What story?

Steven had said, 'That old drummer fox . . .'

Huxley had taken no notice, and Jennifer had simply responded to the shock of losing all their hens.

Who was that 'old drummer fox'?

He looked at the scattered books, searched among them, but found nothing. He called for Jennifer and she came into the room, frowning at the mess. She looked as tired as she felt. It had been a long night, and a long talk, and Huxley had told her much that she should have known before, and explained about the supernatural event that was occurring.

Not unsurprisingly, Jennifer was shocked, and was still shocked, and had spent an hour on her own, fighting a feeling of nausea. He had left her alone. It had seemed inappropriate to try to explain that in a way she had slept only with her husband, that no man from this, the real world, had touched her apart from Huxley. But that was not how she saw it, and there were other considerations too, no doubt.

'Drummer Fox and Boy Ralph? That was Steven's favourite story for years, when he was much younger. He was – obsessed with it . . .'

'I've never heard of it.'

'Of course,' she said acidly. 'You never read *anything* to the boys. I did all the reading.'

'Rebuke accepted,' Huxley said quickly. 'Can you find the book? I must see that story.'

She searched the shelves, and the scatter of books on the floor, opened the wardrobe where albums, school books, and magazines were stored, but couldn't find the volume of tales that included Drummer Fox.

Huxley felt impatient and anxious. 'I must know the story.'

'Why?'

'I think it may be the key to what is happening. What can you remember of it? You said you'd read it to him—'

'Hundreds of times. But a long time ago.'

'Tell me the story.'

She leaned back against one of the desks and gathered her thoughts. 'Oh Lord, George. It's so long ago. And I read so many stories to them, Christian especially . . .'

'Try. Please try.'

'He was a sort of gypsy fox. Very old, older than any human alive. He'd been wandering Europe for centuries, with a drum, which he beat every dawn and dusk, and a sack of tricks. He either played tricks on people to escape from them, or entertained them for his supper. He also had a charge, an infant boy.'

'Boy Ralph.'

'That's right. Boy Ralph was the son of a Chief, a warrior of the olden days. But the boy was born on a highly auspicious day and his father was jealous and decided to kill the infant by smothering him. He was planning to use the carcase of a chicken for the vile deed.

'Drummer Fox lived at the edge of the village, entertaining people with his tricks and sometimes giving them prophecies. He liked the boy and seeing him in danger stole him and ran away with him. The King sent a giant of a warrior after the fox, with instructions to hunt him down and kill them both. So Drummer Fox found himself running for his life.

'Wherever Drummer Fox went he found that humans were tricky and destructive. He didn't trust them. Some were kind and he left them alone. He always paid a small price for whatever he had taken from them. But others were hunters and tried to kill him. At night he would make his bed in their chicken sheds, making mattresses and blankets from the dead chicks—'

Huxley slapped his knees as he heard this. 'Go on . . .'

'He used to say [and here, Jennifer put on a silly country voice], "Nothing against the chicks but their clucking. They'd give me away. Give me away. So better a feather bed than a nice egg in the morning. Sorry chicks . . ."'

'And then he'd silently kill the lot of them.'

'Of course. This *is* a story for children.' Huxley shared Jennifer's smile. 'Anyway, that isn't all. Drummer Fox made the infant Ralph a plaything of the heads of the chickens, threaded on a piece of string.'

Huxley was astonished and delighted. 'Good God! That's exactly what had happened in the chicken house. And Steven never saw inside! He didn't know about that particularly gruesome piece of Ash's game. Go on. Go on!'

'That's more or less it, really. The fox is on the run. He gets what he can from the human folk he meets, but if in danger he tricks the humans into the forest where they invariably get crushed under the hooves of the Hunter who's following the fox. It's quite murderous stuff. The boys lapped it up.'

'And how is it resolved? Is it resolved?'

Jennifer had to think for a moment, then she remembered. 'Drummer Fox gets cornered in a deep, wooded valley. The Hunter is almost on him. So the fox makes a mask and puts it on and goes up to greet the giant warrior.'

'What mask?'

'That's the clever part. For a child, at least. He puts on a *fox* mask. He tells the Hunter that he's a local man who has tricked Drummer Fox by pretending to be a renegade fox as well. Drummer Fox has revealed his weakness to him. To destroy the fox all the Hunter needs to do is to disguise himself on horseback with dry rushes and reeds.'

'Aha. The ending loometh.'

'The Hunter duly ties reeds all over his body and—'

'Drummer Fox sets light to him!'

'And away he gallops, trailing flame and cursing the Fox. The nice or nasty little coda is that one day Drummer Fox and Boy Ralph are making their way back through a dark wood when they hear a hunting horn and the smell of burning.'

'The stuff of nightmares,' Huxley said, pacing about

the room, thinking hard. 'No wonder the boy is afraid of horses. Good God, we've probably traumatised him for life.'

'It's only a story. The stories the boys tell each other are far more gruesome. But then they've leafed extensively through the copy of *Gray's Anatomy* on your shelf.'

'Have they! Have they indeed! Then at least their stories will be colourful.'

'Does it help? Drummer Fox, I mean?'

Huxley swung round and walked up to Jennifer, gathering her into his arms and hugging her. 'Yes. Oh yes. Very much indeed.' She seemed startled, then drew back, smiling.

'Thank you for letting me know about your madness,' she said quietly. 'Whatever I can do . . .'

'I know. I don't know *what* you can do for the moment. But I feel deeply relieved to have told you what is happening. The grey-green figure frightens me, even though I know it is an aspect of *me*.'

Jennifer went pale and looked away. 'I don't wish to think about that any more. I just want you to be safe. And to be near me more often . . .' The look in her eye as she glanced at him made Huxley smile. They touched hands, and then went downstairs.

15

A wonderful example of convergence, or perhaps *merging*: Steven's imagination is inculcated with the legend and image of the fox: but *Drummer Fox* is just a corruption of a more powerful mythological cycle concerning Ash. Ash *herself* is a 'story' reflecting an ancient event, perhaps an incident from the first migrations and movements of a warrior elite of Indo-Europeans, from central Europe.

Ash, the inherited memory, is present in Steven's mind, and the corrupted form of the folk-tale/fable is also strongly present. So Ash – *created by Steven* – emerges from the wood with associations of Drummer Fox: hence the killing of chickens, the necklace of hen heads.

But this Ash has no child!

Drummer Fox: shaman? The drum, the classic instrument of shamanic trance. And Fox's bag of tricks. The same as Ash's bone and wood bag, her magic.

And Ash carries a tiny wrist-drum!

The story of Ash, then, has been shaped by a time nearer to her own origination as a *legendary tale*. Later, as the tale corrupts further into Drummer Fox and other tales of that ilk, so certain shaman trappings return.

Steven summoned Ash. Ash came, half myth, half folklore, and called to Steven. Her gift at the gate – the bone and wood pieces – is part attraction to Steven, part the price she pays for her night's stay on the carcases of the hens.

She wants Steven, then. But why? To replace the lost child? Drummer Fox protects Infant Ralph. In one story – the Ash story – has she. I wonder, *lost* the child? Does she then seek to replace the lost child with another, perhaps so that she can pretend that the true 'prince' is still alive?

How I wish I knew more of the Ash legend.

Wynne-Jones and myself are seen as 'intruders, not to be trusted' and sent to the 'hooves of the horses' by Ash. But she selects a key moment, a primary event in mythological time, when images occur that will last into the corrupted form: the burning man, the horses riding wild, the crushing of men below hooves.

So is it Steven who has directed this aspect of Ash? Or is it Ash conforming to the *older* ritual?

And how do I convince Ash to return me to that moment? And once there, how do I return Wynne Jones safely?

And how did my alter ego slip into this world from his own?

A primary moment, a focus, may be the meeting point of many worlds simply because of its importance . . .

I *must* return to that moment. Something happened there, something was there, that will explain the complication!

You will have to offer her Steven. You fool! Don't you see? You will have to offer her the boy. And then trust her. Can you trust her? Can WE trust her? She will not perform her magic without the gift she seeks. Fool!

But I came *back*. She cast me away, into a landscape both remote in time and place, but it was not a

424

permanent dislocation. She is Steven's mythago. This
has tempered the fury that might otherwise be present
within her. I still have the necklet of wood and bones
with which she dispatched me before; now I will hope to
reason with her.

He left the journal open on his desk and went through
the house to begin to collect his supplies and equipment
for the trek. At some point during the next ten minutes
he was aware of the wafting smell of undergrowth in the
house, and the sound of movement from his office. The
visit was brief, and he caught sight of the shadow as it
ran with uncanny speed back across the field to the
woodland edge.

A brief response, then, and without much interest
Huxley returned to read what had been written.

'Damnation!'

He ran to the garden, dropping the journal as he went.
'Come back!' he shouted. 'You're wrong. I'm sure!
Damn!'

Now he was frightened. He swept up the journal,
turned again to the scrawled line: *Steven is not safe
from Ash. She must be destroyed*, and then flung the
book into its hiding place.

Now there was no time to lose. He roughly packed
his sack, crammed whatever food lay to hand – bread,
cheese, a piece of cold mutton – and almost demolished
Jennifer as he ran to the garden.

'Wait until dawn at least . . .' she said, recovering

from the impact and helping him gather the spilled items from his sack.

'I can't.'

'You're in a lather, George . . .'

Furious, eyes blazing with panic, he hissed, 'He's going to kill her! That will undo everything. Wynne-Jones, gone forever. Maybe . . .' He hesitated, and bit back the words, 'Steven too—

'I have to follow him,' he went on, 'and fast. God, he's so fast . . .'

Jennifer sighed, seemed sad, then kissed her husband.

'Off you go then. Be careful. For the boys' sake, and for mine.'

He made a feeble attempt at humour. 'I'll return *with* Wynne-Jones, or on him . . .'

'But lose his pipe, if you can,' she added, then turned quickly away as her voice began to break.

16

It took Huxley over four hours to locate the Horse Shrine, the longest search ever. He had been confident of the route, but became distracted by the sudden change in the wood from a stifling, chirruping zoo of green light and intense shade, to a silent, gloomy dell, where the overpowering smell of decay set his heart racing and his senses pounding. By moving too fast through this deadly glade he disorientated himself, and took hours to find some part of Ryhope Wood that prompted memory.

At one point a blur of movement swept past him, noisily disappearing into the deep wood. At first he thought that it might be the grey-green man, overtaking him on his passage inwards, but then remembered that his shadow was far ahead of him. More likely, then, the movement was one of the various forms of the Green Jack. As such he took precautionary manoeuvres and measures against attack, keeping his leather flying jacket firmly buttoned to the throat, despite the humidity, and holding a small wooden shield on the side of his face nearest the disturbance.

It was maddening to be so lost, and to be so desperate to find a shrine that, over the years, he had found with no difficulty.

By a stream he washed his face and cleaned his boots, which were heavy with clay from a tree-crowded mire into which he had stumbled. His lungs were tight with pollen and the damp, heavy air. His mouth was foul. His eyes stung with dust, tiny seeds, and the endless slanting, slashing light from above the dense foliage cover.

The stream was a blessing. He didn't recognise it, although the ruins of a building on its far bank, a building in Norman style, high earth defences, compact and economic use of stone, reminded him of a place he had seen three years before. He knew from experience that the mythagoscapes changed subtly, and that they could be brought into existence by different minds and therefore with slightly different features. If this building was a corrupting form of the river station – from a story-cycle told in the courts of William Rufus – which he had recorded before, then the Horse Shrine lay behind him.

He had come too far.

There was no use in using a compass in this wood. All magnetic poles shifted and changed, and north could be seen to turn a full three hundred and sixty degrees in the stepping of four paces in a straight line. Nor was there any guarantee that the perspective of the wood had not changed; hour by hour the primal landscape altered its relationship with its own internal architecture. It was as if the whole forest was turning, a whirlpool, a spinning galaxy, turning around the voyager, confusing senses, direction and time. And the further inwards one journeyed, the more that place laughed, played tricks, like old Drummer Fox, casting a glamour upon the eyes of the naive beholder.

No. There was no guarantee of anything, here. All Huxley knew was that he was lost. And being lost, yet being comforted by this encounter with the river-station of the piratical *Gylla*, from the eleventh-century story, he felt suddenly confident. He had nothing to use but his judgement. And he had something of great value to lose: his friend of many years standing . . .

So he summoned his courage and returned along the trail.

The sound of a horse screaming finally allowed me to locale the shrine, but on arrival at the wide glade I found only desertion and shambles. Something has been here and almost utterly destroyed the place. The monstrous bone effigy of a horse, with its attendant skeletal drivers, is shattered, the bone parts spread throughout the glade and the wood around. They are overgrown, some even moss-covered, as if they have lain like this for many years. Yet I know this place was intact just a few days ago.

The stone temple remains. There are withered leather sacks inside it, some decayed form of food offering, fragments of clay, two wristlets of carved, yellowing ivory pieces resembling crude equines, and carved, I imagine, from horses' teeth. There is also a fresh painting on the grey stone of the outside of the place, a mark, like no animal or hieroglyph that I have encountered. It is complex, of course symbolic, and utterly meaningless. Depicted in a mixture of charcoal and orange ochre, it is tantalising. My sketch, over the page, does not do it justice.

No sign of the horse that screamed.

Light going, night coming. No sign of Ash, and no movement around. This place is dead. Eerie. I shall make a single foray in a wide circle, then return here for the night.

He finished writing and packed the book away in his rucksack. With a nervous glance around he entered the dense woodland again, and ducked below the branches, hesitating as he orientated himself, then striking away from the glade by measured paces, constantly stopping and listening.

He had intended to walk a wide circle, but after a few minutes the abrupt and noisy flight of dark birds, behind him, caught his attention and induced in him a state of frozen silence. He hugged the dark trunk of a tree, peering through the light-shattered gloom for any substantial movement.

When, after a minute or so, he had seen nothing, he began a hesitant return to the glade.

The sound of a scream, a woman's angry, fearful cry, shocked him, then set him running.

A small fire was burning, close to the stone walls of the shrine. The intensity of the flame, the sharp crackle of wood, told Huxley instantly that the fire was new. He was tantalised by the thought that Ash had been near the clearing all the time, watching him, waiting for him to leave.

He approached, now, crouched low in the cover. Ash was a running shape, a twisting, struggling form, caught darkly in the light from her own fire. Something was grappling with her, hitting at her. He could hear the blows. Her cries of anger became groans of pain, but she fought back with vigour, rough skirts swirling, arms swinging.

Huxley dropped his pack and stepped quickly into the clearing. The process of murder was interrupted and Ash looked at him angrily, then with puzzlement. Behind her, the wood shimmered and the grey-green shape of a man moved swiftly to the right. He still had hold of Ash and the startled woman stumbled as her head was wrenched back, dragging her over.

'Let her go! Let go of her at once!'

Huxley snatched a piece of burning wood from the small fire. He dropped it at once and yelled as flame curled round his fingers, singeing the hair on his skin. More carefully he selected a fragment of branch that was burning only at the end—

And grimaced as he realised that the whole of the wood was at what felt like red heat!

—And charged at the shadow of his alter ego.

Ash was being throttled. Her body had pitched back, her naked legs thrashing. Her head and upper torso were hidden by the brush. Her cries were stifled, choking.

Huxley leapt through the undergrowth and thrust the burning brand at the shadow.

'Get away from her! I won't have this, do you understand me? Stop at once!'

The fire at the end of the brand went out. He shook the wood vigorously, hoping to restart the flame, but the life had gone from it.

Then his face erupted with pain and he felt himself flung back into the clearing. He moaned with genuine discomfort and struggled to stand, but all strength had evaporated from his legs, and he fell back, onto one elbow, reached to hold his face, now numbed and oddly loose around the jaw.

Distantly he heard a sharp crack, a half cry, fading quickly, a woman's cry, dying.

'Oh Dear God, he's killed her . . . I've killed her . . .'

Fire burned into his eyes and he shrieked and struck against the brand. A foot crushed down upon his belly, and when he doubled so he felt a further blow, by foot or hand it was hard to tell, against his eyes, striking him flat again. The fire waved down, the flames took on his shirt, and he patted a hand at them, before again fingers closed around his wrist and wrenched him up, to a sitting position, half blinded by flickering yellow fire, and—

Rope around his neck!

Tightening!

He snatched and scrabbled at the thong, managed to cry out. 'Stop this! You have no right! Stop this at once . . . !'

He was lifted, turned, swung. He struggled to retain a degree of dignity, but felt his feet leave the ground and his stomach turn over as he was dragged around by the creature, swinging him with astonishing strength, finally flinging him against the stone of the shrine.

He looked up, then felt burning and realised he was half in the fire. He scrabbled away from the heat, but had the presence of mind to fling gleaming shards and hot ashes against the blurry shadow that had come to tower over him. Where they impacted he caught the grim outline of a naked man, leaning down, and he could tell the smile, and the glitter of menace in the eyes that watched.

A voice like bubbling water hissed, 'Let her die . . .'

'Animal!' Huxley spat. 'You sicken me. To think that you are a part of *me*. Dear God, I hope I never live to see the day that—'

'Steee-vaaaan . . .'

It was an animal howl. It shattered Huxley's concentration. It rattled his nerves. There was such desperation in the cry, such need, such fury. The grey-green shadow bent to its task of killing, but on its lips, on the green-shadow gates of hell that were the exit from its heart, on that invisible, yet tangible mouth was his son's name, and love for his son, *love*, and compassion too, a misguided, misdirected shadow that fought and killed to save the life of

'Steee-vaaaan . . .'

Again the howl of anguish, and then the creature went to work; and with what energy, what power it began to rend the prone and failing body of the man, the human creature that lay before it!

Huxley experienced the scientific process of his death with abstract, disconnected ease . . .

He had no strength left. There was nothing he could do.

That he witnessed the leather thong that suddenly appeared around the shadow's neck was more a testimony to the strength of the scientific curiosity that inhabited the man than any strength of will, or need to survive. He had documented the punishment to his body, and thought only of how this grey-green shadow, this dissection of his mind, his personality, loose in an alien world, could summon the forces of nature such that it could be tangible, whole, and sexual . . .

It was a beast at large, a creature formed from mind, myth and manhood, substance crowning the power of its thoughts, its needs, its desires, its baser hungers. And within that hunger lurked the higher mind that Huxley was proud to call his own, the awareness of love, the curiosity that formed the exploring nature of a man like

Wynne-Jones, or young Christian Huxley, or George himself. Poor George. Poor old George.

On the strangling leather, two pieces of wood and a sharp shard of bone showed up clearly by the scattered light of the scattered fire, and the grey-green man shrieked and drew back, swung on his own noose, caught by his own animalistic arrogance as Ash, one arm hanging quite limp, the other wrapped around the thong, dragged the shadow backwards. The eerie sound of his cry was suddenly drowned by the violent flight of birds from all around, a massive flight that filled the glade of the Horse Shrine with leaves and feathers, and the darkening sky with a streaming blur of circling shapes.

There were horses in the wood. They snorted, stamped and shook their manes, with a rustling of woodland and a rattle and clatter of crude stone and bone trappings, slung on hair twine and stretched and softened leather . . . They were everywhere, all around, and Huxley groped his way to his knees, watching the dark woods.

Movement everywhere. And sound, like chanting: and the rapid beating of drums, the rhythmic rattle of bone and shell . . . It was all so familiar. He could hear the cries of tortured men, and the shrieking laughter that had so unnerved him in a recent encounter. All of this was taking place deeper in the wood, almost out of sight.

Ash had let go of Grey-green man and now stood shakily at the edge of the glade, her good arm flexing as she used the wrist drum to beat out a frantic tattoo. And behind her, light . . . *fire* light . . .

And passing quickly across that light, as it came nearer, a stooped, running shape, a man's shape, swathed in cloak and hood. Which vanished into darkness.

In the centre of the glade the grey-green shadow rose from where it had fallen, tall, frightened, arms reaching out from its sides, head turning this way and that. Again, Huxley watched its sleek, virile form, the hard musculature, the animal litheness as it stepped swiftly to one side, then prowled, half crouched, back across the glade.

The woods were on fire. Flame began to streak into the darkening night. The grey-green man rose from his cowering position, darted to Huxley, bent close.

'Wrong . . .' he breathed.

Huxley backed away, still frightened of the raw power that emanated from the creature. 'What is wrong?'

'I . . .'

Huxley tried to understand, but his mind was befuddled by beating and fear. He said, 'Don't kill Ash . . .'

But the creature seemed to ignore him. It said simply, 'Return.'

'What do you mean? What do you mean *return*? Who?' Huxley struggled to sit. 'Who do you mean? Me? You?'

'I . . .' said the grey-green man, and the hand that reached suddenly to the flinching Huxley merely touched a finger to his lips, closed Huxley's mouth, lingered, then was gone.

And with it, the grey-green shadow, fleeing towards the flame-horse, which burst into the glade, a mass of burning rushes, wrapped around the stiff corpse strapped to the horse's back.

The horse screamed. It was huge. It was higher at the back than a tall man, a giant of a beast, burning, to be sacrificed along with the flaming cadaver that rode it to hell and beyond.

The grey-green shadow seemed to fall beneath its hooves, but then a blur of colour, of light and darkness, moved effortlessly up behind the flaming corpse, and reached around almost to hug the flames. The horse reared, scattering burning strands of rush, fire that filled the noisy glade. The animal turned, struggling through pain and panic, then kicked forward again, the body shifting and shaking on its back, streams of fire like flags, rising and waving in the night wind.

And Grey-green man followed it, and went out of the Horse Shrine, riding to hell, riding home, riding through the breach in whatever fabric between the worlds had been tended in that earlier and near fatal encounter with the horses, and the time of sacrifice.

I felt sure that my shadow had been taken back to its rightful body, that version of me that had unwittingly and unwillingly shed its darker aspect.

With the departure of the shadow there was, in myself at least, a sense of inordinate relief. I saw Ash across the glade, a bruised and battered woman, the wrist drum in her hand being flexed with almost urgent need.

I understood that she had helped me. And I suppose she helped me because she had recognised that I had helped her, that the two forms of Huxley with which she had come into contact were not the same at all, and that I was a friend, whereas the violent *anima* was not.

All was not finished. I had underestimated (I probably always shall) the subtle power of this mythago form, this Ash, this shaman, this worker of magic within the *frame* of weirdness that is Ryhope Wood.

She had not sent me to the time of horses. She had – perhaps through gratitude – brought the time of horses to the shrine . . . She had located the event further away from the shrine itself, so that as I wrestled with the primogenetic manifestation of the grey-green man so I was also watching the sacrifice at some way distant. That hooded shape, passing before the flames . . . myself, perhaps, of the earlier encounter. The flame-horse had ridden on to recapture the errant part of the personality that had played truant from my alternative presence in the wood . . .

It makes me shudder to think of it, but surely *I* was the corpse in the flames; in that other world, from which Grey-green man had come, Ash's banishment of me to the past had ended in cruel murder.

Grey-green man had written: *I was riding the horse when it collided with the hooded man. I remember falling. The horse was bolting. It had two bodies on its back. One alive (me) beginning to burn badly. One dead. The hooded man was struck. I fell, the horse ran on.*

But there had been only one body, flaming, and only the animal survival of the dying, screaming man within

437

the rushes allowed one part of its *anima* to escape, to cling to me, to haunt me.

Poor George. Poor old George.

These sinister thoughts fled rapidly when, with a feeling of joy almost childlike in its power and its simplicity, I saw Wynne-Jones again . . .

Three giant horses, their riders strapped to their backs, encased in an armour made from nature: already rush and reed, flaming, had fled the glade. Now the chalk-white corpse rode around the stone shrine, white rider on a black steed, limbs pinned and positioned by the frame of wood that held the victim upright on the crude cloth saddle. Then came the rider all decked out in thorns, a weave, a suit of branches and berries that allowed only the face to show, a face as dead, as barren as the chalk escarpments of the downs.

But the fourth of the horses carried the man of animal rags, the skins and limbs and heads of the creatures of field, forest and wood, the gaping heads of fox, cat and pig, the hides of grey, brown and winter-white creatures, all draped, bloodily and savagely, around the wild rider.

Crucified in the saddle, but alert and alive, the ragman was ridden round the glade on the back of a stallion whose face showed its pain, its torture, and whose snorting scream told of its fury. It stamped as it waited, pawed the ground, kicked back against the stones of the shrine, and eyed the wood, listening to the whooping calls of the herders, the men who chased the sacrifices through the woodland.

Around its neck dangled a necklace of wood and bone – three pieces!

'Edward! Dear God, Edward!'

The eyes of the man swathed in the rags of creatures widened, but no sound escaped the lips of the face that suddenly flexed with recognition and hope.

As the horse bolted towards Huxley, intending to again penetrate the forest, Huxley flung himself in front of the creature, watched it rear and stamp against him. He backed away, then darted to its side, reached up and *tore* the crucifix from the great beast's back, bringing the wood down upon him, Wynne-Jones and the stink and slime of freshly cut pelts with it, so that the two men tumbled in blood and rot, while the horse entered the wood and was lost.

Huxley unbound his friend. Ash hastened to them, grabbed at Huxley's sleeve and drew them swiftly away into cover. She also tugged the necklet from his chest, indicating that Wynne-Jones should do the same.

When Huxley glanced backwards he saw the tall herders enter the glade, dark shapes in the dying fire, beating at the space with flint tipped weapons, calling for their mares and stallions. But rapidly, as if fading into a sudden distance, the sound of chanting and drumming drifted away, became a mere hint of sound, then was gone completely.

At some time during the night, as Huxley huddled in half sleep against the shivering body of his friend, Ash slipped away into the darkness, abandoning the men.

She took with her the necklet of wood and bone that had earlier transported Huxley to the ancient version of the Horse Shrine. But she left the small wrist drum, and Huxley reached for it and twirled it, watching the small stones strike the taut hide on each side of the decorated box.

A gift for Steven, he wondered? Or something for himself, something with a hidden power? He decided not to beat the drum, not in these woods.

They found a stream during their walk in the raw dawn, and Wynne-Jones washed the blood and filth from his body, drawing on Huxley's spare clothes gratefully.

'I've lost my pipe,' he murmured sadly, as they began the long trek back to Oak Lodge.

'Someone, or something, will use it as a talisman,' Huxley said. Wynne-Jones laughed.

CODA

Steven came running across the thistle meadow, kicking with skinny legs through the high grass. One flap of his white school shirt was hanging loose over the belt of his short grey-flannel trousers. He looked upset, hair unkempt, shirt buttons undone.

He was calling for his father.

Huxley crouched down, huddled back behind the ruined gate that almost blocked the access at the woodland edge to the muddy stream that wound so deeply

440

into Ryhope Wood. He hunched up, hugging the under-growth in the dark, slippery area where the stream widened and dropped a few inches to weave its way inwards. The trees here were like sentries, reaching inwards, outwards, towering over the ramshackle gate, their roots a twisting snake-like mass that made entry all the more difficult.

Brightness entered this gloomy gateway to hell from the summer's afternoon beyond, and Steven at last came to the high bank that dropped to the stream. Here he called for his father yet again.

Behind him, Wynne-Jones and Jennifer were crossing the field more slowly. Huxley rose slightly, peered at them, and beyond them at the house . . .

Wrong! There was something wrong . . .

'Dear God in Heaven – What has happened?'

'Daddy!'

The boy was in earnest. Huxley looked at him again, out on the open land. All he could see, now, was Steven's silhouette. It disturbed him. Steven was stand-ing on the rise of ground just beyond the brambles, the thorns, and the old gate that had been tied across the channel to stop animals entering this dangerous stretch of wood. The boy's body was bent to one side as he peered into the impenetrable gloom of the forest. Huxley watched him, sensing his concern, and the anguish. Steven's whole posture was that of a sad and earnest young man, desperate to make contact with his father.

Motionless. Peering anxiously into the realm that perhaps he suddenly feared.

'Daddy?'

'Steve. I'm here. Wait there, I'm coming out.'

The boy hugged him delightedly. The house in the distance was a dark shape, bare of ivy. The great beech outside the boys' bedroom was as he remembered it. The field, the overgrown field, was four weeks advanced from when he had left it.

Something was wrong.

'How long have I been gone, Steven?'

The boy was only too glad to talk. 'Two days. We were worried. Mummy's been crying a lot.'

'I'm home now, lad.'

'Mummy says it *wasn't* you who shouted at me . . .'

'No. It wasn't. It was a ghost.'

'A ghost!'

(Said with delight.)

'A ghost. But the ghost has gone back to hell, now. And I'm home too.'

Jennifer was calling to him. From his crouching position Huxley watched her as she walked quickly towards him, her face pale, but her lips smiling. Edward Wynne-Jones staggered along behind her, a man exhausted by his ordeal, and confused by Huxley's sudden terror as he had reached the edgewoods and refused to emerge into open land.

There was so little time, Huxley thought, and took Steven by the shoulders. The boy gaped at his father, then shut his mouth as he realised that he was about to be addressed in earnest.

'Steven . . . don't go into the woods. Do you promise me?'

442

'Why?'

'No questions, lad! Promise me – for God's sake . . .
promise me, Steven . . . *don't* go into Ryhope Wood.
Not now, not ever, not even when I'm dead. Do you
understand me?'

Of course he understood his father. What he couldn't
understand was the why. He gulped and nodded, glancing nervously at the dense wood.

Huxley shook him. 'For your own sake, Steve . . . *I
beg you* . . . don't ever again play in the woods. Never!'

'I promise,' the boy said meekly, frightened.

'I don't want to lose you—'

From close by Jennifer called, 'George. Are you all
right?'

Steven was crying, tears on his cheeks, his face
fixed in a brave look, not sobbing or breaking up: just
crying.

'I don't want to lose you,' Huxley whispered, and
gathered the boy to him, holding him so very tightly.
Steven's hands remained draped by his sides.

'When did the farmer last mow this meadow?' he
asked his son, and he felt Steven's shrug.

'I don't know. About a month ago? We came and
gathered hay. Like we always do.'

'Yes. Like we always do.'

Jennifer ran up to him and quickly hugged him, a full
embrace. 'George! Thank God you're safe. Come back to
the house and get washed and freshened up. I'll make us
all some food . . .'

He stood and let Jennifer take him home.

*

Edward has read the entire account of the Bone Forest and is much exercised by its detail and implications. He was puzzled by my reference to having 'destroyed mythagos in the Wolf Glen', a statement I made when warning the grey-green man away from Jennifer. He seemed bemused when I explained that this had merely been a bluff to win the fight: after all, Grey-green man – myself of an alternative reality – was fully aware that our experiences in the mythago-realm of Ryhope were subtly different, so how could he be sure that at a time when he – Huxley – had failed to destroy an aggressive mythago, I – Huxley – had not succeeded? It was a sufficient bluff, I believe. Grey-green man was discouraged from the house and held to the wood, although in retrospect my decision came close to being fatal for Ash.

WJ agrees with me that Ash – the *original* mythic tale of Ash – is closely related to horses, perhaps to the Horse Shrine itself, and that in her original form she was a female *shaman* who exercised particular power over the untamed horses of the valley of her origin.

My regret is that I did not communicate with her on the subject of the primal myth, the core legend: I wonder if she might have had—

Daddy?'

Huxley looked up sharply from his desk, the words in his mind flowing and becoming confused.

'What the devil is it?'

He turned in his chair, furious at the interruption to

his train of thought. Steven stood in the doorway, in his dressing gown, looking shocked, nervous. He was holding a mug of hot chocolate.

'What is it, boy? I'm working!'

'Will you tell me the story?'

'What story?'

Huxley glanced back at his journal, laid his finger on the last line, trying to summon the words that were fading from mind so fast.

Steven had faltered. He was torn, it seemed, between running upstairs, or standing his ground. His eyes were wide, but there was a frown on his face. 'You said as soon as you came back you'd tell me a story about Romans.'

'I said no such thing!'

'But you *did* . . . !'

'Don't argue with me, Steven. Get to bed with you!'

Meekly, Steven stepped away. His mouth was tight as he whispered, 'Goodnight.'

Huxley turned back to the journal, scratched his head, inked his pen and continued. He had written – concerning Ash – that she might have had:

some awareness of what I believe was called the *Urscumug*? But probably she dates from a time considerably later than this primal myth.

The mythago that is Ash can *manipulate* time. This is an incredible discovery, should it be confirmed by later study. So Ryhope Wood is not just a repository of legendary creatures created in the present day . . . its defensive nature, its warping of time, its playing with time and space . . . these physical conditions can be imparted to the mythago forms themselves: Ash's magic – perhaps legendary in her own time – seems to become *real* in this wood. WJ and myself *have* travelled through time. We were sent, separately, to an event that had occurred in the cold, ancient past, an event of such power (for the minds of the day) that it has drawn to it not just *our* space and time, but others too, similar times, alternatives, the stuff of fantasy, the stuff of wilder dreams.

For one brief instant, the wood was opened to dimensions inconceivable. Grey-green man came through, returned. And for my part, my memory was affected, a dream, perhaps, like many dreams . . . I had thought the meadow to be newly cropped, but clearly this had been a dream, and I had misremembered.

Ryhope Wood plays tricks more subtle than I had previously imagined.

I am safely home, however, and WJ too. He talks of 'gates', pathways and passages to mythic forms of hell. He is becoming obsessed with this idea, and claims to have found such a gateway in the wood itself.

So: two old men (no! I don't feel old. Just a little tired!), two tired men, each with an obsession. And a wealth of wonder to explore, given time, energy, and the freedom from those concerns that can so interfere with the process of intellectualising such a wondrous place as exists beyond the edgewoods.

Huxley capped his pen, leaned back and stretched, yawning fiercely. Outside, the late summer night was well advanced. He blotted the page of the journal, hesitated – tempted to turn back a few pages – then closed it.

Returning to the sitting room he found Jennifer reading. She looked up at him solemnly, then forced a smile.

'All finished?'

'I think so.'

She was thoughtful for a moment, then said gently, 'Don't make promises you don't intend to keep.'

'What promises?'

'A story for Steven.'

'I made him no promise . . .'

Jennifer sighed angrily. 'If you say so, George.'

'I do say so.'

But he softened his tone. Perhaps he had forgotten a promise to tell Steven a Roman story. Perhaps, in any event, he should have been gentler with the boy. Reaching into his pocket he drew out the wrist drum that Ash had left.

'Look at this. I found it at the Horse Shrine. I'll give it to Steve in the morning.'

Jennifer took the drum, smiled, shook it and made it beat its staccato rhythm. She shivered. 'It feels odd. It feels old.'

Huxley agreed. 'It *is* old.' And added with a laugh, 'A better trophy than that last one, eh?'

'Trophy?'

'Yes. You remember . . . that raw and bloody bone in my study. You kicked it and called it a trophy . . .'

'Raw and bloody bone?'

She looked quite blank, not understanding him.

Huxley stood facing her for a long while, his head

reeling. Eventually she shrugged and returned to her book. He turned, left the room, walked stiffly back to his study and opened the journal at the page where Grey-green man had left his second message.

The message was there all right.

But with a moan of despair and confusion, Huxley placed his hand upon the page, upon the scrawled words, touched a finger-tip to the part of the paper where, just a few days ago, there had been a smear of blood, confusing and concealing part of Grey-green man's script.

And where now there was no blood. No blood at all.

He sat for a long time, staring out through the open windows, to the garden and the wood beyond. At length he picked up the pen, turned to the end of the journal and started to write.

> *It would seem that I am not quite home*
> *Confused about this.*
> *Maybe Wynne-Jones will have an answer*
> *Must return to Shrine again*
> *Everything feels right, but not right*
> *Not quite home*

Afterword

Merlin's Wood:
The Vision of Magic

The legend of the powerful enchanter, seduced by a young, ambitious protégé, is a well known story, and of all such tales, that of Merlin and Vivien is arguably the most profoundly engaging. The poet Alfred Lord Tennyson devoted a wonderful chapter in his epic *The Idylls of the King*, his re-exploration of Arthur, and the Matter of Britain, to these two wily characters. It is, in my view, the most startling and powerful of the scenes that Tennyson recreates, and very inspiring.

Merlin's Wood is a short novel, in four parts, each distinctively written, designed around the theme of 'the stealing of power'. Of all the novels I have written over the years, this is perhaps the most challenging: nearly two hundred pages of deception and trickery, a collection of moments both of magic and mayhem, of alternative worlds and the recognisable realm.

It is a novel told along the narrow path that divides real existence, as we would understand it, from the possible world that might have arisen had our older and more naturalistic (pagan) beliefs remained profoundly present in European society, rather than having been absorbed by Christianity. There are versions of folk songs, as well as of the poem *The Night Before Christmas*!

Merlin's Wood is also a tale of possession, both physically, and in the form of the intense need we have to *know*, to satisfy the craving that is curiosity.

And it is a tale of murder driven by lust and longing – which is the essential tale of Merlin and Vivien.

The *genesis of Merlin's Wood* can be found in my short story 'Scarrowfell', which deals with a similar world, close enough to our own to recognise, but different because the reality of what we (these days) call 'paganism' is still informing the imaginary society – both from its landscape, to the thinking and beliefs of its people.

And it took only one visit in the late 1980s to the *Fôret de Broceliande*, Merlin's fabled birthplace, and a vacation in Brittany, camping among the tangled woods and monumental stone remains of the prehistoric people who had once inhabited that part of the country, to become entranced with a 'Vision of Magic' that simply *had* to be written.

I wonder if Tennyson visited Brittany, and was equally entranced?

Finally, there is one phrase in that long poem by Tennyson that struck me at once, and which inspired and underwrote the horror and the terror of the family tale that is central to *Merlin's Wood*:

How from the rosy tips of life and love.

Flash'd the bare-grinning skeleton of death!

—two powerfully evocative lines that have so many

different meanings! And in this short novel, I have tried to tease out as many as I can.

The stories that accompany *Merlin's Wood* all draw on the same notion of 'a vision of magic'. The earliest, 'Earth and Stone', was written out of a passion for imagining the landscapes and beliefs of pre-historic Ireland, a time of amazing conceptual and artistic development. I explored the landscape with a very close friend. There are wonders there, still buried below the clay, waiting to be found. A trick is played on my hero, an arrival from the future. The young boy who tricks him – Tig (his full name means: Never-touch-Woman, Never-touch-Earth) – became central to *Lavondyss*, in the Mythago Cycle. I have always had a soft spot for that young trickster. In the 1970s I crouched in the tomb mounds and walked the rain-shallowed earthworks, the remnants of kings and of the stories of the glory of those kings, and I was astounded. Much affected. I felt very much like a visitor from the future, though in truth, it was as if the forgotten years had come alive for me.

'Scarrowfell' was written to be read aloud, with music, preferably folk music, something jaunty. The opening verse is from the Albion Dance Band's *Morris On*. I read it one Hallowe'en. It is set in an alternative world to ours where the absorbing and corrupting of older beliefs, by Christianity, has not been fully achieved. My intention was to explore how blind power (cf Odin) corrupts innocence. It is not the newest of ideas, a fact I know, but I found it powerful when I wrote it.

'Thorn' shows the process by which this failure to destroy the old ways occurs, albeit in the life of one simple stonemason working on a new cathedral in the twelfth century. The story was selected for *The Oxford Book of Fantasy*, edited by Professor Thomas Shippey. I cannot, and will not, deny a debt of honour to William Golding's wonderful novel *The Spire*. My tragic hero is far less inspired than Golding's priest, Jocelin, but his fall tells it all.

Finally, 'The Bone Forest': this is a Mythago tale, though set before the rest of the Mythago Cycle. I wrote it to fill in background and back-story to *Mythago Wood*, and at the request of the screenwriter who was adapting that first novel for film. As with Merlin, so with Mythago: there are many levels and layers, many depths; many discoveries to be made. 'The Bone Forest' is a story of love and horror, of the weird, and of the despair that will eventually lead to the love and delight of *Mythago Wood*. The grey-green man who inhabits the tale is a reflection of the birth of conscience and consent, but hateful: a trickster.

Robert Holdstock
London
November 2008

454